Wicked REVENGE

WICKED ANGELS #1

REVENGE
Wicked

ZOEY DERRICK

COVER:

Cover Model: Jeff Hoffman

Photographer: Bob Vanderford Photography

Cover Designer: Designs by Dana

Formatting Design (e-book & paperback): Parajunkee Design

Editing: Raw Books Editing – Mandy Smith

e-book ISBN: 978-0998937618

paperback ISBN: 978-0998937625

For Emily & Shelley - Thank you for inspiring and encouraging me to write this one. But most of all, for telling me that I didn't suck at it. Love you both!

OTHER BOOKS
BY ZOEY DERRICK

Contemporary Romance:
Finding Love's Wings
Chasing Love's Wings
Irresitibly Undeniable - Standalone
Fractured Breaths - Standalone

Contemporary Erotic Romance:
One Week - Standalone

Erotic Romance:
Claiming Addison
Craving Talon
Redeeming Kyle
Taming Dex
Devouring Raine
Defining Us

Contemporary Erotic, M/M Romance:
Aryn's Desire
Caden's Command

Paranormal Romance:
Give Me Reason
Give Me Hope
Give Me Desire
Give Me Love

"*Hot and sexy biker* plus a female lead who was no wallflower made for a page turner that hooked me and wouldn't let me go. If you adore MC books like I do, grab this one."

- USA Today Bestselling Author, Terri E. Laine

FORWARD

THE WICKED ANGELS MOTORCYCLE CLUB was formed in 1970 by three brothers who enjoyed the ride. They wanted nothing more than to turn that ride into a lifestyle that would feed their families.

The club quickly grew and they branched out beyond the borders of Arizona.

One brother moved to Boulder, Colorado, taking a few senior members with him.

The other brother went to Roswell, New Mexico where he set up his own charter.

The eldest brother stayed in Arizona with the main charter.

Life went on, children were born and the club grew by leaps and bounds.

By the mid-eighties, the Wicked Angels were well-known throughout the West and had many alliances with other area clubs, but they also gained even more enemies. The Wicked Angels did things differently and that pissed people off.

Sure, they have their hands in legal and illegal business practices, but they are some of the most hardcore one percenters around.

When the original three founding members became too old to ride, they stepped down, handing their charters over to their sons. Big Daddy D, Sticks and Tripp.

Tripp is dead. The New Mexico charter is in shambles. At the time of his death, his eldest son, Tryke, though he had the respect of the New Mexico members to become President, wasn't old enough to sustain the club. So, the club was handed over, albeit temporarily, to Rooster, VP of Roswell. As Tryke grew older, he learned the business, gained respect and had the attention of the entire charter. They looked up to him, went to him for answers and came to him with concerns about the direction of Roswell.

PART ONE

CHAPTER ONE
Where it all begins...

"WHY? WHY ARE WE DOING this again, Kellen?" I beg. "We've been over this a million times."

He grabs me by my shoulders. "Because, you need to listen to me. You need to know what to do in the event that something happens to me in order to save yourself, to protect yourself."

"Jesus, Kell, you're acting a fool here. I know what I have to do, but I don't understand why you're making this such a big damn deal right now," I whine.

"Because you're not listening to me, Lily-bean."

I fight the prickling of tears in my eyes. "I am, but I don't care, nothing is ever going to happen to you," I tell him with false conviction.

He turns on me, hard. "You can't say that. You don't know that."

"Then why are you so convinced that something is going to happen to you?" I beg him to explain this to me, but I know it's feeble. He's never been very forthcoming with me and odds are good that this has something to do with club business, which means his lips are sealed.

"Just promise me, please?" he begs.

"Fine," I snap and go charging for the back door.

Kellen grabs me hard around the upper arm and pulls me back. "Lily, don't! I need you to stay here," he snaps before slamming the inside door shut.

"What the hell is your problem?" I argue with him. My blood pressure is rising with each tick of my heartbeat.

Kellen never treats me like this.

My brother is pissed and on edge for reasons I don't know or understand. If this is club business, I'll never know. According to Kellen, my place isn't in the club, but in school and eventually away from here.

"What's wrong with you?" I all but growl at him.

"Nothing," he snaps before opening the door again. I follow him, but he slams the door in my face as he marches into the back yard. "Stay inside," he hollers through the closed door.

Where's he going? He never goes back there.

I turn around, racing for the stairs and my room. It's on the backside of the house and I can see him better from up there.

Time seems off. Like I'm living in a dream. Running slowly through murky water, but I'm not. Something is going down and I can't even begin to wrap my mind around what it is. It irks me to know that Kellen is keeping me in the dark. If something's about to happen to him, the least he could do is tell me instead of being pissed at me for wanting answers.

I reach my room and slam my door shut behind me. In the off chance he hears me, he'll know I'm pissed at him, but he knows my anger towards him never lasts.

My brother has done some fucked up things in the past, but I can't stay mad at him.

He's all I have left.

Pissed off and irritated, that seems to be the name of his little game the closer I get to eighteen. I already graduated from high school. I spent too much time in my room studying and overachieving because it kept my mind occupied and kept me busy.

In a little over a week, my choices are my own.

I've never made a secret about my desires to be a part of the club. It's something I've always wanted, ever since I was a little girl, and he knows that once I'm eighteen, technically, he can't stop me. Over the last four or so years, I never could understand his desire to keep me out of club business, but he's done everything in his power to do just that. He won't talk about it to me. Every time I broach the subject with him, he gets pissed, he shouts and stomps off. We were raised in the club, he's a part of it, why can't I be, too?

2

WICKED REVENGE

In a way, I understand why he doesn't want me around the club. Four years ago, when I was only thirteen, our mom and dad were killed. Though Kellen tells me it was a car accident, I knew better then and even more so now. The only true explanation for it is that something happened inside the club's walls that changed the dynamic of the Wicked Angels MC. I tried for years to convince myself that it truly was a car accident and nothing more, but that's hard to fathom when mom and dad never drove a car unless I was with them. When they went anywhere without me, they were always on dad's bike.

Up until their deaths, I'd always been surrounded by my brother, his friends, my parents and their friends, and extended club family. I was old enough to catch onto a lot of conversations going on between the older people, yet young enough to be naïve about the things they were talking about.

Kellen is nine years older than me. He was twenty-two when our parents died which meant he was old enough to take care of me. He was also old enough to be a fully patched member of the Angels.

Within a couple weeks of our parents' passing, Kellen started disappearing for long periods of time. There were many days when I heard him leave long before I had to get up for school, and other times when he wouldn't come home until sometime in the middle of the night. I learned quickly that even though Kellen was old enough to care for me, to keep me out of the state system, he didn't do a very good job at taking care of me. Unless you count the roof over my head, the clothes on my back and a kitchen full of food, then I guess he did alright. I fed myself, did my own laundry, cleaned the house and made sure my homework was done. Kellen was here, but I was on my own.

A couple of years after their deaths, Kellen started staying around more. He was home more often and things seemed to be settling into a routine. Though he would be home for dinner, that I cooked, he often took off shortly after and wouldn't come home until three or four in the morning.

His being around more meant Kellen and I got into many arguments about school work. In the beginning, I argued that I didn't need school

3

because one day I was gonna be an old lady. That sent Kellen over the edge. He refused to let me anywhere near the club and all but told me that being an old lady was for whores. He never explained to me why I wasn't allowed around the club, or why no one ever came around the house anymore. I haven't seen any of the men or women who used to come over for summer bar-b-q's, and holidays got lonely with just Kellen and me. It was like when my father died, so did the rest of my family.

I didn't understand why.

Kellen spent his life consumed with business, Wicked Angels MC business. It's where my father used to spend his days, too, and somewhere I was never allowed to go.

So, I went to school, I made friends, I did everything to fit in, but something always nagged at me. I never fit in with anyone. I always felt like an outsider with them and until the last six months or so, I could never understand why.

The club is where I belong. I'm the daughter of a Wicked Angels leader.

I haven't stepped foot inside that clubhouse since I was thirteen, but I know where I belong. My mother was an old lady and she was happy to be just that. My father was a badass biker who loved my mother more than life itself, and I want that.

My attention is brought back to the reason I came up here when I see Kellen come out from between the trees that create our property line in the backyard. I watch as he paces around the backyard, something he rarely does unless something is really bothering him. He has light brown, almost dirty blonde hair that is cut short on the sides. Around the time mom and dad died, he wore it in a faux-hawk cut. But now he keeps the sides short and the top, from his forehead to the base of his skull, is longer, too long to make a Mohawk anymore, but he likes it that way. He often has it pulled back in a ponytail at the crown of his scalp. Today it's down, blowing in the breeze. His eyes are a gorgeous green, pretty enough to make me envious of his eye color. Though mine are more emerald green in color, his are bright, vibrant.

4

WICKED REVENGE

His fists are clenched tight at his sides and his face is red with anger. The only time I see him relax is when he looks toward the house, almost as if he's waiting for something or someone to show up.

"Loki?" I ask myself as I cock my head, watching Kellen below.

I shake my head; my brother wouldn't look so tense if he was waiting for Loki to show up.

Loki is Kellen's best friend and while I know Loki is his club name, I can't remember his real name. I've only really ever known him as Loki except on the rare occasion when my brother would call him by his real name.

Loki and Tryke (Kellen's club name) have been friends for as long as I can remember. They're the same age, and if you didn't know any better, they could be brothers.

Kellen disappears from my line of sight as he ducks into the garage. I sit in my window watching, waiting for him to come back out, but time passes and he never does. After almost an hour I give up and toss myself on to the bed face first.

I scream into my mattress with frustration overload.

Kellen can be such a pain in my ass.

Lying there, my mind wanders back to Loki and all his sexiness and the wicked little way he smiles at me. It never fails to send shivers across my flesh, igniting my deepest desires in my core.

Ever since I can remember, I've always staked a claim on him. At one point, I called him *my Loki*, and he never stopped me. In fact, I think he liked it. He's always been mine. But he's always kept me at arm's length, despite my best efforts to get closer to him. He might not know it, but I think I was three when I fell in love with him and it's only gotten worse as I've gotten older and he's just gotten sexier with age.

Loki is the only Wicked Angels MC member I've seen, besides my brother, since my parents', passing. It was like Kellen did everything he could to keep the members out of our house and while I hated being alone, it was a welcome relief from the late-night parties that I had to try and sleep through before.

Having Loki around to keep my brother in check was a godsend, both for my brother and for my infatuation with him. I would notice his little sideways glances at me when I'd throw on something skimpy to get his attention. Eventually he returned the infatuation with little sexy smiles and flirty advances. The occasional weak drunken moment confirmed all I needed to know about how he felt about me.

One of those times, not so long ago, he told me that one day, soon, I would be his woman.

I would happily be his woman if Kellen wouldn't stand in the way of it. Loki is a club member, my brother's best friend, and he represents everything my brother has tried to keep me away from since our parents died.

Loki is tall, about six-three, maybe six-four, and compared to my tiny five-six, skin and bones frame, he's massive. With electric blue eyes and dark brown hair that's long, stretching down to the middle of his back when it's not braided – which is more often than not.

I smile at the memory of braiding Loki's hair when he'd come over to chill with Kellen. He'd sit on the floor next to the couch and let me play with it. I chuckle a little, washing away other memories of my brother's erratic behavior when I was fourteen and braiding pigtails in Loki's hair.

I blush when I remember that he kept those pigtails in his hair for two days. A big, bad, cut wearing, scary ass biker with pigtails is a sight to be seen and Loki rocked it like it was a badge of honor. I think I fell in love with him a little more after that. But he never made a move. Sure, when he'd get too drunk, he'd get me pinned against a wall. My head would spin out of control at the scent of bike grease, faint cologne and the hint of body wash whenever he got close like that. It was like my brain would short circuit and I'd be a helpless animal, ready and willing to turn myself over to him if he said the magic words. But he never did. Eventually his mind would clear and he'd back away, leaving me bereft and needy.

Thoughts of Loki keep my mind occupied until I doze off.

WICKED REVENGE

I'm not sure what wakes me up sometime later, but the setting February sun is streaming through my window.

I rub my eyes and roll over.

Then scream at the top of my lungs.

"Jesus, Lily, relax."

"What the hell are you doing in here?" I snap at Kellen who hasn't moved from where he was standing next to my bed.

"I came up here to wake you up." He sits down on the side of my bed. He has a composed and somber look on his face. It's the same face I remember him having when he'd told me about mom and dad and my heart sinks into my stomach.

"What's wrong? Did something happen to Loki?" I cower away from him, wrapping my arms around my legs, holding them to me. He scowls at me but shakes his head, ignoring my question about Loki.

"I need you to do something for me."

"Anything," I whisper without hesitation.

"No matter what happens, remember that I will always love you. That you'll always be my baby sister. Can you do that for me?"

Just as his words leave his lips, there is a roar of motorcycles from down the street.

"Get in the safe room, now!" he growls as he stands up. "Do not come out until you know it's safe. Do you hear me?"

I stiffly nod, not understanding what he's implying or what's happening.

After my parents died, Kellen went a little crazy. Paranoia was his middle name and it showed. He spent thousands of dollars turning a closet into a safe room. A room we've never had to use until now. After he'd finished the project, he spent weeks teaching me how to use it. Anytime he made upgrades to the room, he would always spend time showing me the new features. There are cameras that cover every inch of the house, every detail, and most importantly, the pictures are crystal clear.

"I mean it, Lily, go, and do not come out until you see it's safe. No matter what happens."

I stand up and he pulls me into the tightest hug I've ever felt from him. He kisses the top of my head. "Love ya, kid."

I squeeze him a little tighter as the reality of what's about to happen starts to wash over me. I start to sob.

He grabs me by my shoulders and pushes me back. "Promise me, Lily. Promise me that you will stay in there. Promise me?"

Through tear filled eyes, I nod my head.

"Go, now," he orders as he stomps from the room. I go out the door of my room and I place my hand on the knob. My fingerprints open the door and I step inside.

Tears flow down my face as I close and press the switch to seal the door.

I never understood why Kellen had this thing installed, until a couple of unexpected club members showed up and he sent me into the room to hang out until they left. I never thought anything of it.

Until I walk into the room tonight.

I shake my head in disbelief as it occurs to me that maybe this is more than paranoia with Kellen.

He's been protecting me, keeping me safe. Keeping me away from the club meant keeping me away from someone who wants to hurt me. By keeping the guys away, by keeping the families away, he's been keeping me safe. "Damn you!" I curse him loudly.

I shiver. The room is cold and grey, with steel walls and no windows. There's a bed, a couple of computers and a wall of monitors tied to cameras all around the property. Apparently, paranoia is his motivation and protection was his game.

I watch the monitors as two bikes pull into the driveway. I immediately recognize Loki, but his face is grim. He's staring daggers into the back of the head of the other guy he's with. I don't recognize the guy from anywhere, but their cuts are obviously Wicked Angels, the same as what my brother and father wore. Though Kellen wears one with similar patches to the one my father wore, Loki's isn't all that different from theirs, but it's enough to be able to tell them apart.

I continue to watch on the monitors. Kellen has made his way into the kitchen. He is standing stiffly with his hand on his hip, no doubt grabbing hold of the gun he always carries at his side.

Something is off.

Something is wrong with this situation.

I don't understand what's going on and I fight every ounce of my being to not flee the room. I look at the wall. "Dammit," I mutter as I realize that Kellen got in here first. I shake my head as I watch the countdown clock slowly tick down. Twenty-nine minutes and fifteen seconds left. Twenty-nine minutes before I can even consider opening the door. "You bastard," I growl at the screen.

Something is off, something is very wrong. I'm so confused. Nothing makes sense. They've come for Kellen, *why?* Tears start streaming down my face, again.

The room is not only a safe room, but also fireproof and soundproof. Nothing happening in here can be heard outside this room and vice versa. I return to the cameras and press a couple buttons, increasing the volume so I can hear what's happening in the kitchen and throughout the rest of the house.

I know where all the cameras are, but you can't see one of them from any room in the house. I don't know how he did it exactly, but he's managed to conceal every single one of them, which makes it easy to record everything and no one is any wiser.

I hear a door burst open through the speakers and my eyes land on the living room camera. The two men, Loki and the other man, come stomping into the house. The older guy calls out for Kellen. "In the kitchen," he replies. His voice is calm, steady and there is conviction in his voice.

"Where is it, you son-of-a-bitch?" the older man snaps as he steps into the kitchen.

"What the hell are you talking about?" Kellen asks with a cold stare in his eyes. I've only ever seen that look when Kellen was lying to my parents about something. It's like his own little way of ensuring he can't be read.

"The money, motherfucker, where is it?"

What money? Not that Kellen would tell me anything, but money isn't something he's ever had a problem with. Why would this asshole be looking for money from Kellen?

Kellen just shakes his head and my eyes wander over to Loki who is looking at my brother, pleading with him behind the old man's back.

"I don't know what you're talking about," Kellen says and I watch as Loki shakes his head in disbelief. It's almost as if Loki believes that Kellen has done whatever it is that's gotten them to this point. But I know Kellen, and he'd never do anything to put himself in danger like this.

Then everything shifts and the next thing I know, Kellen and the old man are pointing guns at each other. "No!" I scream.

"One more chance. Where's the money?" the old man snarls.

"Go fuck yourself," Kellen states as he steps closer to the old man.

Everything falls into a surreal slow motion.

Yet it all happens so fast.

Loki pulls his own gun from his side holster, under his cut, and points it directly at my brother.

Then everything shifts again.

Shots go off.

I can't tell for certain, but it looks like they come from Loki's gun.

"Noooo!" I scream.

The shots stop.

Kellen's chest is splattered red with blood.

WICKED REVENGE

The old man drops his gun and grabs his shoulder. *He's hit, right? Please tell me someone got him.*

Kellen's limp body goes crashing to the floor. His head ricocheting off the refrigerator.

His eyes meet mine in one of the cameras.

Tears pour down my face, making it impossible to see anything. I swipe at my eyes, clearing them as best as I can, just in time to see the light in my brother's eyes go out.

"No, no, no, goddammit, Kellen," I cry.

My eyes roam to the other cameras and I see Loki step over to my brother and place his fingers on his neck. "He's gone."

"Fuck you! Goddammit, Loki!" I scream at the camera.

"Good, let's get out of here."

"If you're so fucking convinced he stole the money, why aren't you looking for it?" Loki questions him angrily. He's trying to sound hard, but I know Loki well enough to know that he's anything but alright after that. His best friend is dead.

"We will," the old man growls in irritation. "Let's just get out of here, let the heat cool off, clean up this fucking mess." He points to his shoulder. "Then we'll come back to search and level the place." He heads for the front door, leaving Loki behind with my brother.

The screen door slams shut and I jump. The sound ricochets around the eerily quiet safe room from the speakers.

"Lily," Loki says softly as his eyes look up at me through the camera. His voice is a soft, an unwanted comfort. Without thinking I reach out to touch the monitor, secretly wishing I was touching him instead. "I know you can hear me. I'm sorry, but you have got to get out of here, now. You know what to do." He disappears off-screen.

I wish I could respond to him. Tell him that I don't want to go anywhere, that I can't leave, but he won't hear it. He also won't let me deviate from Kellen's plans. No matter how hard I beg him to let me stay.

My eyes roam over to the driveway camera. The old man is still clutching his shoulder as he fires up his bike. Loki follows him, swinging his leg over and starting the engine. I lower the volume on the monitors and the roar of the bikes fades into the background.

The old man backs out first and Loki's eyes find the driveway camera. They're narrowed at me, pleading with me. I know what has to be done, but I don't know if I have the strength to do it.

Loki backs out of the driveway and takes off down the street. Within a second he's gone from the camera's line of sight and I'm left alone. Locked in a safe room, unable to get out, unable to do anything. *What if they come back before I can get out of here?*

My eyes roam back to my brother. His eyes have closed some, but they are facing the direction of the camera. "Fuck you, Kellen," I cry into the camera.

The house is eerily quiet.

Dark.

Scary.

I'm alone.

Not even two weeks from turning eighteen and I have no parents, no brother, and no family.

"You're gonna pay for this, you dirty old son of a bitch," I growl.

MY HANDS ARE STILL FUCKING shaking when Gunnar and I pull up in front of the club. I climb off my bike before Gunnar even has his turned off and I storm into the club. Slamming the door back as I go.

"Is it done?" Rooster, the President of Roswell's Chapter of Wicked Angels asks as I enter.

I ignore him and walk up to the bar where the prospect behind the bar slides me a shot of whiskey and I slam it back. I'm so fucking numb right now that I barely even feel the burn. I nod to the prospect again and he produces another shot.

Rooster steps up behind me. "Is it done?"

I glare at him. "It's fucking done, but you know as well as I do that Tryke had nothing to do with this," I growl at him. It's about the hundredth time I've used the argument today, and it was a futile. Case in point, where we're at right now.

Finally, Rooster says nothing. *Thank fuck for that.*

I know damn well that Tryke had nothing to do with it. In fact, I'm certain this is all Rooster's doing. He knows Tryke was getting close, getting the right amount of people to stand behind him when he challenged Rooster for Pres. Now I just have to find a way to prove it to the club's President in Tucson. That's easier said than done. If I could have proved it before now, I would have and Rooster'd be the one going to ground, not Tryke. Tryke was moving in on Rooster's position and Rooster knew it. He also knew that Tryke has more respect in this club and throughout the entire Wicked Angels MC than Rooster will ever have. Rooster had to do something and he found the perfect excuse to do so. No doubt a similar excuse was found when Tripp, Tryke and Kiwi's father, was killed four years ago.

Despite the events of the night, I fight the urge to smile at the memory of Lily when she was just three or four years old. Her strawberry blonde hair was in pigtails as she walked through the kitchen. She had two brownish green orbs in her hands. "Unkie Loki, want some?" she'd asked, holding one of the orbs up to me.

I knelt before her with a smile on my face. "What you got there, kiddo?" I asked her.

"Kiwi." She smiled.

That wasn't the last time I saw the kid double fisting kiwis in her hands. It was, and still is, one of her favorite fruits. Hence the nickname I gave her. I'm sure I fell in love with her that day. I've always felt protective of her, even at fourteen, just like tonight.

Rooster has very few men in this club in his back pocket. Though every member respects Rooster as Pres, it doesn't mean they like him, but as the chapter Pres, they don't have much choice unless they're going to take Rooster down.

There's one man in particular that's crawled so far up Rooster's ass he's tasting Rooster's food for him. That would be Gunnar. The dumbass hasn't a fucking clue what he's doing. He was supposed to be the one to pull the trigger tonight, but I beat him to it. Kiwi is going to hate me for the rest of my life because of it. I can only hope that one day I get a chance to explain it to her, to explain why it was me who put three in her brother. But for now, I have to comfort myself with the fact that it was a pact Tryke and I made a long time ago. I can only hope that one day Kiwi can forgive me for what I've done.

Rooster talked Gunnar into doing his dirty work tonight. Though I can't say I'm surprised. Gunnar was once a notorious hitman for the Angels. He's a hot-headed, short-tempered motherfucker who will do anything if he feels it's justified, or if Rooster orders him to do it.

In Gunnar's eyes, Tryke's death is justified. Regardless of Rooster's order, Gunnar was gonna do it anyway. His justification comes because he's trying to cover someone's ass. Rooster's or his own is the mystery of the moment.

The door slams open again and I know it's Gunnar. I don't bother looking. I simply slam back my shot and nod to the prospect for another.

"We still got work to do, asshole," Gunnar grunts behind me. His voice is hoarse; obviously that gunshot to the shoulder is taking a toll on him.

Good.

Bastard.

I purposefully nailed Gunnar in the shoulder right before I shot Tryke. I knew if Gunnar had his chance, he'd have made sure that Tryke was good and dead. I had to take the chance in hopes that maybe he would survive. I may be a biker, but Tryke and Kiwi are my family.

I put my hand on my chest, feeling the cool metal of my father's dog tags pressing to my skin. I look to the ceiling – toward the sky – silently asking my father for guidance and forgiveness.

My father spent fifteen years in the service before he was wounded and discharged. He and Tripp were good friends. My father loved to ride, and Tripp gave him the golden opportunity to join the Angels. My father was beyond thrilled to be a member of the club, but despite his best efforts, he never earned his 1% patch. He died when I was ten from colon cancer. My mother succumbed to the bottle after that. Tripp and his old lady, Tryke and Kiwi's mom, took it upon themselves to look after me after dad died. I lived with my aunt, my mother's sister, but I was rarely ever there. As soon as I was allowed, I pledged to the Angels.

"We should have taken care of it before we left," I growl back at him. I knew Kiwi would be safe, even if we tore that house apart looking for the *money* they were looking for. Tryke knew what was coming for him and he had a choice to make- protect her, as he's done since their parents' deaths, or run. Tryke wasn't the running type.

"Fuck that, let him rot for a while. That son-of-a-bitch deserves worse than what he got."

I turn around and grab Gunnar by his cut and slam him against the wall. "Fuck you," I growl as I press my right fist into his shoulder. Gunnar doesn't make a sound but sweat beads on his forehead from the added pain I'm inflicting. Looking into his eyes, I see something I've never seen before from him.

Fear.

Good. I push into his shoulder a little harder and his teeth grind together. "Get your fucking ass cleaned up. I'll handle Tryke's house."

"Like hell you will," Rooster chimes in. "Get off him, now."

With Tryke dead, Rooster has everything to gain from this. He will have no one pushing for Tryke's position and more importantly, he thinks he will gain the respect of the club members by killing off Tryke. But the truth is he's lost what little respect he had earned in the last four years.

The Wicked Angels have a long-standing tradition that the presidency is a handed down position. The club was started by Tryke's great-grandfather and his two brothers. When he moved on, Tryke's grandfather took over the club's operations until Tripp, Tryke's father, did. When Tripp died, it would have been handed down to Tryke, but he wasn't old enough and had only had his cut for about a year before Tripp's death. Big Daddy D – head of all Wicked Angels – suggested Tryke learn the ropes, earn the respect, then take over. Tryke was working hard at earning the respect a true president deserves even though he didn't have the title. His fight was because he refused to let Rooster take the club down a path none of the Roswell charter members want to go down.

Aside from learning the ropes, at least as much as Rooster was willing to teach him, Tryke and I began investigating what happened to Tripp and his old lady. We did everything we could, including taking out a couple members of Roswell in an attempt to find out the truth. Someone ordered Tripp to be killed. Someone was dumb enough to follow the order and it was just a matter of figuring out who ordered it and who carried it out. Or if that person is one in the same.

The best we could come up with was pointing the finger at Rooster. Without solid proof that Rooster is responsible for it, the other heads won't act. Come to find out, Rooster is a great-nephew of one of the founding members of the club and the Wicked Angels are a family first organization. Prospecting with the Angels is a given if you have Beaumont blood running through your veins. What you do as a prospect determines whether or not you get your colors and cut.

At the time of Tripp's death, Rooster was desperately trying to push Tripp in a different direction with the club. Sure, we do our fair share of illegal shit, but there are lines that Tripp, Tryke, myself and several other club members of Roswell won't cross. Like human trafficking.

I release Gunnar.

"I'll take care of the house," I snap at Rooster as I grab my shot off the bar and slam it back.

"I want it leveled," Rooster says.

"It will be," I tell him as I nod at the prospect again. One more should be enough to numb the pain.

"I want pictures."

"Yup," I tell Rooster as I finally look around the clubhouse. It's nearly empty. No wonder Rooster is out here running his mouth about shit.

The clubhouse being nearly empty on a Tuesday isn't unusual. But on a night like this, when everyone knows shit's going down, they scatter. When Rooster gets on a power trip, no one's safe and it's made worse by the fact that the shit is Tryke. No one will go near Gunnar for a least a week. When he's amped up like this, there's no telling what he'll do.

My eyes land on Taz, a fine, albeit well-used piece of ass, cleaning up one of the tables. Her shorts are practically crawling up her ass, her tits are barely concealed beneath the half-shirt she's wearing. Typical attire for her around here. She's been a club whore for years, even has a kid that belongs to a lowlife member. Remember the whole – family first rule – well, you knock up a whore, you deal with the fallout. Ignore that fallout and you lose respect.

I walk over to her, grab her arm and drag her down the hall toward one of the rooms. "Hey baby, I've missed you," she coos as we walk down the hall. I'm holding on to her pretty tight but she knows better than to say anything to me about it.

"No talking," I grunt as I push open a door and push her inside.

"Naked, now."

She doesn't hesitate. She throws her shirt over her head and unbuttons her shorts, sliding them down her legs before kicking them off along with her heels.

My cock lengthens and hardens behind my jeans as she starts to climb onto the bed.

I shake my head at her. "My cock is going in your mouth. Then if you're lucky, your ass," I snap and she smiles wide.

"Anything for you, baby." She winks as she climbs off the bed. She comes over to me just as I rip open my button fly and pull my cock free.

"Such a big, gorgeous cock," she coos as she wraps her hand around it.

"Shut the fuck up and suck my dick."

I watch a pout play on her lips. I'm not in the mood for conversation. I simply want to get off and get on with my life.

Her warm lips wrap around the head of my dick and my blood starts racing and my mind starts wandering. I close my eyes and Taz isn't who I'm thinking about sucking my cock.

No, I'm thinking about a cute, five foot six inch, seventeen-year-old strawberry blonde.

Taz's mouth isn't working me fast enough so I grab hold of her face and start pushing my dick deeper into her mouth, not giving a shit if she chokes.

I finally open my eyes and am disappointed to see Taz and not Kiwi sucking me off. "Play with your tits," I tell her and she smiles around my cock.

She removes her hand from my dick and cups both tits in her hands. Taz has been around this club for a long fucking time. I'm sure there isn't a brother in here who hasn't used her or abused her more than a few times. She's not one of my favorites but she'll do in a pinch, like tonight.

"Enough," I snap. "On the bed, face down," I tell her and she moves quickly. I don't even bother removing my shirt, boots or pants. I simple pull a condom from my pocket and tear it open with my teeth before rolling it down my hard length.

I kneel on the bed behind her and to no surprise, she's soaking wet. I slide my cock up and down her slit before lining up with her entrance and slamming home.

"Oh, yeah, baby, give it to me," she moans.

I smack her ass, hard. "Shut your fucking mouth, whore," I tell her before I start pounding relentlessly into her. My goal, come before she does.

I fuck her hard, her body bouncing on the bed. Her ass cheeks wiggle with each thrust in. I take a firm hold of her hips before forcing her up and down my cock. Other than being warm and wet, I'm getting very little pleasure out of this, but given enough time, she will make me come.

That time comes a little faster after I close my eyes and imagine a much tighter, much prettier pussy surrounding my cock. Her reddish blonde hair splayed down her back, her beautiful curves at my disposal.

Three more pumps into the loose cunt at my disposal and my orgasm roars. My cum explodes into the latex barrier.

I grind out my orgasm before pulling out of her.

"That's it?" she snaps.

"Fuck off," I growl back as I rip the used condom off my dick, tie it off and toss it in the trash before buttoning up my jeans and storming out of the room.

Walking back into the common room of the clubhouse, the few members that were lingering are gone. All that's left is Momma Bear, Pitbull's old lady, who is standing over a heavily breathing Gunnar.

As I get closer I see she's stitching him up. I walk up and kiss her on the cheek. "Leave a nasty scar," I tell her.

She laughs, "You know I can't do that."

I wink at her just as she slides the needle through Gunnar's skin again. "Fuck, watch yourself, bitch," Gunner grunts in pain. I smile in satisfaction as I step out of the club and into the warm night air.

I look up to the sky, hoping I've given Kiwi enough time to get out of that house.

CHAPTER THREE

Lily

"If anything goes down, I want you to do it." It's Kellen talking. I'm sitting on the stairs, out of sight from the kitchen. Loki is here having beers with my brother.

"Do what?" Loki's sultry voice reaches my ears.

"To be the one..."

"The one what?" Loki asks.

"The one to kill me."

TWENTY OR SO MINUTES PASS and I can't stop staring at the monitor attached to the camera in the kitchen, the one where my brother lies dead.

The airlocks disengage.

With each passing minute, the fear and sadness turns to rage and to what I'm going to do next.

"You can't do anything if you don't get moving," I tell myself.

I take one more look at my brother. For about the umpteenth time, I swear his chest moves. But then I remind myself that he was shot three times in his chest and there's no way he survived that.

"Damn you, Loki."

The faded memory rattles around my mind again. "Just because you wanted him to do it, doesn't make it right," I mutter.

Kellen knew this was coming.

He knew he was going to die.

His behavior earlier. The argument we got into about what I'm supposed to do if anything happens to him.

Not to mention the weird behavior over the last few weeks. Just a couple weeks ago, Kellen showed up with a car for me. A nearly brand new Nissan Altima. I didn't understand at first. Especially considering his excuse had everything to do with his contingency plan if something happened to him. I blew it off, thinking he was just being overprotective and overly paranoid.

I didn't need the car. He taught me how to drive a motorcycle before I learned how to drive a car so I could have just taken a bike instead. If he'd been smarter about it, he could have pawned it off as a graduation present, but instead he made sure to go over the contingency plan with me one more time.

Coupled with the erratic behavior today, the going to the backyard into the woods.

It explains everything.

"Oh, my god, the woods," I all but shout.

What did he put back there? I ask myself.

"Only one way to find out," I mumble as I reach for the door knob on the safe room and let my fingerprints disengage the lock. I pull the door open. It's eerily quiet outside the safe room. At least inside I had the buzz of all the monitors and the visual of seeing the rest of the house to keep me company. Out here, there's nothing. I've spent many nights alone in this house while Kellen was gone, but never have I felt this alone. That alone was temporary, this is permanent. Tears streak down my cheeks.

I swipe them away with my fingers. I need to focus. I'm running out of time. I need to get out of here before they come back to finish the job. Loki, that old man, other club members, doesn't matter who, but they'll be back here soon enough to verify my brother is dead. Once that's done, they'll destroy the house and all the evidence they've left behind. They'll stop at nothing to cover their tracks and keep the heat off the club.

A shiver of fear slices through me at what they'll do if they catch me. Keeping myself alive long enough to get out of here is more important than anything. My brother didn't die tonight so I could die too. He died to keep me safe.

I turn for my room and go to work.

There's not a lot of time.

WICKED REVENGE

Heading straight for my closet, I grab the three suitcases I keep in there. Again, another present that leads me to believe Kellen knew this was coming a long time ago. Though the suitcases came from Loki and not Kellen, I suspected Kell had everything to do with it when Loki gave them to me. I brush it off as I toss the largest of the three on my bed, opening it. I start emptying drawers, grabbing clothes, shoes, everything within reach that I want to take with me. I don't take time to decide on anything, I just toss it all in there.

I fight the urge to cry several times in the process, but then I start to think about why Kellen didn't send me packing this afternoon, when there was time. Why did he keep me around to see that shit?

Because you'd have never left. The voice in my head is right. I wouldn't have left. There would have been nothing Kell could have said to me to make me leave. He knew that, I know that. He knew that I had to see this for myself. He also knew it would save Loki from having to track me down and explain it to me.

With each passing minute, each item tossed in a bag, my mind and body succumb to the numbness it so desperately needs to get through this.

When we're faced with disaster, we, as humans, have a natural inclination to fight or flight. Right now, I'm running with flight because I have to. To honor my brother's wishes. The fight will come later.

I don't know how much time passes while I'm packing because I wasn't paying attention to the time. I just know that exhaustion threatens to overcome me as I look around my room. Compared to a few minutes ago, it's practically bare. I zip up the suitcases, my backpack and another bag that I used for all my bathroom stuff. I toss my backpack on my back, the bag crisscross across my chest and grab two of the suitcases. I take them down to the garage.

A sense of relief washes through me when I realize I don't have to go through the kitchen. It's taking everything I have not to go in there. I know if I do, I will turn into a blubbering mess and I will never get out of here before they show up. Seeing him, up close and personal, will be my undoing and right now, I need all the strength I can manage to get out of here.

I put the suitcase next to the car Kellen bought me. In hindsight, I understand why he bought me the car. Sure, I can take a bike, but I'd have to leave all this shit behind, leaving behind further evidence of my existence. He hasn't been protecting me this hard for me to destroy it now.

If anyone comes back here and starts tearing apart the house looking for whatever they think Kellen stole, they won't think much of my room as it is and Kellen's bike will still be here. If I take his bike, it will look suspicious. He's dead in the kitchen, after all.

I load my suitcases into the trunk of the car. My eyes narrow on a bag that's already in the trunk. I want to open it, figure out why it's here, but I ignore it. Once my stuff is inside, I run back upstairs, grabbing the last suitcase and the final thing from my room.

I round my bed and kneel in front of the nightstand. I reach under it and pull the metal box from its resting place. There's a keypad on top of it and I punch in the code. 5 6 5 4 and the lock clicks open. I lift the lid and take a look at the purple and silver plated Glock 22 from its resting place. I pop the clip, it's full. Pull back on the slide and it's loaded. I double check that the safety is on and I tuck it in the waistband of my jeans.

Kellen taught me how to shoot a year and a half ago. There was never an argument from me. I wanted to learn, so he taught me. Then I started kicking his ass on the range and he regretted it, but he never stopped taking me.

I fight the urge to let the numbness slide away by closing the box and tucking it under my arm. On my way out of the room, I grab my last suitcase and haul it down to the car. It's the biggest one and it won't fit into the trunk with the other stuff, so I go to the driver's door and open it. I unlock the back door. I press the button before my eyes land on a white envelope sitting in the driver's seat. On the outside, in my brother's script,

24

WICKED REVENGE

is my nickname, the one given to me by Loki when I was three- Kiwi.

"Fuck you, Kellen," I growl and put the letter in my center console. I know better than to read it now.

I need to get into the backyard before I leave.

Before they get back.

I go through the back door, the same one Kellen used earlier today when he disappeared into the garage. Stepping into the backyard sets off the security light over the door, but it won't last long. I pull my phone from my back pocket and turn the flashlight on to illuminate my way. I go through the same two trees Kellen came out of earlier and follow the barely visible footpath.

It's overgrown now from lack of use, but it's the same path Kell and I would take whenever we went into the woods to hide from mom and dad.

The walk seems much longer than I remember as a kid but eventually I reach the small clearing and the dilapidated building we once hung out in. It was our little secret, our own little clubhouse.

My heart squeezes in my chest.

I open the door and shine the light inside.

The floor we once sat on is gone. Replaced by a dirt floor that's littered with broken down hunks of wood from the old floor. The dirt looks like it's been disturbed with an area free of floor debris and a rather large boot print smack in the middle of it.

Using my flashlight, I look around the building for a shovel and I find a small garden one in the corner. I grab it and start digging through Kellen's footprint. I don't get very deep before the rusty shovel scrapes something.

I flip the shovel over and use the handle side to poke around until I find the edges of whatever's buried down here. Once I have it, I flip the shovel over and dig around the outside. It's about the size of a briefcase. I toss the shovel aside and put my hands on the side, prying it up.

Within a few seconds, I'm pulling up a steel briefcase. With my flashlight, I look it over. There's a padlock on it and on the handle, is a bag that's tied to it. I tug on the bag and it comes free. I put my fingers in the bag and pry it open.

Inside is a very large bank roll of what appears to be all hundred dollar bills. Around the bills is a piece of paper that has my name written in Kellen's handwriting.

Freeing the letter from under the rubber band, I unfold it to find a letter from my brother. With my flashlight pointed at it, I read:

> Hi, Kid,
>
> I'm sorry you're finding this letter like this, but what's done is done. Time to move on; time to get away from Roswell. You know what to do, where to go, now go. Do it. On your way, take this to Uncle D. He'll know what to do with it.
>
> Love,
>
> K
>
> P.S. Don't be mad at Loki, I asked him to do it.

"Motherfucker," I growl at the piece of paper. The numbness fades just enough to allow a few tears to escape my eyes. I take a few deep breaths, hoping the numbness will return, but it doesn't.

I don't know how long I stay in the building but gradually the numbness I needed to get moving returns. I stand up and leave the last remnants of my brother behind. I'm traveling back through the trees and I'm almost to the backyard when I hear a motorcycle coming down the road.

"Fuck, fuck," I growl and start running toward the house. My heart is racing in my chest. They've come back to finish the job and I'm still here.

I stop for a second to listen further. When the bike switches gears, the noise drops out completely. There's just one. Thank God, I can handle one.

WICKED REVENGE

I switch the briefcase to my left hand and reach into my waistband as I approach the tree line of the backyard and free my gun. They crossed a line tonight. I will stop at nothing to make sure I'm safe. It's the least I can do to honor my brother.

As the bike draws closer, the noise louder now, but still not quite at the house, I set the briefcase down and fish my phone from my pocket. Unlocking it as I remember the app my brother installed a few months back when I got the phone. The app is tied to the cameras in the house. Kellen set up alarms and alerts on both his phone and mine that would let us know if someone entered the house. There's also access to the live feeds. I'd never needed it before now.

I wait for the cameras to load on the screen and find the driveway one just as the motorcycle engine draws closer to the house.

As soon as the bike comes into the camera's line of sight, I close my eyes and shake my head before tucking the phone back in my pocket.

I grab the briefcase before I take off for the house. I know I won't make it inside before he does, but I'm hoping like hell to corner him somewhere, somehow.

I head straight for the back door of the garage. My only other option is the kitchen door and I'm not about to go in there. I shouldn't have trusted Loki to declare my brother dead. He shot him after all, but I can't bring myself to look at him. I will lose it again.

Once inside the garage, I throw the briefcase on the floor of the backseat and gently close the door before I pull my phone back out of my pocket. I start checking cameras, looking for him.

He's in the kitchen.

He's looking over my brother with sadness in his features and the tears for his pain spill from my eyes. Using the back of my hand, the one with the gun still in it, I wipe my tears from my eyes so that I can see the picture more clearly. "Lily?" I hear him ask. "Can you still hear me?"

"Yes," I breathe.

Loki turns, leaving the kitchen and I switch to the living room camera feed. He goes up the stairs and turns toward my room and stops outside my bedroom door. I watch the sense of relief that washes over his features as he realizes that I've packed up my room. He doesn't yet know that I'm still here.

He moves from my room to the safe room door. I'd closed it after I left, but he places his hand on the knob. I watch the two green lines light up next to the door. The lights are recessed in the wall and covered, so until they light up, you can't see them. "He has access?" I ask myself. Another sense of relief can be seen in his taut features. He looks up into the hallway camera and nods, but he doesn't smile, no, he looks almost disappointed. Did he come back to kill me too?

He goes back down the hallway and then down the stairs, through the living room and instead of returning to the kitchen, he turns toward the garage door.

Shit! I jam my phone back in my pocket and spread my legs, taking my stance and pointing my gun toward the door.

All I can really hear is my heartbeat in my ears as I wait for Loki to come to the door. I won't shoot first, I need answers. I need to know why he killed my brother.

I watch the knob turn and finally the door opens revealing Loki standing there, staring at me.

He puts his hands up. "Don't shoot me, Kiwi."

My nickname sends my heart into panic mode. "Why?" I breathe; it's all I can manage.

"Why are you still here?" he counters.

"I was just leaving when you showed up," I tell him, and my voice cracks with fear and sadness.

"What would you have done if it wasn't me?" he asks as he steps down into the garage.

"Exactly what I'm doing right now. Only difference is, I'd have pulled the trigger first, asked questions later." I reaffirm my stance and cock the gun.

WICKED REVENGE

"I did what I had to do to protect you," he tells me with his hands still in the air. "To protect Tryke. Please understand that."

A stray tear streaks down my cheek.

"I remember. When he told you that you had to be the one to do it?"

He cocks his head at me. "You heard us?"

I nod. "I've heard a lot of things over the years, Loki. I'm not the dumb naïve little girl with pigtails anymore," I remind him.

He shakes his head. "No, no you're not, Lily, you're a woman, and you deserve far better than this. So now you have a choice. Kill me now and run, or get in your car and get the fuck out of here before anyone else shows up."

"There are two choices in life. You can let it go and move on or you can do what I'm going to do."

"What's that?" Loki asks.

"Get revenge," I breathe.

Loki lets a small smile spread across his lips as he comes within striking distance. "That's my Kiwi," he tells me as he snatches the gun from my hand and the next thing I know, I'm scooped up in his arms.

My world shatters as I collapse into a ball of tears in Loki's arms.

CHAPTER FOUR

Loki

"GO, YOU HAVE GOT TO get out of here," I snap at Kiwi.

Having her in my arms, despite how upset she is, is the best feeling in the world, but she cannot stay here any longer. I've covered her ass up to this point, but I no longer have control over who shows up next.

She looks up at me and her eyes are wide with fear. "Why can't I just stay with you?"

"Because it's not safe and you know it. You've got to get away from here, Lily. Get out of here and never look back."

"But I…"

"Dammit, Lily, do it. Do what your brother told you to do." I let her go.

Her stunned expression rips me in two, but if I'm not hard with her, she'll never leave.

"Go, goddammit. I don't know who else is coming. I can't protect you against them." My voice grows harder with each word.

Her eyes narrow at me. "Give me back my gun," she snaps.

I give her an evil smirk. I pull the clip from the gun and push each bullet out one by one. She folds her arms across her chest with indifference. I know damn well there are more bullets where these came from, but by the time she reloads, I'll be back in the house.

Seven bullets on the ground and one final one in the chamber. I give her a tsk of disappointment because the magazine isn't full. I return the clip to the gun and pull back on the slide, discharging the final bullet and turn the safety back on with a flick of my finger before handing her back her gun.

She snatches it from my hand.

"Get. The. Fuck. Out. Of. Here," I growl at her.

"You killed my brother and you treat me like shit," she snaps.

I get in her face. "I'm protecting you. Now get the fuck out of here before I kill you myself."

Her eyes widen in fear, but then harden as she steps up, toe to toe, with me, despite her smaller frame. "Go ahead, motherfucker. I ain't got nothin' left to live for."

I close my eyes as pain and anger wash over me. She can't begin to grasp what she has to live for. She's too young to see it and I'm not about to show her one of her biggest reasons for living, not now.

I smirk at her. "Yeah, little girl, you do. Revenge." Realization slides over her features as her stony, indifferent mask slides back into place. She turns, opening the car door and sliding inside. A heartbeat passes before the garage door is sliding up and the engine turns over.

As soon as she's clear of the door, she throws the car in drive and speeds out of the garage. I hold my breath, praying she doesn't take out my bike on the way out.

Once at the end of the driveway, she hesitates before she turns left. Away from Roswell and the Wicked Angels MC.

I watch her go. I can't seem to get my feet moving for a few minutes. Eventually the reality of what I should do comes into focus and I head for the door, punching the garage door closed and waiting before I step inside the house. I walk down the short hallway to the kitchen and my best friend.

"Who was that?" a voice asks and I turn around, drawing my gun and pointing it at the man standing behind me.

CHAPTER FIVE
Kiwi

FOUR DAYS LATER

"YOU'RE IN THE WRONG PLACE, darlin'," the gate man says to me as I pull up outside the Wicked Angels Headquarters just outside Tucson, Arizona. My gun rests in my lap, just in case I need to throw down. It's not what I want to do. I need answers and there is a man inside this building that can give them to me.

"I doubt that. I need to see Big Daddy D."

"And just who might you be?" I can tell the guy is a little irritated at the name I use. He is, after all, head Wicked Angel, eldest in the line of living Beaumont men and the reason the Angels are as successful as they are.

"Kiwi," I tell him. Loki gave me the nickname long ago and it's the only credit I have here.

After I got to a hotel just inside the Arizona border the other night, I unloaded my luggage, including the bag Kellen left for me in the trunk and dragged them inside. I should have kept moving, but the seedy motel was the perfect place to hide out for a few days. Get my head about me and pull myself together enough to do this.

Two days ago, I opened the bag from Kellen.

Two days ago, I learned the real reason Kellen wanted me out of the house and away from Roswell.

I'm dead.

At least as far as the Angels are concerned.

My brother, in all his infinite wisdom, decided it was best to pretend that I died in the same car crash as my parents.

WICKED REVENGE

This explains why I never saw another Wicked Angels member, except Loki.

"You don't look like no Kiwi to me." The man guarding the club leans into my window.

I catch one of the clubhouse doors swinging open from the corner of my eye. My eyes narrow in on the three men walking out. They're headed toward their bikes until they see my car at the gate and turn in our direction. I'm doing my best to look at them and keep my eyes on the dick whose patch says Whistler, that's giving me a hard time about getting in. I pull my eyes from him long enough to see that one of the three men coming our way is the one I'm here to see.

"What the fuck, Whistler?" one of the men walking towards us shouts.

"She wants to see Big Daddy, says her name is Kiwi."

"Bullshit," says the tallest, and biggest of the three of them. "Kiwi is dead."

With my gun still in my hand, I open the car door, hitting Whistler between his legs. The three men scramble toward me as I climb out of the car.

"Like hell I am," I snap at Big Daddy.

His eyes bulge in pure undiluted shock. Something I had expected, but hoped I wouldn't see. I'd secretly hoped that I was only dead to the Roswell members, but apparently not.

Why would he send me here with this shit if he'd passed it around that I'd died with my parents?

"Jesus fucking Christ, kid," Uncle D says as he shakes his head. "Open the gate."

After a beat, the gates start to swing open. "Whistler, get out of there before she shoots off your balls," someone says and my lips twitch with a smirk as I slide back into my car, putting my gun back in my lap.

The guys clear the driveway and I pull forward until I'm parked on the side of the clubhouse building. I take a deep breath, controlling the adrenaline spike I got when Whistler started giving me hell about letting me in.

I breathe in again, bracing myself for what's going to happen next before I climb out of the car. Gun in one hand, briefcase and my purse in the other.

As I stand up my eyes roam over the four men standing in a semi-circle watching me. Whistler and Big Daddy are the only two I know. Seeing as none of them have weapons drawn, I tuck mine into my waistband along my back and kick my door closed before walking toward the group of men. I send a silent thank you to Kellen for teaching me how to shoot and manage a gun. After mom and dad died, he felt it was important for me to learn, even though I was only thirteen.

"What are you doing here, kid?" Big Daddy asks me. His tone is hard to read, a little gruff, a little confused and something else, concern maybe.

I hold up the briefcase. "Tryke sent me."

He cocks his head. "Why didn't he just come himself?" he asks.

Anger slices through me. One of the reasons I waited so long to come up here was because Tryke should have been honored by the club. All members of the club, including Tucson and Boulder. The anger makes it easy for me to slide my cold, hard demeanor into place. "Because he's dead."

"Fucking Christ, are you kidding me? When?" Big Daddy asks. Anger roars again, a biker is dead and they're doing nothing to honor him.

"Four days ago," I share. "Now, can we talk, privately, please?" I ask a little softer.

"Yeah, kid, let's go." He gestures for me to follow him.

He leads me into the clubhouse, holding the door for me. I duck under his arm and step inside.

There are several club members and half-naked women throughout the big, open common room. It's hard to gauge its size compared to Roswell because it's been so long.

WICKED REVENGE

There are two pool tables along the back side, a bar to my right and several couches lining the walls around the room. There are also several tables, high and low, with chairs and barstools scattered around the place. If you didn't know better, you'd think it was a hopping nightclub most nights. Most night's it's probably hopping but you couldn't pay me enough to sit on a couch in this place.

All the male eyes are on me as I walk behind Big Daddy toward some place quiet for us to talk.

My outfit isn't leaving much to the imagination. I knew coming in here would be a mess to begin with, but I had to do something to either make them drool or ward off the crazy.

I went with the former.

I'm wearing leather pants with a corset top. My hair is done with wavy curls cascading down my back. I'm also wearing peep-toe, black fuck-me pumps and a gold necklace that's tied to a locket my mother gave me when I was about seven. My intention was to present myself as hard-ass as possible. Whether or not it's working, I'm not sure yet. I suppose the gun I got out of the car with is handling a lot of that by itself.

We step into a hallway that runs toward the back of the clubhouse and Big Daddy leads me into his office. His goons from outside try to follow us in and I slam the door in their faces.

"Those are my men," D snaps.

I give him a hard look. "I don't give a fuck. What I've got to talk to you about doesn't involve them," I snap.

The next thing I know, his hand is flying through the air and slamming into my left cheek, sending my head flying to the side. I put my hand on it, trying to soften the sting and I glare at him. "What the fuck, Kiwi?" He looks at me with concern and my hardened exterior softens some. "Are you done being a bitch or do I need to remind you of the rules, again?" he asks.

Sucking in a deep breath, I soften a little more. "Forgive me, but there are very few people I trust right now."

He nods and takes a seat in the chair behind his desk. "What the fuck is going on around here?" he asks. He's pissed. Good.

"What do you mean?"

He looks pointedly at me. "You're alive, let's start there."

I shrug. "Honestly, I have no fucking clue. All I know is mom and dad were killed in a car accident. Once that happened, Tryke got hard, he changed. I didn't understand it, I thought it was grief. But then none of the members came around anymore. I saw only Loki, Tryke's best friend, and that was it. He got paranoid, built a safe room, rigged the house with cameras and sent me to a private school. He used the guise of a better education but now I see it was to keep me away from the family."

"You have any idea why he was so paranoid?" he asks.

I shake my head as I set the briefcase and my bag in the chair opposite him and reach into my bag to produce a DVD that I'd burned of the other night. It killed me to watch it again, but I did. I hold it up., "I have no idea why he was paranoid, but it paid off. You can see for yourself what happened four days ago."

"They got taped?" He narrows his eyes.

I cock my head at him. "Because Tryke was paranoid," I remind him and then ask, "How well did you know Tryke?" Big Daddy is, after all, our uncle and the President of Wicked Angels Motorcycle Club.

"Well enough," he says deadpan. "After your parents died, I wanted him in the President's office, but he, along with a few other people, agreed that he needed some time to get the club under his belt. He was twenty-two at the time. He'd had his cut for what, two years?" I nod, acknowledging him. When Tryke got his cut, it was a huge deal in the house. "He was ready, going to make a run at Pres. From what I knew about it, he had more than enough support to make it happen. But other than that? I get the feeling I'm about to be schooled by my niece on the doings in Roswell."

"Why was he going for president?" I ask.

"Because family first, and like your father, they respect the hell out of him. If there is anyone in that outfit that would make a better Pres, I'd like to know about him," he says confidently.

I roll my eyes. "I'm not all that interested in clubhouse business, Uncle D. I just want to know who ordered the hit on Tryke."

He puts his hands up in defense. My uncle may be the President of Wicked Angels MC, but he's never shown me anything but kindness and love and I respect him for that.

"It certainly wasn't me. Had I known that Rooster had plans on taking him out, I would have taken Rooster out."

"Who's Rooster?" I ask him.

He leans forward, putting his bare, tattoo covered forearms on his desk. "He took over Roswell after your father..."

I give him a hard stare. "You do realize that Tryke never accepted the fact that Daddy died in a car accident, right?"

He nods. "I do, darlin'. But until someone can come to me with hard, physical proof that it was Rooster or anyone else in the club, who ordered a hit or carried it out himself, my hands are tied. There ain't much I can do."

"But you're the club president," I remind him.

"Thank you for that reminder, doll. Yes, I am."

"Then why not do something about it?"

He snorts, "Because we have rules, guidelines in place. Rooster was voted in, albeit because there were limited other options at the time and no one challenged his appointment, not even your brother. Rooster has to be voted out. And if your brother was killed because Rooster was feeling threatened, I need proof. If there are other extenuating circumstances as to why your brother was taken out, that's different."

"But he can't just take someone out without coming from you, can he?"

He glares at me. "No, but it happens."

"He was your nephew for crying out loud. You mean to tell me you're going to sit there and do nothing about him being murdered? Hell, you didn't know he was dead. I waited four days to come to you because I'd assumed you'd gone to Roswell for the burial and yet here you sit." I challenge him and his face reddens. "I thought this club respected its dead."

He stands up, sending his chair flying back. He slams his fist into his desk. "Do not challenge me, little girl," he growls. "He obviously died for an acceptable reason for someone to keep me out of the loop."

"So that warrants no funeral? No respect?"

"Enough," he barks. "You're making some pretty strong accusations here, sweetheart, and you'd better have some proof to back this up."

"Maybe I do," I say, holding up the briefcase. "I found this after Tryke was killed. It came with a pouch that had a note attached to it."

"What did it say?"

I hand him the note from my purse, the one my brother wrote to me, and he reads it over then he looks up at me with murder in his eyes and I take an involuntary step back. "Loki?" he growls and I nod hesitantly.

"I overheard them a few years ago, after mom and dad..." I pause, trying to gain control of myself again. I swallow. "Tryke hid me from the club and the only person he let around the house after their deaths was Loki. I overheard them one night talking about how Tryke wanted Loki to be the one to do it. If it ever came to that. Once I understood that, I realized Loki was doing it to protect Kellen and me." His name slips off my tongue and I bite it, hoping to stave off the tears.

"Do you know why they wanted him dead?" he asks as he reaches back for his chair, pulling it up and sitting back down. I let out a rush of relief. Sitting is good; it means he's calming down.

"I have an idea. It might involve the briefcase or something else, but the other guy who came with Loki kept sputtering something about money and how they know Tryke stole it."

Uncle D leans back in his chair and steeples his fingers against his lips. "It's club business and I can't go into detail about it, but there's been some inconsistencies in that part of the business. We've not been able to break it down enough to figure out who's behind it. If Rooster is saying that Tryke was behind it, he'd have the right to take him down without consulting me."

"So, they become judge, jury and executioner with Tryke?" My uncle just nods and right now I hate him more than I hate Loki. "So, to cover their asses, to make it look like a good hit, they accused Tryke of stealing money from the club?"

My uncle laughs without humor. "Fucking morons." His face turns red with anger. "I may not be there, in Roswell, but I know Tryke better than most and I know damn well he'd never do that. He has no reason to. He's got enough money that he could get a major drug addiction and still survive." I shudder at the idea of Tryke addicted to drugs. Sure, he smoked pot once in a while, but that's it. All the guys did at one point or another. Beer, pot and cigarette smoke were staples in my house growing up.

"I assure you there were no drugs in his life and no reason for him to be skimming money from the club. We had everything we needed and then some. He dropped money on that safe room, those cameras, and security measures around the house like it was chump change," I tell him. "We always had food in the house. I had clothes on my back and a substantial allowance that came without fail every week. He never griped or bitched about a lack of money and he even loaned Loki money from time to time. So, I can tell you, Tryke is not your thief."

"Fucking idiots." My uncle leans forward, putting his arms back on the desk. "I'll get to the bottom of this and handle it."

"I want at him first." I narrow my eyes at him, conveying my seriousness. "I want to take him down."

He just stares blankly at me for a moment. "You're joking, right?"

"Don't patronize me. Between my father, my mother and now my brother, I deserve my chance."

My uncle shifts behind the desk, his hand coming up to play with his beard. Big Daddy is a big guy, about six-five, with broad shoulders and hips to match. At one point in his life, he was healthy and ripped. Too many beers and sitting around has changed that. He's not unattractive, though the belly button length beard is a bit much. He thinks something over for a moment before he points to the briefcase in my hand. "We'll come back to that, later. What's in there?"

"I was hoping you would tell me. All I know is Tryke buried it, I found it with a note telling me to bring it here to you. Trust me; I wouldn't be here if it wasn't for that briefcase." I take a deep breath, digging down to my toes for the strength I found when I finally left that hotel room. I stare at him. "He died for this briefcase," I remind him as I set the briefcase down on the desk in front of him along with the DVD of Tryke's murder.

"You got someplace to stay?" he asks.

"I'll manage."

"Stay here, at the clubhouse." He gives me a look that says it's not an invitation but an order.

"No," I tell him sternly.

"You want a chance for revenge or not?" he asks me.

"You know I do, but not here, not like this," I tell him. "I need time."

"Fuck that," he snaps.

"I'm seventeen," I remind him.

"Fuck," he groans. "For how much longer?"

"What day is it?" I cock my head at him.

"The sixteenth."

"Three more days," I tell him.

His eyes widen briefly before he relaxes. "Well, then I don't see what the problem is."

I put my hands on his desk and lean forward. "I'm not a club whore," I remind him.

He smirks, "No? You walk in here looking like that and expect me to believe you're not a club whore?"

I stand up and try in vain to cover myself. "I needed someone to take me seriously."

"Oh, I'm listening, darlin'."

"I can't stay here," I tell him.

"You don't think we can protect you?" He raises an eyebrow at me.

"I know damn well you can protect me, Uncle D. But you have too many Roswell guys coming up in here too often. My brother did a damn good job of keeping me away from them for four years. Do you honestly believe I'll let you ruin that with your over-protective big daddy complex?"

"Then go north, Boulder. Roswell has no business up there and no need to be there."

"I'm going to my aunt's in Colorado Springs," I lie. The truth is I'm headed to Boulder. Headed to my uncle's.

He narrows his eyes at me. "Your mother's sister?"

"That's where Tryke wants me."

"Does your aunt even know you're coming?"

I shake my head.

"Christ, Kiwi, have you even thought this through?"

"I have enough money to take care of myself and three days until I turn eighteen, then I can get a place of my own," I snap at him.

"You're family, Kiwi." His eyes soften a little. He may be a Pres, a badass biker, but for the Wicked Angels, family has always come first.

"Forty-five minutes ago, you thought I was dead." I narrow my eyes at him.

"That reminds me," he drawls. "I thought you were dead because your brother said so. We buried your ass with your parents. How the fuck was I supposed to know we buried an empty coffin? Whatever Tryke was doing, he let very few people into that inner circle."

"That son of a bitch!" I growl. My anger turns my vision red. "If that bastard wasn't already dead, I'd kill him myself."

"Whoa there, kitten, what are you talking about?"

I shake my head and start pacing around the room. "Will you just open that damn thing so I can get out of here?"

"Not until you tell me what the fuck is going on?" He stands up hard, pushing his chair against the wall behind his desk, again. Jesus, Lily, how many times you gonna piss him off in the course of an hour?

I stop, staring at him. "He brought home two urns. Told me it was easier that way." Tears swim in my eyes and I bite my lip. I've held it together this long, I don't need to lose it now.

My uncle shakes his head before shouting, "Whistler, Spike, get in here!" I jump at the loud boom of his voice.

"Yeah," one of them says behind me, though I don't bother to look to see who.

"Who can we send to Roswell?"

"Depends. What do you want done?"

"I want someone on the inside. We need to figure out what the fuck is going on down there," my uncle explains to the two men who just came into the room.

"Then send someone from Boulder or somewhere else. You send someone from here and they ain't gonna let them near anything."

I try my best to ignore them talking about Wicked Angels business but they're openly doing it in front of me. "Alright," my uncle concedes. "We'll talk about it later. Let me finish with Kiwi." He sits back down and glares at me. "Your brother did the right thing," he states stoically.

"What are you talking about?" I narrow my eyes at him in frustration.

"Club business."

"Fuck that bullshit. You can't drop a cryptic statement like that and not answer it."

WICKED REVENGE

My uncle is out of his chair and rounding his desk faster than I can react. He has me pushed against the wall, his hand at my throat before I can blink. The impact knocks the air out of my lungs. I fight for breath, but he gives me nothing. I don't fight him. "Listen, and listen good. Club business is club business and not meant for some little bitch, you get me?" he growls at me.

I fight for air again before nodding and he releases me. I double over, pulling in deep breaths, trying to right myself as he returns to his desk.

"What's the combo?" he asks as if he didn't just have me pinned against the wall.

I shrug while standing back up, straightening out. "The note says you'll know what to do with it."

"Well fuck," he grumbles but he starts fiddling with the combination. It's one of those turning wheel ones.

"How many numbers?" I ask.

His eyes look up from the briefcase and he responds, "Six."

"Birthday," I tell him.

"Whose?"

"How the fuck should I know?" I retort. His eyes narrow at me again and my heart skips a terrified beat in my chest, but he doesn't move. "Try yours, mom's, dad's, Tryke's, mine?" I throw my hands up in frustration. "Fuck if I know." I go back to pacing around the room while my uncle goes to town on the lock.

After a few heartbeats he asks, "What's yours?"

"February nineteenth, two thousand," I tell him.

He fiddles with it some more, putting in my date of birth and pushes the button, the latches pop up. "Well, aren't you a lucky charm," he mutters.

I shrug and move around his desk to look inside the briefcase.

"Money? I thought you said he didn't steal anything," my uncle snaps at me.

I look closer at it. There's something off about it. I don't understand it completely, but the color is bad, the numbers askew. "It's counterfeit," I breathe.

"How can you tell?" He looks up at me, skeptical.

"Look at it?" I tell him. "You got a twenty?" I ask and he digs into his back pocket, pulling his chain wallet from its resting place and he goes digging for a twenty. After a few seconds, he produces one and holds it next to the bills. "See, the color is off, not enough to raise too many eyebrows when they're all together and away from a real one."

"Fuck me," my uncle breathes.

"He died for a pile of fake fucking bills?" I snap.

My uncle just shrugs before he pulls a stack of the fake twenties from the briefcase and then the next thing I know, he's pulling them all out. Beneath the row of bills are a bunch of metal plates. "They're print plates," my uncle says as he grabs one from the briefcase and beneath it is a manila envelope.

Again, he pulls the plates from their resting place before reaching for the envelope. It has my name on it. "Fuck me," I breathe and my uncle looks at me as if I've lost my damn mind. I'm sure that I have. He hands it to me and I flip it over, unclasping it then opening the flap. Inside are a stack of papers stapled together with a note on top.

> Lily-bean,
>
> If you're reading this, you've done exactly as I've instructed. Thank you for listening to me. I need you to do one more thing for me.
>
> Attached to this note is all the proof that Big Daddy needs to track down the missing money. With a little investigation, he might be able to finish what I started and figure out who's skimming off the top. I recommend he starts at the top.
>
> I'm sorry I couldn't tell you any of this, but the less you knew the better.

WICKED REVENGE

I owed it to mom and dad, but more to you. You deserve a life better than I've given you, go and find it, Lily-bean.

There's no signature, but it's clearly my brother's handwriting. I pull the note from the stack of papers and I look at them briefly. They look like accounting ledgers. I hand them over to my uncle. "The letter says that this," I point at the stack I handed to him, "is enough for you to track down the missing money and with a little investigation, you should be able to finish 'what he started' and find out who's behind it." I take a deep breath. "Loki may have killed my brother, but he didn't do it without orders. I assure you of that. The other guy that was there with Loki got hit in the shoulder during the struggle, but Loki got nothing. If my brother was shooting, he'd have clipped Loki too. I think he did what he needed to do to make sure that Tryke died with a little dignity, considering he was being falsely accused." I chew on my lip for a second before I add, "Loki might know more about this." I nod at the briefcase.

"Why would he kill your brother?" my uncle asks, his voice is soft, sad almost.

"Because my brother asked him to," I state simply. "My guess is that the guy who was there with him is working for someone else inside the club or maybe he's responsible for the missing money or knows who is. They kill Tryke to cover their asses and Rooster takes out the one man vying for his position. He wins all the way around.

"But, if money continues to disappear, then they've still got a problem and Tryke wasn't the right man. Thus, producing a reason for you to take down whoever ordered the hit. If the money stops disappearing and the books stay legit, the person who took the money to begin with..." I swallow, "is dead already, or they're covering their tracks. But in the end, when they get in over their heads again, the money will start disappearing again. It's an addiction, Uncle D. Whether it's drugs or gambling, or just money in general, whoever is really behind this will not stop forever."

"Jesus, how old are you again?"

I smile at my uncle. "I'm a lot smarter than the strawberry blonde lets

45

on. I pay attention. I'm smart. Private school wasn't just to get me away from club members' kids." I wink and go back to the other side of the desk.

"We'll get to the bottom of this," he says without a hint of promise, but more of a 'don't get your hope us' kind of tone as he fishes blindly for his chair and takes a seat once again.

"Whoever is behind this, I want my crack at him. Whoever it is took out my parents and had my brother killed."

"Revenge is an ugly game, sweetheart."

"And it's all mine."

My tone leaves little to misinterpret and my uncle nods in understanding.

CHAPTER SIX

Lily

ROSWELL TO BOULDER, COLORADO BY way of Tucson, Arizona.

I stretch as I get out of the car in front of my Uncle Sticks' house in Boulder.

The house is gorgeous, considering it's a bachelor pad. White with hunter green shutters on either side of the windows. Two stories and a wraparound porch.

The front door opens and my uncle comes out with eyes narrowed on me. He's older, sixty, a couple years younger than Big Daddy, but Sticks looks every bit his age. "Well, I'll be damned," he grunts as he steps off the porch steps. I meet him halfway between my car and the stairs.

"Hey, Sticks." I smile and he wraps his arms around me.

"I was hopin' you'd skip that aunt of yours and come up here." His face lights up with a smile as he lets me go. Unlike his brother, Sticks maintains a nice goatee, though it's longer off the chin, it's not unattractive considering his age. His hair is salt and pepper and his eyes are my same shade of blue. The family resemblance is uncanny.

"So, Uncle D called you?"

He laughs, "Of course he did. Our niece, whom we thought dead, shows up after four years, damn right he called me." The cold hits me then and I shiver. "Come on, let's get you inside." He's actually happy to see me, which is a good sign.

He helps me with my bags, bringing them all in the house. "How long you gonna stay?" he asks as we set the bags at the foot of the stairs.

"Not long. I just need some time to get on my feet up here," I tell him. It's the truth. I never intended to be a burden on my uncle.

"You cook?" he asks, raising an eyebrow at me.

I smile wider, relief washing over me for the first time in almost a week. "I do."

"Well?" He cocks an eyebrow at me.

"I've not killed anyone yet," I tease.

"Good, you're staying."

I laugh.

The night goes much like that until he stomps his way up the stairs to his room. Sticks was married for a very long time to a woman I adored as a child. She died when I was ten and Uncle Sticks has been alone ever since. Well, as alone as a biker with a clubhouse full of club whores can be.

As I climb into the guest bed next to his room, I start to think about his open invitation to stay. I can't help wondering if he knew more about my being alive than he lead me to believe. It also makes me wonder if he'll give me the information I need about Roswell. The best I got out of Big Daddy was Rooster's name. I still don't know the name of the man who was with Loki that night.

I also need some time to learn as much club business as I can. I need to know how to get inside the walls and hopefully I can do it as something other than a club whore.

My uncle has been the Boulder charter Pres since he was twenty-two. The same age as Kellen when our parents died, but Boulder's charter was smaller in numbers and already had some well-established businesses to keep it afloat during his transition. Under Sticks' guidance and leadership, Boulder now rivals Tucson for the largest charter and it is still the most profitable.

During our talk tonight, I learned that the Boulder charter has several stores, shops and bars between here and Denver that they run. The money flows into the entire club through Boulder, and while Roswell and Tucson have their own store fronts, Boulder, for whatever reason, is the bread winner. There are several smaller charters throughout the West Coast. California, Oregon and Nevada are three states that I know for sure have charters.

Uncle Sticks, named because he was always drumming away with whatever he could get his hands on when he was younger, seemed happy to see me at first. Until I told him my plan to get revenge on the asshole who killed my parents and Tryke.

"Revenge is left to the big boys, darlin," he said, but there was a twitch in his lips that told me he wasn't all too disappointed in my intentions.

"Yeah, well, if anyone has a right to it, it's me."

He didn't have much of an argument after that. But he looked me up and down, scrutinizing me in my loose-fitting jeans and light colored t-shirt. The longer we talked the more I think he realized just how serious I am about it.

I'm formulating my plan to get Sticks' help when I doze off.

I'm awakened by the sun the next morning. I move around upstairs, hitting the shower and getting dressed as quietly and quickly as possible. I want to make him breakfast this morning.

I got here too late last night to make him a proper dinner, so breakfast will, with any luck, make up for it and put him in a talking mood.

I move around the kitchen and I can't help thinking about Sticks' wife and old lady. I wonder why he never took another one. It's not uncommon for members to take old ladies and lose them, either by their own stupidity or something awful happening to them, and then they find new ones. Sticks isn't like most members, though. He loved his old lady more than life itself.

Just as I'm finishing up the bacon, Sticks sits down at my breakfast spread. I can't help smiling as he devours the entire table in a matter of minutes. Grunting and groaning in appreciation of my cooking. "Yeah, you ain't goin' nowhere," he smirks.

"For now," I remind him.

"Listen, buttercup, you want revenge on these assholes, you're gonna haf-ta find a way to toughen up."

"So, show me." I smile at him.

He grunted with a smile on his face. "When you turn eighteen?"

49

"Tomorrow."

"Well, fuck me sideways," he laughs. "I'll find you a job, get you something inside the club walls, and give you a chance to learn the ropes, but you're gonna need new threads." He looks at my clothes again before dipping into his back pocket for his wallet. I notice then that Sticks' standard attire is a black t-shirt, black jeans, black motorcycle boots and his cut, but unlike most of the men, no chain on his wallet. Then again, he's pushing sixty.

"I got money," I tell him as he brings his wallet out.

He tucks the bills back in his pocket. "You sure?" he asks.

"Yeah, Tryke didn't leave me empty handed."

He nods before he takes off toward the front door. "We got some business at the compound tonight. I'll be home late."

I shake my head with a smirk on my face and off he goes. The familiar roar of his Harley brings a strange sense of comfort I didn't realize I needed.

I'm not sure I'd be able to live my life away from motorcycles, despite the wishes of my brother.

After more than six hours of shopping, a couple stops ended up being Wicked Angels owned shops, and more than a thousand dollars, I have enough clothes to get me started. After I start working, I'll work on enhancing some, but for now, this will have to do.

I haul all my new stuff up into my room and am trying shit on when the roar of a Harley coming down Sticks' long driveway captures my attention. I know almost immediately that it's not Sticks. I know enough about bikes to distinguish one from another and this one is alone.

"What are they doing here?" I mumble. *Is it a club member coming by?* They've got no business here without Sticks. Then again, he could be running late. I walk quickly and quietly over to my window and pull back the curtain enough to see out.

I narrow my eyes. "No way," I whisper as my heart leaps into my throat and I watch the man on the bike pull off his helmet.

50

CHAPTER SEVEN

Loki

3 HOURS EARLIER

I turn off my engine, throw the stand down and look around, taking in the two prospects who are keeping an eye on the bikes parked outside the clubhouse. They're young and smaller than I'd have thought, but then again, things are done differently up here. The family genes don't run as deep here as they do down in Roswell or Tucson and they bring in real recruits off the streets. It works. The more the merrier.

The door to the clubhouse pops open and the man I'm here to see comes out to greet me. "Loki." He grabs my forearm and we bump chests.

"Sticks," I smile. "What's goin' on?"

"I should ask you the same. Come on, let's talk."

He leads me inside the clubhouse. Not much different than Roswell just shaggier. Maybe even a little dirtier. Judging from the couple of club whores, they've been around way too long.

Sticks leads me back toward an office in the back of the main floor of the clubhouse, past the common room. I've been here before and have stayed upstairs where there are loaner rooms to crash. They're nice enough, but not something I'd want to stay in long term. Roswell, at least, has that going for them. Each room is equipped with its own bathroom and fridge, making long term stays easier.

Regardless, Boulder is a nice house.

Sticks ushers me into his office. "Beer?"

"Yeah."

He reaches into the small fridge behind his desk, producing a beer and he hands it to me after I close the door behind us. "She make it up here yet?" I ask softly. I don't have to go into details about who I'm referring to, he knows. I called him a couple days ago.

"Yup, at my house right now."

I nod, pulling a long drag on my beer. "She alright?"

"All things considered, she's fine. She's planning on staying here a while," he tells me as he takes a seat behind his desk. "What about you? You gonna transfer up here?"

I snort a laugh, "You really think Rooster would let me?" He answers my sentiment with his own humorless laugh. "He needs me too much," I remind him.

"Tell me what happened," Sticks says, not as a question but rather, in a spill your fucking guts kind of way.

So, I launch into the details surrounding Tryke's death while he sits behind his desk hemming and hawing with forced interest. I knew that Big Daddy got a hold of him the moment I showed up. I'd stopped there a few days ago, following Kiwi on her path. I needed to make sure she got here and that she finds what she's looking for while she's here.

Another two hours pass as Sticks and I exchange words and club business, before I'm kicking my bike over and headed out of the compound. I'm not staying long, but I do have some business to attend to while I'm here in the form of a five foot, six inch nearly eighteen-year-old.

CHAPTER EIGHT

Lily

PRESENT TIME

I surge down the stairs and out the front door.

Loki doesn't know what hits him when I slam into him.

I should be furious with him.

I should hate his fucking guts. I should want to add him to my list of revenge targets, but I can't seem to bring myself to do it. Not today, at least.

"Jesus, Kiwi, knock me on my ass, why don'tcha." His voice is meant to be hard, pissed off, but I can tell he's just as happy to see me as I am to see him when he wraps his arms around me, lifting me off the ground. He squeezes the air from my lungs, and he doesn't let me go.

Fine with me.

He's all well-defined muscle, long brown hair, and sleeve tattoos and madness. "Why are you here?" I ask him softly.

He sets me back on my feet, then brushes the hair from my face with a gentle touch that sends my heart into its own orbit. "I got business with Sticks," he tells me.

"He's not here," I inform him.

"I know, I saw him already."

"Then why are you *here*?" I emphasize.

"You eighteen yet?" he asks and I blush.

I shake my head then look at my watch; it's just after five in the afternoon. "Less than seven hours to go," I tell him.

"Jesus, that's too fucking long," he groans.

"Why is my turning eighteen so important to you?" I ask with a little sass in my voice.

"Don't worry about it." He takes a step back. "You gonna make me dinner or what?"

I smile at him. "Come on." Grabbing his hand, I lead him into the house. As I climb up the steps to the porch, I turn back slightly and the big bad biker dude's eyes are locked on my ass. "Enjoying the view?" I ask with a sultry tone, or what I think is. He snaps to attention and comes with me.

I make Loki his favorite- roasted chicken with ranch potatoes and green beans. He stoically sits in the kitchen while I cook for both of us. Then as we eat, we talk about all kinds of shit. Everything from Roswell to my brother. The way he talks about my brother makes me miss him so much more. Loki knew him better than I did and I want to be angry at him for that. But then I remember that the two of them have something in common, the Wicked Angels.

The more he talks about my brother, the more pissed off I become that he doesn't seem all that emotional about his death.

"What's wrong with you?" he asks.

I glare at him. "You killed him, for fuck's sake, Loki. How the hell can you sit there like nothing's happened?" I snap.

"Because I took care of business, I didn't have a fucking choice," he bites back. I can see the anger in his eyes.

I pull my eyes away from him and shake my head back and forth more than is necessary, trying to find my voice and hide the tears.

"Look, it's club business, and you know better than to ask too many fucking questions, Lily."

The use of my real name sends a slice of anger through me.

He never calls me that.

I realize arguing about this isn't going to get us anywhere. I'm left suffering the consequences of 'club business' while he gets to hide behind it like it's an iron curtain.

I turn to the sink and start washing dishes and loading the dishwasher.

WICKED REVENGE

All while I work, he doesn't leave the kitchen, in fact he hardly moves unless it's to grab a new beer from the fridge. I want to throw a knife at him, but a part of me is afraid I'm going to really hurt him. My reaction is irrational. I should want to hurt him, kill him, make him suffer. If he were suffering emotionally from what he's done, it would be easier, but he's not. So, it makes me want to hurt him that much more.

I close the dishwasher and start it before double checking I didn't miss anything. I set the pans to soak in the sink before drying off my hands and turning to him. "You staying here tonight?" I ask.

"I've got more business with Sticks, so yeah, I'm staying here."

"Then I'll see you tomorrow," I tell him, false anger in my voice, before I stomp up the stairs and into my room.

When he showed up, I abandoned all the clothes I had bought in the middle of my bed, so I shove them onto the floor before I strip out of my jeans and t-shirt in favor of short shorts and a tank top for bed.

I can't wrap my head around what he's done.

I can't imagine it's easy for him.

He killed his best friend for crying out loud.

Fuck.

I can't wrap my head around why in the fuck I can forgive him so easily. I know Kellen wanted it that way, but fuckin' A. I'm the one left behind, alone, without a family because of some fucked up 'club business' bullshit that no one seems to want to talk about. I basically handed them everything they need on a silver platter, the least they can do is let me in on the details of what's happening, right?

I roll my eyes at myself.

That's never going to happen.

At best, if I manage to weasel my way behind club doors, I'm a club whore. Unless, by some miracle, someone decides to make me an old lady, but even then, I'd be out of the loop regardless. Unless the Wicked Angels magically decide to start allowing women into their inner circle, my only hope is as a club whore. At least in that capacity, I'm capable of keeping my head down and my ears open. If someone claims me and I'm privy to information shared between the old ladies, which is like a gossip circle. Sometimes they know more than their men do, but still, it doesn't get me any closer to Rooster.

I shudder at the thought of being a Roswell club whore.

The idea of being a whore, period.

My eyes land on the clock sitting atop the nightstand next to my bed. The minutes slowly tick by until it hits eleven fifty-eight. Two more minutes. Then it hits me.

Loki will return to Roswell, Kellen is dead, and my parents are gone. I'm all alone and I feel every bit of that loneliness as the clock ticks closer to midnight. No one should ever feel like this, regardless of how old they are.

I miss my brother most of all. I miss his smile, the way we laughed, the way we were just Kellen and Lily, brother and sister, surviving the loss of our parents. But now it's just me.

Twelve o'clock strikes on my clock and I quietly wish myself happy birthday before rolling over and closing my eyes.

My eyes squint tight. Despite my best efforts, I hadn't fallen asleep, when blinding light brings my eyes to the door. The light coming off the hallway is blinding me as I try and see who's standing there. At first I think it's my uncle come to check on me, though I didn't hear him pull up. Then the figure shifts, and I can see better as his body blocks the light. The light illuminates him from behind, casting his face in shadow. "Loki," I breathe. "What are you doing?"

He steps into the room, his boots hitting the floor heavily as he turns back toward the door and closes it.

He hasn't answered my question, nor does he say a single word to me as he strips off his cut and lays it across the foot of my bed. His shirt comes next. My eyes adjust slightly to the change in light, and I can see the moonlit outline of his pecks and abs. "Loki," I whisper as my body ignites with a desire I'm unfamiliar with. My clit aches to be touched as he pops the buttons on his jeans, followed by kicking off his boots. He slides his jeans down his legs then stands back up. His father's dog tags clinking together and the sound of my breathing are the only noises I hear in the house. As long as I can remember, he's worn his father's dog tags. He never takes them off. I wonder if he'll take them off now.

Through the dim light of my alarm clock and the moonshine coming through the window, I can see he's completely naked. "Loki, what are you doing?" I ask again but my voice is weak, laced with an unwanted attempt at stopping him.

He walks over to the side of the bed, grabbing ahold of my covers before throwing them back, exposing my shorts and tank top clad body to him.

The bed dips as he climbs into bed.

In the next heartbeat he's rolling over, holding himself just above my body. His father's dog tags fall on my chest, right between my breasts. His proximity and warmth sends a wave of goosebumps across my flesh and hardens my nipples.

I catch the scent of beer on his breath, but it's barely noticeable with the scent of musk, wind, the road and Loki.

A new thrill roars in my veins as I breathe him in deep. Committing his scent to memory.

He leans down and gently brushes his lips over mine. The sparks of desire ignite everywhere as he presses his lips to mine. They're soft, gentle, and passionate at first, but then he fights to deepen the kiss by nipping at my lower lip. His legs shift, separating mine and then he's between them, pressing his hips into my core, stroking along my center.

I gasp.

He steals his chance and slides his tongue into my mouth, flicking it against mine.

I moan when he thrusts his hips again, his cock stroking along my covered slit.

His kiss, the thrust of his hips and my labored breathing makes my head spin. I can't stop myself from pulling away from the kiss to suck in a deep breath. When I turn my head to the side, he takes the opportunity to kiss along my jaw, down my neck, to my shoulder where he pulls the strap of my tank top down along my arm. His fingers hook into the top seam before he pulls it down, exposing my left breast. He wastes no time sucking my hard nipple into his mouth.

I moan again as he sucks and licks my pebbled flesh. I can't help the flick of my own hips against his and he grunts. The vibration sends a new sensation through my nipple that roars through my body before settling in my sex.

Once he's satisfied, he releases that nipple and moves across my chest to the other. He quickly pulls my tank down, exposing it and pulling it into his mouth in the same manner as the other. With his right hand, he pinches my left nipple between two fingers, rolling it around while he licks and sucks on my right.

I slide my hands into his hair, holding his head to me, keeping him in place as he flicks his hips again. His cock is hard, thick and long pressed against my slit and desire explodes. I suddenly need him inside me as fast as possible.

I let my hands slide down his neck to his shoulders and I push him toward my crotch, gently. I manage to mask the fact that my hands are shaking, or at least if he notices, he doesn't say anything.

He grunts again but releases my nipple. His hand pushes my tank up toward my breasts so that he can kiss my stomach on his way south. My nipples are wet and exposing them to the cold air makes them pebble further and ache to be sucked again.

Loki reaches the waist of my shorts with both his hands and he tugs them toward my knees. He's smothering me, making it impossible to move, but I manage a little leverage to lift my ass and he rips my shorts down just below my crotch. He has his eyes locked on the apex of my thighs. I fight the urge to cover myself up. There is a strange look in his eyes, but I can't make it out because of the darkness in the room. Still, he's says nothing.

WICKED REVENGE

The next thing I know, my legs are in the air, my ass is falling back to the bed and my shorts are hitting the floor. His hands creep in under my ass and he lifts me to his mouth. Loki's tongue slides flat, hot and wet down the center of my folds. I cry out and my legs twitch when he sucks my clit into his mouth.

He slowly lowers me back to the bed.

His mouth never leaves my clit as he does. With his hands still under my ass holding me to his face, I slide my hand down my body, feeling the wetness left on my nipple. The light touch of my own fingers sends a ripple of goosebumps over me and my nipples harden again.

I reach out, putting my hand in his hair as his tongue starts flicking, sucking and nibbling on my clit. Wave after wave of pleasure rockets through me and I lift my hips against his mouth.

I feel a tingle and tremors course through my veins. My body locks down as something explodes out of me and I cry out his name.

Realizing it's an orgasm, I start to panic a little, but Loki doesn't stop sucking my clit, my legs twitch with each swipe of his tongue until his hand is between my legs. His fingers, callused and dry, touch my center. He spreads his juices along my entrance before he slides a finger inside me. I cry out again. He only dips his finger in a little, but it's enough to make my legs quake again.

After a few small strokes in and out with his finger, he releases my clit from his mouth and sits up. I can barely see him as he wraps a meaty hand around his cock before he's sliding it up and down my slit. I moan. "Loki, I…"

"Shh," he says before he's pressing into my entrance. "Fuck me, you're tight as hell," he groans as he pushes a little farther into me before pulling back.

I grunt as the pain registers.

He's huge, spreading me wide open, but he doesn't stop. I don't want him to stop. I've been waiting a long time for this.

He continues moving with tiny thrusts in and out of my sex for a few more strokes, then his hands slide under my hips, lifting me up, giving him a better angle and once he's satisfied, he pushes in hard and fast.

I scream as pain ignites in my body as he rips through my virginity and growls, "Fuck," in anger. "Why didn't you stop me?" He's pissed, but he doesn't pull out or push in farther.

"You wouldn't let me talk," I counter, tears stinging the backs of my eyes as rejection slides through me. He's going to pull out, get dressed and end this. I feel it in my veins.

"You're a fucking virgin," he groans.

"Not anymore," I mutter. He goes to sit up and pull out. "Don't," I say, wrapping my legs around his waist. "Finish it," I tell him.

He shakes his head, but I clench my muscles involuntarily and it's like an animal takes over and he starts thrusting in and out of me in little bursts. It hurts at first but then the longer his strokes get, the more rhythmic, the less it hurts and the more it starts to feel amazing.

A sensation similar to earlier starts to creep through my sex and outward through my body. I feel my muscles tighten around him and he grunts.

"Fuck," he groans, this time the anger is gone. "So, good. So, fucking tight. Tight fucking cunt." He starts pushing into me harder and faster. My orgasm builds again. It doesn't take but a few more strokes before the pleasure overwhelms me and my orgasm takes over.

My inner walls clamp around his cock and he pushes into me hard and fast until I feel a hot rush inside me and he grunts out my name.

His body twitches with his orgasm.

He collapses on top of me, our breathing ragged and uneven. He presses his forehead to mine, but he says nothing, just lets his breathing return to normal while his cock softens and he rolls over, taking me with him as he wraps his arms around me, holding me tight. My back to his front. His hand comes to rest over my left breast, his fingers twitching slightly against the tight, sensitive pebble of my nipple.

WICKED REVENGE

After a few minutes, his breathing levels out and he starts snoring softly in my ear.

My heart explodes with something I'm not sure of. I've been in love with Loki for years. I'd always hoped he'd be the one to take my virginity. I snuggle into him a little deeper, his cock hardens between us, and I know I've gotten my wish. I follow him in slumber moments later, wrapped tight in his arms.

While it's still dark in my room, I awaken to Loki's fingers pinching my left nipple and his mouth wrapped around my right. I moan.

The next thing I know, he's pushing back inside my sore, aching center, but within a few strokes the ache is gone, replaced by an overwhelming orgasm. He pushes into me harder and faster as if he's reading my mind. I moan and cry out his name when my orgasm consumes me and he pumps in once, twice, three times before he explodes inside me. We fall back to sleep without words.

The sun is hot and pouring in my window.

I roll over, breathing deep, pulling in the scent of Loki on the pillow until realization hits me that I'm alone. Disappointment slices through me and I sit up. His boots, jeans and cut are gone; the only thing left is a black t-shirt, the same one he was wearing during dinner. Excitement fills me. There's no way he left without his t-shirt. I head for the bathroom, but something on the bed catches my eye and I pause to look.

The reddish brown evidence of my virginity lingers on the sheets. A shiver slides up my spine as I remember him between my legs. Desire ignites and I swing open the bathroom door, only to close it again when I realize I'm nearly naked. My tank is askew and my shorts are nowhere to be found.

I look on the other side of my bed and nothing. "Where?"

Then I look out the window, the same one I saw him pull up through yesterday and his bike is gone. Sticks' bike is in his place. My heart sinks into my stomach.

I find a pair of pajama pants in my suitcase and throw them on with a t-shirt after righting my tank top. I leave the t-shirt Loki left behind in my room as I head downstairs to find Sticks sitting in the kitchen drinking coffee. "Where's Loki?" I ask him.

He shrugs. "Wasn't here when I got home."

"When was that?" I ask.

"About an hour ago."

I look at the clock on the microwave- it's six forty-five in the morning.

My virginity is gone.

Loki is gone.

It's only now when I realize that I lost my virginity to a badass biker douche who couldn't even face me in the morning. Or wear a condom.

PART TWO

CHAPTER ONE
Loki

SIX YEARS LATER

"YEAH, I GET YOU, BIG Daddy," I say into the phone before pressing the end button. Shit is finally going down around this hellhole of an MC club.

Rooster is about to fry.

Gunnar and the rest of his goons are going down with him.

I step into the clubhouse. Taz, one of the clubhouses long-time whores, is putting her tits in the face of Rack, one of the recent additions to Wicked Angels. He's all too willing to suck one of her huge nipples into his mouth.

My cock hardens.

Ignoring the slut desperate to get laid, I approach the bar where Pyro is sitting and flicking his lighter. He has long hair, dark chocolate brown, and a wicked scar on the side of his face from hairline to his Adam's apple. I asked him once where it came from and he just grunted in his gravelly voice and that was the end of it.

When he showed up here a few years ago, he was already sporting it.

He was sent down from Boulder because we needed some more muscle here.

At least that's what Big Daddy told Rooster.

I'm the only one who knew the real reason for his visit, or rather, extended vacation. But that's beside the point. Big Daddy and the Tucson guys are finally ready to make their move on Roswell to extricate Rooster from his post.

Since Tryke's death six years ago, no one has dared challenge Rooster for president, no one except Pyro and me. Though we're not exactly running toward that opportunity. It's something he and I have talked about, privately. It's not something you bring other people in on. You do that, you get dead.

Pyro flicks his lighter again. "What's goin' down, brother?" I say to him.

"Same shit." His voice is gravelly, like he's smoked a dozen packs of smokes a day for years. The truth is the wicked scar caused some damage to his vocal cords. The girls around here find it sexy as fuck. Swear to God, this man gets more pussy than a strip club on payday. I shake my head. My eyes land once again on Taz, who's moved to hike up her skirt and straddle Rack. It takes everything I have to not walk up behind her and slip it in her ass while she rides him.

"Leave it," Pyro says. "She don't deserve a double team," he grumbles before swallowing back his whiskey.

He's right, but still, it would be fun as fuck to watch Rack's eyes bug out of his head as I did it.

The prospect behind the bar moves away. "One more," I whisper so only Pyro can hear it.

"About fucking time," he whispers harshly back.

"It's been six years, what's one more month," I whisper back.

"Pyro," a voice calls from the hallway. We both look over to see Rooster standing there.

"Yeah?" he says.

"Need you and Loki to get over to Iron Wings, Loni's got somethin' for you," Rooster says.

"What would that be?" I ask.

"A new piece of ass? How the fuck would I know? Just get ya'asses o'er there and find out," Rooster orders. The man has not aged well these last six years. His face is lined with wrinkles, he cut off his hair because he couldn't take care of it, and he's lost a hell of a lot of weight. Frankly, he looks like shit. Good.

"Yup," Pyro says before slamming back the rest of his whiskey and setting the glass on the bar and heading for the door. I follow him out into the warm Roswell sun and we climb on our bikes. He kicks his over first, I follow and off we go down the street.

Ten minutes later and we're pulling into the Iron Wings Saloon, a Wicked Angels owned bar that's just off the highway and our biggest money making joint in Roswell. We don't hold a candle to Boulder, but it works well for us.

There are a couple cars in the lot, none of which I recognize, not uncommon, but the bar doesn't open for another couple of hours. Odds are we're here for a pick-up. Loni, the bar's manager, usually holds funds until the end of the week, but on big nights, she has it picked up the next morning.

The bar is a front for many things, including, but not limited to, drugs and prostitution. The bar's lot is shared with a truck stop. Best marketing plan on the planet, fuck you very much. You get bikes, dykes, and trucks, most of the time, in the same night, every night.

I lead the way inside. Pyro hates coming over here. I can't say it's my favorite either, but I do it because I have no choice.

We step inside and I pull my shades off my eyes and tuck 'em into the back of my cut. Easier to keep them back there. "Loni," I call out.

"Back here," she answers and I head toward the back office.

"Thanks, Skit, for coming in."

I hear a soft laugh that rattles a memory in the back of my brain, but I bury it before I let it consume me.

"Skit, that's a new one," I hear the voice say and it's sexy with a southern twang worked in.

Loni laughs back, "The hair, it looks like skittles."

I shake my head. Must be a new hire. Which means Rooster wasn't too

66

far off. Then again, Loni hires who she wants, when she wants, and she doesn't give five shits if anyone else is interested in them.

"Can you start tonight?" Loni asks whoever she's speaking with in her office.

"Absolutely, what time?" the girl replies, and again the southern accent is almost sweet, or maybe it's just her voice.

She has to be a new piece of ass, though I doubt Loni had time to call Rooster about it before she offered her the job.

"Six to close?" Loni asks.

"I'll be here, thanks Loni," the girl says.

They exchange good-byes and the next thing I know, this gorgeous five-foot something in hooker heels with green hair and black streaks that remind me of the inside of a kiwi, slams face first into my chest. The scent of strawberries assaults my nose and my mind flies back to six years ago and the night I took the virginity of my best friend's sister.

No way.

CHAPTER TWO
Skit

"SORRY 'BOUT THAT," I DRAWL.

"Where's the fire, sugar tits?"

"Back off," Loni, the woman I just interviewed with, snaps.

I don't bother lifting my eyes to look at the man I ran into, I simply skirt around him and head for the door. I can feel his eyes boring into the back of my head as I look up into a pair of chocolate brown eyes framed with full lashes. A wicked scar runs down the side of his face. The eyes narrow at me in confusion. There's something familiar about them, I can't place them before he shies away from me. Putting his scar on full display. The ragged looking line runs from hairline, over his jaw and down his neck.

"What the hell, Lon, hiring virginal newbies to work for you?" I hear the man I ran into ask.

"Fuck off, she'll be fine. She's been working in a biker bar for the last five years. I'm pretty sure your hulk-ass being in her way didn't help."

"Whatever. What you got for us?" I don't stick around to find out why she'd called these two over before I'm plowing through the front door and headed toward my car.

The moment I finally look around, I realize I am in a shit ton of trouble when I see a very familiar bike sitting in the parking lot.

"He'll be back," I mutter.

I climb in my car, throw off my hooker heels before turning on the car and backing out. Just as I'm about to pull from the lot, the bar's door opens and out steps the two men I ran into before.

"Shit," I grumble before turning away and peeling out of the parking lot.

Once I get home, I head into my ensuite bathroom to strip myself out of the getup I'm wearing.

I stop to look in the mirror and my eyes land on the picture of me that was taken a couple days after arriving in Colorado. I had it taken so I could remember who that girl is, regardless of where I am.

I had shorter, strawberry blonde hair, barely visible eyebrows because of the blonde tint to them. My nose was perfect, small and innocent looking. I have no make-up on. That used to be a standard for me. I never wore it. In fact, I hated it with a passion. I never understood why a girl had to cover her face in order to *look pretty*. My eyes are bright green in the picture. My shoulders were small, just like the rest of me.

My eyes roam to the mirror now. My hair is long, just kissing the top of my butt; my shoulders wider, my arms are stronger, more toned and defined from hours in the gym lifting weights. I pop out the contacts in my eyes and see the purple hue that covers the lens as I place them into the solution until tonight.

My chest is bigger than it was back then. I barely filled in a C-cup before and now I'm overflowing a D. My nose is a little misshapen, complements of a cat fight a few years ago. I got the bitch pretty good, but she broke my nose in the process. My eyebrows are dark, colored, waxed and plucked to perfection and my face is layered in make-up. Everything from foundation to colored-in eyebrows, giving them a fuller look, down to heavy eye shadow, today it's green with eyeliner, mascara, a little blush to highlight my cheekbones and lipstick. Today it's red.

It took me a long time to learn how to do my make-up, but working in a biker bar taught me a lot about what men like.

I no longer own baggy jeans and t-shirts, except the shirts I wear to bed. I now have an entire wardrobe of low-rise, boot cut jeans, various skirts, and leather pants, corsets, tight tank tops, basically anything that will show off the womanly figure I have compared to the girlie figure of six years ago.

All in preparation for this, right here and now. But running into him so fast wasn't exactly part of my plan.

CHAPTER THREE
Loki

"WHY WE GOING BACK THERE?" Pyro says.

"I want another look at that sweet piece of ass from earlier," I tell him.

"Not a good idea, brother." He groans, "You know how Loni is about us fucking with her newbies. She'll bust your fucking balls."

"Better than sitting around this shithole working the same pieces of ass I've been tapping for the last eight years. At least there I can pick up a piece of passerby." Or Skit, I add in my mind.

"Yeah, don't go there," he warns.

"Why the hell not?" I ask.

"I don't know, something about her bugs me."

I shrug it off.

Pyro is well-known around here for being paranoid, then again, he has a right to be.

I throw my glass back on the bar and turn toward him. "You comin' or you gonna stay here and sulk in your beer?" I shoulder check him.

He slams back his whiskey, sets the glass down and we're out the door. "I can't believe I'm letting you talk me into this."

I shrug as I throw my leg over my bike and fire it up. Toss it into neutral and push it backward, clearing the other bikes in the gravel before throwing the throttle wide open and peeling out of the parking lot.

CHAPTER FOUR
Skit

THREE HOURS INTO MY FIRST shift at Iron Wings and my feet are starting to ache, but I will do as I always do and suck it up.

I've been out of work for the last six weeks, but that was by choice. Wearing these shoes was a choice too, but it's playing out to be a big mistake.

Give it some time, I remind myself as I carry a tray of shots and drinks to one of the bigger tables in the joint. Tonight, my make-up is done with tones of blue and silver on the eyes, a light pink blush on my cheeks, a dark cherry red lipstick and my hair is pulled back off my face. The length still running down my back. I'm wearing a high-backed corset that wraps around my neck at the top. It doesn't clasp, but it gives the illusion that it does. I chose this for tonight, not wanting to reveal all my secrets at once.

"Alright, boys." I smile wide as I set the tray down and start handing out drinks and shots. I think I get them all right, and what I don't get, they're handing down the line anyway. As soon as we're done, I stand up and the unattractive guy on this end grabs my ass. He really grabs it and it hurts, but I plaster my best flirtatious smile on my lips and look at him. He removes his hand, good. "Can I get y'all anything else?"

"Not at the moment, doll," the nicer, more attractive one says to me.

"I'll be back." I smile again and turn back toward the bar.

The door to the bar swings open, like it's done all damn night and I don't know why, at this moment, I decide to look and immediately I wish I hadn't. "Fuck," I mutter under my breath before bending over another table.

"Hi there, what can I get y'all tonight?" My phony accent serving its purpose and they smile up at me.

After a few more moments, I'm headed toward Loni and the bar with my order.

"Whatcha need?" Loni asks.

I give her the drink order and I do everything I can to stop my eyes from roaming around the bar to look for him, but I fail. My eyes land right on his as he's looking at me. I pull my eyes away quickly. No need to blow my cover so early. If he finds out who I am, I'm gone, and I won't be able to do what I need to before skipping town for good.

If I get mixed up in a man, I will lose my focus and I will never get out of here. I have no choice.

Loni finishes my order, setting the drinks on the tray. "You got a new table." She darts her head in the direction of the man I'm trying to avoid and his friend with the familiar eyes and nasty scar.

"Thanks," I mutter and she laughs.

"Oh, take this to table eight." She slides me a handmade paper envelope. I know the drill. I tuck it into my pocket, leaving just a tail hanging out.

"How much?" I ask.

"Twenty."

I nod in understanding and Loni smiles at me.

It came as no surprise when she told me about the backdoor dealings of Iron Wings Saloon. It's a biker bar and owned by the Wicked Angels. No matter how much I know they've tried to clean up, they can't make the money necessary to get out of the drug trade and keep the members happy. At least not yet. I'm sure without goons like Rooster and Gunnar running this shit, this charter could run like a well-oiled, drug free machine.

The sluts are another story.

I drop my drinks at the right table, add empty glasses to my tray and stop by table eight. "Hi boys." I wink.

"Where?" the guy asks.

"Right hip pocket, twenty," I tell him and he shows me the bill before stuffing it into my pocket and taking his drugs in its place. I wink and move on to the dirty drop bucket before making my way to fuck-knuckles one and two.

I set the tray down on the table and lean forward, giving both men a

72

shot of my assets. Catching names on their cuts. Though I knew the first one immediately, the other is a familiar mystery that's making me crazy trying to figure out.

Loki smirks, looking down at my rack and the other guy, Pyro, turns his eyes away. Maybe he's celibate or some shit. I shrug it off. "Evenin' boys, what can I get ya?" I ask, chewing my gum.

"Whiskey, neat," Pyro says.

"Same," Loki adds while leaning forward to get a little closer to me. His eyes are a little wild as he grabs a strand of my hair, bringing it to his nose before it falls from between his fingers. "Strawberries?" he says in a voice that has my sex heating up hotter than fireworks on the Fourth of July.

I give him my best 'try me' look and he smirks, sitting back and stretching his arms across the back of the booth, an invitation or cocky-asshat, I'm not sure which just yet.

I make a show of letting my eyes roam slowly over his body, landing on the outline of his gorgeous cock in his tight jeans. I slide my tongue over my upper lip. "Two whiskeys coming right up." I grab my tray and take off.

The next thing I know, a hand snakes its way around my waist and I'm pulled backwards until I'm sitting in Loki's lap. His erection pressing into my hip. "What time you off, sugar tits?" The name grates on me and I want to roll my eyes.

"Long after your bedtime, sweet cheeks." I gently smack his cheek, both in warning to watch it, and just so that I can put my hands on him.

He's changed, grown broader, more muscular, as if that was possible. His hair is long, landing between his shoulder blades, but shorter than it was six years ago. His face is covered in a well-kept beard that makes me want to rub my legs together to find relief. His eyes are still blue, but they've darkened some, or it's just bad lighting.

He gives me a knowing smirk but releases me when I stand up. He gets one more dig in by smacking my ass as I walk away.

I get about five steps away before I let out the breath I was holding.

The son-of-a-bitch still smells the same.

Nothing's changed.

No, everything has changed.

"G'night, Loni," I call as I head for the door.

"You coming back tomorrow?"

I smile at her. "Bet your ass I am."

"See you at six," she hollers as I step through the doorway. It's late September and the night is cooler than I expected it to be, a cold shiver slides down my spine. The bar was hot, so it's a welcome relief to the sweat.

I'm walking out, on my first night, a Wednesday no less, with over seven hundred dollars in tips and my percentage of drug sales. Only two percent but still. This bar moves some serious narcotics.

As I approach my car, I realize how much I miss my trusty Altima as I'm stuffing the key in the door. I had no choice but to get rid of it. I couldn't bring it back here.

I turn the key and the light clicks on in the car at the same time I catch a glimpse of someone behind me. I'm about to scream when the man behind me presses into me and covers my mouth with his hand.

The scent assaults my senses and my heart skips a beat. It kills me that after all this time he still has this effect on me.

"Don't scream." Loki's sinful voice slides over me.

"What…" I mumble through his hand, fighting the urge to lick it. He removes his hand. "What are you doing?"

"Taking you home."

I laugh a humorless laugh. "Hardly. You're drunk. You think I'm climbing on the back of your bike?" I ask incredulously, but secretly, I want him to take me home.

"Then you can drive me home," he counters with a nonchalance I wish I could own the way he does.

"Call a cab."

He presses his cock into my ass. Desire explodes through my veins. What I wouldn't give to have that cock inside me one more time.

"Get in, slugger." The words are out before I can process their meaning. Fuck, I'm driving him home.

"You make habits out of taking random guys home?" he asks with a raise of his eyebrow and disbelief in his voice.

"Well, you're Wicked, right?" I ask.

"Right."

"Loni runs this joint, right?"

"Yeah," he answers.

"And I'm guessing Wicked Angels own Loni?"

"So?"

"You fuck with me, I tell Loni, Loni tells your Pres and your ass is grass, right?"

"Huh?" he says with disbelief about my understanding of the order of things around here. It was obvious the moment I met Loni that she's an old lady. The cut she wears is a dead giveaway. It wasn't until tonight that I saw she's owned by an Angel named Cowboy. When I asked her about him tonight, she said he's usually at the bar with her, but he was taking the night off. She hinted that he was probably hanging around the clubhouse, but never confirmed it.

I turn, raising an eyebrow to him when I realize he hasn't moved. "Am I taking you home, or not?"

"Yup," he says then sways slightly before he rights himself to walk around my car. A part of me wishes I'd driven my bike tonight. Wouldn't that have been a fun turn of events? Riding bitch behind a woman. I want to roll my eyes. I know that will never happen, no matter how drunk.

He stumbles his way to the passenger door and climbs in. I go to climb in and a momentary slice of panic runs through me as my eyes land on what's sitting on the backseat. I blow it off. It's directly behind him for one, and two, he's too drunk to give a shit, he ain't gonna notice.

"Where to, slugger?" I ask him, maintaining my southern accent. Though in his state of mind, I doubt it matters. I could be a brick wall for all he cares.

He mumbles his address. I shake my head; some things never change. He's still living in the same house he grew up in, a house that's right down the street from mine.

He leans over the center console, again taking a strand of my hair and pulling it to his nose. "Strawberries," he slurs.

Is it possible?

Nah.

It's been six years.

Too many things have changed, I've changed.

He's changed.

I risk a glance in his direction as I pull off my heels.

His scent assaults me in this confined space, sending little pulses of desire to my clit.

I catch his arms in my peripheral and I can see quite a few more tattoos covering his arms than before. Regardless, he's sexier now than he was six years ago when he snuck into my bedroom, stripped me naked and stole my virginity.

We drive in silence, but I keep looking at him to make sure he doesn't pass out on me. He's studying my features. If he honestly looks too closely, he'll put two and two together. I'm not ready for him to do that just yet.

The hours in the gym, coupled with the heels and a more defined and curvier figure helps throw off the similarities enough that in his drunken state of mind, there's no way he's putting two and two together. I hope.

My tits are significantly bigger and my hair is much longer, though it's no longer strawberry blonde like it was back then. Instead, this week, its lime green with black streaks. I'd done it on purpose. I'd hoped to see Loki and torture him with the prospect that my hair looks like a kiwi. I guess wanting him to figure me out always played in the back of my mind. I wanted him to pine for me, to make him crazy while I kept him at arm's length.

That is gonna be much easier said than done.

In Colorado, I was away from him, out of sight out of mind, but now, being here, having him in my car, I want him to put two and two together.

There's a small part of me that wants to show him the woman I've become, the woman he's missed out on for the last six years, but right now, this is too much fucking fun.

A little payback is in order.

I turn down his street. "Alright, slugger, which one?" I ask him though I already know the answer. I don't need him to know that I know where, exactly.

"That one, on the left, the blue one." He points and I nod as I pull into the driveway. I put the car in park and reach for the parking break. His driveway has a steep decline headed toward the garage door, better safe than sorry. He reaches over and turns off the ignition, but leaves the keys in. Then he grabs my hand on the parking break and he puts it on his crotch. "Here's a better knob to grab hold of," He mumbles.

"Oh really?" I tease him back. I let my hand roam up and down his length, feeling the thickness beneath his jeans. "You want a blowjob right here or would you rather fuck me in your bed?" I ask bluntly and his eyes widen at my brazenness.

"Did you just...did I hear you right?" he asks.

"Blowjob in the car or sex in your bed?" I ask again.

"Fuck me," he breathes.

"I'm tryin'," I tell him.

"Bed," he slurs.

I roll my eyes but grab my keys from the ignition as I open the door and climb out. I slide my keys into my pocket before slamming the door shut.

He hasn't moved.

Way to go, genius, put him off with your forwardness.

I grab my phone from my back pocket so I can shoot off a quick text.

Running late, be there soon.

The recipient of my text is sound asleep so I don't expect a reply, but in the event she wakes up, I don't want her to worry. I tuck my phone back in my pocket before he finally stumbles his way out of the car. "Where's your keys, big man?"

"Pocket," he grumbles as he walks toward me. His hand on the hood of my car holds him steady. I meet him near the front fender.

I put my hand on his chest, with the sole intention of teasing him. I let my hand slide down his chest, over his abs and finally I brush his cock on my way to his pocket. I reach inside, feeling the head of his cock just below the bottom of the pocket. Yeah, he's that big.

He shivers as my fingertips tickle the head of his cock. I wrap my fingers around his keys and pull them out.

Hooking my finger through the ring, I hold them up to him. "Which one, slugger?"

He looks at them. "The orange one." He doesn't slur as bad this time, making me wonder if this is all just an act on his part to get in my pants.

I guess we'll see.

I grab the orange one between my pointer finger and thumb and grab him by the buckle of his belt, pulling him along toward the door. "Well, well, aren't you eager," he says as he follows along behind me. I reach his door and insert the orange one into the locks and undo both of them before I open the door.

78

WICKED REVENGE

"Your house, lead the way," I tell him. He nods and steps inside first, I follow closely behind him. My hand still on the waistband of his jeans. He stops just beyond the reach of the door and he closes it behind us. His body presses against mine and I'm pushed against the door.

He wastes no time before he slams his lips against mine. The contact short circuits my brain momentarily.

I've waited six long years to have him back in my arms, six years to tell him everything and yet here I stand before him and he's completely clueless about who I am. I let that thought clear my mind and bring me back to the present and what I want to do tonight.

Loki continues at his frantic pace and slides his hands up my sides and cups my breasts, squeezing them, coaxing my nipples to harden beneath my corset. I feel his fingers tug downward on the tight leather until he realizes the material is going nowhere. I pull away from his kiss. "Let me help you," I whisper softly and his hands move back to my sides. I unhook the front of the corset. His impatience gets the better of him about halfway through the hooks in the front and he starts pushing the material aside. He has just enough room to slide his hands inside my corset. The closer I get to the bottom of the corset, the less tension there is against my chest and my tits fall free.

Reaching under the material for both my nipples, only to stop short of rolling both of them between his fingers. He growls as he blindly takes in my piercings with the tips of his fingers.

His fingers side to the underside of my breasts, his fingers brushing along the tattoo he can't yet see and I shiver. His thumbs slide over the tight pebbles of my nipples between the hoops I'm wearing.

He flicks his thumbs over them, hardening them and the sensation sends shots of desire pulsing to my clit. The little bundle of nerves is a live wire like they were our first night and I grind my hips looking for friction or release.

His lips press into mine again as I moan.

Somewhere in there I find the strength to undo the last two hooks on

79

my corset and pull it wide. Exposing my breasts and abdomen to him.

He pulls away from the kiss and looks at my body. A hiss cuts the silence in the house as his eyes widen at the sight of my tattoo.

Underneath my breasts, I've added a tattoo that consists of ivy type vines with a tribal twist to them. The line goes from one side to the other. His hands slide along the ink and further south to my pierced belly button. That's the newest of my additions. "Gorgeous," he groans before wrapping his lips around my left nipple, sucking it in and flicking his tongue against it like he needs it for survival. Tiny clicks of metal can be heard with the passing of his tongue. He's pierced. That's new.

Slivers of memories slide through my mind and I shake them off. I reach for his shoulders, pushing his cut down, trying to tell him that I want it off. He releases my other breast and my side so I can finish what I started. Once his cut is off, I want to throw it on the floor, but I know better, so instead I hook it on one of my fingers, waiting for him to take it from me.

His eyes dart to it and he takes it while releasing my nipple from his mouth with a pop.

The lack of sensation gives me a moment of clarity. This seemed like a brilliant idea when I told him to get in the car, but now I'm beginning to wonder if I've lost my mind.

Hold it together, you got this. Give him a taste of his own medicine.

He hangs his cut on a hook next to the door before he comes back to me. Tramping down my guilty conscience, I reach for the hem of his t-shirt and start tugging upwards. He gets the hint and lifts his arms.

Once he's free of the t-shirt, it's my turn to hiss because his stomach, though littered with tattoos before, is now completely filled in with various designs. Some of them are rather harsh, skulls and snakes, while the others are a little softer, more delicate, like a flower. I narrow my eyes at it. It takes everything I have not to fall to pieces before him and explain everything when I see the delicate lily tattooed just to the left of center, over his heart. I put my hands on his stomach and slide them up,

80

giving me the chance to touch the tattoo. I notice that both his nipples are pierced, too, and they weren't back then. Each one is adorned with silver barbells. I lean into him, moving his father's dog tags to the side before kissing just above my tattoo It's close enough to his nipple that my little secret kiss goes unnoticed when I lick and kiss my way to his nipple, sucking it and the barbell into my mouth.

He growls again and I smile.

The last time we did this, I wasn't much of a participant, but times have changed and I'm determined to make him feel as good as humanly possible. I want this to hurt.

Once I'm satisfied with its hardness, I leave that nipple for the other, leaving a trail of wet kisses across his chest. The small smattering of chest hair tickles my nose, but I keep going. I suck his other nipple into my mouth briefly, but frankly, I'm bored.

I start kissing my way down his chest, his abs, until I find the happy trail that divides the perfect V disappearing into his jeans. I take the button between my hands and I free it, then lower the zipper. I stand, sliding my hand between his boxer briefs and his stomach until my fingers wrap around his meaty, rock hard cock. He groans above me. I smile and lower myself to my knees. I bring his jeans with me as I go, bringing them around his thighs, freeing his cock.

I look up at him through my lashes and lick my lips. "Take it," he growls.

With my left hand, I coil my fingers around his stiff cock, squeezing and tugging before I wrap my mouth around the head of his dick.

The second my warm, wet mouth contacts his shaft, he curses above me and a smile plays on my lips. I set myself into a zone, letting my body take over, my mind shutting down as I begin to suck his cock deeper into my mouth.

His hands slide into my hair, coaxing me, but before he can take control of my head, I start to fuck his cock with my mouth. Letting it go deep, hitting the back of my throat, swallow, release and repeat.

His grunts and groans above me, telling me all I need to know, and I keep going. His hands never tighten in my hair and I smile internally as satisfaction slides over me.

I keep fisting his cock and letting it fuck my mouth as best I can with his girth. He really does have a fat cock, and I won't lie, I've never had one bigger than his.

"Stop," he barks.

I release his cock. "What?" I snap back at him.

"You're gonna make me come," he snarls.

"Isn't that the point, big man?"

"I want your cunt," he says, his voice surprisingly free of slurs and drunkenness.

I stand between him and the door and reach for the button on my jeans. I kick off my heels and shrink about four inches. He smiles. I reach into my back pocket and produce two condoms before lowering my jeans down my legs. I leave my lace panties in place as I kick my denim and shoes to the side.

He steps back, enjoying the view.

His eyes land on my thigh and the intricate tattoo design there. It's a combination of lilies, orchids and ivy - similar to what's under my breasts. His hand glides up from the base of it, near my knee to my hip.

I shrug off my corset and grab hold of his dick, leading him further into the house. "Where'm I goin', slugger?" I ask.

"Left," he breathes. No doubt drooling over what's coloring my back. The tension between me and his cock lets up as he steps closer to me. "You have an amazing ink-slinger," he says.

That I do, but I don't need to go into that detail, considering it's from a Wicked owned shop near Denver. "Thank you," I say softly. "Now where?" I say as I turn down the hallway.

"Door, straight ahead."

His drunkenness is the only explanation for why I'm able to lead him through his house by his cock. Either that or I've got him so raging hard that it doesn't matter.

I step through the portal and he pounces on me, arms wrapping around me, taking my breasts into his palms and his fingers rolling my nipples. There's a twinge of pain and a mountain of pleasure that spikes with each pinch and roll.

"Where'd you want me, cowboy?"

"Face down," he grunts.

I climb up on the bed. It is filled with all scents of Loki and my mind goes blank. I have never forgotten this scent, despite the smell fading from my sheets and the t-shirt he left behind, the same t-shirt I still wear to bed almost every night. I can hear him shuffling behind me as he kicks off his boots and jeans.

His hand slides onto my ass cheek before sliding to the other one then down the middle of my back as he climbs onto the bed. Then his fingers are in the thin band of my thong and I feel him pull on it, snapping it and the scraps fall away. "Oops," he laughs.

I roll my eyes. They're hardly panties anyway.

He presses into me. "Oh no, you don't." I sit up, bringing the condom packets I grabbed out of my jeans before sliding them off.

I pull them apart, setting one between my teeth and tossing the others on the bed behind me.

I tear the foil packet and pull the condom free of its covering. "No glove, no love, slugger," I tell him.

I'm not on birth control, but I'm clean. Him on the other hand? Who the fuck knows. I slowly roll the condom over his cock, he smirks. Once the condom is in place, he spins me back around, pinning me to the bed as he lines back up with my entrance. He pauses briefly. The brief pause turns into a few heartbeats and its getting annoying. I push into him, my pussy taking the tip of his cock and he grunts, then slides inside me in one swoop. Nothing like the first time, but still quick and he's huge. I squirm, allowing my body a moment to get used to his size, but he has no intention of waiting for me before he's pulling back out and pushing in.

I cry out as pleasure explodes.

"Jesus, for a bar slut, your cunt's tight as a glove."

I clench my teeth.

He slams back into me and I cry out again.

Fuck him.

He deserves this shit.

I start meeting him thrust for thrust. Getting off is no longer a priority for me, but I'm determined to piss him off and if that means fucking him and leaving him, or fucking him and insulting him, then by all means, I'm ready.

He starts grunting harder. Despite being pissed off and desperate to hold back my orgasm from him, it's growing hotter by the minute.

Fucker.

He continues pounding in and out of me. The dog tags clink together. He's close, his strokes becoming uneven.

I bite my tongue, hoping to distract from the building pleasure. I hate that despite everything this man has done to me, he still sends my body into a fury of lust and desire.

His grunts get more intense. He's holding back, waiting for me to come first. That satisfaction makes me smile slightly until he releases one of my hips and slides his hand around front. He searches out and finds my clit. His finger flicks against it then he pinches it between them and my orgasm explodes, consuming me. My pussy clenches his shaft harder.

Tears of frustration threaten to leak.

My plan is falling apart.

He thrusts into me as my orgasm subsides and he grunts and groans as his cock hardens, jerks and explodes with his release. The rubber barrier, my safe haven.

After he's done rubbing out his orgasm inside me and the condom, he withdrawals. I hear him pull off the rubber. What he does with it, I have no idea because the next thing I know, he's plopping down on the bed next to me.

I stretch out, refusing to look at him. He wraps his arms around me, pulling me into his side, my back to him. I hear him sniff my hair. "Missed you, Kiwi."

I freeze, then I'm met with gentle snoring and I realize that my cover isn't blown just yet. I wait patiently until his gentle snores turn harder and his hold on me loosens enough for me to extract myself.

Thank God, my shit's in the living room.

I carefully climb off the bed and as I'm walking out of the room, something on his nightstand catches my eye. It's a picture. I pick it up and hold it toward the hallway light. "Fuck me," I breathe.

It's a picture of me, sleeping in my uncle's house, six years ago. My tank top is askew, but nothing is showing, he covered me up before he took it. Judging from the light in the room, it had to be right before he left.

Asshole.

CHAPTER FIVE
Loki

I ROLL OVER, *FUCK.*

My eyes bolt open and I look around. "Huh?" I mumble.

Must have been a dream.

I roll over again, this time with my face landing in the blankets. All I can smell is her. *Kiwi.*

I bolt upright. It's still dark outside and I'm lying across my bed buck ass naked. "How?" I ask no one and I look around the room. I see my pants, but by t-shirt and cut are missing.

My eyes roam around the room and they land on the picture next to my clock. I shudder when the night comes roaring back to me.

The chick, at the bar. Skit, that's what Loni called her earlier in the day. She served us, we drank.

Pyro left…

"Fuck," I groan as I stand, heading for the front door. My shades are pulled back on the picture window near the door and I can see my driveway- no bike. "Fuck, fuck, fuck." I turn and see my cut hanging on the hook by the door. My eyes roam down to the floor and I find my t-shirt and nothing else.

I shake my head and stumble back to my room.

"What the…?" I breathe as I pick up the skimpy black lace thing lying on my floor.

Then I remember snapping her thong right before I tried to plunge inside her. The only other woman I've ever gone bareback with was her, Kiwi. *Why did I all of a sudden want to do it again?* I ask myself, but I have no logical answer.

She stopped me. Rolled on a condom.

Jesus, for a bar slut, your cunt's tight as a glove.

I pull the fabric to my nose and inhale her scent. Strawberries and sex.

WICKED REVENGE

My mind wanders back to that night in Boulder when I plunged face first into her beautiful cunt.

"What the fuck is wrong with me?" I groan before plopping back on the bed. My head roars with the start of a hangover as my eyes land on her picture next to my bed. Asleep, sprawled out on the bed, tank screwed up, hair slung over the pillow. The picture of perfection.

You walked away from it, asshole.

That's the last thought that rolls through my mind before I pass out, again.

Lily

"LILY," I HEAR BEFORE A knock against my bedroom door.

I scrub my face, praying my eyes are no longer red and swollen from the crying jag I let myself have before passing out around three this morning.

"What is it, Emily?" I ask.

"Piper, she's not feeling well," Emily tells me through the door.

"I'll be right out."

I hear Emily's retreating footsteps as I climb out of bed, my eyes roaming around the room looking for something to put on. I grab Loki's old t-shirt then check myself in the mirror. I'd washed off my make-up before I started in on myself last night. So, I'm really just checking to make sure the emotional breakdown isn't evident.

I can't believe I thought for one second my plan would work. I should have known he'd pass out, or wouldn't give a shit. Especially after he called me a bar slut with a tight pussy. It was at that point I felt completely used and I hated that my body responded to him the way it did.

I've always had a hot spot for Loki, ever since I was a little girl. First, it was just that he was sweet, nice to me, babysat me when my parents were busy or when Tryke was unable to. Then, as we both got older, he got hotter and hotter and I got more and more infatuated with him.

I shake off the memories and cover myself with the t-shirt and throw on a pair of pajama shorts before leaving my bedroom. I stop at Piper's room and she's not there so I make my way into the living room. It's bright, too bright in the house. It must be early afternoon when I find Piper laying on the couch.

"What's the matter, Pipes?" I ask her as I sit next to her.

"I not feel good, mommy." Her voice is soft, sad and pathetic. I put my hand on her forehead.

"You're not running a fever," I tell her.

"I know, I just…I miss Uncle Sticks," she says sadly.

"I know, baby, I do too, but I promise, things will be alright here." I take a deep breath. I was waiting for this to happen. She and Sticks were like two peas in a pod. Sticks despised my leaving Boulder, but he understood that the time had come for me to do what I needed to do. He relented when he realized that even six years later, despite my daughter, I wasn't going to let them get away with the things they did to my family. "Can we just give it a little time?" I ask her softly and she nods. "Good, thank you, baby girl. Now, what can I get you to make you feel better?"

"Ice cream," she states, her voice more confident now.

I raise an eyebrow at her. "Have you had lunch yet?"

She nods enthusiastically before coming off the sofa and wrapping her arms around my neck, squeezing tightly. "You have to work?"

"Not for a while, baby. Tell you what, let's have Emily get you some ice cream while I go get in the shower, then you and I can watch that movie you like?"

"The one with the yellow guys?" she asks sheepishly.

I laugh lightly. "That's the one," I tell her and she lights up before hopping down and going into the kitchen.

WICKED REVENGE

"Emi, Emi..." she practically shouts as she runs into the kitchen.

"What, baby?" Emily says back to her.

"Mommy, say I can have ice cream."

"She did, huh?"

"Uh huh," Piper answers back.

I smile as I stand up from the couch. A distant sound catches my attention and I listen intently as the roar of Harleys draws closer to the house. Three of them roar past the house, all wearing Wicked Angels cuts. They go too fast for me to be certain, but I don't think any of them are Loki.

The bikes continue down the street until the noise disappears. Then it comes back. This time it's just one bike. It slows in front of the house. I can't tell who it is at first, not until they pause right in front of my house. Eyes locked on my bike as it's parked out front. He seems to be looking it over, almost as if he's trying to decide who it belongs to. After a moment, he turns his head and I see the jagged scar down the side of his face and I know it's the man who was with Loki last night.

I can't place him, but there is something oddly familiar about him and its really starting to bother me.

After a few moments, the bike roars and takes off after the other three. Loki's house is right down the street, though out of earshot of the bikes, close enough that he could drive by and see my car in the driveway. That is if he was that alert last night.

"Here you go, sweetie," I hear Emily say.

"Thank you," Piper replies and I scoot down the hall for my room, a shower and clean change of clothes.

It's now quarter after five and I have to be to work in forty-five minutes. I kneel and Piper wraps her arms around me. "See you tomorrow, mommy," she says.

My working nights, in a bar, is nothing new for her, which is why Emily is here. We became friends after she stopped at the bar where I was working at the time. I don't know what it was, but we just clicked. She was doing everything she could just to pass through town and move on with her life.

We never discussed her reasons for running away, but I managed to convince her to stay. She was barely nineteen at the time and I wasn't about to let her take off. So, I gave her a job as my nanny. When it came time for me to move down here, I offered her more money, and she didn't hesitate, much. She has her own room, and she takes care of Piper for me. I look past Piper to Emily. "I left your salary and some grocery money on the counter for you," I tell her.

"Thank you, Lily," she smiles.

Emily is twenty-two now and I hated pulling her away from Boulder, but she was more than willing to come with me. She's a sweet girl and amazing with Pipes. She is making plans to go back to school and I offered to help her pay for it. I'm not broke and working at a bar is hardly what I need to do to make a living and it kills me to pull so much time away from Piper, but I have to do this. If I don't, and I'm discovered, she'll never be safe.

"Love you, baby girl. Have a good day at school tomorrow." I squeeze her.

"I will," she says enthusiastically. It was evident that school was going to be a great place for Piper and it has been. She's in kindergarten, but her school doesn't offer full day, so she's there in the mornings. "Love you," she smiles as she lets me go. She turns toward Emily. "I want mac n' cheese for dinner." I smile at Emily who nods and takes Piper into the kitchen for dinner.

I secure my leather and head out the front door, a bag in hand. I can't very well wear leather bike boots, though I'm sure Loni is gonna give me an eyeful when I show up on my bike at the bar tonight. I don't give a shit. I don't want to take my car. The temptation to give Loki a ride home again, should he show up, is too great. I have to put some distance between us or I won't get this shit over with so I can go back to Boulder with my heart in one piece.

Big Daddy is keeping Sticks in the loop on what's going down in Roswell. Sticks is keeping me in the loop on the side. I need to know when Arizona plans to make their move so I can have my crack at Gunnar and Rooster before Big Daddy gets his claws into them.

I fling my leg over my bike and start it. Feeling the rumble and hum of the engine between my legs gives me a feeling of power and invincibility. I look to the sky and silently thank my brother for teaching me to ride before he taught me to drive.

Old ladies don't drive, they ride bitch.

I guess maybe I was never meant to be an old lady. I love the rumble of the bike between my legs and the control in my hands as I drive.

I put my shades on and slowly back the bike down the driveway before kicking over the gears and taking off down the street.

The wind in my face is the best feeling in the world, second only to looking in my daughter's eyes.

The eyes of her father.

CHAPTER SIX
Pyro

THE BIKE TAKES OFF DOWN the street. Whoever owns it, isn't an Angel and curiosity got the better of me after I saw it this afternoon. So, I'm hiding down the street when I see it rolling down the driveway before peeling out.

"Fuck," I growl as she roars past me.

I give her a head start, long enough to get through the light at the entrance to the neighborhood. No need to follow her, though. I know where she's going. Loki on the other hand?

I turn the opposite direction of where she went and head straight for his house.

I pull up in front of it and park behind Loki's car. Loki and I took it back to Iron Wings to get his wheels this afternoon and I reamed him a new asshole about taking home bar sluts. Loni is an absolute ballbuster when it comes to her girls, and a new one is no exception.

Loni is Cowboy's old lady. She's been running Iron Wings for the last twenty plus years and has no qualms about busting your ass if you fuck with one of her girls, especially the new ones. Even ones, like Skit, who've had a long-standing career as a bar wench.

Loki opens the door as I climb the steps. "Back to bust my ass again?"

"She rides."

"Who?" He narrows his eyes at me.

"Skit, that's who. She rides, man."

"No shit?" he says skeptically. "What's Rooster gonna do?"

I shrug. "I'm not telling him. But to be fair, she's riding to work, so it's her ass if anyone sees it and you know damn well Loni will."

"Then let her deal with it," he grumbles.

"What's your beef?"

He shakes his head. "I can't stop comparing her to Kiwi."

WICKED REVENGE

I stiffen at the name. "Why would you be comparing her to Kiwi?" I say through gritted teeth.

"Don't fucking start with me, dick," Loki snaps.

I debate on telling him about the little girl's bicycle I saw in the front yard of her house, but I let it go.

Then again, if he knew she had a kid? He'd never have taken her to bed. That's his number one rule. Maybe if I tell him, he'll leave her the hell alone. "She's got a kid, dude."

He freezes and turns back toward me. "What?" he says harshly. "How the fuck you know this?"

"The same way I know she rides. When I was coming up here this afternoon to get your shit, there was a new bike on the street, well, in the driveway, and I stopped to check it out. Didn't want anyone riding in on us unannounced. So, I went back and watched, waiting for it to leave."

"Where?"

"The old Mason place." I jerk my head north.

"How old's the kid?" he asks.

"You're asking a lot of fucking questions," I snap at him.

"How old?" he growls

"Fuck if I know. I didn't see her."

"How do you know it's a girl?" He widens his eyes at me.

"The bicycle, moron. It's a girl's bicycle," I snap back at him. "Why the fuck you care, asswipe?"

"I don't" he answers quickly.

"And your shit don't stink either," I counter.

He glares at me and shakes his head.

"What are we doing tonight?" I ask.

"I'm going to I.W."

"What in the fuck for?"

"I think I owe her an apology," he says.

It's my turn to narrow my eyes. "I say again, what the fuck for?"

He sighs, "Forget it."

I roll my eyes. "Grab your shit. Let's bounce."

He nods and heads into his bedroom. I want to punch his fucking lights out. What in the fuck is his deal with this chick?

I admit she has some familiar qualities about her, but there are a lot of Beaumonts around these parts, so for all I know, she's a family kid. She certainly doesn't look like *her*. I don't say the name, I can't.

"Hey, you talked to Pixie lately?" I call down the hall.

"Nah, why?"

I shrug, even though he can't see me. "No reason," I tell him.

He comes back into the living room, his cut on, his boots half-zipped. "Bullshit, why?" He narrows his eyes at me.

"Forget it."

He shakes his head. "She's fine," he tells me.

I nod before we take off.

Lily

I PARK AROUND THE BACK of the bar, like I did last night when I got here. There are several cars and several more bikes in the lot, considering it's just before six. The backdoor to Iron Wings swings open just as I'm throwing my leg over. "Girl, you got brass balls in there I don't know about?" Loni, my new boss, asks.

I narrow my eyes at her. "No, why?"

She shakes her head. "Take that shit home and get your car," she snaps.

"What the hell for?" I ask.

"Rooster or anyone else sees you riding that, you're gonna have hell to pay. Girls don't ride in these parts unless they riding bitch on their old man's bike."

"I rode in Colorado, what's the big deal?" I ask. Though I get the impression I already have the answer.

"Sticks let you ride?"

Oh shit. "Yeah," I tell her hesitantly.

"Well, Rooster ain't gonna let it fly here. So, get it home before he sees you."

"Loni, I can…"

"No, Skit, you can't. Trust me on this one, please. You can ride that shit anywhere you want, just not on MC property. Get me?"

I nod. "I get you."

"Take it home, come back, and get to work, yeah?" she says, though I can tell she's really not mad at me, just giving me a heads up.

I flip my shades back on, sling my leg over and turn over the engine. I'm thankful for the bandana covering my hair, at least if someone sees me, they'll know it's a girl, but not necessarily me.

Within ten minutes, I'm pulling back in front of the house when I hear the roar of bikes, two to be exact, coming from the direction of Loki's house. "Shit," I sputter as I run for the door, but I'm not fast enough.

The next thing I know, two bikes are pulling onto my lawn and their engines cut out.

I pull the bandana from my head before I freeze when I hear their stands go down. "Brave, bitch." It's Pyro's gravelly voice.

"Excuse me?" My heartbeat is racing a million miles a minute and fear grips at me when I realize that Piper is inside.

"Brave bitch riding in Roswell," Pyro says and I turn toward him.

"I take it someone tipped you off?" Loki asks. His hair is pulled back into a…I have no idea what he's doing with his hair and Pyro's is braided down his back.

"Loni, when I pulled in," I share with narrowed eyes.

"Good," Loki says. For some strange reason, Pyro is staring daggers at me and Loki looks like he's ready to tackle me to the ground and fuck me.

"Message received, boys, no riding to Angels' territory. Got it. Now I need to go change." I turn toward the door.

"Where'd you learn to ride?" Pyro asks me. My heart stills again before I turn back around.

"Someone who could kick both your asses. He told me if I could learn to ride a bike and drive a stick, I'd never be stranded."

Pyro freezes in his tracks. His eyes turn from daggers to murderous in a matter of seconds.

"Mommy…" Piper's voice reaches my ears as the screen door slams shut.

Fuck.

"Hey baby, can you go back inside? I'll be there in a minute." She looks from me to Pyro, then to Loki and then back to me.

"Okay," she says, slowly backing away toward the door. No one says anything until she's inside.

"Skit, who is that?" It's Loki's voice, but it sounds, I don't even know, freaked out?

"My daughter."

"How old is she?" Loki asks.

"Five," I answer automatically and he relaxes. I don't tack on that she'll be six in a couple months.

Pyro on the other hand looks like he's about to spit nails. "Message received?" he says through gritted teeth.

"Yes, Pyro, I got it from Loni," I tell him. My heart still hasn't found a normal rhythm in my chest.

WICKED REVENGE

I don't say anymore, I just walk into the house and close the front door. "You alright, Lily?" Emily asks me. "You look like you've seen a ghost."

I suck in a deep breath but I don't move. I wait patiently for the sound of Harleys kicking over. It takes a few moments before the bikes roar to life outside. "I'm fine, I just need to change and swap my rides."

"Something wrong with the bike?" she asks.

I shake my head. "Nope, not at all." I leave it at that and I head for my room, Piper follows behind me.

"Mommy, who those guys?" she asks.

"They're just friends, baby."

"Oh, okay," she says before heading into her room. I sit down on the bed waiting for my heart to return to normal. Once steady, I exchange my pants for a short skirt and black fuck-me heels before saying my good-byes again and leaving for Iron Wings.

CHAPTER SEVEN
Loki

PYRO AND I PULL UP to the clubhouse and my mind is consumed with the little blonde girl with curly hair at Skit's house. Something about her looks ridiculously familiar and all I want to do is drink it away. Who knows? Maybe fuck it away, too.

Pyro is in a mood when we step inside.

"What's your beef?" I ask him.

He shakes his head and doesn't answer me.

"What the fuck, man?" I growl at him and he turns on me, getting in my face.

"Are you so fucking stupid or just blind?"

I shove him off me. "What the fuck are you talking about?" I snap and my eyes narrow at him.

"Pyro, Loki, get in here," Rooster snaps from down the hall interrupting us and whatever scuff we're about to get into.

"This isn't over," I tell Pyro as we both walk down the hall toward Rooster's office.

"Need you guys to ride," Rooster says as we enter his shitty office. He doesn't bother to clean up after himself, ever. "I don't give a damn what your beef with each other is, get the fuck over it," he snaps.

"Where we goin'?" Pyro asks.

"Boulder."

My heart sinks into my stomach and Pyro glares at me through narrowed eyes.

We finished our business with Rooster and returned to the clubhouse common room. We're taking off early tomorrow morning. Sticks wants us in Boulder by tomorrow night. According to Rooster, something's going down up there and Sticks needs some muscle, which usually comes from Arizona, but they're having their annual ride this week and can't spare anyone.

I had to fight rolling my eyes during our meeting. I know it's all bullshit. Sticks needs us in Boulder for other reasons, but they're using it as cover for what's really going down.

We were in the front of the clubhouse all of fifteen minutes before Pyro disappears to stuff his dick into Taffy. He knows as well as I do that the Boulder girls aren't the best, so he's gonna get his while he can.

Taz comes down the stairs looking freshly fucked and she smiles at me in invitation, but I shake my head. I have other ideas. The prospect behind the car slides me another whiskey and I slam it back before leaving out the front door of the clubhouse.

I should go home, do some laundry or some bullshit like that, but instead, my bike heads opposite my house and before I know it, I'm pulling up in front of Iron Wings. I didn't consciously decide to come here, but apparently, I need to be here.

I climb off my bike and head for the door.

The Angels have prospects here too, watching over bikes and the doors. Anyone who's not MC has to pay a cover to get in so I bypass the line and instead of a prospect, I see Rack standing at the door. He nods as he lets me inside and the place is packed. Every seat full except for one of the two tables Wicked usually occupies, so I head there. My eyes roaming around the room until I find her.

My heart stops in my chest as I take in her backside.

She's not wearing a bra and some backless number, showing off her ink. I'd seen it last night but was too drunk to really look at it. Though I can't fully see it from here, it's glowing slightly under some of the black lights of the bar. But that's not the only thing I see glowing. On her left shoulder, she has something else tattooed, but I'd not noticed it the night before and now I understand why. It's been done in white. Nearly invisible, unless you're looking for it or standing under black lights.

My eyes roam down to the small of her back, graciously free of ink.

The first thought that comes to mind is how great my ink would look dipping into the crack of her ass. I shake my head. *Where in the fuck did that come from?*

She turns back around, headed for the bar, and her eyes immediately land on mine. In the light, she looks younger, years younger, and a memory slides into place that won't leave as I remember the soft features of the one I drove away all those years ago.

I try and shake it off as I head to the table and grab a seat. The only reason I'm thinking about her is because I'm headed back to Boulder for the first time in six years. My cock hardens at the prospect of seeing her again. Will she want to see me? Is she still there?

I shudder and ignore my thoughts. It's fucking ridiculous that I would want to see her again. She's ancient history.

Skit dutifully comes over, leaning on the table like she did last night. Her left shoulder is closest to me and I'm disappointed at the lack of black light over my table. I want to see her tattoo. "Back for more?" she asks. Her tone a little harsher, more pissed off, and I like it. My cock stirs in my jeans.

"The same," I tell her, narrowing my eyes at her.

"Where's your friend?" she asks referring to Pyro.

I lean forward. "Why? You interested in a tag team?"

"You couldn't handle this last night. What makes you think the two of you can handle it?" There's a wicked smirk playing at her lips.

"Oh, trust me, sugar tits, we could take you."

"Sure, you can." She wiggles her eyebrows in invitation before she saunters off toward the bar. I debate briefly on texting P, asking him to come help me put her in her place.

The ass chewing he gave me earlier about taking her home sends ice through my veins and I keep my phone tucked away.

The night progresses and I take it much slower on the whiskey so that

I can get my own ass home tonight. Besides, riding hungover isn't good for anyone.

Around eleven the bar starts dying down, earlier than normal, so I take the cue and leave. I don't see Skit before I go and I'm disappointed. I wanted to see her one more time before I bail. I won't be back 'til early next week.

Pussy ass.

I roll my eyes at myself before leaving through the front door. Rack is still there and I nod to him before climbing on my bike and taking off for home.

CHAPTER EIGHT

Lily

"YOU OKAY TO WORK TOMORROW and Saturday?" Loni asks me.

"Absolutely," I tell her.

"We don't open 'til six on Sunday and shut up around eleven. It's usually dead in here and we're closed on Monday. So, would Wednesday through Saturday be alright for you?"

I smile. "Absolutely, Loni, whenever you need me."

She smiles back. "Get out of here. See you tomorrow night."

"G'night," I tell her before I go out the back door to my car. I look around, seeing no one. Loki left a couple hours ago. I don't imagine he's hanging around out here hoping for another chance.

I'm leaning down to unlock my car when a hand covers my mouth and I'm pressed against my car. I breathe through my nose and smell stale cigarettes and alcohol, maybe even some chick's pussy. I shudder. "Loki," I growl. Then again, Loki doesn't smoke.

"Guess again." Pyro's gravelly voice of Pyro meets my ears. "You gonna scream?"

I shake my head and he releases my mouth. "You don't have to assault me to get laid, you know," I tell him without turning around.

"I don't want you," he growls at me.

I try and turn around but he stops me. "Then what's the point?" I snap.

He whips me around and leans down so he's inches from my face. "You were told never to come back here."

My heart freezes in my chest as Pyro's voice no longer sounds gravelly and vaguely familiar. "How'd you?" I narrow my eyes at him, but the darkness back here makes it impossible to really look at him.

"Why are you here?" he asks.

"That's none of your fucking business. Now, if you'll…"

WICKED REVENGE

"It is my business," he murmurs close to my lips. There's absolutely no sexual tension between us and I find that rather odd. Again, I try and look into those familiar eyes and I can't seem to focus on anything. "Tryke made it my business." His voice has turned arctic on me and I shiver at the mention of my brother's name.

"I have shit I need to take care of," I mumble.

"It's being handled, go home."

With that, he pushes away from me and disappears into the darkness surrounding the bar.

I let out a rush of breath that I didn't know was stuck in my lungs.

He's seriously scary as fuck.

Why in the hell would Tryke bring anyone else into his little secret besides Loki? Big Daddy and Sticks know because I brought it to their attention and I never had to ask for them to keep it a secret. It's what they do and no one, outside of them, needed to know. The guys that were with Big Daddy that day were just collateral. None of them seemed to even have any recognition about who Kiwi was, so I let it go.

I shake my head. It's been six years. Who the fuck cares anymore?

Wicked Angels think Lily Beaumont died ten years ago. Anyone who looks into my property agreement for my house will see that it's registered to Reggie Beaumont, also known as Uncle Sticks. Worse case, they'd assume I was his kid or some shit like that. That was the one concession I'd let Sticks have about us moving back here.

My mind wanders over all the different reasons why Pyro is so pissed off at me as I drive home. It's just before one in the morning and I'm exhausted when I pull in my driveway and stumble my way to my front door.

Emily and Piper are asleep when I get in the house so I try to be quiet as I go into the kitchen looking for something to munch on.

I hear the roar of a motorcycle coming down the street. From back here I can't tell what direction its going so I hurry to the window and peel back the curtain a little bit to see. It's coming from Loki's house and it stops in front of mine. I watch intently, waiting to see who it is, or for them to decide what they're doing. The bike shuts off. The rider kicks his leg over and then stands. I know immediately it's Loki, even before he passes under the light of the street lamp.

"Fuck," I sputter.

I go to the door and open it, stepping outside before he reaches it. "What are you doing here?" I ask, my tone sharp and pissed off.

"I came to see you," he says clearly, not drunk.

"You do realize I have a daughter asleep in the house right now and it's the middle of the night?" I make sure my little southern twang is in my voice. If I let my normal voice, sans accent, come out, he just might put two and two together.

"Yeah," he says as he runs his hand through his hair. It's not tied back tonight, just loose flowing down his back. Little kinks in it from it being pulled up earlier. Jesus, he's fucking gorgeous. Black jeans, boots, white t-shirt under his cut. I lick my lips. "About that?"

"What about it, Loki?" My defenses rise immediately and I try not to let it come out through in my voice.

"She's a gorgeous little girl."

My eyes flutter closed. Hearing those words from his lips melts every hardened part of my soul. "Thank you," I manage to say through gritted teeth.

He doesn't seem to notice. "What's her name?"

"Loki, come on, it's the middle of the night."

He gets a little flustered before his eyes bore into mine. "I'm leaving in the morning. Club business. I just wanted to see you before I left." He turns to leave.

"Wait," I say as I move down the three little steps from my door and into the grass. He stops and turns back toward me. My heart is overruling my brain right now and as much as I want to be pissed off at him for all the shit he's put me through, he looks so sad and broken that it hurts my heart.

I stop, just a few feet in front of him, and he closes the distance between us. He presses his forehead to mine. "I'm gonna be back next week."

I put my hands on his biceps, holding myself to him. "Okay?" I can't withhold the skepticism from my voice. "Are you afraid I'm not gonna be here or something?" I ask.

"I'd deserve that," he mutters, his voice so low I'm not sure it was intended for me to hear. Unfortunately, I can't argue with that statement.

"I'm not goin' anywhere," I breathe.

His eyes come to mine, searching, asking, begging. I don't know, but they're desperate for something. Answers maybe. My heart freezes, then kicks up in double time as I feel like spilling everything to him. Explaining it all.

He gently kisses the tip of my nose, something he always did to me when I was a kid. I don't know if he's ever done it to anyone else, or if he's figured out who I am. I let my eyes flutter closed briefly and then he's pulling back from me. "Wait for me," he whispers as he steps out of my hold and turns back to his bike.

My heart is pounding so hard and so loud in my chest that it's halfway to China before I catch up to it. He kicks over the engine on his bike and takes off. He goes a little ways before turning around and roaring back down the street toward his house.

It takes until I hear the roar of another bike, this time from the right, to I get my feet moving. The last thing I need is Pyro coming down the street and seeing me standing here like an idiot.

I race for my door and manage to make it inside before the bike goes roaring past. Though he doesn't stop, I see his head turn in the direction of my house as he flies past.

Somehow, I made it from the front door to my room and a shower before wrapping myself in Loki's old t-shirt and climbing into bed.

That night the dreams come at me in rapid, vivid detail.

Changing from Sticks, my friends and Boulder, to Loki, Roswell, then finally landing on Pyro. But it's not Pyro I'm looking at when the dream ends abruptly and I bolt upright on the bed.

I couldn't get back to sleep after that. Just before six in the morning and I pad quietly through the house to the kitchen where I make coffee. My mind bounces from six years ago, to now, and back again.

If you didn't know better, Big Daddy or Sticks could be my father. The three of them, despite the large age gaps between them, all look the same. They have the same eyes, Kellen's eyes, and I keep trying to figure out if either one, Big Daddy or Sticks, had any sons who would be old enough. I know Sticks doesn't. He and his wife never had kids. But Devon – Big Daddy D – on the other hand… I debate picking up the phone and calling Sticks to ask, but it's too early for that.

I pour myself a cup of coffee and return to standing in the patio window in the dining room looking out at the open field behind my house. I'm so zoned out that I didn't even hear Emily come into the kitchen, she makes me jump and I spill coffee on the floor.

"I'm sorry, Lily," she murmurs as she grabs a towel from the counter. "I didn't think you were up."

"No, it's fine, it's my fault," I tell her as I take the towel from her. "I'll get it." I kneel and wipe the floor. "You're up early," I remark.

She shakes her head. "I'm usually up this early, gives me a chance to shower and get ready before Piper wakes up."

I give her a sad smile. "You should have told me no," I mutter.

She cocks her head. "No to what?"

"Moving down here. You're so young, Emily. You shouldn't have to be tied to my daughter like this." Thinking of my brother has me in a melancholy mood.

She smiles at me. "I love your daughter, Lily. She's a joy to be around and I like having a steady job. Most people I know my age can't say the same thing."

I nod in understanding. "I just don't want you to feel like I'm holding you back from something."

She shakes her head. "You're not."

"If I ever start to, will you tell me?" I ask her.

She nods and smiles. "Besides, you said I could go to school if I wanted to."

I smile at her and ask, "Have you found something?"

She nods again. "I'd like to check out Roswell Community."

"Get me the information, we'll make it happen," I tell her.

"Thank you, Lily." She smiles wider, her whole face lighting up with excitement. She's a great kid. Shit, she's only a few years younger than I am, but I feel so much older than I am, so she'll stay a kid in my eyes. "I'm gonna hit the shower," she tells me as she pours herself some coffee.

"What's your plan today?" I ask.

"I need to go to the store while Piper's at school, or I could wait and go after and bring her with me. If you'd like?"

I nod. "I'm gonna end up passing out again soon." I can feel the weight of sleeplessness already. "I'm working tonight. I'm gonna be working Wednesday through Saturday, six to close," I tell her.

"Okay, that will work." She smiles before heading down the hallway to the bathroom and her shower.

My mind wanders away from my brother to Emily and going to school. If she goes Monday through Thursday, I can make that work, as long as she has a morning class on Thursday. I can get up and take care of Pipes on those days. Having Sundays, Mondays and Tuesdays off will really help. I hate being away from Piper so much.

ZOEY DERRICK

The roar of bikes catches my attention. My eyes land on the clock. Its seven fifteen in the morning and I move to the front window to see who's coming down the street. The sound draws closer from my left, its two bikes. Then I see Loki in the lead followed by Pyro. They're both wearing road vests that have Wicked Angels written on the back, but no colors, no patches. I take a deep breath. Both of them are riding together. A few days without drama will be really nice around here.

"Mommy." I turn to see Pipes still rubbing her eyes.

"Hi, baby, you're up really early," I say as I go over to her after setting my coffee cup on the table. She yawns. "Come on," I tell her and I lead her down the hallway. "Em, I'm gonna snuggle with Piper," I tell her as we pass.

"Okay," she says and I take Piper into my room. She climbs up on my bed and I follow behind her, wrapping my arms around her. She's laying on her back under me. She grabs a chunk of my hair and she starts playing with it. Something she's done since she was a baby and breastfeeding. It brings me as much comfort as it does her and she dozes off. I nuzzle my face closer to hers, breathing in her fresh Piper scent and fall asleep shortly after.

This time, I don't dream.

CHAPTER NINE

Loki

WE ROLL INTO BOULDER ABOUT six o'clock, after stopping outside of town to fill up and swap our road vests for our cuts before rolling up to the clubhouse. It's Friday night, which means the clubhouse is full of bikers and bitches when we step in the main door.

It takes only a few minutes before Sticks comes out of his office and pulls us back with him.

The closer we got to Boulder, the more agitated Pyro got and I'm not entirely sure why. Whatever is biting his ass is pissing me off. He's not normally this irritated. He usually lets shit just roll off his back and there's nothing I can possibly think of that would piss him off this much.

By the time we step into Sticks' office, the tension is rolling off him in waves and I want to put him through a wall.

"What's crawled up your ass?" Sticks asks Pyro.

Pyro just narrows his eyes and shakes his head, but says nothing further.

"Where is she?" I ask Sticks.

"Who you talkin' 'bout?" Sticks plays dumb, but I know he knows damn well who I'm talking about.

I glare at him, "Kiwi, where is she?"

He puts his hands up in defense. "She's long gone, man. Rolled outta here about a year ago." His voice is calm. I have no reason to doubt him, but Pyro growls at him. After Pyro asked me about talking to Pixie, I got to thinking about it and it's been more than a year since I called up here to check on her. So Sticks' answer doesn't surprise me.

"Bullshit," Pyro snaps.

"What's up your ass? What the fuck you care where some broad is?" Sticks bites back at Pyro. I can't say I blame him.

Pyro slams Sticks against the wall, hand in his shirt. "Where is she?"

"Fuck, Pyro, what the hell, man?" I try pulling him off Sticks but he just rolls his eyes at me.

"Gone for fuck's sake. She moved on, moved away."

"Where?" I ask him.

"What the hell do you care? You were here once, asswipe, and you left her." Now I can see Sticks is pissed as fuck. He glares at me and then shifts his eyes to Pyro. But Pyro's eyes are on me instead. The same murderous glare that was directed at Sticks a second ago is now pointed at me.

"What the fuck did you do to her?" Pyro snaps, releasing Sticks and moving in on me.

"Fuck you," I growl at him, ready to throw down. "What the fuck you care? You abandoned her," I remind him.

"Both of you, knock it the fuck off," Sticks says in a tone that makes us both cringe. "Or I'll throw you both the fuck out of here, and trust me, there's some nice piece of ass coming in tonight and you don't want to miss it."

I roll my eyes. Sticks' solution to everything is a fine piece of ass.

"I mean it, she's gone. She rolled up out of here, looking for something more from life. Last I heard she was headed for Kansas City. She's an adult, perfectly capable of taking care of herself." He sits down in his chair behind his desk. "But don't let that fool you two fuck-knuckles. There ain't a man in that room out there that won't throw down for her, so you two better get your shit together and quit fighting about this shit before you drag it out of my office and get yourselves dead, you get me?"

We both turn to look at Sticks. "You were supposed to keep her out of the club," I remind him.

He shrugs. "There ain't nothing you can stop that girl from doing once she puts her mind to it. She came up here after Tryke died." I don't miss Pyro's stiffening at the mention of Tryke's name but I let it go. "She needed a place to crash, I gave her one. She needed a job, I gave her one. When she was ready to leave, I let her go. She survived five years up here and she did it without much help from me. She made friends with the right group of people and wormed her way into the hearts of every biker in this house."

WICKED REVENGE

"She has a way of doing that," I mutter.

Pyro relaxes a little as Sticks tells us what's what.

After one final stare down between the three of us, we move on to business. Discussing our purpose for being here.

It's the better part of two hours before we're armed with all the information we need and we finally join the party in the main room of the clubhouse. We're to leave here in the morning and get down to Tucson where we fill Big Daddy in on all that Sticks knows and what we've learned over the last several months. Neither Big Daddy nor Sticks trusts the phone lines. He'll cover for us up here while we journey south. From there we will return home, but not before we establish our plan for taking down Rooster. At this point, the only thing that will take him down is a bullet between the eyes and Pyro will be more than happy to care of it.

Kiwi's disappearance isn't a good thing.

She's wanted revenge against Rooster since the night Tryke died. If she gets wind of what's doin' she's gonna be all over him like white on rice and I can't say I blame her one bit.

Rooster ordered the hit, Gunnar carried it out. Well, made sure it was carried out, and Kiwi is gunning for both of them.

Pyro and I start mingling amongst the other members and club whores.

Pyro

LOKI OCCUPIES HIMSELF WITH A club whore and I slip back down the hall, finding Sticks' door and knocking.

"Enter," comes from the other side and I open the door and step inside. Our eyes meet.

"Hello, Reggie," I say in a menacing tone that puts his guard up instantly.

"Not many people know that name…"

"Family, right?"

He nods, shell shocked by my being in here and using his real name. "What do you want, Pyro?" he asks as he stands up.

I cock my head. "I'm not here to hurt you if that's what you're afraid of. She's lost enough in her life. She doesn't need to lose you, too."

"What's your beef with Lily, Pyro?" For the first time in six years, that name grates on a few nerves and I try and shake it off.

"Where is she, Reggie?"

He narrows his eyes at me. "I think you already know the answer to that question, you're just hoping I'll confirm it for you."

I flick my zippo, the sound causing Sticks to jump a little. "Maybe, maybe not," I whisper.

"Then why ask the question? What do you want with her?"

"What I wanted for her was a club free life. It's what she was supposed to get by coming up here. Instead, you hand her exactly what she wanted."

"And that's what, exactly?"

"Revenge," I breathe.

CHAPTER TEN

Lily

THE WEEKEND PASSES WITH NO sign of Loki or Pyro.

I finished my shift on Saturday night, went home and climbed into bed without incident. Emily made plans for Sunday, knowing it was my day off and I was going to want to spend as much of it with Piper as humanly possible. When I asked her what her plans were, she laughed and told me she was going to be a Roswell tourist. I laughed a little harder after that. She deserves a day off and I get to spend the day with Piper. Win-win.

Piper and I made cookies, sang silly songs and watched movies until it was time for her to go to bed or rather, until she passed out on the couch with her head on my lap. Being with Piper, just the two of us, makes me miss Boulder a little more. Sure, I had a bigger support system up there, between the old ladies, a couple of the girls I worked with and Sticks, but I had to practically runaway with Piper to spend time alone with her. Down here, I have more time with her, but I'm working more. It's a job I love and yet it's unnecessary financially and it irks me to leave her.

Monday afternoon, while sitting down to do homework with Piper, my phone rings, it's Loni.

"Hey boss," I say when I answer the phone.

"Hey, sorry to call on your day off."

"No worries, you need me?" I ask.

"Not today, but the clubhouse is throwing a shindig tomorrow for a visiting club and we need all the girls we can get." I shudder. This is my least favorite part about being a bar back.

"What time?"

I hear her sigh in relief. "Seven, the clubhouse. You know where it's at?"

"I do. What time you want me there?" I ask her.

"Can you come at six?" she asks, and I can tell she's reluctant about it.

"I'll be there."

"You're a lifesaver, Skit."

I smile. "No problem. See you tomorrow."

"Thanks again," she says and we disconnect.

"Em," I call and she comes into the living room. "I have to work tomorrow night. I don't know what time I'll be home," I tell her and it's the truth. Early on, in Boulder, I would do club parties and I would often crawl home around nine or ten in the morning.

"No problem." She smiles. "Pipes and I are gonna go see a movie on Wednesday after school."

"Yeah," Piper says excitedly.

"You're a lifesaver," I tell her.

"Don't forget, she needs to get registered for dance class."

"Shit!"

"Mommy!" Piper snaps at me.

"Sorry, baby," I tell her with a smile. I look back at Emily. "Thank you, I will take care of it." I'd completely forgotten and classes start in just a couple weeks.

Tuesday comes, still no sign of Loki or Pyro.

As the day drawls on, I'm more and more relieved that Loki hasn't driven past my house. I'm hoping like hell he doesn't show up tonight, but I'm not sure I can get that lucky.

I went to the dance school this morning and got Piper all signed up. She starts the middle of next month, giving me just a little over a month to handle what I need to take care of. Registering her implies that I'm staying here. It might not be a bad idea, but we might not have much choice.

WICKED REVENGE

On my way home from registration and stopping by the store, Sticks called me. He didn't say much other than things were in motion and he'd be in touch. The plan is to get the club vacated somehow, with the exception of Rooster, but that might be easier said than done. I have a backup plan in place that involves his house. Which I'd like to avoid, but the son of a bitch did kill my brother in his own home, maybe I can do the same to him.

"Mommy," Piper calls from the kitchen when I get inside the house.

"Hi, baby," I call back. "Whatcha doin'?"

"Emi and I are coloring." I hear the chair scoot as she jumps down and comes running toward me. "Am I going to dance class?" she asks. Her excitement is palpable and I smile wide at her.

"You are, baby, in a few weeks, okay?"

"Okay, does this mean we get to go shopping?" She smiles wide at me.

She's worse than I am when it comes to shopping. This girl loves to do it, and she knows exactly what she's doing too. "Absolutely," I tell her.

She runs back to the kitchen, arms raised in the air shouting, "yay," as she goes.

I hear Emily's laugh from the kitchen. I round the corner. We exchange a look of, 'oh boy' before she sits down with Piper.

"Piper, baby, I'm gonna go lay down, okay?"

"Okay, mommy," she says without looking up and I nod to Emily and head toward my bedroom. Tonight's gonna be a long night, and I need to catch a little more sleep. I've been up since just before seven when Piper came in bouncing on my bed. She's really excited about dance class and it warms my heart. She'd been in one back in Boulder and I promised her that I'd get her into a school for it down here. Now she just has to wait for the session to start.

I change into a t-shirt, draw my curtains tight and climb into my bed. It doesn't take more than a few minutes and I'm out.

"WHAT ARE WE DOING?" PYRO says into the phone.

"What choice do we have?" I remind him.

I can almost hear his eyes rolling. "When all this shit goes down, I'm never entertaining again," he mumbles into the phone.

I hear that. "I'll see you there. I need to get wet."

"I'll be there."

We hang up and I toss my phone onto the bed and strip out of my riding gear to jump in the shower. I'm happy to be home. My ass is numb and my eyelids weigh a hundred pounds, but we'll never hear the end of it if we don't show tonight.

It's seven thirty when I climb out of the shower. The shit and shebang started half an hour ago, but I don't rush. I couldn't care less tonight. All I want is to go see Skit at work, drink and pass the fuck out.

Another twenty minutes and I'm flying down the street headed toward the clubhouse. I drive past Skit's place and there is light coming through the curtains, but Skit's car is gone. Her bike is in the driveway, up near the house. Good, she learned her lesson. The only bike she needs to be riding is mine.

I blink as I pull up to the light. I keep blinking for no reason at all, perplexed by the direction of my thoughts. Where the fuck did that come from?

She's not mine, never has been, and never will be.

I walk into the clubhouse. No joke, dude, the place is packed. Wicked Angels and Critical Chaos members filling up the chairs and couches.

WICKED REVENGE

Two pool tables full of bikers and bitches. Tits hanging out, asses bouncing like there ain't a care in the fucking world. I roll my eyes. Only this charter has tits and ass hanging out all over the fucking place.

My eyes land on Taz who's working on some ugly ass dude from CC with one of the other chicks who works at the strip club owned by the Angels. Taz's eyes lock on mine for a moment and she winks at me before locking lips with the blonde. Now that's exactly what I need tonight. I give her a wicked grin before my eyes continue around the room. That's when bright green and black catches my eye over by one of the pool tables. I blink in shock that she's here. Then I blink again when I see Rack has his hand down the front of her tube top. I watch his fingers move as he rolls her nipple between them and I can see the other one is as hard as a rock beneath the thin fabric.

Mine.

I shake my head. *Get it together, fuckshitiot. She ain't yours and she ain't someone else's either. She's a bar cunt, nothing more. A great piece of ass that you want to tap again and again, but you can do that shit with any girl in here.*

She hasn't seen me yet, so I duck to my left, toward the bar and lots of fucking alcohol.

I'm three drinks in when Pyro finally shows his face. He roams the room, and I'm not sure if he's looking for someone or not, but his face grows angry when he catches an eyeful of Skit and Rack. He shakes his head and I turn back to the bar. What's his deal with her?

He moves next to me. "You see that shit?" he asks.

"What shit?" I counter, trying to play stupid.

"Skit and Rack."

"What about it?" He glares at me. "What? You hot for Skit?"

He visibly shudders.

"You wanna 'explain?" I ask him.

"Hell no."

"You fuck her?" I ask point blank.

"Fuck you, and fuck no. Not my flavor," he says in a way that begs me to argue with him.

"Bullshit. Hot piece of ass like that and you're telling me you don't want to tap it?"

"Shut it, Loki," he snaps.

I roll my eyes. "I don't understand what's crawled up your ass and died lately, but you'd better figure it out." I lower my voice and get in his ear. "Find your fucking head, man, you're running out of time."

"Fuck off," he growls, his raspy voice catching.

I let it go. I'm obviously not getting anywhere with him on the Skit front and I don't want to talk about it anymore. If he wants to claim her, fine.

My chest grows heavy at that thought and my heart skips in my chest.

She's not mine, I remind myself as my eyes wander over to her. She's now straddling Rack's lap, her tits in his face. She's facing my direction so I get an eyeful of her nipple as Rack switches from one to the other.

Skit's eyes are locked on mine.

She lets her mouth fall slack as she feigns enjoyment. I shake my head at her and she puts a little more effort into it. I roll my eyes.

Just then Taz walks past me and I grab her wrist, bringing her toward me. Her eyes widen briefly as I wrap my arm around her, pulling her into me. I whisper in Taz's ear, "Play along," She grunts in understanding and I give her a couple kisses along her shoulder before dipping my head lower. Taz, on her game as always, lowers her tank top, offering me her tits and I suck a nipple into my mouth. My eyes never leave Skit. Taz's hand slides into my hair, holding me to her tit just a little longer and I flick my tongue against her hard peak and she lets out a rush of air. She is enjoying it, where Skit is not.

WICKED REVENGE

I smirk at Skit, making a show of licking and sucking on Taz's tit and Skit's eyes narrow.

She leans down and whispers something in Rack's ear. Whatever she says springs him into action and he stands up. She quickly pulls her top up and he grabs her by her hand, pulling her toward me and the door.

I release Taz's tit from my mouth, she pulls up her top. "Thanks, doll," I tell her.

"Anytime," she smirks, winks and off she goes.

Rack and Skit walk past me, out the door. I go to follow behind them, but Pyro grabs my arm. "You're a dick, but let it go."

I shake my head and try, but I can't. I pull my arm free and step through the door into the cool night. My eyes find them quickly when I hear a hog turn over. I narrow my eyes at both of them. Rack's already on his ride. Skit steps on the skid and flings her leg over expertly. My eyes narrow and a growl escapes my lips.

She wraps her arms around Rack's stomach, holding herself to his back. He's paying attention to what he's doing, she is watching me.

Rack switches gears and revs the engine and they disappear briefly as he turns around and when they come back into my line of sight, she's looking at me. She releases her hold on Rack long enough to flip me the finger.

"Fucking cunt," I growl. It's one thing to let a brother suck your tits; it's a whole other thing to be the bitch on his ride.

CHAPTER ELEVEN
Lily

A SLIVER OF SATISFACTION SLIDES up my spine and settles over my heart, mending one of the many broken pieces left by Loki over the years. The look on his face was fucking priceless when I climbed on the back of Rack's bike. It was only made better when I flipped him the fuck off as we sped out of the compound.

I'm a couple blocks from home. I asked Rack to take me home. I claimed to have had too much to drink and he was all too quick to oblige me. If there was anything I learned about one of the newest members of Wicked Angels, it's that he's human and still has his heart. He may have his colors, but he's yet to get his 1% patch. An honor the Wicked Angels only bestow to its members after they prove themselves. Rack is well on his way, but he's got a long way to go.

Loki is furious with me.

Good.

Fucker deserves it.

I direct Rack to my house and he parks in front of it. "You got a bike?" he asks as he kills the engine.

"Yup, it once belonged to a good friend of mine."

"You ride?" He raises an eyebrow at me, incredulously.

"I do," I challenge him.

"Nice," he grins wide. "Not many chicks 'round here have the balls."

I smile. I'm going to like this guy. If he can keep hold of his heart a little while longer. "Thanks for bringing me home," I tell him softly and give him a small kiss on the cheek.

"Anytime."

He fires up his bike and I back away, waving at him as he takes off down the street. I wait for him to disappear before I head for the door when I hear another bike roaring down the street. I close my eyes. I know exactly who it is. Thank God Rack went the other way. I'd hate to think what Loki would do to him. I turn around and cross my arms over my chest and wait for him to pull up. He does, but he stops at the curb. I half expected him to come roaring up in my front yard.

"Get on," he says over the engine.

I shake my head.

"Get the fuck on," he growls.

"Good night, Loki," I smirk before turning toward my house.

I hear the bike roar down to neutral. I speed up, but I don't get far before Loki wraps his arms around me from behind. "Run from me again, sugar tits, and I'll make you regret it," he growls in my ear. "Your daughter is in there and I want to fuck your goddamn cunt dry, so you have two choices."

I should kick and scream at him, fight him, but I can't. My body is alive with the promise of more things Loki and I'm having a hard time responding any other way.

"We can do this here, with your daughter in the next room, or you can get over your self-absorbed ass and get the fuck on my bike, where you fucking belong," he growls in my ear and I melt further. His claim of my belonging on his bike has my heart doing flutters in my chest. My stomach roars with butterflies and I give in to my body's desire for the man who's acting like a caveman.

"Yours," I tell him with a whisper and he releases me. He turns toward his bike and I follow behind him. He kicks over; holding the bike steady and I step up, flinging my leg over and wrapping my arms around him. I press my cheek to his back. His heartbeat hammers in my ear. Unlike with Rack, I let my hands roam lower and my fingers tickle his hard cock through his jeans.

He growls through his teeth, the vibration tickling my ear. "You're gonna fucking kill me."

He pops the clutch and off we go, racing down the street toward his house.

The ride is too short.

I just started to get comfortable and we're pulling into his driveway. He kills the engine and holds the bike for me to climb off. He turns the ignition and pulls his keys from it and hands them to me. I take them, reaching for the orange colored key and I hand them back to him with his house key poised and ready to go.

He takes them from me and leads the way down the sidewalk and up the steps. He hasn't said anything, not that I expected him to, but it would be nice if he would, instead he unlocks the door and ushers me inside before kicking the door closed.

"I may do a lot of things, sweet ass, but sloppy seconds ain't one of them. Go clean yourself up," he snaps and I glare at him. He raises his eyebrows at me in waiting.

"He sucked my tits," I counter.

"He had his grubby ass hands and nasty mouth all over my favorite part of your body, next to that sinful mouth and that tight fucking cunt of yours, so if he touched either one of those, brush your teeth and wash it."

I stand there and cross my arms over my chest. Short of tapping my foot in a way that a child would, I don't know what else to do to protest his choice of words. Then again, I have a feeling I've poked the bear tonight and he'd fuck me without touching my mouth or my tits and I don't want that either.

"Go," he orders gruffly.

I rip my top off and he hisses through his teeth. I kick off my heels and unbutton my denim. I bend at the waist, pushing my jeans and thong down my legs before kicking them off and standing naked before him.

As I suspected, the bear has been poked. He slams into me, pushing me against the wall. His lips brush mine. I smile over my victory, then he moves his mouth away and his hands wrap around my ass and he's lifting me in the air. I wrap my legs around him. My wet slit brushes along the rough zipper on his jeans. I moan in pleasure and pain.

WICKED REVENGE

He then lowers his lips just over my nipple and I can feel his hot breath against the left, but that's it. I groan in frustration at him. He ignores me completely and moves to my right nipple, repeating the torture, taunting me with his delicious mouth wrapped around my now pebbled nipples.

Then his hand slides between us. I think he's going for the fly of his jeans, but instead his fingers brush feather light against my sex. "Oh god," I cry out. "He didn't touch it."

His fingers slide through my folds until he finds my entrance and he slips one inside me. I cry out. He shifts his hand so his thumb can strum my clit while his finger moves in and out of me.

I slide my hands into his hair, holding him to me gently and awareness lights his eyes. He cocks his head at me, really looking at me. His hand stills between my legs. I buck my hips, looking for friction and release and he's still as stone.

"Loki, please," I beg. "Finish it."

In the next breath, his lips are slamming against mine. His tongue darts in immediately and his fingers move inside me. My orgasm is balancing on the edge but he won't let me tip over the edge.

"Loki," I cry out again as I pull back from his kiss.

He presses his forehead against mine. "I fucking knew it," he growls as he pulls his fingers from my pussy and he steps back, lowering me to the floor.

His hands slide into mine, wrapping our fingers together, his eyes searching mine, a million questions swim in the silvery grey orbs. "Kiwi?" he breathes.

"Yes," I breathe as a tear falls free and slides down my cheek.

His hands release mine only to slide into my hair, my face between his palms. "I don't know whether to throw you out or fuck you senseless right now."

"I'll take the latter," I mumble and he growls, pulling back from me. The loss of his warmth sends a shiver down my spine. He traces a single finger from the base of my neck, down between my breasts, and across my stomach before he lets it fall away.

"Am I dreaming?" he breathes.

"No." I should say more, but I need him to process his discovery.

"How?" His eyes still haven't left mine. "How did I not..."

"You did, you knew that first night."

He shakes his head. "That was a drunk man's dream." His voice is low, almost menacing.

"No, Loki, it wasn't."

"I fucking hate you," he groans.

His word sting, sending a shot straight to my heart. "No, you don't."

"I fucking do, Kiwi. You fucking left me."

I pull back from him. "I left you? That's rich, Logan," I snap with his real name.

"You should have stayed."

"You wouldn't fucking let me stay, remember? You stood in that goddamn garage and told me to do what my brother said to do. I did. Then you followed me to Colorado. You snuck into my room in the middle of the night and stole my virginity and then my eighteenth birthday because you were gone."

"I had to leave."

"Why?" I breathe.

"Because, Kiwi, you deserved better than a fucked-up biker sneaking into your bedroom on his way through town. Because Tryke would have killed me if I pulled you back into the club life."

"Tryke's dead," I state. Though I said the words, I'm not sure I believe them anymore. I don't know why, but I just don't.

His eyes narrow at me. "You deserve better."

"That's my choice, Logan. Not yours, not Tryke's, no one, only mine.

Sticks respected that. Now it's time you do too."

"Your daughter deserves better."

At that, my breath freezes in my chest. "Our daughter," I whisper.

"What?" he snaps.

"You heard me," I bite back. Suddenly I become acutely aware of my nakedness and I want my clothes. I need to cover myself up.

"How?"

I glare at him. "What do you mean, how? You fucked me, Loki, twice," I remind him. "Both times without a condom. Do I need to go into how the birds and the bees work with you?"

"She can't be mine."

"Oh, believe me, she is one hundred percent yours. All you have to do is look into her eyes, Loki. It's all anyone has to do. Why do you think no one knows about her? No one, except you and Pyro, because you can't keep the fuck away from me." I pull my arms up, covering my chest. It's all I can do because he won't let me make a move for my clothes.

"Why are you here?" he asks.

"Because you brought me here."

He stalks closer to me, tightening the distance between me, the wall and his rock-hard body. "Why are you back in Roswell?"

I look up at him with bewilderment. "Why the fuck do you think?" I growl. "Arizona is about to make a move. It's the last fucking chance I have to get revenge for my parents, for Tryke."

He punches the wall next to me. I don't flinch. "I killed Tryke," he growls.

"You had no choice," I yell back.

"Do you honestly believe that?" he asks me in a tone that challenges everything I know about that night.

"Yes," I breathe.

"Why?"

"Because Kellen only ever wanted to protect me, keep me out of the club, away from the danger it presented and you would do anything to protect me from that danger because no matter how hard you try to be badass and hide it, you fucking love me and you loved him." Tears swim in my eyes. "You'd do anything for him. You'd die for me."

"Don't kid yourself, sweetheart." He pulls away from me.

"Bullshit. Drop the badass act, Loki. You'd die to protect me. You'd kill if it meant keeping me safe. I'm yours. I've been yours since I was three fucking years old. I've never wanted anyone but you."

Again, his eyes narrow, this time in anger. "Bullshit."

"I did what I had to do to survive inside the club's walls, Loki. You fucking know that as well as anyone. If you didn't kill Tryke, he'd have had to kill you or you'd both be dead. So, don't think for one second that I don't know that you did what you did to save me."

He slams into me, pressing me against the wall. His hand comes to my chin as he lifts it toward his face. His eyes are on mine, alive and alight as he growls, "You're right," before slanting his lips over mine in a soul-stealing kiss that melts every piece of ice around my heart. My entire body comes alive under his skillful lips. His tongue slides into my mouth and I stop breathing momentarily as I feel his cock press against me, hard and ready.

Our breathing is ragged and uneven when he pulls back. "Finish it, Loki," I urge.

He grabs my wrist and pulls me down the hall toward his room.

CHAPTER TWELVE
Loki

WE ENTER MY ROOM.

She's naked.

I'm hard.

She had my kid.

Fuck.

"What's her name?"

"Piper," she whispers.

"You never thought to tell me?"

"I called you, several times," she mumbles.

"I should have never…"

She glares at me. "Don't you dare. I don't regret it. Not one second of what we had that night. She's my everything, Loki. Everything," she emphasizes.

I sit on the bed, my elbows on my knees and my head in my hands.

She kneels before me and puts her hands on my hips and vies for my attention by getting in my line of sight.

"I don't regret it," she says again before taking my head in her hands and pressing her lips to mine. I groan and wrap my arms around her, pulling her into me. Her body is warm, naked, willing.

Her hands roam down my neck, over my shoulders and she wraps them around my waist. "Finish it," she breathes.

I stand, pulling her with me and her arms move back to my shoulders, sliding off my cut. I release her, letting my cut fall from my arms and she lays it across the bed gently before returning for my t-shirt. She pulls it off in one swift movement and then she's at my jeans, unbuttoning them, sliding down the zipper and pushing them down to my thighs.

She lowers herself to the floor, my cock free and in her face. She slides a fat, wet tongue from base to tip and I shiver. My eyes roll up in my head and my head spins. I feel her lift a pant leg, looking for the zipper on my boot and she lowers it then taps the back of my foot. I lift it and she pulls it off my foot and tosses is aside. She repeats the process on the other foot and I sit back down.

She pulls my jeans and socks from my legs and I fall back on the bed. Emotions overwhelm me. She's here, she's with me, and she brought my daughter.

My daughter.

Her hands slide up my thighs and her body presses between my legs. One of her hands wraps around my dick and she gently strokes up and down. I groan. Her touch obliterates me in every way imaginable. I felt it that first night in Boulder, then again during the first night here. It's why I went in without a cover six years ago, and tried to again last week. I can't think straight around her.

Her body slides up farther and then she straddles me. Her wet cunt sits atop my dick and he twitches. "Fuck," I growl and I see a smirk of satisfaction on her lips. She leans down, pressing her pussy further onto my crotch. I want to be inside her, buried deep. She flicks her hips. Then she's kissing my chest, but not my nipples, no, her lips land on the lily tattooed over my heart.

"It took everything I had not to kiss this that first night," she breathes, her breath cool against the wetness she's left behind and my nipples harden. The barbells feel like vices as the skin tightens. "When?" she asks.

"As soon as I got home," I tell her. It's true. I wasn't home twelve hours and I was in the shop. "I left because I promised Tryke I'd walk away," I whisper. "He wanted you safe, away from this life. If I'd have stayed, you'd have gotten sucked right into it."

She sits up, the motion making my eyes roll as her pussy slides along my cock. "Did it ever occur to either one of you that it was my choice to make? Or that the safest place for me was and is as an old lady?"

My eyes widen at her. "Is that really what you want?"

"It's what I've wanted since I was ten, Loki," she admits.

WICKED REVENGE

I sit up fast, wrapping my arms around her, holding her to me, my face in her neck, my cock shifting between us. "Finish it," I tell her.

Her hand slides between us, but she hesitates. "I'm clean." I breathe. "You're it, the only one I've ever..." I don't need to say anymore. She's shifting herself to line up with my cock. Her entrance is right there. "Piper," I breathe.

"I'm covered," she whispers.

"That's disappointing," I mumble before pulling my face out of her hair. Her eyes are wide as she looks at me.

"She's my everything, but I won't do that again, alone." Her voice is barely above a whisper.

"Never alone again," I grunt as I push into her.

Her eyes roll back and my body burns for her. "So, fucking tight," I say through gritted teeth, holding back the overwhelming rush of sensation and desire to come.

"For a bar slut?" she tacks on with a raised eyebrow.

"Fuck," I groan as I flip her over, pressing her into the bed, my cock pressing farther inside her.

She cries out my name and I start to move inside her. So wet, warm and tight. "You feel amazing," I grunt as I continue to thrust inside her, hard.

I lower my face and brush my lips against hers. "Mine," I growl and I start really fucking her, harder and faster.

Her body locks down and I know she's close, so close. I push in and out faster as she explodes around me. "Logan!" she cries and my orgasm explodes inside her clenching tunnel.

Something wakes me. I'm not sure what and I don't care. I roll over, looking to wrap my arms around my woman and she's gone. I bolt upright in bed when I hear a pounding at the front door. "Kiwi," I say, but I get no answer. "Fuck."

I get out of bed, grabbing my jeans and stumbling my way down the hall, putting them on as I go. I look through the window in my door and see Cowboy standing on the other side.

"What's doin', man?" I ask as I open the door. The look on his face wipes away all thoughts of looking for Kiwi.

"We got trouble."

"Figured, where?"

"Clubhouse. Get dressed," he snaps and I race down the hall to my room. Kiwi's scent lingers around the room and my cock hardens. She fucking left.

My eyes land on the clock, her picture and a note. It's nearly eleven in the morning. I grab the note.

Hey Slugger,

Had to get home to Piper.

-L

Like a moron, I sniff the paper and it smells just like her.

"Let's go, bro," Cowboy calls from the living room. I put her note down and get dressed.

I'm throwing my cut over my shoulders as I walk down the hall. Cowboy is standing there holding something in his hand with a wicked smirk on his face. "Have fun last night?" I snatch Kiwi's panties out of his hand.

"Didn't you?" I raise an eyebrow at him.

"Always. Perk of having an old lady."

I shake my head but only to hide the fact that I'm not ready to admit publically that I've found my own old lady.

"Let's fly," Cowboy says and we take off across the yard. He's climbing on his bike as I pull my phone from my cut. There are several missed calls and two texts.

I click the first one.

Miss you, slugger.

I smile like an idiot at my phone then flip to the next one and my smile fades.

From Pyro:
Rack's dead

"Fuck," I growl as I kick my leg over. "What the fuck happened?"

I direct my question to Cowboy but he doesn't answer me as he starts his bike. "Critical Chaos," he finally says as he pushes up my driveway.

"Fuck."

It's after eight when I'm roaring down the street toward my house. I drive past Kiwi's place and her car is gone. The other car and her bike are still there. She's at work, should be.

I speed up. I want to take a shower before I head to Iron Wings tonight. Cowboy shut it down for the night, but it's where the Angels are meeting. Rack's ink has barely healed and he's gone. He was a good kid with a lot of potential and all the guys recognized that early on. He was a little soft, not sure he'd have ever earned his 1%, but he wasn't gonna stop trying.

His death was caused by stupid male chauvinistic bullshit. Completely unnecessary, but he will be buried as a brother in two days.

Rooster will be at I.W. tonight and I need to be there to keep Kiwi in check. As far as I can tell, they've not crossed paths yet and who the hell knows what frame of mind she'll be in.

I take a fast shower, ignoring my hard cock. The thought of seeing Kiwi again, knowing she's Kiwi, has my mind roaming with all kinds of crazy ass ideas.

I get out, get dressed and within ten, I'm on the road to Iron Wings.

CHAPTER THIRTEEN

Kiwi

"WE NEED ANOTHER ROUND," I tell Loni. None of us want to be here tonight, but Rooster's given us no choice. I wanted to ask why they weren't doing this at the clubhouse, but I bit my tongue and let it go. Iron Wings is one of the Angels' biggest money makers in Roswell. Shutting it down for a night so these guys can drink themselves stupid isn't exactly the smartest business decision.

Either that or I'm just pissed because I have to serve the asshole responsible for killing my brother, mother and father. I clocked him the moment he walked in the door. Don't ask me how I knew, I just did. Immediately after him was the other guy, Gunnar, and my blood boiled when I saw him.

I've also gathered from the other members that Rooster and Gunnar are not their favorite people. They respect them, sure, it's who they are, but that's where it stops and I take comfort in that. Rooster has run this charter into the ground and I get the impression no one is gonna care when he's dead.

"Here you go," Loni says softly. Her eyes are red from crying. Losing a member takes a toll on everyone and this one hits me harder than I expected. I didn't know Rack well, but I knew enough to know he was good people. Hell, I wound him up tighter than a drum last night and he took me home without a second thought and never made a move to further our evening. I had mad respect for him after knowing him only a short time.

I grab my tray off the bar and walk toward the pushed together tables in the middle of the bar. Nearly everyone is here. Pyro got here a few minutes ago and his eyes keep landing on me. I don't understand it. I don't get what his obsession with me is. It's not like he's made a move on me. The one time I thought he was, he told me he didn't want me. That still stings.

I pass drinks around the table. The guys are animated despite the circumstances and they're telling stories about Rack. Apparently, he was a prospect longer than most, so he was hanging around the club a long time. Everyone seems to have a story to tell about him.

The door to the bar opens and my heart stops in my chest as Loki strolls in. As he walks closer to me, my heart kicks up in double time. He wraps his arm around my waist and pulls me into his side. The next thing I know, his lips are pressing into mine and there is a chorus of hooting and hollering from the men in the room.

I blush and pull back. "Nice to see you too, slugger."

He squeezes me again and lets me go, finding a seat next to Pyro, who is glaring at him with daggers shooting from his eyes.

About an hour later, the old ladies show up wearing their colors. I've never seen most of them, but they quickly slide in beside their men and settle in. New drinks are served by me and one of the other girls, Kat. Loni has joined Cowboy, her old man, at the tables.

My heart clenches when I see Loki looking at me. He cocks his head and I try to hide my jealousy of what Loni and Cowboy have but Loki sees it and offers me a sad smile.

No one else shows up. No whores, no free pussy, just the men and their old ladies. Kat and I serve them throughout the night. Eventually the evening turns rowdy as the amount of alcohol they consume goes up, but they're not dicks, just angry, hurt biker dudes cutting loose.

When the party dies down and everyone but Cowboy, Loni, Kat and myself are left, we clean up the bar, putting the tables back and getting ready for tomorrow's crowd. The members didn't pay a dime for their drink fest, which means Kat and I made nothing for the night, which is okay by me until Loni comes over and hands us both envelopes. "For tonight," she says sadly. "I couldn't have done this without the two of you." Her eyes well with tears again and her man, Cowboy, comes over and wraps his arm around her.

We take that as our cue to leave. Kat and I walk out together.

"You alright?" she asks me.

"Yeah, you?"

She nods. "I liked Rack. He was always sweet, and a great tipper when he wasn't working the door." She winks.

I smile at her as we both climb into our cars. As I'm sitting in the seat, I see something, though I don't quite know what because when I turn back, it's gone, but I swear Kellen was just watching me outside the bar.

I shake my head and shake it off as I drive away.

My phone chimes.

I look at it when I come to a light.

From Loki:
Want to see you tonight.

To Loki:
I'm exhausted.

From Loki:
Please.

To Loki:
Be right there.

The light changes and I drive through town. I keep checking my rearview. I don't know why, but I feel like I'm being followed. It's two in the morning and Roswell is a ghost town. I'm being paranoid.

I drive past my house, it's all dark inside. I don't want to wake Em, so I don't text her. I don't plan on staying at Loki's long.

I pull into the driveway next to his bike and kill the engine. My eyes are on his bike and a shiver slides through me. I don't know why, but tonight, I can't keep Kellen out of my mind.

Loki meets me at the door. He's only wearing jeans. No socks, no shirt and no cut. My mouth waters.

"You alright?" I ask him.

He nods softly. "You?" he asks.

"I think so. I didn't know him well, but he…he was a good kid."

He chuckles, "He was older than you are, sweet cheeks."

I narrow my eyes at him. "So?"

He shrugs. "Just sayin."

He closes the door behind me and I take a moment to look around his house. I've been in here three times and all three times I've had sex on the brain and no lights to show me around.

It's simple, a little dirty, but that's to be expected. A few plates scatter the coffee table in front of the couch, there's some papers on the dining room table, shit like that, but all in all, it's what I expected of a bachelor pad. The big flat screen sort of gives it away, too. It's half as big as the wall and you'd have to be in China to see it all.

"Like it?" he asks.

I smile at him. "It's definitely you," I tell him. He smirks and wraps his arms around me. "Thanks, by the way."

"For?"

"Outing me tonight."

He looks at me with narrowed eyes. "Oh, the kiss." He smirks. "Jealousy looks good on you," he adds.

I glare at him. "I'm not jealous."

He snorts a laugh and spins me around, holding me to him. His hard cock presses against my stomach and I hold back a groan as I remember feeling him inside me last night. "I saw the look on your face when the old ladies showed up."

I shrug nonchalantly. "What about it?"

136

WICKED REVENGE

"Since you were ten, huh?"

I soften at his tone. "I was old enough to understand that old ladies rock and…" I stop.

He gives me a little shake. "And?"

"And I was old enough to realize I was in love."

His eyes narrow. "With who?"

I look him square in the eyes and answer, "Robert Pattinson."

"Oh really? You like that dead, vampire shit?"

I shrug, smirking. "Maybe a little."

"I'm crushed," he teases.

"Why ever for?" I mock him back.

He leans down, his lips a mere inch from mine. "Because it wasn't me," he breathes and then he claims my lips. My mind goes blank at his words and his touch, but I find it somewhere in there and kiss him back. Our tongues start dancing, my body humming, racing and igniting with the desire to have him between my legs again.

When my breathing grows shallow and ragged, he pulls back, his eyes locked on mine. "I never said it wasn't you," I share.

The truth is it was him.

He smirks again.

"I have to get home," I tell him and his smile falls.

"I want to come with you."

I pull back a little and he lets me go. "I don't know, Loki."

"Why not?"

I fold my arms over my chest. "You know why," I tell him.

"She's my daughter."

"You know that, now, but she doesn't. Well, I don't think she's put two and two together yet."

"What's that mean?" He's getting angry and I don't like it.

"It means that she's seen pictures of you, but they're old, Loki." I put my hand on the side of his face, my fingers brushing through his beard. "No beard, shorter hair. She's only five."

"I want to meet my daughter," he growls.

Tears well in my eyes. If I'd known he'd react like this, I'd have driven down here while I was pregnant.

"What did I say now?" he snaps.

"Nothing, it's just…"

"Just what?" His voice is still harsh.

"I stayed away because of you. I was petrified of what you'd say. What you'd do, what you'd make me do if you knew I was pregnant."

"Back then, I can't honestly tell you what I'd have done because I didn't know. But now…" he trails off.

"Now?" I prompt.

"Everything's changed," he breathes.

"Give me a couple days, okay?" I ask him.

"Two, tops," he agrees. "Now, as much as this is killing me," he brushes a finger from my temple and down my jaw before pinching my chin between his fingers, "Go home." He presses his forehead against mine. "I'll see you tomorrow."

I give him a small smile and his lips brush mine. I wrap my hands in his hair and pull him to me, kissing him like my life depends on it.

After a few heartbeats he pulls back. "Not helping, Kiwi," he grumbles.

"Oops," I smirk.

"Go home," he says in a tone that's not to be argued with. I turn toward the door and he smacks my ass. I squeak. "See you tomorrow."

"Tomorrow," I tell him and I'm out the door, down the steps and at to my car. My eyes land straight ahead and it's there again, the sense of being watched, having eyes on me. The street lamp flickers and I see it again, a face watching me. I shiver as Kellen comes back to my mind.

I climb in my car and back out. I'm back home in less than a minute and no one followed me. I hurry inside and to my room.

I hit the shower and grab Loki's t-shirt from six years ago and wrap up in it as I snuggle into bed.

Like the other night, the dreams come at a rapid fire pace.

Loki, Piper, Colorado, Sticks, Big Daddy, Rooster…I'm tossing and turning.

The faces start changing, morphing from one person to another until they land on Pyro. He's the only one to speak to me in my dream.

I'm staring at him, scrutinizing him when he opens his mouth. "Lily," he says and I bolt upright in bed.

"It's not possible," I breathe.

Suddenly it hits me like a freight train- the cameras at the house, the videos. He stored them on an online storage site. I fling the covers off my bed and go for my laptop on the dresser before bringing it back to my bed and sitting cross-legged, laptop in my lap as it warms up.

I log in and type the website address in and wait for it to load.

I wrack my brain, trying to remember the login.

After a minute, it comes to me and I sign in and put the password in and it loads.

Pyro

MY PHONE CHIMES.

I pull it from my pocket.

It's a text, I open it.

> From Unknown:
>
> Login attempt successful.
>
> You're receiving this message because you requested notification when...

I drop the phone and dive for my clothes on the floor of my room.

"She knows," I breathe.

CHAPTER FOURTEEN
Lily

THERE ARE A LOT OF video logs on here. Each one is tucked into a folder by date. I sort them by most recent and come to the day my brother died.

I click on it.

The folder opens and it's separated by camera, though not labeled as such.

I click on each one until I find the kitchen feed.

I start it.

Then fast forward through it.

I see my argument with Kellen in the kitchen before he stormed out of the house and disappeared into the backyard.

I fast forward, a little slower now.

Kellen comes back into the kitchen and grabs a beer from the fridge, then he turns around and he's talking to someone. I turn up the volume and back it up a little.

"It's all set." I hear a voice I recognize immediately as Loki's. "Where is she?"

"Sleeping," my brother says. "You got it?" he asks and Loki comes into view on the kitchen feed. He hands something to my brother. I can't tell what it is because it's in a bag.

"It's rigged, ready for anything. If you're hit in the chest, it will work. Anything else will be legit pain, but no blood."

I cock my head at the screen.

"You're using pellets?" Kellen asks.

"The first will be real. I'm gonna clip him in his gun shoulder, take him out of the equation, then I'll hit you three times. It won't really hurt to the point of making you scream, but the impact will be real," Loki says.

"Thank you," my brother tells him.

Loki looks at him, and there's a sadness in his eyes that I don't understand just yet.

"Take care of her. Promise me?" Kellen says and my eyes well with tears. He knew. He knew exactly what was coming for him.

"Promise," Loki tells him. "I'll make sure she gets where she's going. Then I'll leave her to find her own way."

My brother gives him a small smile. "Thank you," he says softly and they give each other one of those big, man hugs that lasts for long moments.

My eyes well with tears as I watch the video.

After a few minutes, Loki leaves with the promise of being back in an hour.

The kitchen feed now shows nothing but empty kitchen and Kellen has disappeared. I leave that video up and playing as I go in search of other videos, fast forwarding them to the same time stamp.

I finally find him. He's in his room. I can't see him completely because the camera is in the hall pointing toward his room.

I watch him remove his cut, then his t-shirt. I almost look away thinking he's changing but then he reaches into the bag Loki gave him and he pulls something out, some type of vest and he places it over his head. It almost looks like a bulletproof vest and my heart flutters in my chest.

I wipe the tears from my eyes then press fast forward on the kitchen feed until Loki and Gunnar show up. I put it in slow motion.

Loki shoots Gunnar first, then quickly shoots Kellen. The slow motion gives me more detail than it did when I watched it in real time originally. Once the shots are fired, I back it up and slow it down further. I watch as each impact hits Kellen and how each impact sends blood flying out, as if something has popped on his chest and the vest suddenly makes sense now. Loki rigged it with pockets of fake blood.

I speed up the video until around the time Loki showed up. While we were dancing in the garage, I watch Kellen get off the kitchen floor. Slowly at first, and he grabs his head. He'd hit it pretty hard when he went down. But he gets up nonetheless.

After a few minutes, Loki comes into the kitchen.

"Who was that?" Kellen asks.

"Your sister," Loki replies.

"She gone?" Kellen asks.

"Yes, on her way to Tucson with the briefcase you left her." I see Kellen nod, sadness in his eyes. "She'll be alright, Kell, trust me. She knows what to do and she'll do it. I'll follow her to Tucson, make sure she gives Big Daddy what he needs to know and then I'll go up to Boulder and make sure she made it. Once I know that, I'll leave her to her life."

"Thank you," Kellen says softly.

"It's what we do, Tryke. You know that." There's a brief pause and an exchange of looks then Loki says, "We got work to do."

Kellen nods and they disappear from the kitchen feed. I don't know what they do exactly, but eventually I hear the roar of a bike on the feed. My guess is it's Loki's. I don't bother looking for the driveway feed. I'm sure Kellen climbed on the back of his bike and off they went.

I continue staring at the feed until fire consumes the kitchen and kills the feed.

Pyro

AFTER BREAKING INTO HER HOUSE, I'm ready to bust down her door to stop her, but I get distracted when I'm walking toward Lily's bedroom. My eyes land on a wall with several pictures, most of them have her daughter in them. I move to the far end of the hall and see a few pictures of Lily right around the time everything went down. She's smiling, happy. She's blowing out a one and eight on a cake. Several of Sticks' members around her.

The pictures change then, she's still the same girl, had to be just a few months later but she's pregnant. Eighteenth birthday…Right after Tryke's death.

Then there is another picture, Lily's nineteenth birthday. She's still smiling, wider than normal, trying to blow out candles while she holds a baby to her breast. I grit my teeth.

I follow the line of pictures, more of Lily and her little girl. One of the pictures says 'Happy First Birthday, Piper', I narrow my eyes, scrutinizing the little girl. She looks like Piper, but also like someone else I know.

"Son of a bitch," I growl softly before I leave the house.

I flip my leg over my bike and go roaring down the street. I don't go home. The sun is barely up, but I don't give a shit. I'm gonna fucking kill him.

Loki

I BOLT UPRIGHT IN BED as the banging continues on my front door. My eyes land on the picture of Lily asleep at her Uncle's house, then on the clock. It's just after seven in the morning.

"Open the door, you son of a bitch."

"Pyro?"

I stumble out of bed, not bothering with my jeans. I'm wearing boxer briefs as I stumble down the hall. His banging gets more insistent.

"Open up, asshole."

"What's your…" I don't even get the door open and the question out of my mouth before he's pushing in the door and connecting with my face. "Fuck," I growl. "What the fuck was that for?"

"You fucked her! You fucked her, knocked her up, and left her to deal with a child all by herself?"

WICKED REVENGE

He attempts another right hook but I see it and dodge it.

"How..." I narrow my eyes at him.

He moves in again. This time I block it and sock him in the stomach. He doubles over briefly but when his eyes land on mine, they're on fire. Rage boils behind the contacts he wears. "You were supposed to make sure she was safe, not fuck her and leave her. Hurt her." He grunts as he slams into me, sending me into the wall behind the door. The same wall I had her up against the other night. Fuck, head in the game. "Of all the bitches around here, you had to fuck my sister," he growls before landing one in my gut.

"How long have you known Skit was really Kiwi?" I ask, trying to defuse the situation a little before things get way out of hand.

"A few days."

"Before Boulder? Is that why you were chewing Sticks' ass?"

"The bike," he growls before shoving me into the wall and backing away. "What she said about the bike, that's the shit she was fucking told years ago." He sighs. "I'd had suspicions that it was her, but there were too many differences, it was hard to determine. After we left Sticks' office, I went back, got the answers I needed."

"That's why you're so pissed off at her."

"I'm pissed at my fucking self," he growls at me.

"What the fuck for?"

"We didn't protect her," Pyro says.

"It wasn't your choice." Both our heads snap in the direction of the front door. "I made the choice to be involved in this club. I made the choice to have my daughter, and I made the choice to live my life in a way I wanted."

She's pissed, that's obvious, and she's glaring at Pyro, as if trying to place him somewhere and my heart freezes in my chest. "You left me. You left me alone, to fend for myself."

"He was protecting you, Lily," Pyro snaps at her.

"I went back and found the tapes from the house that day," she says and my heart sinks into my stomach. "Now it all makes fucking sense. You," she turns on me, "at Sticks', when I got pissed at you for showing no emotion at that fact that you'd killed my brother, you knew he was alive and you didn't think to tell me? To stop my pain? No, instead you sneak into my room, steal my virtue like the animal you are and walk the fuck away, causing me even more pain."

Pyro's fist connects with my face again. "You son of a bitch."

"Stop it," Lily screams at the top of her lungs. "Both of you. Grow the fuck up." She steps into Pyro, her finger in his chest. "Who the fuck are you? Who I fuck, and what I do is none of your concern. I don't know you." I cringe. She knows Tryke is alive, but she still has no clue. It's either that or she is unwilling to let herself see what's right in front of her.

Pain washes over Pyro's features. He nods.

"And you," she turns to me again. Her open palm connects with my face and my head snaps to the right. "Fuck you, you son of a bitch, you knew, all this fucking time that he was alive and you kept it from me. What the fuck?" She steps back. "Go to hell, both of you," she snaps and walks out the front door of my house.

"Kiwi!" I shout after her. She doesn't stop. Pyro goes after her, but she doesn't acknowledge him and he comes back inside. "I just got her back," I mutter to him.

"Me too," he breathes.

"Want a beer?" I ask.

He nods.

CHAPTER FIFTEEN

Kiwi

I KEEP LOOKING OVER MY shoulder as I walk back to my house. I don't know what possessed me to come over here, but I did and I'm not sure I'm happy about it. I heard a bike fire up close to the house. At first I thought someone was stealing mine. By the time I got to the living room, there wasn't anything to see. Something about it sent me out the door and down the street.

Those fucktards. "God," I groan in frustration as I get closer to my house. Tears of frustration well in my eyes, making it hard to see where I'm going. I want to punch something, anything. I don't care. I'm so fucking pissed off at both of them, when I should be happy.

I got Loki back.

My brother is alive.

And yet I want to shoot both of them.

I open the front door and Piper is sitting on the couch, cartoons on the television. She looks at me and greets, "Hi, mommy."

All my anger, frustration and the pain I feel at the two idiots down the street melts away. "Hi, baby. Whatcha watchin'?" I ask.

"Cartoons," she smiles and turns back to the TV.

"Where's Em?"

"In the shower," she says without looking away from her show.

I move around the couch and sit next to her. She snuggles into me and we watch the rest of the show, then the next and the next one after that before I finally come out of my haze of disbelief. Piper should have gone to school but she fell asleep in my lap and I let her stay home.

Of all the people in my life I expected to hurt me, Kellen certainly wasn't one of them. When he died, yes, it hurt, but it was acceptable because it was out of his control. But he's not dead,. He's alive and he didn't trust me with his secret and that hurts almost more than the day he died.

My cell rings in my room. I want to ignore it, but I scoot out from under Piper and jog down the hall. I miss the call, but see that it's Loni and I rush to call her back.

"Hey, sorry, I didn't get to it fast enough," I tell her when she answers.

"No worries," I hear a lot of bikes revving in the background.

"Where are you?"

"The clubhouse. Listen, there are a lot of people coming into town today, I can really use your help."

I shudder. "I don't…"

"No, no, not with that. Um, can you cook?"

I laugh into the phone, "I can."

"Thank God, I need some help in the kitchen. We're trying to feed a lot of Angels today and it's gonna be impossible without some more hands to help."

I smile into the phone as I walk down the hallway toward the living room. "I can, but I have a problem."

"Oh, what's that? The bar's closed tonight and tomorrow," she tells me, as if working is the issue.

"No, it's not that, uh, my daughter."

"You have a daughter?" she says, her voice raising a couple octaves at the surprise. "Sorry, I just, I had no idea."

I smile again. "It's okay. I gave her nanny the day off."

"Bring her. My kids are here too. It's not that kind of party. Promise."

"Okay, how soon you need me?"

"You showered yet?" she laughs.

"I'll be there in less than sixty," I tell her.

"Thank you, Skit, you're the best."

"I try."

We hang up. "Where we goin', mommy?"

148

WICKED REVENGE

"Wanna come to work with me?" I ask her and she flies off the couch, headed for her room hollering, 'yeah' as she goes.

Emily comes around the corner. "You didn't give me the day off?" she raises an eyebrow at me.

"I did now." I wink and she smiles at me.

"Thanks," she says and I head for my room.

I trade in my hooker heels for my most comfortable pair of boots, the ones I usually ride in. My short skirts and ripped jeans in favor of more sensible low-rise boot cuts, and my corsets for two, well-fitting tank tops, the top one is black with the Harley logo printed on it.

I do my make-up, though not as hooker-like as I do for work, but still enough to keep the real Lily buried behind the paint. I also put my contacts in and pull my hair back.

Piper comes bounding into my room. "What do you think?" she asks and twirls around.

I kneel. "Well, look at you," I tell her and she giggles.

She's wearing her own biker boots, only she has leggings on with a short, ruffled skirt and a t-shirt that says, 'bad to the bone' in pink glitter letters. It was the same kind of outfit she wore the first time she stepped foot in Boulder's clubhouse and all the men melted like butter in her palms. She was two years old.

"What do you want to do with your hair?" I ask her.

"Nothing. I like it like this." She smiles wide. Her face is framed in blonde ringlet curls.

"Earrings?" I ask and she lifts her hair.

"My pink ones." She smiles.

"Well, you're ready to go, aren't you?"

She jumps up and down before bolting out of my room. Emily moves out of the way with Piper's bag in her hand. "I put all her stuff in here, her tablet, some snacks and juice boxes."

"Thank you," I tell her softly. "I appreciate it."

"No problem. Day off or not, I need to run some errands today. I'll be on my cell if you need me to come get her. I'd be more than happy to."

"Depending on how long this goes, I may have you come pick her up tonight."

"No worries." She smiles and turns to leave before turning back. "I hung her dress up, the black one you asked me to. It's ready to go for tomorrow with her tights and shoes."

I give her a sad smile. "Thank you."

She smiles back and leaves my room so I can finish getting ready.

Another fifteen minutes and Piper is in the backseat, buckled in her booster and dancing to the music on the radio. Then when her favorite song comes on, she squeals, "my Adam," and starts singing.

Most parents would be concerned if their five-year-old was singing 'Sugar' by Maroon 5, but not me. I love watching her sing and dance.

We're both rocking out as we reach the clubhouse. The fun comes to an end as I roll down my window and turn down the volume. The guy at the gate is a prospect I haven't seen before.

I'm about to say something when Piper lowers her window. "Hi there, handsome," she says and the guy blushes as red as a cherry.

I bust out laughing. "Sorry," I say through my giggles. "I'm K..." I stop myself. "Skit, I'm here to see Loni."

The prospect, recovering from the shock of a five-year-old calling him handsome, waves us through and I park off to the side of the clubhouse.

Loni wasn't kidding. There are way too many bikes here. One stands out among the rest of them.

I turn around, looking at Piper. "Someone's here you're gonna wanna see," I tell her.

"Yeah," she leans forward as if it's a conspiracy, "Who?"

WICKED REVENGE

"Well, let's go find out."

I made no secret of my biker bartending career. Loni knows I came from the Boulder charter so Piper getting excited over seeing her Uncle Sticks isn't going to be an issue. "Mommy, my door," she says and I chuckle as I climb out and reach back, opening her door and she jumps down. "Finally," she says deadpan as she brushes her hair off her face. I shake my head, laughing and I close our doors. She takes my hand, my eyes go toward the clubhouse and they lock on someone I'm not sure I'm ready to see just yet.

"Who's that?" Piper asks.

"Go ask him," I tell her and she looks at me as if I'm crazy. "It's alright, go ask him."

I look both ways and release her hand. She goes running toward Loki. His eyes widen momentarily as Piper bolts toward him. I shrug as if to say, you figure it out.

I follow right behind Piper and she looks up at Loki, who's a good three and half feet taller than she is. "Who are you?" she asks him. He looks at me and I nod.

He kneels to her level. "My name's Loki, what's yours?" he asks. His voice is sweet, gentle and nothing like this morning.

"I'm Piper. Do I know you?" she asks him and again, Loki's eyes meet mine.

"I'm a friend of your mom's. Is that okay?"

"Yup," she says then without prompting or preamble, she wraps her arms around his neck and I watch the big cut wearing biker dude turn into a puddle of goo on the ground. He wraps his arms around her and stands. "Whoa," Piper says. Then she looks down. "That's a long way down." She laughs.

Loki and I join her. Loki reaches out for me and he wraps his arm over my shoulders, then kisses my forehead. "Thank you," he whispers. I nod. I'm still pissed as fuck at him, but Piper doesn't deserve that.

"I came to help Loni. I gave my babysitter the day off," I lie. "Loni said to bring her."

Loki nods in understanding.

"Mom?" I look at Piper.

"What, Pipes?"

"Is this who you said was here that I would want to see?"

I shake my head. "Nope, there's more," I tell her and Loki looks at me. I shake my head softly, she'll hear. He sets her down and she goes for the door.

"Who?" he asks when she's out of earshot.

"Sticks," I breathe.

"He's in the garage," Loki says quietly

I follow after Piper. She's trying to open the door. "Not there, baby, come here," I tell her and she steps aside and takes my hand. I lead her around the side of the clubhouse building and Loki comes with us.

As soon as we round the corner of the building, I can see Sticks and a couple of the other Boulder guys talking to a couple of the local ones over a pretty sweet looking bike.

Piper squeals, and runs straight at Uncle Sticks. "Sticks," she yells. At least eight pairs of eyes land on Piper and Sticks' face lights up.

"Pipes," he says and opens his arms. She jumps straight into them. He stands up, catching me in his line of sight. I walk up to him and wrap his arm around my shoulders the way Loki had. Though it's not possessive, just what Sticks does.

"How you doin' kid?" he asks me.

"Good to see you." I smile at him. He squeezes me harder and then turns his attention to Piper. "I'm gonna go help in the kitchen, can you keep an eye on her?"

"Of course, I'll bring her in the back door. The guys are itching to see her." He smiles at me. I nod and ruffle her hair.

WICKED REVENGE

I lean down. "Behave. I'm gonna go help Loni, okay?"

"Bye, mom," she says without even looking at me. I roll my eyes and laugh as I turn toward the kitchen.

Loki grabs my arm and I look up at him. He doesn't say anything, but I can see the war happening in his eyes. "Keep an eye on her?" I ask and he grunts. I shake my head and he releases me.

I step through the portal on the garage side of the building to find the kitchen and Loni. She puts me to work immediately after introducing me to a couple of the other ladies in the kitchen. I notice immediately that they're all wearing cuts and Angels' colors. They're old ladies. It feels comfortable and normal back here surrounded by them but I can't help questioning why it is they called me in over any of the other females.

We work in the kitchen for a while before Piper comes bounding in the back door. She has something around her neck and I narrow my eyes, trying to make it out. "What's that, baby?" I ask her.

"Uncle Sticks gave it to me," she squeals and lifts it to show me.

My eyes go wide. "Oh shit," one of the women behind me says.

Then Sticks comes into the kitchen after her. I look at him. "She's Wicked Angels now, darlin'," he grins. Following behind him is Big Daddy D and I notice a couple of the girls behind me gasp when he comes into the room.

"You gave her family colors?" I ask him.

It's Big Daddy who answers me, "All the kids get them."

"But I'm not Angels," I remind both of them.

"Not technically," Loki says as he comes in behind the other two. "Not yet anyway." There is a gleam in his eyes that sends my heart fluttering in my chest.

"But she is," one of the old ladies says. I turn to see which one and it's Kara, she belongs to Opie. She's pointing at Piper. "Am I the only one that sees it?" she scoffs.

"No, woman, you're not," Sticks says.

All the other girls are looking at Piper, then they look at Loki then back to Piper before finally landing on me. "Oops," is all I can say.

The women laugh. I turn red as a cherry.

"Skit, you crazy ass, why didn't you tell me?" Loni says as she wraps her arms around me. "She looks just like him," she whispers in my ear.

I just shrug, unsure of what else to say. "I look like who?" Piper says. "Mom says I look like my daddy."

"You can say that again," Sticks grumbles, but I see him elbow Loki who stands there dumbstruck.

We stand around for a few minutes. I never answer Piper's question and then Loni shows the guys from the kitchen and grabs Piper and puts her up on the counter next to where she's working.

Loni and Piper carry on a conversation for more than twenty minutes and it warms my heart to watch until Piper says she's bored. I run out to the car and grab her bag.

There's a couple of chairs in the kitchen and she makes herself comfortable with her tablet and she curls up with it watching a movie with her headphones on.

There's a scuffle in the common room and a couple of the old ladies go running in there. I stay behind, not really caring what's going on out there. There's alcohol, drugs, sex, who the hell knows. I look over at Piper and she's fallen asleep. I smile at her as I reach for my phone to call Emily.

Ten minutes later, I'm handing Piper over to Emily outside the gates. Piper doesn't want to leave, but she's satisfied when I tell her she can see Sticks tomorrow. "What about Loki? I wanna see him too."

His name on her lips warms my heart. "Him too," I tell her.

"Good," she yawns and off they go.

I turn back toward the clubhouse and Pyro is standing on the other side of the gate. "Hi," I breathe as I approach him.

"Why did you bring her?" he asks me.

154

WICKED REVENGE

"I didn't have much of a choice," I tell him.

"Bullshit," he snaps.

"She wanted to see Sticks and the rest of the guys."

"She's got no business being here."

"That's rich," I snap at him. "She's been around them ever since she was born. She misses her Uncle Sticks." I put a little more emphasis on the word uncle and the steely expression on his face fades away.

"Not fair."

"No, what's not fair, Pyro," I sneer his name, "is living in a world where I tell her about her Uncle K, who's dead." I drop it after that. I don't want to say too much. I have my suspicions about Pyro. He obviously knows about Kellen because his attitude toward me speaks volumes.

I go back toward the backdoor of the kitchen. A couple of the guys, Cowboy and someone else, are out back of the kitchen firing up burgers, brats, hot dogs and other shit for dinner. I join them.

Cowboy turns to me. "Hey Skit, this is Opie."

I look over the man with Cowboy. He's about Loki's age, his hair is cropped short, almost military, he's wide in the shoulders and his arms are completely covered in ink. I hold my hand out to him. "Nice to meet you, Opie. I met Kara, she's great."

His face lights up at the mention of his old lady. "She is, isn't she?"

I laugh, "She is. I gotta get back in there. It was nice meeting you, Opie," I smile.

"Likewise."

I reach for the door. "Skit?"

"Yeah," I turn back to Cowboy.

"Thanks for helping out in there."

I smile. "Anytime."

For the first time since I met him, Cowboy gives me a genuine smile that reaches his eyes. They crinkle a little at the corners. He's probably in his late forties, been riding a long time and he's called Cowboy because when he doesn't have a helmet on his head, he wears a cowboy hat. Odd thing for a biker, but the hat has metal medallions that run around it. Giving it a more badass look. I saw his bike once and he has a special saddlebag for it.

I go back inside and get back to work setting out the food along the row of tables pulled from the clubhouse and lined up outside. Plates, silverware, potato salad, fruit salads, all the fixings you could possibly want to go with a cook-out. The guys are busy arranging picnic tables and the sun is on the verge of setting below the horizon when the first pans of burgers and dogs are added to the table.

I'm watching over the food when I feel warm arms wrap around me. His scent assaults my nose and my sex heats.

"She asked about you," I tell him.

"Yeah?"

I chuckle. "She didn't want to leave. I told her she could see Sticks tomorrow. That was okay, but then she asked about whether or not she could see you tomorrow. When I told her yes, she got excited."

I can't see his face but I hear his breathing shift and change behind me. "She's a great kid."

"Yeah, she is," I add to his sentiment.

"Thank you," he whispers in my ear.

"How many times you gonna say that today?"

He chuckles, "A few more maybe."

"For what, this time?" I ask.

"For stepping up and helping the old ladies with this."

"Why me? Why not one of the other girls?"

"Because none of the other girls will be old ladies one day." His voice is soft in my ear and I turn around in his arms, hooking mine behind his neck.

WICKED REVENGE

"What are you saying?"

He smirks at me then moves to kiss me, I turn my head. He growls.

"Not fair," he mumbles.

"Totally fair, you're dodging my question," I tell him and he leans to look at me.

"Mine," he growls and presses his lips to mine.

My head swims, my body hums, my sex ignites with desire and lust for the man I'm trying to hate. My body is betraying me and he knows it. His tongue slips into my mouth and I stop breathing.

"About fucking time." I hear Sticks.

I release Loki's mouth and turn toward him. "For what?" I ask.

"That he made an honest woman out of you," Sticks remarks with a chuckle as he walks down the food line.

I look back at Loki, who quickly raises and drops an eyebrow then he smirks, "About time."

CHAPTER SIXTEEN
Loki

"I'VE BEEN ON MY FEET all day, I'm exhausted."

"At least let me drive you home," I tell her.

She looks at me. "I have my car, and I'm going to need it tomorrow." I remind him.

"You can ride with me tomorrow."

I start chewing on my bottom lip. "I planned to bring Pipes," I say softly. "She wants to see Sticks again. Besides, old ladies are the only ones that should be on funeral rides."

"So, are we just gonna sit here arguing about me taking you home? You coming up with all kinds of excuses?" I accuse.

She narrows her eyes at me. "It makes sense and you know it." She yawns.

I shake my head, trying not to get pissed at her for not wanting to ride with me. "Alright," I concede.

"Thank you," she smiles and leans up on her toes and kisses my chin. "I'm still pissed at you for this morning," she snaps. "So, if you want to be a baby about shit, go do it somewhere else."

She turns for the back door of the clubhouse, not wanting to go through the common room and I don't blame her, they're pretty obnoxious in there right now. After food was done, the old ladies left, and the bitches showed up. Needless to say, there's tits, cunts and dicks flashing everywhere in there.

I snatch her elbow and spin her around. "This how we gonna play this?" I ask her, my tone clipped.

"You're the one making a big fucking deal out of this, Loki, not me."

I release her elbow and she turns again without another word. It takes too long for my mind and body to get in sync with each other and when they do I make it around the clubhouse to see she's pulling out of the lot. "Fuck," I groan. I should jump on my bike and follow after her, but maybe she needs some time to cool off. Fuck, maybe I need to cool off.

I turn back toward the club and Sticks is standing there watching me, a smoke hanging from his mouth. Sticks is a big guy, bigger around the middle, with long silver hair and a beard that practically reaches his belly button. "What'd ya do this time?" he asks me.

I shake my head. "She's pissed at me."

"Well, no shit," he smirks. "It's what they do, man."

"Huh?" I laugh a little.

"You know?" He raises an eyebrow in question.

"Yeah, I know. I've known for twenty-four hours and I've already managed to piss her off."

"How?" he asks. Sticks has always been a man of few words so this conversation surprises me.

"She wanted me to figure it out. She used a line that I've never heard except from her." I lean up against the wall next to him. He offers me a smoke and I take it from him, pulling a lighter from my pocket. I light up. It's been a while since I've had one.

"Piper?" he asks.

"Yeah, I know," I breathe.

"She tried to tell you," Sticks says with anger lacing his tone.

I didn't want to get into it with Kiwi, Sticks or anyone else, but the last time she called me, about three months after I left, I was 'occupied' and didn't answer. I listened to her voicemail for weeks, but never called her back. "I never expected she was calling to tell me that."

"Pipes is a good kid. Don't fuck her up the way you fucked Kiwi over." His voice is deadpan, but the inflection is there.

"I'll do anything to keep her safe."

"She's an Angel now. You fuck her up, we fuck you up." Sticks' comment isn't an empty threat. I've been on the giving end of punishments for fucking with Angels' kids, it's no joke.

"Don't plan on it," I tell him before pulling a drag off the smoke burning in my hand.

"Do right by her." He throws his smoke out into the gravel before walking in front of me. "You owe her that much. She don't want to be with you, then be a father to your daughter and leave her be. She wants you, then you know what you have to do. So help me God, color that bitch before someone else does."

"I intend to."

Sticks grunts as he passes me on his way to the common room door. I pull another drag before tossing the smoke by his and I stomp it out. I stare up to the stars above us.

It's a clear night and for the first time in my life, I don't want to step inside that common room.

My mind wanders back to the last voicemail I ever got from her.

I was upstairs, Taz was on my dick. I saw her name come up for about the tenth time in the last month or so and I ignored it.

I can hear her voicemail plain as day.

"Loki, I need to talk to you, please," she sighs into the phone, "I really need to tell you something," there's a pause on the line, "I won't tell you over voicemail, so answer your phone." The line went dead.

I never called her back.

I could have avoided all this bullshit if I'd have just called her back. Maybe I could have convinced her to abandon her plan for revenge against Rooster and whoever else she blames for her parents' and Tryke's deaths.

I can't help wondering if her knowing that Tryke's alive will get her to abandon her plan.

I shake my head. Not likely. She's just as stubborn as her fucking brother.

I go back into the clubhouse.

WICKED REVENGE

I regret it immediately.

They've laid lines on the bar and nearly every club whore is topless.

Whistler takes a line off Taz's chest and then she turns around and takes one off the bar. We know where they're gonna end up tonight.

Whistler is Big Daddy's VP in Tucson. He wasn't always that way. When I first met him six years ago, he was Sergeant-at-Arms. I don't remember what happened to D's Vice, I just remember hearing that Whistler had moved up. He's in his late forties and been a club member for close to thirty years. Short of being a Beaumont, Vice is as high as you're ever gonna get.

Rooster, despite his Beaumont blood, took the club by force, rather than letting the natural order happen.

I'm going to take it from him by force, if I have to.

A shiver runs up my spine.

I get the impression that's happening sooner rather than later.

Before it goes down, I need to drop my challenge on the members. Once Rooster's gone, the spot will open and the Vets will decide who takes over.

With our inner circle behind Rooster's takedown, I have enough votes. It's just going to be a matter of getting the vote off before Rooster manages to take me out.

I get an eyeful of Pyro giving it to Trixie, one of the club whores. This isn't the first time I've seen them go at it. He catches me watching and gestures for me to join him. I shake my head and he laughs before pushing back into her, bent over the pool table.

Sex and drugs.

Cannibal Corpse starts playing over the sound system and the party kicks up a notch.

Sex, drugs and death metal.

I gotta get out of here.

On my way home, I drive past Kiwi's house. The lights are off, except for one in the living room. I slow down outside and I see her peek through the curtain. I stop. She shakes her head.

I turn off my bike and climb off.

She meets me at the door.

"What are you doing here?"

I don't answer her. I just press her against the screen door she just closed behind her.

"Loki," she breathes.

"The less you know, the safer you are," I tell her with a whisper.

"Okay," she breathes as she wraps her arms around my neck, pulling me down to her, and her lips press against mine. My cock, already hard from clothing choice, tank and short shorts, jumps in my jeans.

I press myself into her, wrapping my hands around her ass and lifting her up, she breaks our kiss. "You gonna fuck me in my front yard?" she asks softly.

"Come home with me," I grunt like a caveman.

She smirks and squirms out of my hold, so I set her back down. She pushes me back and I think she's gonna send me packing, but instead she grabs me by my t-shirt and opens the door, pulling me inside behind her. "Be quiet," she whispers. "Emily and Piper are both sleeping."

"Who's Emily?" I ask.

"My nanny."

"Oh." I don't know what else to say to that as she leads me down the hall. My eyes land on the wall of pictures and I stop.

"Tomorrow," she whispers, tugging me down the hall. I follow her.

Once inside her room, she quietly closes the door and pulls her tank over her head. Her nipples pebble and she lowers her shorts. I growl at her. "Caveman." She laughs lightly.

WICKED REVENGE

I grunt again and she smiles. She saunters toward me, reaching for my shoulders and my cut. I let her slide it off. I take it from her and toss it back on her bed before reaching for the hem of my shirt and pulling it up and off, letting it fall to the floor. "Don't kick me out," I tell her.

"In the morning I will." She sounds disappointed by that prospect.

"I don't like this," I tell her.

"I have one more day, remember?"

I grunt again and she reaches for the button of my denim, undoing it and sliding my jeans down my legs. I toe off my boots and kick off what she started. Her hand wraps around my cock, stroking up and down gently. My eyes wobble around in my head at the sensation.

Now free of my pants, I wrap my arms around her, pulling her to me, forcing her hand from my cock and pressing it between us. She lets out a rushed breath and I claim her lips with mine.

I turn her toward the bed and press her backwards until her legs touch. She's off balance and breaks the kiss as she lays down. I lean over her, kissing her again. She reaches for my cock and I grab her hand and pin it beside her head. I feel her smile against my lips as she moves her other hand. I snag that one too and hold her there. Trapping her beneath me as I lower my lips down her jaw and her neck, kissing and licking lower until I suck a taut nipple into my mouth. Her back arches and her arms flex. I lick and kiss my way to the other nipple and give it the same treatment before licking my way down her stomach. I release her hands from mine, but I keep them pressed to her wrists as I go lower and I bring my hands with me, trailing feather light over her skin. I feel her shiver under me as I draw my hands closer to her tits and nipples.

As soon as my fingers ghost over the peaks, she moans softly. My lips kiss a path along the inside of her left thigh. I kiss up and over her pelvic bone and kiss down the other side.

As I do, I roll her nipples between my fingers, tugging on the rings running through them. She cries out softly.

"Shh," I remind her right before I run my tongue through her slit. She tastes like fucking strawberries and heaven. Her hand slides into my hair, her fingers curling, holding me in place. I flick my tongue against her clit and her whole-body twitches as the pleasure spreads.

"Loki," she breathes.

I smile into her slit and flick my tongue harder and faster. Her body starts to vibrate beneath me. She's getting close. Next, she'll lock down. I move my left hand off her nipple and bring it between her folds to spread her wide before pushing my thumb inside her. Her body locks down beneath me so I suck her clit into my mouth and pull my thumb out before sliding it back in.

The hand in my hair tightens, it's almost painful, but I don't stop.

Her orgasm explodes and I feel the warm rush of it surround my thumb as her sex heats and clenches at my thumb. "Loki," she breathes again and I slowly pull my thumb back and slow my mouth on her clit. I release her nipple and I pull back completely.

She trembles from the lack of contact, but I don't leave her there long. "Scoot," I tell her and she slides farther onto the bed, giving me room. "Better yet, move," I tell her and she looks at me, puzzled. "On top," I clarify.

"Caveman," She says with a hint of a laugh, but she moves. I lay down in the middle of the bed with my head on the pillows and she comes back over me. Her pussy at my cock.

"Condom?" I grunt.

She shakes her head and presses the head of my dick at her hole and I shudder at the warmth and wetness. She slides it up and down her slit, getting my cock wet with her juices before she lines it up and starts to slide down on me. 'Fuck," I groan.

She smiles and steadies herself before she starts pumping up and down on my cock in tiny bursts. She's letting herself coat my cock, each pass gets easier to slip in and out of her tight cunt.

Her pussy squeezes and releases as she does this, her eyes roll up, her nipples are hard and nearly in my face. I take both her tits in my hands and squeeze. She throws her head back and slides all the way down my shaft. "Oh, God," she cries softly.

She doesn't pull up. Instead, she flicks her hips and her cunt clenches and releases a few times around my cock. I close my eyes tight. "You feel so fucking good," I tell her.

"You're fucking huge," she remarks but she doesn't stop the flicking of her hips. Her hands come to my chest, my hands still around her tits. I grab the hoops in her nipples and pull on them gently. Her eyes flutter and she starts sliding up and down my cock in a faster rhythm. Her fingers press into my nipples and she starts playing with my barbells. The added sensation sends tingles of pleasure straight to my balls. I feel them flex and I bite my lip to hold off my orgasm. I want her to take me for everything she can, get her fill before I fill her up.

The way she works her hips as she fucks my dick makes her look like the most amazing stripper I've ever seen. So fucking gorgeous. I grunt when she slams down hard. It feels so fucking good being buried inside her. I release her tits and put my hands on her hips, helping her on my cock and she smiles down at me. She leans forward, pressing her lips to mine and she claims my mouth.

My balls tighten and I nip her bottom lip. "Come, dammit," I growl. She presses her pelvic bone against me, grinding her clit against me. I reach between us and find it for her. I flick it a couple times and she's coming. A warm rush of juices pours over my cock, sending me over the edge and I empty myself inside her.

She falls onto my chest, panting.

I pull my hand from between us. My cock still inside her for now. I wrap my arms around her and play with her hair. "I like the hair color."

I feel her cheek twitch. "I did it for you," she breathes.

"Kiwi," I say softly.

She nods.

I let my hands trace down her back lightly. Tickling her a little as I do, but she doesn't move. My cock softens and falls from her slit and I put my hands on the small of her back. "This would make a great spot for my brand," I whisper, my fingers tickling her sensitive flesh. Her cheek hardens against my chest as she smiles, but she says nothing.

Once our breathing normalizes, she pulls her sex off mine and snuggles into my side with her head on my shoulder, her body pressed to my side and her leg hitched over mine. I continue playing with her hair until I hear her breathing even out and I know she's fallen asleep.

Sleep doesn't come for me. Instead, I start planning what I'm going to do next.

The sun is coming up when I wake her for another round.

I give it to her quick, at her request, because she doesn't want to wake Piper. When I finish, I leave her with the promise of seeing her later. As much as I want to see my daughter, I promised her one more day.

CHAPTER SEVENTEEN

Kiwi

"MOMMY," PIPER YELLS FROM THE hallway.

"In the bathroom, baby," I holler back and she comes racing into my room.

"Look," she says with a hint of excitement in her voice and I look at her.

I smile wide. She's wearing a black baby doll dress, black tights and her black Mary-Jane shoes. Around her neck is the necklace Sticks gave her yesterday. It looks like a dog tag with a purple background and the Wicked Angels MC logo on it. The boys get a red one and the girls get purple.

I kneel in front of her. "You look gorgeous. You want to keep your hair like that?" I ask and she nods. Her golden curls frame her face and she looks adorable, but I'm bias. She's my daughter. "Okay then, I'm almost done," I tell her as I stand up.

"Is Loki my dad?" she asks innocently.

I look over at her, tears prickling the backs of my eyes and I kneel again. "What makes you ask that question, sweetie?"

"He has my eyes." I cock my head at her. "I was looking in the mirror and my eyes remind me of Loki's."

She's ridiculously observant for a five-year-old and I don't know what to say. "How about you ask Loki that, today, when you see him?"

Her face lights up. "Okay, I will." She's satisfied with that as she skips out of my room. I debate warning Loki, but I think it would be better if she surprises him with the same question she asked me.

I finish putting my make-up on and fluff my hair before turning off the lights and going toward the living room. "You sure you don't want me to come?" Em asks me.

"If you want to, you're more than welcome to," I tell her. "You won't know anyone."

Em shrugs. "I don't mind. Besides, I wouldn't mind making new friends."

I hide my cringe. I'm not sure she has a real clue about what she's getting herself into, but it would be good for her to meet some new people. "How long do you need to get ready?"

"Ten, maybe fifteen." My eyes widen at her. "I was hoping you'd say yes." She blushes.

I smile and jerk my head toward her room and she scurries down the hall.

Piper is sitting on the couch, playing on her tablet and I grab a few things to throw into her bag to bring with us.

Following the funeral, the guys will ride through town, making a giant loop before landing back at Iron Wings. Loni told me yesterday that they were having today catered because none of the old ladies want to be stuck in the kitchen all day. They're also bringing in tables and chairs to fill up the back lot for all the members of Wicked Angels and the bar is closed again tonight. The strip club owned by the Angels, on the other hand, is another story. Between the clubhouse and the strip club, there will be plenty of pussy to go around. I shudder at the idea of getting pulled in for that.

Would Loni seriously ask me to do something like that after yesterday? I close my eyes. I already know the answer to that. Until I've been given a cut or I quit working for Iron Wings, the answer is yes, she will.

"I'm ready," Em says and both Piper and I turn to look at her.

"Wow," Piper says mesmerized. I can't say I'm not a little stunned myself.

Emily is a gorgeous girl with long black, stick straight hair, and she's well-endowed in the chest department. She's my height with gorgeous legs, which she is showing off in a short, A-line dress that's black with a wide white belt that comes to rest under her chest. She's also wearing a block high heel with black straps and she's thrown a little make-up on that accents her bright blue eyes.

WICKED REVENGE

"You look nice," I tell her and then I nod for her to join me in the kitchen. She follows and Pipes goes back to her tablet.

"You know I'll always be straight with you, right?" I ask her and she nods, confused. "You're about to go to the funeral of a biker. You're going to be around slimy, sleazy, horny as fuck men."

"I'm not a virgin," she blushes, "I can handle myself."

"I know you can. I just want to give you a heads up because once they get an eyeful of you, they're going to want more," I tell her and she nods in understanding. "You can say no," I remind her. "And don't take drinks from anyone except me, okay?"

"I'm not..."

"That won't matter, not to these guys, and whatever you do, don't get on the back of anyone's bike." She nods.

"I'm not going to drink. I figure at some point I'll be bringing Piper home."

"Probably after the funeral. We're not going to the clubhouse, so it will be a little more civilized, for a little while."

Her face lights up in a wide, excited smile. I wink at her.

Not ten minutes later, we're headed for the car when a bike comes roaring down the street from Loki's direction. Piper gets excited and tugs on my dress. "Is that Loki?" she says.

"I think so, baby," I tell her.

"Can I ask him now?"

I smile down at her. I'd hoped that she'd have gotten sidetracked, but it's obvious this is something she's going to find out one way or another. "Wait until we see him later, okay?"

She pouts and climbs in the car. Loki pulls up behind my car. He's wearing his shades but I can tell he's staring at me. So, I put my arms out to the side and twirl around. When I'm facing him again, he lowers his shades slightly so that I can see his steel grey eyes looking at me and a spark of desire ignites in my veins. "I have something for you," he smirks.

I walk up to him and he wraps his arms around me, pressing me into his side. He's still on his bike, but the engine's off. He leans his head down and presses his lips to mine. I kiss him back with gusto, and he growls, pulling back from my kiss. "Is that all?" I tease.

"No," he says with a growl. "But the fact that our daughter is in your car is the only thing stopping me from bending you over my bike right now." His voice is gravelly, rough and breathless. He releases me and I step back from him. He turns toward his saddlebag and flips it up. "I was gonna give this to you later, but since you're here."

He pulls something out, it's black and leather and I cover my mouth as his rough fingers open it. He turns it around and my jaw falls to the ground. "Loki," I breathe as I take in the black vest with the Wicked Angels colors on the back and across the top of the logo it says, 'Property of Loki'. It's an old lady cut. He turns it back around and opens the flaps on the front for me to put my arms through. I stand there staring at it like an idiot.

"You're killing me, woman," he growls.

I try and smile at him. "Are you sure?" I finally manage.

"If I wasn't sure, I wouldn't be handing this to you." His voice is a little harder, a little irritated maybe. "I realized last night, after you left the clubhouse that I couldn't enjoy myself. Even surrounded by lines, booze, sex, and rock music, because you weren't there. Now," he shakes the vest, "you can be there whenever the fuck I want you there and I ain't gotta worry about some prickhead motherfucker sticking his dick in you."

I smile at him and step forward, turning around and shifting my purse to put my arm through, then shift again for the other arm. It fits like a fucking glove. He growls again. "I'm fucking you tonight wearing only that." He grabs me by my waist and pulls me into his side again. "I mean it," he whispers before pressing his lips to mine chastely, "old lady."

WICKED REVENGE

I pull away from him. "Give me a moment," I tell him and I go to the car where Em and Piper are waiting patiently.

"Mommy, your back matches my necklace," she squeals.

I hand over my keys to Em. "You mind taking her?"

"Not at all." She climbs out and looks back at Loki, he smiles at her and she returns it with a blush. I want to roll my eyes, but she has a point, Loki is fucking gorgeous.

I hand over my purse and she takes it, putting it in the car with her. "I'll be right back," I say and dart toward the house. I can't ride with these fucking shoes on.

I'm in and out of the house in a hot fucking second, shoes on my finger, boots on my feet and I'm running toward Loki and the bike. He has a wicked grin on his face. "That's my woman," he moans, flipping open the saddle bag my cut came out of so I can drop my heels inside before I climb on. The skirt I'm wearing is tight, so I hike it up, giving me barely enough room to put my legs on either side of his hips. Then I slide my arms around him and let my fingers trail over his cock. He growls almost as loud as his bike when he kicks it over.

He pulls out. Em and Piper follow us.

When we pull into the funeral home parking lot, there are no less than fifty bikes and Em finds a place to park toward the back of the lot. Loki steadies the bike for me to climb off, and once I do, I push my skirt back down.

"Son of a bitch," a gravelly voice says and I turn to see Pyro a few feet away from us, staring daggers at Loki.

I roll my eyes and Loki ignores him.

"Oh, my god!" I hear a squeal and then suddenly I'm being spun around and Loni's arms are wrapped around me. She looks past me at Loki. "You sneaky devil you. When you suggested her yesterday, I thought you were nuts, but now it all makes perfect sense." She squeezes me tighter.

I raise an eyebrow, catching Pyro in my peripheral; he doesn't look as pissed as he did a moment ago. Thank God.

"Mommy," Piper squeals and Loni releases me.

"Welcome to the family," she says softly.

"Thanks," I tell her.

"Piper," Loni says excitedly and Piper jumps into her arms.

"Hi, Loni!" She smiles at her and wraps her arms around Loni's neck. Then she turns to Loki. Her face lights up in a big, beautiful smile as she looks at him. If you ever want to watch a biker's heart melt, have a kid look at him the way Pipes is looking at Loki. "We need to talk, Loki," Piper says completely serious and Loni laughs as she sets her down. Piper walks right up to Loki, tugging on his cut and beckoning him to her level with a crooked finger.

"What's up, buttercup?" Loki says when he's face to face with her.

"Are you my daddy?" she asks him.

Loki freezes, his eyes coming to me and I nod my head, letting him know he can answer her question and he looks back at Piper. There is so much love radiating out of his eyes when he does that my heart melts. "I am, baby girl," he tells her softly.

"Yay!" Piper squeals and she wraps her arms around him so tight that he nearly falls over from the impact.

I look at Loki and for the first time since I've known him, his eyes are full of unshed tears and my heart flutters in my chest.

"Does this mean I get to see you whenever I want?" Piper asks as she pulls back from their huge hug.

Again, Loki's eyes find mine. I shrug, raising an eyebrow and I let my fingers slide over the collar of my cut. "Yeah, baby girl, it does," he responds and she squeals again. Loki picks her up and flips her around so she's riding on his back. "Hang on," he says and her little hands wrap around his neck, holding on for dear life. "I'm gonna kiss your mommy now, is that okay?"

Her face scrunches up. "Ewwww," she snickers.

Loki leans over to me and I lean up on my tip toes and he presses his lips to mine then pulls back. "Thank you," he whispers.

"There's those words again," I smirk.

"You gonna stand here all day?" Piper asks and bucks on his back.

Loki laughs and takes her toward the funeral home doors. We've managed to amass a crowd of bikers, including Big Daddy, Whistler, Pyro, Sticks and Pixie.

Sticks gives me a wicked grin then grabs his cut, straightening it before he winks at me and heads for the funeral home.

Big Daddy comes over and he wraps his arm around my shoulders and kisses my temple. "Welcome home," he says. "You do realize that you just made him Pres, right?"

I turn to look at him, narrowing my eyes in confusion.

He cocks his head. "Angels rules, family first. You're the last of the Roswell line, female or not, he's Pres."

"Well, fuck me sideways," I breathe.

"That's his job, darlin'." Big Daddy squeezes my shoulders and releases me. I pull my heels from the saddle bag and set them on the ground before kicking off my boots and climbing into them.

I readjust and Emily is standing behind the bike with my purse. "So, does this mean Loki's moving in?" she asks with a hint of a blush on her cheeks.

"Uh, shit, I have no idea." I laugh. "I guess we have some things to talk about."

She laughs, "Looks like you've got time."

I put my boots back in the saddle bag and close it up before taking my purse from her. "Thanks," I tell her.

"She's happy?" Em asks.

I look over at Loki and Piper. Loki is bouncing her all over the place and her giggles can be heard from here. "I think so," I tell her.

"Good," she sounds concerned.

I look at her. "This doesn't change anything about our arrangement."

She lights up at that. "I'm not…" I give her a knowing smile. "Okay, good." She breathes a sigh of relief.

"Come on," I tell her and I lead her to the lawn in front of the funeral home where Piper is trying to climb up Loki as he's talking to someone.

"Pipes, come here, baby." She wraps her arms around Loki's leg and looks at me like I've lost my mind. Loki's eyes meet mine in a silent apology and I smile before joining him.

Immediately he wraps his arm around my shoulders and tucks me in close to his side, holding me there. He's posturing and I know he's reminding everyone that I'm his. If my cut doesn't prove that enough, his arm will.

He continues talking, not about me or anything I truly care about, so I just people watch.

I see a few of the old ladies walking into the building with their old men in a similar fashion to how Loki is holding me and it makes me smile.

I shouldn't have wanted to be an old lady. I should have wanted to keep as far away from the club as humanly possible, but standing here now, a biker's arm draped over me possessively, I feel like I'm home. Piper is vying for Loki's attention and he gives it to her without a second thought. "What is it?" He lets me go and kneels at her level. I don't hear what she says to him, but whatever it is, he laughs and picks her up. He settles her in one arm, his right, and wraps his left around me and we go into the building.

"What'd she ask?"

"She said she was bored and wanted to go inside," Loki tells me. His voice has a hint of humor and maybe even happiness in it that I never expected to hear and regret swims in my veins as we approach the door to the funeral home.

"Mommy, why are we here?" she says as we stand in line to pay our respects.

"A friend of Loki's passed away, sweetie."

"Oh." Her mouth makes a little 'O' and she looks around. There are a couple of kids about her age playing quietly in the corner of the room. She leans over to me, whispering, "Can I go play with them?"

"What do you say?" I tell her.

"Please?" She scrunches up her face in a way she thinks is cute and Loki chuckles.

"Sure," Loki says and sets her down. She runs over and I hear her introduce herself. The two kids tell her she can play with them and she sits right down.

"Whose kids are those?" I ask.

"The girl is Opie and Kara's daughter, Jess. The little boy belongs to Taz." The name sends ice through my veins. That's the chick whose tits he was sucking the night I ran off on Rack's bike. "His dad's Shifter," he answers my unasked question.

"Oh," is all I can manage. I have no business asking a question like I nearly did. Sticks let me in the clubhouse with Piper and I worked in the bar. But Boulder's clubhouse is run a little differently. There's very little sex in the common rooms. Making out is about as intense as it gets in there. If it goes beyond that they'd go to one of the rooms upstairs in the clubhouse. But Angels' kids are all you'd see in there. The whores, if they had them, kept them away. So seeing one of Roswell's whore's kids shouldn't be the shock that it is. Being a member's kid changes things.

He looks at me, wondering where my mind has wondered, but doesn't say anything.

We spend thirty more minutes in line to pay our respects to Rack, but I notice something's missing. "Where's his cut?" I ask Loki.

He gives me a sad look but shakes his head. "Tell you later," he whispers in my ear. I let him go ahead of me. He knew Rack longer than I did, but I need a moment with him too. If I'd have brought him into my house that night, and slept with him instead of sending him packing, he might be alive and that notion has been eating at me since I learned he was killed. I don't know the details, just that someone from the visiting club got a wild hair up his ass, got pissed, they got in a fight and Rack ended up dead.

Rack's missing cut could only mean one thing- either the asshole who killed him took it as a trophy or they can't find it. Burning cuts of fallen brothers is a big deal with the Wicked Angels. Their name patches end up on the Wall of the Fallen in the clubhouse common room and their cuts are burned. Loki finishes and he offers me his hand to take. "Can I have a minute with him?" I ask and Loki nods reluctantly but lets me have my moment.

"I'm so sorry," I whisper and a tear slides down my cheek, landing on the back of my hand that's holding onto the side of his casket. He looks so peaceful it's surreal. "I wish I'd have asked you to stay," I mouth because I can't get my voice to work. I kiss my fingertips and then press them to his cold cheek and walk toward Loki.

He opens his arms and I wrap my arms around him. "What did you say to him?" he asks quietly.

"I told him that I was sorry and that I wished I'd asked him to stay that night." Loki stiffens under me. "Stop," I whisper harshly. "If he'd stayed, whether we did anything or not, he'd still be alive," I explain.

He loosens up around me. "Or if he'd told you no to taking you home, you could have been in the middle of it." He squeezes me tighter.

"I was pissed at you. I wanted to hurt you. If he hadn't taken me home, someone would have," I tell him.

He narrows his eyes at me. "Is that all it was? An act?"

I roll my eyes. "You knew that already." His chest shakes with silent laughter and I push him. "Caveman," I murmur.

His arms tighten, pulling me back into him. "Your caveman."

I snuggle into him again. "Mine."

There was a small service in the funeral home before Loki, Opie, Cowboy, Gunnar, Pyro, and someone else I haven't met yet, carried Rack's casket out of the home and it into the back of the hearse. As we're walking out behind them, Em and Piper join me. Then Kara comes over. "You ridin' with Loki?" she asks.

I shrug. "No clue," I tell her, and it's true. I rode here with him but the bikes are for members and old ladies.

"Can Jess ride with Piper? They seem to be having a good time together."

"I don't mind. Emily?"

"Fine with me," she says with a smile looking down at Piper and Jess.

"Thank you, the ladies are riding," she whispers as if it's a conspiracy and then it hits me, Loki colored me.

"Will you be okay if I ride with Loki?" I ask Emily.

"Absolutely, I'll just follow the line."

"The hearse goes first, the family car, which…" I look around the crowd of people and in all honesty, I don't see anyone outside of the biker community here. Huh. "Then the higher ranks of the home club, followed by the other charters, then cars. The rest of the bikes will bring up the rear. There will be bikes on either side of the car." I fill her in on Wicked Angels' funeral protocol and she nods in understanding.

I tell Piper bye, but she and Jess are in their own little happy world. I think she's made a new friend because she doesn't care what I'm doing. Emily takes them to the car and I find Loki. He wraps his arm around me when I do. "Am I riding?" I ask.

He glares at me. "Why wouldn't you be?"

I shrug. "Because you made me an old lady about two hours ago," I tell him.

"You're wearing my colors, you ride with me," he says in a way that brings my favorite caveman to life. "Next it will be my brand."

I laugh. "I need my boots," I tell him and he lets me go. I go straight to Loki's bike and flip the saddlebag up.

"Just because he colored you, don't mean shit."

My blood freezes at the voice behind me. It's not Pyro, but I voice I know all too well. Gunnar. "Why would that change anything?" I say with more confidence than I feel.

"Don't think we don't know who you are, Kiwi." He says my name with such disdain that it makes my blood turn from ice to boiling in a nanosecond. I turn and he's gone. I only get his back as he retreats toward his bike. My eyes roam around, looking to see if anyone saw it and the only eyes I find are none other than Rooster's, glaring at me.

"You alright?" Pyro says and I turn to him. I simply shake my head but say nothing.

"Kiwi?" he says in a tone that begs me not to argue with his question, much the way Kellen used to do when I was younger and once again I find my eyes locked on his. They're similar, familiar, but not the same. Kellen had bright green eyes. These eyes are a dull, seen too much shit in my life, brown. The hair is long, he smokes, he has a wicked fucking scar down the side of his face. There's too many differences. It's not possible, I remind myself.

"Later," I whisper. I have to learn to trust someone. Loki, Pyro? I don't know anymore.

Pyro gives me a small nod before he walks off toward his bike. I drop my boots to the ground and kick off a heel before sliding my foot in. Then repeat the process with the other foot.

"You shrunk," Loki says with a laugh.

WICKED REVENGE

"Heels and bitch riding don't mix." I smile at him, putting my little encounter with Gunnar out of my mind. Now's not the time. "Neither do tight skirts," I say deadpan.

"Oh no, the skirts work." He smirks.

"Caveman," I mumble and he laughs. I pick up my heels and toss them in the saddlebag and wait for him to situate.

"Where's Pipes?" he asks and I smile again at the nickname.

"With Em and Jess, her new best friend," I answer with a hint of bitterness.

"Jess is a good kid."

I huff. "She didn't even say bye to me."

Loki throws his head back laughing at the same time as bikes start firing up. I should have brought ear plugs. I feel sorry for anyone in Roswell we're about to drive past. There's more than two hundred hogs roaring down the streets, revving engines, determined to let God know that an Angel is making his last ride home.

CHAPTER EIGHTEEN
Loki

"GO HOME, BABY," I TELL Kiwi. "You're exhausted."

It's been a long fucking day. The funeral, the graveside service, which was better than expected and full of nothing but Wicked Angels, and now a party.

Rack didn't have any family outside of the Angels and seeing that hurt more than anything. It doesn't help that we have no cut to burn, no final closure for Rack and what he deserves. But by the end of the night, everyone seems to be doing just fine.

Kiwi took Emily and Piper home a little while ago and came back. I tried to convince her to stay home then, but she refused, said she didn't want to leave me alone. "I'm alright," she tells me for the tenth time.

I get in her face. "You're dead on your feet, go home."

"I want you with me," she whispers.

I look around the bar and there are more than a hundred Angels still here, most of which are Roswell charter and I can't leave, not yet. "I will come when I'm done."

She reaches into her pocket, she'd changed out of her dress and into a pair of jeans and her boots with a corset top under her cut. She looks sexy as fuck. The dress was bad enough this morning, this is worse. She hasn't taken her vest off since I gave it to her and it makes me smile when I see it. She's mine, I've staked my claim and she accepted it. "Alright," she yawns as she hands me something.

"What's this?" I ask as I take a key from her.

"It's a key, so you can get in," she yawns again. "I don't want you pounding down my door." She gives me a promising smirk.

I wrap my arm around her shoulders and lead her toward the door. I walk her to her car and she keeps yawning. It's barely ten o'clock, but she's been going since early this morning and I didn't let her sleep much last night. It's a good thing she's going home and she can catch some sleep before I wake her up. "Sleep in it," I tug on her cut. "I'm going to fuck you while you're wearing it."

She rolls her eyes. "Yes, because sleeping in leather is so comfortable."

I kiss her forehead and she leans up, catching my chin. She growls and I laugh and claim her lips. I don't linger because I'm going to end up fucking her on the hood of her car if this carries on much longer. My cock has been hard half the fucking day and it's starting to hurt. "Go before I fuck you on the hood of your car." She literally purrs at me. "Go home, woman," I tell her and she laughs, climbing in her car. I stand there watching her as she takes off down the street.

A good portion of the Angels left the bar some time ago. Most of them disbursed to the clubhouse or Cottontail, our strip joint on compound property. Most of the old ladies have bailed already, all that's left in the pussy department is club whores and bar sluts. A couple of the strippers came over, but for a Roswell Angels party, it's fucking tame and rather boring.

"Hey stranger," a female voice says to me as I start heading back to toward the bar. "Long time no see." I turn to the voice. It's Stoney, one of the strippers from Cottontail.

"Be a lot longer before you see me," I tell her and I start walking back to the bar. She catches up to me, grabbing my arm.

"I miss you," she says as she looks up at me through her eyelashes and my once hard cock deflates.

"You gonna keep on missin' me," I tell her and my tone doesn't leave much room for argument.

"Don't be like that," she purrs.

A moment ago, it was sexy as fuck on Kiwi, but this shit is obnoxious. "I ain't the one with the problem here," I tell her and she starts rubbing her hands all over my chest. She almost has them under my open cut before I grab hold of her wrists and pull her hands from my body. "Go home, Stoney."

"Only if you come with me."

I squeeze her wrists and watch the pain register in her eyes and she sobers. I can't quite tell what she's on, drugs, alcohol or both, but she's six sheets to the wind. "Fuck you, Loks."

I roll my eyes. I fucking hate that nickname and she fucking knows it. She uses it like a badge of honor or something. "In case you hadn't noticed, I ain't interested, so get lost, go find some other dick to suck, but stay the fuck away from mine." I throw her hands downward and the motion throws her off balance. She falls and I don't bother catching her.

"Ashsshole," she sputters.

I roll my eyes and leave her on the sidewalk. I'm about to reach for the door when it opens and Gunnar steps out. "Wasting good pussy now?" His voice is like nails on a chalkboard. Not literally, it just grates on my fucking nerves to no end.

"She so great? Have at it," I snap and side step him. He doesn't stop me and I step back inside. He doesn't follow me in and I see through the window after a few minutes that he's got his arm around Stoney and they're disappearing. I shudder.

Up until Kiwi, six years ago, club whores and bar sluts were amazing. Then Kiwi happened and club whores and bar sluts became a great source of blowing steam and my load. But now? They all make me sick and to think that Kiwi's been one for the last six years makes me shudder again.

I can't and won't fault her for that. How can I? I could have stopped it. I could have made an honest woman out of her and I didn't. So, her past is something I have to deal with, just like she'll have mine to handle.

I grab a whiskey from Loni who winks at me and I head out the back door where all the tables and another fifty or so people are still gathered. I ain't seen Pyro in a while and I don't see him now. We haven't talked all day and I don't know why that bothers me so much, but something's really eating at him.

I wander around the side of the building, into the darkness and the shadows, just watching and listening.

That's when I hear the smack of skin to skin contact, not the fucking kind either. "You had one fucking job, you dumb fucking cunt." It's Gunnar.

"I'm sorry," Stoney cries.

I roll my eyes. Apparently, the little Gun-man has blowjob standards, who knew?

"Get out of my face, you worthless piece of shit. Next time I tell you to do something, you fucking do it."

"He shut me down." I hear her cry, softer now.

I narrow my eyes and turn toward them. I can barely make them out just beyond the bushes that separate us.

"Next time show him your tits or something."

"Loks isn't like that," she cries more.

I see and hear the next smack that comes. "The fuck he's not."

Gunnar's hands go to his belt and he undoes the fly of his jeans. I have to bite back a laugh when he pulls his so-called cock from behind the zipper. "Suck it," he orders Stoney. I want to step in and stop it, but then Stoney rises to her knees, a smile playing on her lips as she wraps her fingers around his tiny pecker and puts it in her mouth. "That's it, bitch, you know your place."

I shudder as shivers of disgust slide through me.

I can't fucking wait to take this asshole down. The first thing that's happening is we're bringing in fresh blood, fresh bitches and getting rid of tiny-dicked-pricks like Gunnar Marsden.

I listen a little while longer as she grunts and groans around his tiny prick. She's really into it and it makes my stomach roll.

I don't move from my spot. I'm well-concealed and I can see a good bit of action from here, not just the sad blowjob behind me, but club members, a couple of the remaining old ladies, including Opie and Kara. I shake my head when I realize that Kara has lost her shirt under her vest and Opie's hand is inside, playing with her tits. He alternates from one to the other.

I hear Gunnar grunt out his orgasm down Stoney's throat. "Now get the fuck outta here," He growls at her and I hear her scurrying away.

After a beat, I see Pyro come out of the bar. He's looking around, looking for me.

"Psst."

He turns, looking right at me and he comes over. I hold my finger to my lips, making sure he knows to be quiet. I go back to watching Opie and Pyro's eyes follow mine.

I see him shake his head and I'm sure he rolls his eyes too, but then Opie frees himself from Kara before leaving her on the picnic table all alone. He walks to our left, where Gunnar was, and I turn to see Gunnar still standing there, but someone else has joined him.

I tap Pyro on the shoulder and point with two fingers at my eyes then one in their general direction. They obviously don't know we're here in the darkness.

"Did it work?" Rooster asks Gunnar when Opie arrives.

"No, he turned her down flat." Pyro looks at me and I cup my ear.

"She needs to try harder," Rooster snaps.

"Get Taz, he can't say no to her," Gunnar says. "Stoney's a dumb cum slut."

You'd know, asswipe.

"He colored Skit today. Good luck getting him to do anything," Opie says and both Rooster and Gunnar look at him like he needs to shut the fuck up. Pyro's eyes turn to me. I give him a small nod.

"Oh, who gives a shit. Ain't no one around here a saint. He sure as fuck won't be either."

Pyro's eyes go from what-the-fuck to glaring at me. I shrug and shake my head.

"I'll talk to Taz," Opie adds. "See if she can't get to him."

Again, I roll my eyes and shake my head. The purpose behind all this is beyond me.

"We need him vulnerable," Rooster says.

I'm still holding my drink in my hand. I set it on the window sill behind me. Pyro nods at me. "Why not just clip his breaks?" Opie says.

Well, fuck.

"You're a damn idiot. That's not a guarantee," Gunnar says.

"So, fucking shoot him," Opie growls.

"Now that's a novel idea," Gunnar perks up.

"Shut the hell up, both of you. We'll work this out later," Rooster snaps and walks toward the front of the bar. Opie returns to the picnic table where his old lady sits, but not before grabbing Taz's ass on his way by.

Gunnar finally takes off toward the front of the bar, following Rooster.

"Well, fuck me," I breathe.

"You knew it was comin'," Pyro says.

"Yeah, but what in the actual fuck? First Tripp, then Tryke, now me?"

"We gotta tell 'em," Pyro says conspiratorially. "But fucking Opie, really?"

I shake my head. "I guess it shows who we can and can't trust. Bottom line, Opie's out when this is over," I grumble and skirt Pyro.

"Where you going?" he asks.

"I got a woman to fuck," I tell him.

"Dude, seriously? Why you gotta point that shit out like that?"

I laugh and shrug before walking through the bar, waving good night to Loni and Cowboy, and then out the front door to my bike.

I don't see Gunnar or Rooster on the way so I double check my brakes on my bike before I take off and see everything is intact before firing it up and taking off toward Kiwi's.

I kill the engine in front of her neighbor's house and push my bike up her driveway and put it in front of Emily's car. It's not hidden exactly, but if someone was driving by they wouldn't be able to tell without stopping and no one is stopping while I'm here. Even if it means sleeping with one eye open all fucking night.

I unlock the front door with the key she gave me. The outside light was on when I got here so I hit the switch by the door. She left a lamp on in the living room and I kill that too before kicking off my boots and heading down the hall toward her room.

Piper's door is slightly ajar as I pass and I stop. Pushing it open a little further, I lean into the jamb as I watch her sleep. She has her hands up close to her head and her covers are kicked off on one side of her body. I smile and tiptoe in. I fix her covers quickly before I lean down and kiss her forehead. "G'night, princess," I whisper softly and I tip toe toward the door.

When I turn around, Kiwi is standing in the doorway wearing nothing but a skimpy pair of black panties and my vest. I jump a little. She puts her finger to her lips, telling me to be quiet and she steps aside, letting me sneak back out. She closes the door behind me, leaving it slightly ajar. "She hates her door closed all the way," she whispers.

All I see is her. I let my hands slide into the front of the cut. They roam up to catch her nipples between my fingers. Her breathing falters as she backs away from me. I walk with her until we're in her room. I let her nipples go long enough to close the door quietly.

I grab the front of her cut and pull her toward me. "You're so fucking sexy in this," I breathe. My cock grows harder by the second the longer I look at her. Her long legs are uncovered, her black panties leave little to the imagination and I can't wait to bury my face in her juicy, delicious cunt.

"I'm sexy in everything," she counters.

I try thinking and I can't argue with her as her hands come to the button fly of my denim. She rips it open. "Yes, you are, but my colors take the cake. Tomorrow it will be my ink," I tell her as she lowers herself to her knees before me, bringing my jeans and boxer briefs with her.

WICKED REVENGE

I cup her cheek in my palm and she leans into it as she wraps her fingers around my rock-hard cock. "Fuck," I breathe and she reminds me with a finger to her lips to keep quiet.

"Just suck it," I tell her with a smirk.

"Caveman," she says before sucking my cock into her mouth.

My legs tremble and my eyes roll up into my skull. She releases me with an audible pop and I look down at her. "Don't stop," I tell her.

She rolls her eyes and I slide my hand into her hair, tightening my fist, taking several strands with me and she whimpers. "That's what I thought," I say and she starts sucking my cock back into her mouth. Her hand strokes opposite her mouth and the entire day of torture comes crashing down on me as I feel my balls tingle. "Not gonna last," I tell her.

She smiles with my cock filling her mouth and she starts sucking and fist-fucking me harder and faster.

"Goddammit," I groan and her other hand cups my balls. "Fuck," I growl at her. She squeezes both my cock and my balls and I glare at her.

She releases me. "Quiet," she whispers. "You wake her and you get nothing," she smirks again before sucking my cock back into her mouth. This time she doesn't stop and a few short pumps later, I'm coming, her little grunts adding sparks of sensation as my cum slides down her throat.

"Evil wench," I tease her and she stands, hooking her thumbs into her panties and pushing them down. I growl as she crawls on the bed.

I slide off my cut, then pull my t-shirt off and kick my jeans off to the side as she lays down on her back, looking sexy as fuck with my cut covering her tits, though barely, and one leg crossed over the other, blocking my view of her sexy cunt. I grab her leg and open her up. She smiles at me as I lower my face to her slick, already wet as fuck pussy. I lap at her juices, savoring her sweet and spicy flavor as it assaults my tongue. Her hand is in my hair, holding my head to her pussy and I slide a hand up, flipping open her cut, exposing her pierced nipples. I push my hand up higher on her body until I'm rolling her nipple between my fingers. She moans and her legs start to twitch. Her free hand goes to her other tit and she mimics my motion. I smile into her slit and use my free hand to push inside her with my thumb and I wiggle it around.

"Oh god," she breathes. "Fuck me, Loki." I chuckle as I suck her clit into my mouth and her body trembles and locks down. She's on the cusp and I pull back. She glares at me.

"I'm gonna fuck you now," I tell her.

"Loki?"

My eyes meet hers. "Yeah, baby?"

"I'm not on birth control."

"Fuck," I growl. "You're mine now, I don't give a fuck," I tell her as I lift her legs, lining the head of my cock up with her entrance and slamming inside her. She cries out and I lean down, pressing my lips to hers, swallowing her cries as I pound in and out of her soaked sex. "So, tight," I groan as her pussy does the clenching thing. "You squeeze me so fucking good," I tell her and she moans. I lower my head, finding a nipple and sucking it into my mouth and her hand slides between us. Her fingers strum her clit and the clenches get harder and more frequent. Her body trembles, and then locks down again.

I fuck her harder through her orgasm and she wraps her arms around my shoulders, putting her face in the crook of my neck. Then I feel the sharp lick of pain as she bites me. "Fuck," I growl and my orgasm ignites, spurting hotly from my dick and coating the inside of her pussy. "Mine," I growl.

"Yours," she replies.

CHAPTER NINETEEN

Kiwi

I FELL ASLEEP DRAPED OVER Loki and woke up with him draped over me. His soft snores are a comfort I didn't anticipate. He claimed me with his cut, then claimed me with his dick, twice.

Sometime in the middle of the night, he woke me up by sliding his cock inside me. I was on my side so he'd hitched my leg up and pushed inside me. I remember rolling my shoulder back to expose my tits to him and his tongue lavished my nipple the entire time he was sliding in and out of me. We came together. My orgasm pulling him over the edge and he poured himself inside me.

I shiver under him, remembering telling him I'm not on birth control and no, getting pregnant isn't at the top of my list of things to do right now, but there's something animalistic about the way he takes me. I can't get enough.

My bladder screams at me to move my ass, but my mind says to stay right here a little longer.

I look over at the clock. It's just after ten in the morning. I can hear The cartoons I hear playing in the living room let me know Piper is awake. I told Emily to keep her home today. I already called the school, letting them know we had a death in the family. It bought her a few days. Kindergarten is a little beneath Piper, but she has to do it before they'll test her for placement. She's a smart kid and having Emily around has been amazing because she's taught Piper so much.

A little slice of fear about Loki being here slides through me, making me shiver and my bladder scream louder.

I try and extricate myself from the caveman, but as soon as I move, he tightens his arm around me. "Where you go?" the caveman grumbles.

"Bathroom," I groan and he releases me. Thank God. He grunts as he rolls over and I shake my head. "Caveman," I whisper and I hear him chuckle quietly as I head into my bathroom.

When I come out, Loki is sprawled on the bed. The sheet is down around his hips and his cock is hard as a rock, standing straight up, tenting the sheet. His even breathing tells me that he's back to sleep and I lick my lips. Time for a little payback.

I go over to the side of the bed he's on and gently pull the covers up and over his steely erection before I straddle his hips. I reach between us, wrapping my fingers around his cock and I stroke. He grunts again, but doesn't wake up. So far, my plan is working.

I line his cock with the entrance of my pussy and start to push down before pulling up slightly. He moans. I smile and keep going until I have him fully sheathed inside me. I reposition slowly, not wanting to wake him up just yet and I start to grind my hips against his. "Fuck," he growls and his eyes open, landing on mine. They're hooded and my nipples pebble.

"Paybacks, caveman," I say huskily as I position my hands on his chest and lift my hips up and push them down. His cock slides in and out of me, filling me with each glide. His hands grab hold of my hips, guiding me up and down his cock a couple of times before he pulls my hips forward and pushes them back, grinding his cock against my g-spot and my clit against his pelvic bone.

My eyes flutter closed as the sensation overwhelms me. Then he lifts me up and back down again, then grinds me against him. I get the picture and take over for him. I arch my back, pushing him in deeper and his hands cup my breasts, twisting my nipples between his fingers, and my orgasm races through my veins. I smile down at him. His eyes are locked on the spot where we come together and I get an idea.

I sit up, pulling my tits from his hands and he pouts, literally. I lean back, putting my hands on his thighs and I feel his muscles tighten to support me. With the change in position, his cock is pressing into that happy center inside me and I lose my focus for a second. Once I come back to the present, using the leverage I have on him, I start sliding up and down his shaft. "Fuck," he growls again and I feel his thumb press against my clit.

WICKED REVENGE

"Oh god," I breathe as I start fucking him harder and faster.

He increases his pressure and pace against my clit. My orgasm climbs to unbearable heights just under the surface. That sweet peak is right there, ready to explode. "Finish it," he growls and I do. Fucking him hard, my orgasm explodes and my body quivers and he empties his seed inside me for the third time in less than twelve hours.

Our breathing is ragged, his cock still hard inside me when I lean forward, bringing my chest to his and he wraps his arms around me. "Did you really mean what you said last night?" I ask him.

"Which part?" His hand moves into my hair, brushing it aside and he adjusts so he can look at me.

"About not caring that I'm not on birth control?"

I look up at him, my head still on his chest. "Yeah, I did," His voice is soft, leaving no traces of doubt at his words.

"We've barely just gotten together," I tell him. Granted, we've had sex a few times without a condom, but there's still time for me to do something about it if he's changed his mind and technically, it shouldn't be that time in my cycle. At least that's what I'm telling myself.

His hand comes to my chin, forcing me to look up at him. "We already have Piper," I tell him, my voice barely above a whisper.

"And I've missed everything when it comes to her. I won't do that again," he tells me. His tone begs not to be argued with.

"I'm sorry." My chin quivers and tears fill my eyes. "If I'd known…"

"Stop." His voice is quiet but forceful. "I assure you, you'll never be alone again."

I want to believe him, truly I do. But he left me once. What would stop him from doing it again? His thumb comes to my cheek and he swipes away a tear. "I mean it, Lily." The use of my name sends a thrill through me. He doesn't use it often, but when he does, it's like lightning in my veins and my heart floods with warmth at his declaration.

I nod because I can't find my voice.

His cock twitches inside me and he rolls us over. He claims my mouth in one of his infamous soul-stealing kisses as he starts pushing in and out of me and starting round four.

We didn't linger in bed after that. He was a little miffed that it was so late in the morning before we crawled out of bed, but my stomach growled and he decided to take Piper and me to breakfast, or in Piper's case, lunch.

We're both dressed before we leave the bedroom and Piper's eyes turn to saucers when she sees Loki behind me. "Loki," she squeals and launches herself off the couch.

"I've been replaced," I grumble.

"You have not," Piper says completely deadpan as she jumps into Loki's arms.

"Hi, princess," he says. "Want to go to breakfast with mom and me?" he asks and she gives him a look like 'are you kidding?'.

"Um, it's lunch time, Loki."

He laughs. "For you, but for mommy and me, we want breakfast."

"Okay," she says as she squirms her way down and Loki lets her go. She runs off to her bedroom and I find Emily in the kitchen. She's working at the computer I gave her when we moved down here.

"Whatcha doin?" I ask.

She smiles at me. "Looking at the class schedule for the spring semester."

I give her a reassuring smile. "Any luck?"

She lights up. "I've found four classes that will work."

"Work with?"

"Piper's school schedule."

"Oh, Em, we will work out whatever we need to in order to get you to school. Don't take classes just because it works."

"I'm not. These are all classes I have to take anyway. I won't get to the fun stuff until next fall." She lights up and continues talking as Loki comes into the kitchen. "The classes would be Monday through Thursday. Starting between ten and eleven and I'd be done by two, giving me enough time to pick-up Piper."

"What about homework?" I ask her.

Piper comes into the kitchen. "We're gonna do homework together," she announces confidently.

Emily laughs and shrugs. "I think she's just as excited as I am." She looks back at the computer.

"We're gonna go get something to eat. you want to come with us?" I ask.

She shakes her head. "I will if you need me to, but otherwise, I wanna look at this a little more."

"Okay," I smile at her as she goes back to looking at her classes.

I grab my purse and my keys from the counter. "You don't need those," Loki says smugly.

"Uh, yeah, I do," I tell him and he just smirks.

"Pipes, you wanna ride on my bike?"

"OH! MY! GOD!" she squeals and goes running for the door. "Let's go, Loki," she says as she throws the door open and I hear her feet hitting the steps.

"How?" I ask.

"She's small enough to ride in my lap." He winks and goes after her.

I should be petrified that my daughter is so excited to ride on someone's else's bike, but instead, I pull her helmet from the entry way closet. "We'll be back, Em."

"Okay," she says, but I can tell she's not really paying attention as I close the door.

Loki has his bike set up and he's lifting Piper up as I come down the steps. She full of energy and excitement as Loki sets her between his legs. I join them, handing him her helmet and he smiles. "Alright, Pipes, helmet time," he says.

"Aw man," she grumbles and Loki laughs.

"No helmet, no ride," I remind her and she stops pouting. Her being on a bike is nothing new. Though I've never put her on mine, Sticks and several other Angels in Boulder have rode with her just like Loki is doing now.

"Come on, mom," she says through the helmet and Loki winks at me.

"You sure?" I ask him.

He gives me a 'don't be ridiculous' look with the raising of his eyebrow and he steadies the bike for me to climb on. Once we're settled, he fires up the bike and Piper squeals with excitement. I wrap my arms around both of them. Loki drops his shades and off we go.

We go to a diner, which come to find out, is owned by the Angels, around the corner from the house. The ownership should've been obvious because there are no less than a dozen bikes in the lot when we pull up.

It's so close that we could have walked, but where's the fun in that. Piper expresses her displeasure at the short ride and Loki promises her a longer one when we're done eating.

The diner is nice, quaint and very well-kept. The food smells wonderful and my stomach growls again. Loki snags us a booth in the front corner of the diner. It's one of those corner ones and Piper climbs between us. Am I disappointed that I'm so far from Loki? Maybe. But Piper is happy to be close to both of us. And she has a lot of time to make up for with her dad.

I notice the guys in the diner and I see several I recognize from the last couple of days, but they're not Boulder charter, maybe Tucson or here for all I know. "Who are they?" I ask Loki.

WICKED REVENGE

"Look at their patches," he says before going back to help Piper decide what to eat.

I notice then that they have Arizona flags on them and my nerves settle.

"Mom," Piper says, pulling me away from looking them over. "I want ice cream and cheese pizza and French fries."

I laugh, "Alright, food first, ice cream last."

"Loki said I could have ice cream first," she pouts.

I glare at Loki who shrugs. I see how this is gonna go but I shake my head and let her order her ice cream first.

Piper ate her ice cream then finished her pizza and most of her fries. I was impressed. We're finishing up when Loki pulls his phone from the inside pocket of his cut.

"Yeah," he says into the phone. "Yup, when?" he asks and I have no clue who he's talking to. "Fuck yeah."

"Loki," Piper scolds him and I can't hide my laugh.

He narrows his eyes but he's not mad. He kisses her on the head. "Sorry, baby," he whispers before returning to his phone call. "We'll be there in twenty." He hangs up.

He looks to Piper and asks, "Can we reschedule our ride?" She folds her arms over her chest. "Just by a few hours?"

"Fine," she concedes before sliding down the bench seat and under the table. She pops out the other side. "We at least get to ride back to the house, right?"

"Yes." Loki smiles at her.

"Good," Piper chirps and heads for the door.

Loki throws a couple bills on the table and we leave the diner.

Loki climbs on first, then he lifts Piper up, putting her helmet on before steadying for me.

Within minutes we're back at the house and Piper is inside with Emily. "Where's the fire?" I ask him.

He beams at me before jerking his head toward the back of his bike, telling me to get on. I roll my eyes and climb on the back of his bike. A little payback is in order for keeping me in the dark, so I grab his cock and he growls as he backs out of the driveway.

He takes off down the street.

Ten minutes later and we're driving past the compound, but we don't stop. Loki drives up to the next street and turns left into a small, Angels owned plaza and Loki parks in front of Wicked Ink. I gasp.

He kills the engine, drops the peg and holds the bike steady. I don't move.

He looks over his shoulder at me. "You're wearing my cut, the least you can do is wear my ink, too."

"Oh alright," I grumble, but I don't really mean it. I climb off and he ushers me inside.

It's a nice place. I worked in one of Boulder's shops for a few days helping them out, but surprisingly, this one is much nicer. Newer, cleaner.

"Hey, Loki," one of the guys says and Loki greets him in the Angels' standard arm grab and back slap.

"Kiwi, this is Axel. Axel, my woman, Kiwi."

Axel's face lights up as he looks me over. "About time," Axel mutters.

"Shut it," Loki says and they both smirk.

"Where we doin' it?" Axel asks me.

I look at Loki who shrugs. "Back?" I say.

"You got it." Axel smiles before leading us to the counter and a light table. He shows me the design and my head spins.

"That's a lot of ink," I tell the two of them.

"It's what you do," Loki says as if I should know this and I do.

I look the tattoo over and it's a replica of one of the two skulls facing each other with tribal wings coming out the backs of their heads that's on their patches. The tribal is both black and white. The drawing has no distinction, but the lines are there showing where the black and white separate.

The skull is facing to the right with the tribal that makes up the wings flowing behind it. Across the top left side, following the curve of the wing, it reads, 'Property of Loki' in an upward direction. Then at the bottom of the wing, in a downward direction it reads, 'Wicked Angels MC'. The lettering is in black.

"I just have one request," Loki says.

"What's that?" Axel asks.

"Instead of white on the wings, use green."

I glare at him. "Why green?"

He smiles at me. "Kiwi."

I laugh a little.

"You got it, man, anything else?" Axel asks and I shrug.

Loki approves the design and we follow Axel back to one of the curtained areas. He already has his chair set up. It looks like an upright massage chair like the ones in the malls at those five-minute massage parlors. The only difference with this one is it sits up higher.

I pull my shirt over my head, keeping my bra on, and I ignore Loki as I turn around to show Axel my back. "Damn, woman," he praises as he looks at the wings already inked on my back. "You sure you want this back here?"

"It's either that, my right shoulder or my right thigh," I say.

"Any one of those will work," Axel says.

I finally look at Loki, his eyes roaming over my body. "Where do you want it?" I ask him.

He gives me a wicked smirk. "I wanted it dipping into the crack of your ass, but I like the idea of your shoulder better."

"Okay," I tell him then turn my head toward Axel. "You might wanna switch the skull around," I say.

"Why?"

"Because," I lean over and show him my right shoulder. "This one's taken," I tell him.

"Oh shit, that's nice." Axel compliments.

"I was wondering about that," Loki says. "I saw it at the bar but I never got a good look at it."

"Got a black light, Axel?"

"Sure do, come on." he stands and leads us to another room in the back, it's another artist's room, but Axel closes the door once we're inside and he flips a switch, a black light illuminates the room.

"Nice," I smile.

"We do a lot of white ink. Especially first timers," Axel says and both he and Loki start inspecting my arm.

The tattoo is of Piper's name. The letters are intricate and the design behind it of various flowers conceals the letters. "Why'd you do this in white?" Loki asks me.

I give him a sad smile. "Because, I wanted the ink, but I wanted to be able to hide it if I needed to." I don't need to explain further. Loki understands why it's that way. "I'd like to color it one day," I say to Axel.

"We can definitely do that. It's a great design. Great slinger." Axel uses the term for artist. Usually they're ink-slingers but slinger is used for artists.

"Denver," I tell him.

"Nice," Axel smiles and kills the black light.

"I have the original drawing of my shoulder."

"Great, that will help, we can schedule an appointment for you after we're done today."

"Awesome," I say and we go back to Axel's station.

WICKED REVENGE

Within thirty minutes he's going to work on me. Loki never leaves my side.

It takes Axel about four and a half hours to complete the work and as each color is added, shaded and filled in, Loki's eyes grow more and more amazed. I'm pretty sure he shed a tear when Axel finished his name on my arm.

We're getting ready to leave when Loki's phone rings in his cut. I'm pulling my cut back on, careful not to bump my arm. It's warm and burning under the black plastic Axel put over it when he finished.

Loki hangs up the phone, and he's not happy. "What's going' on?" I ask.

"Gotta jet, Axe," Loki says. "Thanks, man, I really appreciate it." Loki reaches into his pocket and pulls an envelope from the inside of his cut and hands it to him. It's not overly thick, but there's a few bills stuffed inside it. I don't even want to know how much the ink cost and I don't ask.

We say our good-byes and Loki leads me out the door.

He turns to me as he gets to his bike. "I've gotta go take care of some things. You working tonight?" he asks.

"What time is it?"

"Almost five?"

"Crap, I'm supposed to be in at six," I tell him.

"Well, let's go, I'll drop you off at home."

"Alright." I climb on after he readies the bike and he takes off toward my house.

I change and get ready for the night. I wish I didn't have to go in, but Loki is busy with club business and it's Friday. Iron Wings has been closed for two days and the place is going to be crawling with people. Especially if we still have out of town guests.

I kiss Piper good night and leave for the bar.

199

When I arrive, Loni's eyes go straight to the black plastic on my shoulder. She laughs and shakes her head. "That boy wastes no time, does he?"

I laugh with her. "Not a second," I tell her as I set my purse behind the bar and grab an apron.

Within an hour, the bar is packed, standing room only. The Wicked Angels' tables are full of several Angels from Arizona, Colorado and a couple of Oregon guys.

The demeanor among the Angels is different toward me than it has been in the past. There's no more ass grabbing, very few crude remarks, and nice tips left behind when they leave.

I smile to myself. I could get used to this old lady shit.

Another couple hours in and I pull the bandage off my arm and slather it with Aquaphor while I'm on my break. When I come out without the bandage, Loni whistles at me. I laugh. "Green? That's a new one," she says.

"What color is yours?" I ask her.

"Blue, most of ours are. I guess they couldn't be original," she snickers.

The bar's door opens and Loki, Pyro, Cowboy, Sticks, Pixie, Whistler, and Big Daddy walk in. Loki's eyes roam over me and he smirks when he sees my shoulder uncovered. The guys all make their way to one of the recently vacated tables and I dutifully go over there to serve them.

They all check out my shoulder. Pyro looks annoyed and Loki beams with pride as the guys appraise Axel's work before finally giving me their orders.

They're drinking heavy tonight and before I know it, the bar's shutting down but the guys make no move to leave as Loni, Kat and I clean up the bar area. They're chatting away in the corner, getting a little louder, but they're having a good time. Loni makes no move to kick them out and when we're done, she sends Kat home.

Loni and I join them, her on Cowboy's lap and me on Loki's.

WICKED REVENGE

For the first time since arriving in Roswell, I feel safe, secure and it's like Boulder was before I left. Home. The guys joke around, having a good time. Pyro has gotten much more animated as the night has progressed. He's no longer shooting daggers at me. Though he's not exactly talking to me, it's like a calm acceptance has come over him. It's kind of nice.

Eventually the whiskey runs out and we break up our impromptu party. I drive my car home and Loki follows me.

We're in the house all of five minutes before he strips me of my clothes and he bends me over the bed.

When I wake in the morning, he's gone.

Memories consume me as fear washes over me that he's bailed again.

I shake my head at my idiocy and see a note he left me.

Back later,

-L

"Caveman," I mutter and climb into the shower.

CHAPTER TWENTY
Kiwi

AFTER MY SHOWER, I CATCH the clock, it's about eight-thirty and I know Piper is up because I can hear her laughing at something. It's Saturday morning and she's probably watching cartoons.

I leave my bedroom and find her doing exactly that, curled up on the couch. She looks past me. "Where's Loki?" she asks.

I give her a mock glare, teasing her, "What am I? Chopped liver?"

"Eww, mommy, that's gross," she laughs and scrunches up her nose.

"Sorry to disappoint you, sweetheart, but it's just me."

"Not a disappointment, unless you're not gonna watch cartoons with me."

I laugh and round the couch, plopping down next to her and she curls up with me and we watch some weird cartoon she laughs at repeatedly. I don't get it, but if it works for her, I'm good with that.

Emily brings me a cup of coffee. "Thanks," I tell her as she hands it to me.

"No problem. Thought you could use it. You got home late." I smile at her and notice the excitement in my eyes and her eyes roam over my right shoulder. "So that's what you got?" she asks as she looks at it.

I smile wider. "Yup."

"He branded you?" she laughs. "That was fast."

"Get used to it around here, sweetheart. Men don't waste time when it comes to what they want, they do and they miss out," I tell her.

"Good to know."

"How's the school search going?"

She gets animated as she tells me what she found out, including financial aid and the likes. She says there are a few grants she wants to apply for so I don't have to handle the full burden. I don't bother arguing that it's not a problem, because it's futile.

WICKED REVENGE

Emily's been through a lot of shit in her life, and she deserves a break and a chance to find some real happiness. Her intention is to go to school for early childhood education and it warms my heart. She loves kids, not just mine.

All three of our heads turn toward the front of the house when we hear a bike roaring down the street. I get up and go to the window. Piper follows me.

"Loki," she squeals as she goes to the door.

"Pipes," I tell her, but she flat out ignores me as she goes bolting down the steps.

Loki is barely off his bike when she plows into him. I follow after her. "Hi, princess," he greets her with a smile.

"We go for our ride now?" she asks.

"Not right now, I need to talk to momma."

"Fine," she huffs.

"I promise, we will ride soon," he says before he kisses her cheek.

"We better," she sasses and Loki laughs.

She goes running back into the house and I meet Loki halfway.

He wraps his arms around me, lowering his face to mine before kissing me senseless. All too soon, he releases me.

"I know your brother taught you to shoot. You got one?"

Where is this coming from? I nod to him.

"You need to go get it, get changed and I'll be back in five minutes," he says in a way that isn't meant to be argued with, so I turn for the house. I turn to my left so he gets an eyeful of Loki branding on my arm and he whistles. I roll my eyes and head into the house.

Within five minutes, I've changed my shirt from the t-shirt I had on to layered tank tops, thrown on my shoulder holster and put my cut on over it, swapped my Chucks for boots and I'm waiting outside for Loki.

I'm barely there a minute when he comes roaring down the street. He stops at the curb and I climb on. I'm barely situated when he takes off down the street toward the diner we ate at yesterday. I expect him to turn left toward the club but instead, he turns right.

"Where are we going?" I ask him.

"Pyro's, he has something we need to see."

I nod against his back as he continues down the street. My heart starts pumping a little faster as he's weaving in and out the cars. It's Saturday morning in Roswell so the traffic is thicker.

It takes about ten minutes before we're pulling up to a nice adobe style home. The yard is cleaned and maintained, the garage door is open and there are two bikes inside. The one I've seen Pyro riding and another one that looks like it's in pieces. The image reminds me of home. Kellen always had one bike he was working on and then the one he rode regularly. The one he worked on was usually vintage in some fashion or another, but this one, though not new, looks like it's seen better days.

Loki leads me into the garage and I get a better look at the bike.

My heart freezes in my chest. I'm looking at a nineties version of a Heritage Softail like my father used to ride. In fact, the coloring is very similar to it and it sends my mind into a tailspin, back to my dream, and the videos. Kellen is alive, somewhere. And Kellen loved dad's bike. He spent days out in the garage working on it after dad's death. Eventually the bike disappeared; he'd told me he sold it.

"What's wrong?" Loki asks.

"The bike." I jerk my head in its direction. "Dad used to ride one just like it."

I notice Loki stiffen slightly. "You remember that?" he asks.

I nod. "There isn't much about them that I've forgotten," I share with him. "Kellen said he'd sold it years ago."

"There's a lot of bikes out there like that," he says.

I frown but shrug it off. It's not possible.

Loki leads me into the house. I hear voices, several of them, some

204

louder than others. They obviously match the bikes out in front of Pyro's house.

"What is she doing here?" Pyro asks.

"This is club business, Loki," Sticks snaps and I glare at him.

"She has a right to know," Loki states vehemently. I feel slightly championed and at the same time, I want to leave the house immediately.

Sticks, Big Daddy, Whistler, two guys from Tucson I don't recall ever meeting, Sticks' right hand man Pixie – yeah, we'll discuss that later – and then Cowboy. The last one surprises me.

"Where's Opie?" someone asks.

"Opie is no longer a part of this circle," Loki says. "The night of the funeral, I caught him conspiring with Rooster and Gunnar."

"About what?" Sticks snaps.

"Me," Loki states simply and my heart sputters.

"What about you?" I ask and he looks at me, sadness in his eyes.

"They we're trying to use Stoney to get to me, to make me vulnerable."

"Who's Stoney?" I ask, my blood pressure rising.

"This isn't relationship counseling, darlin," Big Daddy says and I let it go.

"Stoney is a stripper at Cottontail. Gunnar and Rooster had set her up to attempt to set me up. When I shut her down, Gunnar, being the prick that he is, pounced on her. Only he didn't make a secret of it and I caught them."

"They didn't know we were there," Pyro adds. "But the long and the short of it is they were going to move on to Taz, to see if she could get to Loki because they're planning something."

"My best guess is they've found out I'm trying to make a move for Pres," Loki says and I stiffen.

Big Daddy's words come back to me in a rush, 'you just handed him the club.' "He knows," I add.

Nine pairs of steely biker eyes glare at me. "Yesterday, after the funeral home service, I was swapping shoes by Loki's bike and Gunnar came up to me. Said he knows who I am. I didn't buy it for a second until he called me Kiwi."

Nine pairs of eyes start shifting around the room. "How would he know it's you?" Big Daddy asks.

I shrug, but then reality dawns on me. "Loki colored me, claimed me as his old lady. Why on earth would he do so fast if there wasn't a history between us? Couple that with the fact that I brought Piper around. You saw them the other night. They knew instantly that Piper is Loki's. If he managed to gauge her age, or overheard anyone asking how old she is, he may have been able to put two and two together. If Gunnar and Rooster know who I am, that means they know I never died in that crash."

"The only way they could know that is if they..." Pyro stops talking for a heartbeat. "Motherfuckinggoddamnsonofabitch. I fucking knew it."

"Care to enlighten us?" Sticks asks him. His patience is wearing thin, I can tell by the tone of his voice.

"The only way they'd know I didn't die in that crash is if they caused it to begin with," I breathe.

Loki's arm comes around me, holding me to his side. "That was ten fucking years ago," Big Daddy sputters. "You were a kid, what, twelve, thirteen? How the fuck would they even put two and two together after all this time?"

"I colored her," Loki breathes. He brings it back around to what I was saying before. He walks away from me to start pacing the living room.

"What the fuck does that have to do with anything?" I growl.

"Because," he snaps at me. "Because you showed up, in town, with my kid, who looks exactly like me, precisely long enough to be gone for her to grow up. When Tryke died, I handled the house. I took care of it, but there was one thing that wouldn't go down in the flames."

"The safe room," I mutter and Loki's eyes meet mine.

WICKED REVENGE

"I made sure the inside was torched, that I could do, but the shell of it remained." Loki's irritation rises.

"I should've just run when I had the fucking chance," Pyro mutters.

I look at him, his eyes are on me and they're filled with a range of emotions- sadness, anger, frustration, longing. He pulls his hair back, making it appear shorter, then he turns to the side, showing me his scar free side and he closes his eyes.

Three things happen at once. I see a hidden tattoo behind his ear, one he'd gotten after mom and dad died. It's a tiny lily. The profile of his features and then his hand is at his eye, pulling down his lower eyelid and his finger is poking it. The light behind him is such that I can see the curve of a contact lens.

My breathing stops.

My mind races at a thousand miles a minute.

Before I even know what I'm doing, I pull my gun from my holster and I'm charging toward him.

He drops his hair and his hands as he falls to his knees. "You god damn son of a bitch," I growl as I put my gun to his temple.

"Kiwi," Loki snaps at me. I turn pointing my gun at him. He puts his hands up in surrender.

"Don't you fucking start, asshole! You knew, you fucking knew he was alive. You knew he was here, and yet you acted as if he were dead."

"I had no choice," he says with regret.

Pain, anger, frustration, fear. It all consumes me. My heart pounds in my chest like it's going to explode.

Anger drives me.

I turn back to Kellen, my mind still in overdrive as I press my gun back to his temple.

"All this fucking time?" I shout. "All this fucking time I thought you were dead, all this time I've been here, you've been here, you've known who I was and you couldn't even say anything to me. You left me, left me when I needed you most." Tears are streaming down my cheeks, all the emotions filling me up and spilling over.

"Lily-bean," he breathes.

I can't stop the sob that wells from my chest. My hand starts shaking and the next thing I know, Loki's arms are wrapping around me. He disarms me and I sink to the floor.

CHAPTER TWENTY-ONE

Loki

"CAN WE TRUST HER TO keep this to herself?" Whistler asks.

"She'd have been safe with the secret all along," Sticks tells all of them.

Kiwi has completely checked out on me. Her tears have stopped but she hasn't moved from my arms. Pyro disappeared a minute ago, though I don't know where he went.

"She's stronger than you think," I tell them all.

"That's obvious," Big Daddy chortles. "She's been through more shit in her life than any of us can possibly imagine." His eyes glare at me.

"I didn't fucking know," I snap. "None of you thought it was important to tell me?" This is the first chance I've had to vent my frustration in regard to Piper and being kept out of the loop regarding her existence and I'm tired of everyone treating me like I'm a fucked-up animal who abandoned his daughter.

"He's right," Kiwi says and all eyes turn back to her. "But," she adds, my eyes meeting hers, "When you never called me back, I figured it didn't matter to you what I had to say because if it had, you'd have called me back." She moves to stand up and I don't want to let her go, but I do. She stands. "Where's my gun?" she snaps.

"You gonna shoot anyone with it?"

"At the moment, no." She glares at Big Daddy and I hand her back her gun. She pops the clip out expertly, then checks the chamber before holstering it again and straightening her cut. She hasn't taken it off so maybe that's a good sign.

"She's armed again, brother," someone says and I turn to see Pyro – Tryke – coming back into the living room. I narrow my eyes at him. Something's different. Then I realize he's taken out his contacts.

He's looking at Lily and they're both just staring at each other. "How'd I not know?" she mumbles.

"The same way I didn't know you were you, and Loki didn't know who you were," Tryke tells her.

"Why?" she asks. "Why not make them think you were dead, then go after them yourself?"

There's a collective sigh around the room. "We have business to discuss, darlin', so if you don't mind, can we save the family reunion for later?" Big Daddy grumbles.

I watch Kiwi as her face turns stoic and she nods, pulling the mask back on.

"Where were we?" someone asks and I get off the floor.

"Kiwi was telling us about how Gunnar knows who she is. Though I'm not sure how he managed to put two and two together," Pyro/Tryke says.

"My disguise wasn't fooling anyone," Kiwi mutters. "I knew if anyone looked close enough, they'd figure it out. The exception being the old ladies and longtime club members, like Cowboy, Shifter," she looks at me, "and the ones that were under my dad's run as Pres. They were always at the house, and they knew me as well as anyone else. But the last time any of them saw me, I was thirteen years old. So, at best, they'd see a family resemblance and nothing more.

"And when Tryke," her voice chokes on the name and she looks at him, "Told them I was dead, and went to the elaborate ruse of making it seem as such, they wouldn't believe otherwise.

"You guys have to remember," she continues, "that this is a biker club, and when members disappear, or die, they are remembered. Their cuts burned, patches are put on the Wall of the Fallen and they're not forgotten. But kids, old ladies, whores, employees, no one gives a shit about them unless they were close."

"We were close at one point," Cowboy chimes in and Kiwi smiles at him.

"I remember that, we were."

"But I still didn't know it was you, not until now," he says to her softly.

WICKED REVENGE

She gives him a melancholy smile. "What I did, what I'm doing here, is because my parents deserve to be avenged. Their deaths were nothing more than a power hungry, ball-less power trip and I've done what I could to prove that point. Gave Big Daddy everything he needed to make a move. You're the ones who've let it go on this long. Now that someone else is going to try and make a play for his position, and he knows it, there's no stopping him unless we stop him first."

"I want to show you guys something," Tryke cuts in. He looks at Lily, sadness and relief battling for the top spot on his features. "I rigged the clubhouse, much the way I rigged the house," he tells her and she nods. "We needed eyes on the inside and while we couldn't possibly know that whatever they were doing was going to be made known inside the clubhouse walls, I had to take a chance." He picks up a remote and points it to the TV. It flickers to life and the picture shows the inside of Rooster's office.

Standing with him are Opie and Gunnar. "Opie was supposed to get close to Rooster and relay information back to us, that was his role in all this. Opie made no secret of his distaste for Tripp following his death and Rooster used that to his advantage. However," I continue, "over time Opie came to realize that Rooster was too fucked up for his own good. Now the reason we know he's failed us is because we had no idea about their plan to take me out. If Opie'd been the person we thought he was, we would have known before Stoney made her move."

"That's not entirely true," Kiwi cuts in and all of us glare at her. "Look, I'm not defending him, but think about this for a second. Rooster and Gunnar have their guards up now, whether Opie tipped them off and turned against you guys or they found out through some other means is moot for the moment. But if Gunnar or Rooster made their plan to try and take out Loki, on the fly, Opie may not have known about it."

"Then why hasn't he come to us since the other night?" Tryke asks. "I tried reaching out to him to no avail, so again, Opie is still out."

Kiwi shrugs. "What's on the tape?" Whistler asks and the tape starts playing.

I'm watching with rapt attention as Opie, Gunnar and Rooster pull up the linoleum floor in his office after having moved a filing cabinet. Beneath the floor is a safe. Due to the video quality, we can clearly see the combination as Rooster turns the wheel before wrenching the handle and pulling the door open. It's a good size safe. "Get it out of here, take it to my house and put it in my safe," Rooster orders.

"Combo?" Opie asks.

"The same," Rooster says.

We proceed to watch Opie and Gunnar empty the safe. As they do, more and more stacks of bills come out.

"Fuck, there has to be a good two to three million there," Pixie says.

"How long has this asshole been skimmin'?" Sticks asks.

"As best as I can tell, about two years before I was killed," Tryke answers. "But the amounts were smaller, less noticeable, but none-the-less they added up quickly." He pauses the video. "There's more of the same, I'll show you the last part in a minute. During the three-year gap when I wasn't here, while going back through the books, I noticed a few things happening. One being large drug orders would come in, our usual take, and that money would replace the drugs, dollar for dollar, no problem. But then I started noticing more drugs being brought in from different channels and kept off the books. Then I noticed more money being spent on supplies, excess inventory for the shops, but when that inventory was catalogued, it never existed and the drug income stayed about the same. So, the drugs being purchased with the money allocated for inventory never made it into the books.

"That's when I noticed the profits at the shop, Cottontail, Iron Wings, and Pixie Sticks (yup, it's named for exactly who you think it is, only in this case a clothing boutique owned by the Angels were falling in comparison to the amount of inventory being ordered. But purchasing was still increasing, meaning an increase in drugs and overinflating the shop's books."

Cowboy steps forward. "It was around this time that Rooster ordered us to start watering down alcohol and we pushed more and more drugs through the bar. Our alcohol consumption decreased based on the watering, but the profit lines stayed the same and our drug business tripled."

"So, you see where this is going?" Tryke asks the room.

"He was using the legitimate businesses as a front to push more drugs. Offsetting his profits by reducing actual inventory," Kiwi cuts in and everyone looks at her. She shrugs. "Club business," she snarks.

"Go on," Sticks tells her.

"It's a classic coop. If you make it look like you're purchasing more inventory, when in reality you're purchasing less, you're making money. The money allocated for said inventory is getting sandbagged, thereby raising very few questions on the books side of things. Rooster probably used that money to purchase more drugs, a more profitable business in his mind. More drugs meant more business, and more business meant more money going straight into his pocket."

"Huh," someone says.

"Why didn't you stop him from running Iron Wings via the clubhouse?" Kiwi asks Cowboy.

"By then, Tryke was here, running the books, working the numbers, finding discrepancies. We agreed to work together on bringing Rooster down, so we did as he asked, followed his instructions to keep up the ruse. The more we handed Tryke, the easier it became for him to figure out."

"All that combined with the video coverage leads us to today. He's freaking out and that means he's moving the money."

"What if he moves it out of his house?" Kiwi asks.

Tryke points the remote at the TV again. "This was an hour or so later at Rooster's." He starts the video.

I watch as Gunnar and Opie carry in bags of cash from a truck in the front yard. The camera shifts to another angle and they're in an office, bringing in the same bags and setting them in front of a safe hidden in the wall. We watch as Opie puts in the combination, again it's visible with some finagling that I know Tryke has already done. The safe opens and inside the safe are several more stacks of cash. "I can only assume this was moved before the cameras were installed. I have combed through three years of footage on a daily basis and nothing. So, assuming that's the case, this here, is the money they accused me of stealing in order to take me out."

The two on the video don't say much while they fill the safe with money. "Now, here's where it gets interesting."

The camera zooms in and we watch as Gunnar puts several stacks of cash in his cut. "The thief is getting played," Pixie says.

"This isn't the first time I've caught Gunnar dipping into Rooster's pockets. Usually it's during a party at the clubhouse when Rooster is distracted by a piece of ass."

"This is our way to Rooster," Kiwi says.

Tryke pauses the video, and we look at her. "Use it, turn him against Gunnar, let him take out Gunnar, you all know he will."

"And Opie?" I ask her.

"If he's really a traitor to us, then Rooster will pull him in closer. If he's not a traitor, then he will use his new position to our advantage. Either way," she shrugs, "it's a win."

A phone chimes with a loud beep causing everyone to jump. Tryke pulls his phone from his pocket. "Oh," he says and then the screen changes again. "This is live."

"Is it set?" Rooster asks on the feed coming from his office.

"She was reluctant to do it, but I gave her a little persuasion. She'll do it tonight," Gunnar says.

"Do we know where he'll be tonight?"

Gunnar snorts, "Prolly at I.W. with that bitch of his." I can see Kiwi visibly stiffen at the implication that he's talking about her. "Though I think she's the one you need to worry about," Gunnar adds.

"I ain't worried about some dumb cunt," Rooster sneers. "That bitch ain't got nuttin' we can't handle."

"If you say so," Gunner remarks.

"Did you take care of the other thing?" Rooster asks.

"Yup, I suspect he's running back to them right now to tell them about what's goin' down. If he does his job, they'll show up tonight ready to throw down."

"You're certain of that?" Rooster sits in his chair.

"He's gonna tell them you moved the money and where you moved it to. Then he's going to tell them that you're handling some shop business and play lookout for them, keeping an," he uses air quotes " 'eye' on you. This way they'll make a play for the money, but we'll be there when they do."

"You really think they're that stupid?" Rooster asks.

"They ain't got no reason not to trust him. He's been loyal to them from the beginning. Feeding them the information we wanted them to have and him feeding us all their information. How else you think I found out about them making a play for your job?"

Rooster steeples his fingers to his lips and sits there pondering what Gunnar is trying to tell him. "Then set it up. Get Loki out of the way first. Once he's down, get the rest of them to move and we'll be waiting for them when they do. Opie will keep us in the loop about when they're gonna make a play for it?"

I can't help rolling my eyes and shaking my head. Yes, the Wicked Angels wants their money back, but if he thinks we're so stupid as to break into his house, while he's still alive, to take it, he's got another thing coming.

"What if this is a setup?" Kiwi asks. "What if Rooster's found out about the cameras in the compound and he's using them to play you?"

"Get it done," Rooster dismisses Gunnar and as soon as he's gone, he picks up the phone on his desk. "You get with them yet?"

A clicking sound happens on the TV and we can hear who he called reply, "Not yet. I've been trying to reach Loki all morning with no luck." I scowl at the screen, despite him not seeing me as he talks to Opie.

"Go to his house if you have to. Jesus, do I have to do everything for you?"

"No, sir," Opie says into the phone.

"Remember what's at stake," Rooster warns through the phone.

"Yeah, I know," Opie says, his voice full of fear though he's trying to hide it.

"I mean it, I won't think twice about killing her."

"I'll fucking do it, leave Jess out of this."

"Oh fuck," Kiwi growls.

"You know the rules." Rooster hangs up.

"If he knew he was being watched, I can't imagine him doing something like that. You go after an Angels' kid and you're gonna have the weight of all the Angels coming down on your shoulders before you can execute anything," Sticks growls. "We protect our own." He fists his hand and knocks it against his chest.

"Opie ain't telling anyone shit. He's knows better. He's thinking that if he handles this, does what Rooster asks, that Jess will be safe again. I'm willing to bet that Gunnar's idea of persuasion when it comes to Taz is her kid, too. The problem is, unless he's taken down, Jess will never have a chance," Kiwi says then takes a deep breath. Her eyes wander over to Tryke. "I'm walking, talking proof of that," she breathes.

"That's it. I'm done," Big Daddy barks. "We're ending this and we're doing it now." There's a determination in his voice and a steely disconnection in his eyes. Something rarely seen, but Rooster has officially trampled on the Wicked Angels name by going after innocent children and Big Daddy will not stand for it.

"What's happening?" Kiwi asks.

WICKED REVENGE

Big Daddy turns to her, putting his hands on her shoulders and she winces at his strength. "Are you ready?"

She sucks in a deep breath and lets it out. "Never been more ready," she tells him. There's a confidence in her voice I didn't expect to hear.

"I'm here, I'm alive. Please for the love of your daughter, Lily, don't do this," Tryke pleads.

"It was never just about you," she tells him, tears filling her eyes. "It's because of Piper, mom, dad, you. You may be alive but those sons 'a bitches took my family away from me and so help me God, I will not let them have that chance again." She moves her eyes from Tryke to Big Daddy. "What do we do?"

"We give them what they want," Pixie says, speaking up for the first time. The man is a beast and the biggest fucking teddy bear on the planet. He got his name because when his daughter turned one, the man was crazy enough to dress up like a fairy for her. Before Pixie was given to him, they called him by his real name, Bear, literally. He wears the name Pixie like a badge of honor. Or an embarrassment. His daughter is now Lily's age and an old lady. Pregnant with her second child.

The idea that Kiwi might get pregnant again sends a shiver of desire through me, but I tramp it down, we have work to do.

"We let Opie reach out. Loki, you go home, wait for him to show up to give you the news."

"He's not called me, at least not before I killed my phone at home before I picked Kiwi up," I tell him.

"Regardless. Give in to him, let him tell you what he needs to say to you. Tell you about the money, maybe he'll slip and give you more than that, but don't hold your breath. When that's over, take Kiwi to work, stay there with her. Let Taz make her move."

"I don't like this idea," Kiwi grumbles.

"We need to let them think they're in control of this situation. I'm sorry, but it has to happen this way." She reluctantly nods to Tryke. "When she's made her move, he'll make his. Take her down, do whatever you want with her, but don't hurt her. She's not doing this by choice," Tryke reminds me.

"I know that," I snap. I'm irritated because they want me to play this part. I want nothing to do with Taz and I don't know how far it's gonna go before I can get my hands on her.

"Make sure you take her someplace neutral, like the clubhouse or Cottontail," Pixie adds.

"What will you be doing?" I ask.

"Moving in on him."

"It's a trap," Kiwi says.

"Yes, but one we're prepared for. We rolled out of town this morning, doll," Sticks says. "But myself, Pixie and half the Boulder members are here still."

"Tucson too. We rolled out. I sent half my guys packing and kept my best guys here. Believe it or not, sweetheart, we knew this was coming. It was just a matter of when and there's no time like the present." Big Daddy's face lights up at the prospect of a fight.

"Why can't someone just challenge him for Pres?" Kiwi asks.

"I did that once," Tryke says. "The morning I was killed."

"Is that why you were in such a foul mood that day?"

Tryke nods at her. "I'd put forth my challenge, the upper levels were supposed to be voting on it. Instead of conceding, he had me killed."

"Wicked Angels in Roswell lost nearly half its members to Tucson and Boulder because of it," Whistler says. "Every one of them want back here when management is right."

"Why did you wait so long to do this?" she asks Big Daddy. "I don't understand why you didn't act the moment I told you what happened to Tryke."

Big Daddy's face grows red with anger. "Are you questioning me, woman?"

"No," she growls. "I don't understand why you've let shit like this go on for so damn long. You're supposed to be the big bad Big Daddy and yet you've waited so long that it doesn't make sense anymore…"

Big Daddy's hand connects with her cheek. "I don't have to explain myself to you."

"Enough!" Tryke and I bark at the same time. Kiwi's hand is on her cheek and I want to go to her, to comfort her, but she's equally as pissed off as Big Daddy is. Her hand draws under her vest.

"You pull that pistol from your side, you best be prepared to fire it, little girl, because I will not hesitate," Big Daddy growls at her. Kiwi freezes. "Get her the fuck out of here, lock her down."

"No, don't," Kiwi argues with him.

Big Daddy gets back in her face and she doesn't back down, it makes my dick hard. "Why I do the things I do is none of your goddamn business. Up until forty-eight hours ago, you were a bar slut, you held no power over anyone. But we gave it to you because you're family. Always have been, always will be and family is always first, but goddammit, I do not have to explain my actions or choices to you."

"Alright," Sticks says, pulling Big Daddy away from Kiwi and she stands tall, proud, confident. My dick twitches. "Rooster's family, Lily."

"What?" she glares at him.

"He's not a brother, like your dad, Devon and me, but he's a Beaumont. And being a Beaumont affords latitudes, as you very well know." Sticks raises his eyebrows at her. "Get me?"

"Murder is a latitude?" she challenges.

"Until an hour ago, we had no proof that Rooster killed Tripp. You've provided that to us, and now, we're going to act on it," Sticks growls. "As far as Tryke is concerned, we backed off at his request. He wanted the chance to take Rooster down himself. Only difference is he wanted to do it in a way that wouldn't just put a bullet in his skull. Everything he's collected is proof in an ongoing investigation with local LEOs. Gunnar may go down with a bullet through his skull, but Rooster will go down with shackles around his wrists and where he goes from there is up to the guys already on the inside."

"That's not how Angels handle business," she grumbles.

"It's exactly how we handle business. We are not in the business of killing people. When you walked in my door six years ago, you were armed with a wealth of information that I took to Whistler, who passed it on to some of his LEO friends." Big Daddy's expression softens and he jerks his head toward one of the guys Sticks brought with him. "We'd like you meet ATF Special Agent, Jethro Jackson."

The man I know as Sketch, steps forward. "Nice to meet you, Lily," he says extending his hand to her. She takes it slowly. "Your uncle is right, we've managed to gather enough information to finally take Rooster down for extortion, money laundering, illegal firearms sales and distribution, and a whole host of other crimes, including, but not limited to murder."

She shakes her head in disbelief. What else is she gonna say? "We may be the bad guys to most people, the 1%, but we abide by the laws," Sticks says.

Kiwi laughs, "Bullshit."

Sticks shrugs. "Well, for the most part." He smirks.

"So why only Rooster? Why not you or Big Daddy?" she counters.

"Brass balls this one has," Whistler chuckles. "Because we've made friends with the right people and while we may sell drugs, and offer sexual services, we've never adventured into the trafficking of drugs outside our communities."

"Oh yes, because that's better." She shakes her head. "I don't need to know the details. I just want him taken out."

Big Daddy shakes his head and Sketch moves off to the side. "What would you rather have us do?"

"More like what I'd rather do."

"Which is what exactly?" Tryke asks.

"Put a bullet through his skull." Her voice is dead serious and a couple of us, including me, can't hold back our chuckles. Her face goes hard. "What, you don't think I could do it?"

"It's not that, but where's the fun in that?" Whistler asks. "He dies and you live with the nightmares of watching his lights go out."

"Well, I'd planned on putting one in each foot and shoulder before I went there." Again, she's like a feisty fiery kitten that's still got her claws. It's hot as fuck and my cock throbs.

"Now that's an idea," Pixie says. "You that good of a shot?" Pixie challenges her and Sticks busts out laughing.

"I wouldn't challenge her if I were you. Pix."

Pixie straightens up a little. "Oh, this could be fun."

Sticks shakes his head. "Your funeral, man, your funeral."

"Let's go, outback."

"How in the fuck did we go from plotting a take down to a duel in the backyard?" Tryke laughs.

"You got extra ammo?" Pixie asks Kiwi. She reaches into her cut pocket and pulls out two clips.

"That gun legal?" Sketch asks.

"Oh yeah," Tryke answers. "I gave her that gun for her sixteenth birthday."

"Posturing at its finest," I mumble and a few laughs ring out.

The next thing I know, we're in Tryke's backyard, hay bales stacked, targets pinned to them. They're made out of human forms. Tryke runs back into the house and returns a few minutes with pictures of Rooster and Gunnar taken from the feeds in the compound and he pins them to the targets.

"What we playin'?" Kiwi asks and my cock strains in my jeans.

"Whatever you want," Pixie says and I watch as Kiwi checks her clip again and then loads the chamber.

She stands, spreading her legs. Tryke's chest puffs up with pride. She files off four rounds.

"Oh shit," Sketch swears and he starts laughing. Tryke's fighting a laugh and I'm staring like an idiot with my mouth open.

"Uh, sweetheart, you missed," Pixie says as he looks at the target where there are four random bullets peppered through the paper.

Sticks is practically on the ground because he's laughing so hard.

"Let me try that again," Kiwi says, humor in her voice.

She re-poses and fires off the next four.

"Jesus," Sketch says.

My mouth is officially on the ground and Pixie is just glaring at the target. Still no bullets in the body on the target, but she hit the exact four spots she hit originally. She cocks her head in challenge to Pixie. "You're up, slugger."

"Uh huh," Pixie says and he repeats four shots, then immediately fires the next four. The pattern is nearly identical to hers.

"Alright," she smirks. "Kell, you got more bullets?" she asks and I see Tryke's face light up when she uses her nickname for him.

"You know I do," he tells her.

"We're gonna need them."

These two continue posturing for another ten minutes. Pixie goes first on the second round and he clips the armpits of both targets from his position. Kiwi poses and shoots down the same holes Pixie left.

The next round is Kiwi's turn and she walks up to the targets and pulls off Rooster and Gunnar's faces and returns to the invisible shooting line. She reloads her gun, all fifteen bullets locked and loaded. She steadies herself before she fires.

"One, two, three, four, five, six, seven, eight, nine," she says quickly as she fires.

Sticks and Big Daddy are rolling with laughter and I cock my head at the target. She's shot two eyes, a nose and a mouth on the target before sending one flying through the middle of his head. It's nearly perfect.

"Alright, so you can shoot when you're standing still," Pixie says. "Load it." He nods to her hand. Tryke hands her the box of bullets and she reloads her gun. Pulling back the chamber, she's ready to roll. Pixie takes up another target, replacing the one that's been shot to shit. He pulls her smiley face one off and he holds it up to the sun, and the sun shines through it, leaving a smile face shining on his own. He folds it up and tucks it under his arm before hanging the clean one up. He returns the picture of Rooster's head to the target.

From this distance, I can barely make out Rooster's ears. I don't know how anyone can make a shot like that from here, but it's obvious Kiwi is up to the challenge.

"Alright, Kiwi. Give him your best. But you have to look at Tryke," Pixie says. "Not the target."

I look over at Sticks who is obviously biting his tongue to stop from laughing. "Better yet, why don't you stand in front of me, or behind me and you can cover my eyes," she challenges. Now that Pixie is out of her line of sight, he's moved over toward Tryke. She turns to face them both. Her arm extended, she starts walking toward them, firing in rapid succession over her shoulder, shell casings flying, her body moving, her eyes never leaving Tryke, my eyes never leaving the target.

"Jesus fucking Christ," I sputter as she fires off the last bullet.

Four in his head, square, four in his chest and one in the general area of the target's crotch. Her gun is letting off some smoke as she holds it up to her lips and blows the barrel.

Tryke explodes with laugher. Sticks and Big Daddy are staring like idiots. She cocks her head at Pixie. "Care to challenge?"

He puts his hands up in mock defense. "No, ma'am, I don't."

"She keeps this shit up and Wicked Angels just might induct its first woman," Big Daddy says, clearly shocked.

"She rides too," Tryke says, humor in his voice and light in his eyes.

"Oh, now that's one way to get under Rooster's skin," Cowboy, who's been quiet since before we came out here, says. "Let her ride."

I walk up behind Kiwi as she holsters her empty gun beneath her arm. I wrap my arms around her and whisper in her ear, "My dick is so fucking hard right now. I want to bend you over and fuck you stupid, right here in front of everyone."

"Caveman," she murmurs, humor coloring her tone.

"You ever want a job, give me a call," Sketch says. "I know a few guys who could learn a thing or two from you."

She laughs, "It's one thing to shoot a paper target, it's a whole other thing to shoot a living being."

"Don't let her bullshit you. I took her hunting once. Just once. Sticks shakes his head. "She nailed that dear perfectly in the chest, it barely bled it died so fast."

"Oh bullshit," she counters. "Exaggerating much?"

"Okay, it bled, but not as much as it would have, it literally dropped dead." Sticks puffs up proudly.

"I have to get to work," Kiwi says. "So what's the plan?"

We spend the next hour going over the details before we leave. Cowboy calls Loni to let her know Kiwi's been held up but she'd be there before it gets really busy.

Before we leave, she reloads her gun and her two spare clips from Tryke's stash and puts them back in their places. Tryke stands before her, and all the questions, answers, and mixed emotions between them are palpable. I step back, watching from a distance, allowing them a minute to themselves.

Kiwi touches the scar running down Tryke's cheek and he wipes a tear from hers. They don't appear to say anything; they don't need to, not really. I'm just glad the secret's out of the bag. I couldn't stand holding it in anymore. It's bad enough she had a reason to hate me over it, holding it in much longer and I was gonna fucking lose my shit.

It was the unspoken secret between us. Cowboy is the only other Roswell Angel who knew. We never let Opie in on that fact. We were too afraid he'd figure out a way to use it to his advantage. I guess maybe we always knew Opie would turn tail as soon as he could.

She climbs on the back of my bike and her hand traces over my cock. "Bitch," I groan and she laughs against my back. She keeps it up the whole way back to her place.

It's five-thirty when we arrive and Piper is eating when we step into the house. She comes over and gives Kiwi a hug and then latches on to me. "Missed you, Loki," she says then she kisses my cheek.

"What have I become? The invisible woman?" Lily teases her.

"Loki let me have ice cream for lunch," she reminds me.

"This is true." Lily nods and smiles. "He did, didn't he? Yeah, I'd miss him too."

I set Piper down and she takes my hand. "I want to show you something." She pulls me toward the kitchen.

"I'm gonna go get ready," Kiwi lets us know and she disappears.

Piper shows me a drawing she did. "What's that?" I ask her.

"It's you, mommy, and me," she says pointing to each of us respectively.

"What are we doing?" I ask her.

"Riding your bike." Her excitement is clear. Her personality is dripping off the page she's colored, and I can tell she's gotta be a handful in school, but her drawing is really good.

"Well done, princess." I kiss her on top of her head. "I'm gonna go find mommy, okay?"

"Okay," she says but wraps her arms around my neck for a tight squeeze before she lets me go.

Leaving Piper to her coloring, I start toward Kiwi's bedroom. My cock is hard as fuck, but with each step I grow more and more pissed off. There's been a lot of fucked up shit these last twenty-four hours, but what I can't fathom is why revenge is so important to her? I get it, I want Rooster, Gunnar and maybe even Opie, dead, too, but that's my job, not hers. Not when she has my daughter to take care of.

Why? Her parents are gone, left her at a young age so why in the fuck would she risk her life and leaving Piper without her?

I need answers.

I keep walking down the hall and into her bedroom, expecting to see her there, but I don't, instead I find her in the shower.

CHAPTER TWENTY-TWO

Kiwi

"LOKI?" I CALL WHEN THE bathroom door opens, I get no response.

I shrug, must be my imagination.

Then the curtain is drawn back and he's standing there, buck naked, cock hard, a fierce expression on his face. "What's wrong?" I ask.

"Shut up," he growls and steps into the shower, grabbing my shoulder and spinning me around, pressing me against the tile. He places his forearm at the back of my neck, locking me in place.

"Loki, what the fuck?" I growl but it's pointless. His hand slides up between my legs and my body trembles at his touch. The hold he has over me when it comes to sex kills me, but this is so much worse. My body is igniting with desire and yet all I want to do is slap him.

He pushes my legs apart then wraps a hand around my waist, pulling me toward him a little. His arm moves from my neck and his hand slides into my wet hair, gripping it tight and holding me to the wall.

Without warning, he pushes himself inside me, hard, fast.

Angry.

I cry out.

"Loki, please," I beg him. "What's wrong with you?"

"Shut. Up." He emphasizes each word. There's an unspoken threat tacked on to the end of those two and I cringe away from him.

He picks up his pace, faster, harder. My body comes alive with the need to come, despite the tears forming in my eyes. I don't say anything, afraid of what he might do if I did.

A few more pumps into me and he pours his seed into me with a growl.

He pulls out and holds me to the wall as he rinses his cock in the water.

Then he steps out of the tub before letting me go.

My head is screaming that I should slap him, but I can't move. I remain frozen as Loki disappears into my bedroom.

The tears I'd been holding back consume me and my knees give out.

After a few minutes I manage to pull myself together and finish my shower and climb out. I gingerly towel off. He didn't hurt me, not physically at least, but I can't even begin to wrap my head around why the fuck he'd do something like that.

I was in the shower long enough for him to dress and leave, that was the point after a couple minutes. I wanted him gone and out of the house. Knowing he wouldn't stick around after something like that pushes me into motion, I have to go to work.

I towel off quickly and toss the towel in the hamper in my bathroom and go into my bedroom to find my outfit for tonight.

A squeak tears through my throat when I see Loki, fully dressed, sitting on my bed. "What in the fuck was that? What the fuck are you still doing here?" I screech at him and his eyes meet mine. There's some unnamed-never-before-seen emotion playing in his eyes. It's a combination of anger, pain, and something else. "Get out," I tell him.

He stands, rounding the bed and coming toward me. He gets to me before I can make a break for it. His hand slides around my throat, not painfully, but enough to know it's there and he pushes me into the wall next to my dresser. "Give it up," he growls.

"What the fuck, Loki?"

"Your vendetta, give it up."

I glare at him. "What are you talking about?" He shoves against me a little harder, again, not painful, just enough to remind me that he's driving this circus.

"Rooster, Gunnar, give it up," he growls.

"No," I snap.

"How?" His voice softens at the same time as his eyes do. "How can

228

you possibly put yourself in a situation like this and never once think about the consequences of your actions?" he asks and I'm baffled.

"What consequences?"

"What happens to her," his free hand points toward the door, "when you don't come home? Does she deserve that, Lily? Does our daughter deserve to grow up without you just so you can settle a score?"

I let out a rushed breath and sag against him, giving up my physical fight in hopes that he'll let me go. "She's the reason I'm doing it," I breathe. He releases me, but keeps his body pressed to mine. "I need her safe."

"She was safe in Boulder," he snarls at me.

My eyes widen at his tone. He's never been so pissed off at me before and I don't get it.

"You brought her back here, you made her unsafe, Kiwi. She was safe there and now? Now they know about her, they know she exists and if they can use Jess and Hunter to get to Taz and Opie, what makes you think they wouldn't use Piper to get to you?"

His words slice through me like a hot knife through butter and my knees weaken.

Loki's hand comes to my face and I flinch. His eyes widen in shock then his features soften in regret. "I'd never hit you," he breathes. "I may get rough with you, Lily, but I will never, ever hit you." He's growling in anger toward the end.

"Reflex," I whisper.

"Give it up, for Piper, for me? Please. Let me take care of this," he pleads.

"I can't." My voice comes out breathy and barely audible.

"Yes, you can. For her. For me." He lowers his face to mine, inches away from my lips. "I will not let anything happen to you or Piper, not now, not ever. Please, let me do this my way."

"We have a plan," I counter.

"Fuck the plan." The hand near my face gently strokes down my cheek.

"You're more important to me than any plan they make. Let me finish this. Let me finish what we started. Stay out of it, stay away from it. Just let us do this our way, please?" he pleads. His voice grows more urgent with each word. More desperate. His eyes flicker back and forth between mine, unable to focus on one or the other, mine are doing the same. Reading him.

Can I do this? Can I give it over to Loki to handle, for Tryke to do as he's always done and protect me? Protect Piper?

I know the answer. I knew the answer the moment Piper was born. I knew, despite the years behind the gun, taking self-defense classes, learning to fight, that in the end the Angels would handle it. I wanted them to handle it. Sure, I would be pissed, at first, but eventually, knowing those men could no longer harm me would bring me the peace I've been searching for. The club has always protected its own. Why should I be any different? But I want, no, need a finite way to feel that revenge is met.

Can I truly step back now and hand it over to them?

"Okay," I breathe and Loki relaxes instantly, his hands cupping my cheeks, lifting them up to his lips and he presses into me. His cock hard, my pussy still wet from the shower, my need to come balancing on a blade's edge. His lips gently press into mine.

They're warm, soft, everything opposite of the war that was raging through him a minute ago. He gently strokes my cheeks with his thumbs. His kiss is different, he's different. Not just from the shower, but period.

His gentle kisses continue and my heart nearly explodes in my chest. This is it; this is what kissing your lover feels like.

I wrap my arms around his neck, holding him to me as tight as humanly possible. I can't get close enough to him. I can't pull him into me the way I need to feel him.

With my arms around his neck, I use that as leverage to lift my legs. He catches on quickly and presses me further into the wall. I don't care that he's dressed and I'm completely naked.

All the words he's said, all the looks he's given, his demands that I back off, all of it has come to this. He's protecting what's his, he's claiming what belongs by his side and he's doing it with unconditional love and devotion. And he'd do it with or without his brothers at his back. My revenge is his revenge in a sense.

I pull back from the kiss, our hooded eyes meet. "Finish it," I breathe.

And finish it, he does.

"Take your bike," Loki says as we're leaving the house.

I'm an hour and twenty minutes late for work, and even though Loni knew I'd be late, it still makes me crazy. I hate being late. "Are you fucking nuts?"

He gives me a smirk that says, 'well, duh,' and adds, "Want to piss him off, ride the bike."

"One minute you want me in the middle of all this, the next minute you're fucking me in the shower like a caveman because you're pissed off and you want me to back off, the next you want me to rile him up? Seriously, Loki, you're making my fucking head spin."

"Just because I want you safe, doesn't mean you can't have a little fun in the process." He winks.

"Loni will send me home."

He snorts, "No, she won't, I'm calling Cowboy now."

"Where are you going?" I ask him.

"I'm swinging back by Pyro's" I cringe. I don't like that name anymore and he gives me a sad smile. "Then I'm coming to the bar." He winks

I smile and climb on my bike.

"Jesus, one of these days I'm gonna fuck you bent over that thing," he growls.

"Fiend."

"Only for you, baby, only for you." He smirks and sits down on his bike as he pulls his phone from his cut. "Cowboy," he pauses, "Yeah, we're all set. Hey, listen, do me a favor. You at the bar?" He pauses again. "Okay, good. Tell Loni not to freak out on Skit again." I can't hear Cowboys reply. "Alright, see you." He hangs up. "We're good," he tells me.

"She has no idea what she's not freaking out about, does she?"

"Not a fucking clue," he laughs and kick starts his bike. I follow suit and fire up mine.

He leads the way down the street until we get to the light. He's going right, I'm going left, but we're side by side. "I could get used to this," I say over the roar of our engines.

"I'm tryin," he smirks and the light changes. He flashes me a wink and we both take off.

The rumble of the engine brings me a new calm and I find my center as I drive to work.

Loki was right. Loni didn't say a fucking word, but she glared at me when I came in the door. I apologized for being late and she softened. I know she's not mad about my tardiness, she's pissed because her husband, who winked when I came in the door, told her to back off.

A little while later, Loni and I are alone and out of ear shot so I whisper, "I did it on purpose."

"Why would you want to rile that man up?"

I give her an evil smirk. "Because, he deserves it." She shakes her head but smiles nonetheless. "Thanks for understanding," I add.

"I can't argue with that logic," she says and goes back to tending bar.

It's almost three hours later when Loki shows up with Tryke, Pixie and Sticks in tow. They don't sit in my section but I swap with Kat, giving her one of mine in exchange for the boys. She gave me a knowing smirk and a wink before I sashay to their table.

Once I'm there, I lean over and Loki growls at me. I wink at him. "What'll it be boys?" I drawl.

232

WICKED REVENGE

"Fireball," Sticks says. I knew that answer before I asked the question.

"All the way around," Tryke says. I notice now that his contacts are back in, his hair is down, styled in a way that makes him Pyro and not Tryke. But there's still something different about him, weight maybe. A burden is finally gone from his shoulders, perhaps?

"Comin' right up," I say as I push off the table and head toward the bar. Loki smacks my ass as I pass him, hard, and I yelp.

Loni rolls her eyes and shakes her head as I approach the bar. "They drinkin' fireball tonight, Lon."

She raises an eyebrow at me, and I shrug. "Okay then," she laughs.

A couple minutes later I have their drinks in my hand. Loni cracked open a new bottle, poured their drinks then set the bottle on my tray. "Trust me, they'll want it." She winks and I carry it over to the table.

As I'm sliding drinks off my tray, Loki grabs my ass and squeezes. My mouth falls slack when I feel his finger brush along the seam of my jeans that's running right up my slit. "Not fair," I grumble at him.

"Oh, it's totally fair," Loki smirks just before he toasts the others and they shoot down their drinks.

All four of them put their glasses on the table expectantly and I roll my eyes. "Ain't you guys capable of pourin' your own shit?" I ask with a cock of my eyebrow and a smirk.

"Hell no," Pyro says and that's the moment I realize it really is like a weight has left his shoulders. He's never been so animated since I met 'Pyro' about two weeks or so ago.

I smile wide and pour them each another round before leaving them to fend for themselves.

Another hour passes, it's getting close to eleven. I was just beginning to wonder if Taz was going to make her appearance when she comes into the bar. My eyes meet Loki's and he gives me a nod. So far, the plan for tonight is playing out just as Opie said when Loki caught up to him.

Taz doesn't seem like herself when she sits at the bar. Loni waits on her and she orders a drink. Loni gives me the side eye. I don't know how much she knows about what's going down, but even she seems surprised.

I continue serving drinks to my tables and checking on the guys, but Pyro, Pixie and Sticks are getting up to leave so Loki can do what he needs to for the night.

"You alright?" he asks me.

"No, but I will be," I tell him.

"I promise you, nothing will happen between us tonight."

"I know," I breathe.

"I mean it, Kiwi, I'm not like most of these guys. I gave you my patch, you're wearing my brand. Short of putting a ring on your finger, there's no bigger commitment."

My body freezes at the mention of a ring. He leans forward, getting close to my ear and he whispers, "Which I will do." His voice is full of promises at the mention of putting a ring on my finger.

"It's been two days," I breathe.

"I've been waiting a lifetime for you," he adds and backs away from me. I take a deep breath, trying to find my center of gravity before I back away from him. He sits there patiently waiting for me to say something else and I don't know what to say. I simply nod and pull away from the table. My heart races in my chest.

When I approach the bar, Loni comes over to me. "You alright?" she asks, but I'm staring off at nothing. "Yo, Skit?" She snaps her fingers in front of my face.

"What? Yeah, I'm fine."

Loni laughs, "You sure about that?"

I blink. Then blink again. "No," I finally manage.

WICKED REVENGE

"What happened?"

Right as I look at her, I see Taz getting up from the bar after putting her glass on the counter. I turn my focus to Loni. "I'm just... I don't know, but that man seriously knows how to knock me off kilter."

She laughs again. "What he do this time?"

"Told me he was gonna put a ring on me."

She puts her hand on her hip. "You're wearing his patch, his permanent brand on your shoulder and you're freaking out about a ring?" Her eyes are crinkled in the corners as if she's fighting off another laugh. "Girl, to these guys, patching is no different than saying 'I do'."

"Well, shit," I breathe.

"Uh huh," she snickers. "It's only us who freak out about the ring." She leans forward. "Cowboy patched me two weeks into our relationship, he didn't put on ring on it 'til after we had three kids and that was because I begged him to."

"Well, hell, I guess I should've known better."

I glance around and see Taz approach Loki. I turn away from them. "Get used to it," she says, a little disdain in her voice.

"Cowboy one of those guys?" I ask.

"Probably, but I've spent too much time fretting over it, worrying about it, making a big deal about it. The bottom line is, they are who they are." She shrugs nonchalantly.

"I don't know if I can be one of those girls," I whisper.

"Most of them only have the gall to do it away from their old ladies," she sneers.

I try to ignore Loki and Taz. But it's hard. She's not done anything to him but join him and talk to him.

After about twenty minutes, they get up to leave and Loki gives me an apologetic smile as he leaves.

"Seriously? You're gonna let him walk out like that with her?" Loni grabs me.

I shake my head and let it go.

CHAPTER TWENTY-THREE
Loki

TAZ IS IN HER CAR, I'm on my bike, because that's how this rolls. I may be giving into this, but Kiwi is the only bitch I'll have on my bike. We're headed to the back of Pixie Sticks. The club put rooms back there for club members to use and after hours it's usually pretty quiet.

I'm thankful when I get stuck at a light and she goes on ahead. I whip out my phone. "She do it?"

"Yeah," I say into the phone. "When was the last time you swept Pixie Sticks for cameras?" I ask Tryke.

"Yesterday, who suggested it?"

"I did."

"Then you should be alright, but I'll sweep the feeds."

"Thanks," The light changes and I rev, I faintly hear the click on the line and I take off, putting my phone back in my cut and following behind her.

I feel my phone vibrate against my chest, but it just goes once, so it's a text.

A few minutes later, I'm pulling into the back of Pixie Sticks and there is no one else here, as expected.

I park next to her car, and I pull my phone from my cut again.

Pyro to Loki:
Sweep checks out. Watchin.

Some of the tension in my back subsides and breathe a bit easier. My brother has my back.

I put my phone away and grab the keys from my bike. She's waiting by the door. She's nervous and her lack of pick-up tonight has me worried. She's not her usual self and it makes me wonder if she's ready to turn against Rooster.

WICKED REVENGE

I punch in the code to the building and hold the door for her. She reluctantly steps inside and I lead her to the first room on the left. Once inside, I close the door behind us, and she wraps her arms around her midsection and she starts crying.

"What is it?" I ask her.

"I can't do this," she mumbles.

I walk behind her and put my hands on her shoulders. "Talk to me, Leslie." I say her real name and she stiffens.

"They have him," she sobs.

"Who?" I demand with urgency.

"Rooster, Gunnar, they have Hunter."

"Fuck," I groan.

"If I don't do this, they will kill him."

"What are you supposed to do?" I ask her and she produces a syringe from her purse.

"Give you this."

"What's in there, Leslie?" I ask, backing away. She's a woman on the verge of losing it and I don't want her stabbing me with whatever is in that needle.

"I," she sobs, "I don't know. They just gave it to me. It looks like H," she says. "But there's a lot of shit that looks like it, so I have no fucking clue. They told me whatever is in here won't kill you, but it's supposed to take you out and then I'm supposed to call them and let them know the job is done."

Her tears are making it hard for me to understand what she's saying. I reach for my phone.

There's a text from Pyro.

Calling it off. Hunter is more important. Where is he?

"Where is he, Leslie?"

She turns and her eyes are desperate, pleading. "I don't know," she says through quivering tears. "Right before I came into I.W. they sent me this." She pulls her phone from her purse and shows me a picture of Hunter, there's a little blood dripping from his nose and his cheeks are dirty.

I see red, blood fucking red.

"If they want you dead, or drugged, I figured I could trust you to help me," she breathes.

I nod. "You can, but please, give me the needle." She has no problem handing it over to me.

"I want him back, I need him, Loki," she sobs.

"Hey," I tell her as I approach her, having set the needle down on the dresser. I wrap my arms around her.

She sobs in my arms for a moment before sobering. "I'll help you," I tell her.

In a move I didn't think her capable of, she twists in my arms and out of my hold. Something hard presses to my head and I hear the familiar click of a gun being cocked.

"Jesus," I spit and she pushed me to my knees and forces my arms behind me. "What the fuck is with you bitches today?"

She presses the gun harder to my temple and her eyes meet mine, solid green and focused, pointing right at me. "So fucking gullible."

"Are you kidding me?" I tell her. "I'm not your enemy, Leslie. If anyone can save your son, it's me."

"Yeah, by me killing you." The gun rattles a little bit.

"Have you ever fired one of those before?" I ask her. I'm trying to distract her. If she wanted to kill me, she'd have pulled the trigger already.

"Shut up," she snaps.

I fight the urge to roll my eyes. Sure, I have a gun to my head, what else is fucking new. "I know Gunnar threatened you into doing this. Told you if you didn't do it, Hunter would pay. I knew before you walked into the bar that this was the plan and I must admit, you gave off a stellar performance, Leslie."

"Stop calling me that," she snaps.

"That's your name, isn't it?" She doesn't answer me, I didn't expect her to. "I really thought you were scared when you approached me tonight, so well done." I lean into the gun, her eyes widen. I'm not called Loki for nothing. "So if you're going to kill me, do it. But know this before you do, I'm the only one who knows Hunter is in his hands. I'm the only one who has a pretty good idea where he is and most importantly, if you kill me, no one will help you."

"Hunter will be safe," she insists.

"No, Leslie, he won't. You kill me, you do their dirty work, and how long before they hold Hunter over your head again? Next time it won't be as simple as taking down an unarmed man. Next time you could get yourself killed in the process." She doesn't say anything so I continue, "Think about it. You know I'm right. I'm willing to bet this isn't the first time they've threatened you into doing something you didn't want to do." I take a chance, because I need to keep her talking, or at the very least, distracted. "When they kill him, and you know they will, what will you do then? What's stopping them from killing him, even if you kill me?"

I hear the gun rattle again and I take my shot, grabbing her arm and lowering the gun. It goes off, but it doesn't hit anything but plaster behind me. "Oh, God," she cries.

"It's alright, I'm alright," I tell her.

"They're going to kill him."

"No, they're not. A gunshot has rung out. You're going to call them, you're going to tell them that the job is done. Then you're going to find out where they're holding Hunter, or a place to meet to get him back. Do you understand me?" I ask.

She nods, but she's a million miles away.

I tuck the gun in my jeans and grab her shoulders. "Leslie, look at me," I tell her with a little shake and her eyes turn to me, but it takes a minute for her to focus. "Did you hear me?" I ask her.

"Call them. Tell them it's done," she breathes.

"Then find out how you get Hunter back," I say again. She nods, her eyes are glazed over, she's in shock. "I need you to call them, now, Leslie. If there is someone outside, someone that followed you here, they've heard the shot. The longer you wait, the more danger you're putting him in."

"Okay," she breathes.

"Where's your phone?" I ask.

"Purse," she mutters.

Fuck, this isn't going to work. I want to slap her, wake her up, but I'm afraid of hurting her. "Leslie?" I snap. She doesn't move, or even flinch. Fuck. I slap her across the face. It takes a second but she focuses. "There you are," I say softly.

"Why did you do that?" she asks. Tears fill her eyes.

"Because you're in shock, Taz. I need you to focus right now."

"Ohhkay," she says reluctantly.

"I need you to call them, tell them it's done and find out where Hunter is or how to get him back. You hear me?"

"Yes," she says, reaching into her purse for her phone.

I stiffen because I don't know what else this crazy-ass woman has up her sleeve but she only produces her phone.

She presses a couple buttons and puts the phone to her ear. I lean down, listening.

"It's done," she says softly into the phone.

"Good," Gunnar says on the other end of the phone.

"Where's my son?" she asks him.

"Patience, bitch. I need you to do something else for me."

WICKED REVENGE

"No," she snaps into the phone. "I've done what you asked me to do, I've taken him out. He's dead, now give me back my son." The catatonic woman that was standing here a minute ago is no longer here, the mom in her is taking over.

"We're not done with you yet."

"Let me talk to Hunter," she begs. "Let me hear that he's okay."

"Mommy, mommy, where are you? I wanna go home."

She cries, "I'm right here, baby, are you okay? Has he hurt you?"

"I'm scared." His voice ricochets in my brain. He's sounds terrified.

"Now, where were we?" Gunnar returns to the line.

"I've done what you asked, give me back my son," she snaps.

"Not until you've completed your next task."

"What do you want from me? Why can't you do this shit yourself?" she barks into the phone.

"Because it's much more fun watching you do it. Now, I need you to go to Iron Wings, get that bitch of his and put one in the back of her head." The line goes dead.

Kiwi.

"When you dance with the devil, the devil always wins," I mutter. "We've got to get you out of here," I tell her.

"What about Skit?" Tears trickle down her cheeks.

I shake my head. "You're not touching her," I tell her. I grab my phone from my cut. There's a new text from Pyro.

Wow, that was close.

We've got a lock on Gunnar's location. He's in the old warehouse behind the clubhouse.

Rooster is in his house, waiting for us. We have eyes on him.

Cowboy has eyes on Kiwi. They're shutting down the bar early. Stay put.

"Now what?" she asks.

"We wait."

"What the fuck do you mean, we wait?"

Just then my phone buzzes.

It's a group text to all the guys inside the Angels that we trust.

Amber! Amber!

Hunter Ingles – Taken by Gunnar. Compound Warehouse.

Full alert.

Inbound Rescue.

Standby.

The text went to about twenty members of the Roswell charter and several from Tucson and Boulder. Most of which are still in town. "They're going after him," I tell her.

"What do you mean?"

"The club, an Amber has gone out. The guys are in motion. We wait here."

"No!" She charges past me and I wrap my arm around her waist. "I need to be there when they do."

"You'll get yourself killed." She rights herself. "You're no good to him if you're dead," I remind her. She stops fighting me. "Now, I need you to tell me if Gunnar was with anyone when he approached you today?"

"How'd you know it was today?"

"That's unimportant. I need to know if he had anyone with him when he did it."

"No, it was just him."

"Where?" I ask her.

"In the clubhouse. I'd just left Shifter in one of the back rooms."

"You didn't see anyone else?"

"No," she breathes.

"What time?" I ask.

She shrugs. "Early afternoon, maybe around two, two thirty."

I turn my phone back on, pulling up Tryke's number, he answers on the second ring. "We need to go back on the tapes," I tell him.

"From when?" he asks.

"Today, when Gunnar approached Taz."

"What do you want to know?" he asks.

"Was anyone else in the hallway, anyone else watching their exchange."

"No, I checked all the feeds in and around the hallway, the rooms, nothing. Why?"

"I need to know if anyone else has turned against us, working for Gunnar. I need to know if I can get her out of here."

"There's no one else there. I canvassed the whole thing. So, unless they have cameras I couldn't pick up, no one else is there. Inside or out."

"Okay, thanks."

"Yup, they're close," he tells me. "I've got eyes on Rooster via camera and on site. If he moves, we'll know."

"Thanks," I say and hang up the phone.

"I want you to get in your car. I want you to go to Iron Wings." She stiffens. "I want you to stay away from Skit," I warn her. "I will let Cowboy know you're coming. If you don't show up, I will call off the rescue of your son. If you show up and even attempt anything with Kiwi, so help me, God, I will let Gunnar have Hunter. Do you understand me?"

She nods solemnly. "How do I know you won't hurt him?"

"You're alive, aren't you? Unharmed, despite putting a gun to my head?"

"Yesss," she says shakily.

"Then that's your answer. You know you don't put a gun to an Angels' skull and live to tell the tale. You've been around this club long enough to know that." She nods. "That's my insurance. See, if I go spouting about your actions here tonight, you'll have the weight of the Angels coming down on you faster than you can sputter an apology. So, rescuing Hunter is moot. Get me?"

She nods again.

"Good, now get out of here. Get in your car, go straight to Iron Wings and whatever you do, do not step foot on the compound. Hear me?"

"I hear you," she breathes.

"Go, now," I bark.

She jumps and scurries from the room. I follow her to the outer door and listen closely to what's happening outside. I hear her car door shut and the engine turn over. She wastes no time backing out and I hear her engine rev as she goes.

I take a deep breath; my phone vibrates in my pocket. I pull it out, it's Sticks.

"Yeah?" I say into the phone.

"Jesus, you've got brass nuts, man. You alright?" he asks.

"For the moment, what's going down?"

Sticks kept me on the phone for another minute or so, filling me on the situation. They're about to move on the warehouse and I want to get there so bad, but I let him go to call Cowboy.

He answers on the second ring. "Yup."

"Has Taz arrived yet?" I ask.

"Nah, not yet, she coming back here?"

"I told her to get her ass over there, she's to stay there. She even breathes on Kiwi, you let me know."

WICKED REVENGE

"Kiwi's not here," he cuts me off.

"What?" I shout into the phone.

"She left about five minutes ago, said she was going home."

"Fuck," I growl and I charge out the door, drawing Taz's gun from my back just in case.

"I'm coming," I tell him and disconnect the call.

I try calling Kiwi, but she doesn't answer. If she's riding, she wouldn't.

I fire up my bike, tucking the gun behind me again, and I take off out of the parking lot of Pixie Sticks, headed for Kiwi's, not Iron Wings.

CHAPTER TWENTY-FOUR
Kiwi

SHIT'S HAPPENING AND I COULDN'T sit around that bar anymore. Loni kept giving me looks of apology for Loki leaving with Taz. I knew why he did it, but her looks were making it worse and my mind kept wandering around to what it is he could have been doing with her. I'd expected him back sooner and no one is answering my calls. I've tried Big Daddy, Pixie and Sticks. Those are all the numbers I have. I wanted to call my brother, but I don't have his number and calling Loki would blow his cover.

I turn down the street my house is on.

I can't sit here. I have to help in some way.

But how?

I pull in the driveway of my house. The house is dark, considering it's after midnight and both Emily and Piper should be sleeping is normal, but I just don't feel right being here.

I have no idea where Loki went with Taz.

I need to know he's alright.

I back out of the driveway and take off down the street toward Loki's.

A minute later I'm pulling in front of his house and there's nothing going on here. His truck is in the carport, but his bike is gone. He's not here.

My heart sinks. I reach into my vest pocket and pull out my phone. I see a missed called from Loki and I'm about to dial him again when it rings. I idle down the bike and answer the phone.

"Where the fuck are you?"

"Jesus, calm the fuck down. Glad to know you're alright," I snap back at him.

"I'm fine, where are you? You were supposed to stay in the bar," he growls.

"I couldn't take it anymore. Loni kept giving me pity looks because you left with Taz. I couldn't tell her that I knew why. It was pissing me off."

"Where the fuck are you, Lily?"

I roll my eyes. "Maybe I shouldn't tell you."

"She tried to kill me," he barks into the phone.

"You knew that."

"No, she put a gun to my head and tried to kill me. She played me, Lily, like a fucking fiddle."

"Jesus," I breathe.

"When she called Gunnar to tell him I was dead, Gunnar gave her a new target."

"Who?" I ask.

"You," he says and the phone disappears from my hand. Something presses to the side of my head and I know instantly that it's a gun.

"Hello, Loki," a menacing female voice says into the phone. I catch a glimpse in my side mirror and see it's Taz. "I warned you that I was going to get my son back."

She puts the phone on speaker.

"And I told you that if you didn't follow my rules I'd call off the rescue mission."

"Go ahead, she'll be dead in a minute anyway."

"You can't kill her any more than you could kill me."

"I was never meant to kill you, asshole," she sneers and the phone goes dead when she pushes the end button. She tosses it onto the ground and stomps on it. "Now, turn it off." Tells me. I take a deep breath, calming myself down as best I can. I've been in this position before. Granted, the gun wasn't loaded then, but still. I wait for her instructions before moving further. I put my hands up, my keys hooked on my index finger. "Get off," she orders.

I kick the stick down and using my legs, let the bike lean to the side as

I stand up on my left foot. "Off," she orders.

I do my best to gauge her position behind me before I move to kick my leg over. She's standing too close, perfect. At the same time as I kick my leg up and over, I use my arm to knock her arm and the gun out of the way. I kick her in the back pretty hard and she huffs. The gun falls from her hand and lands on the ground. Thank god it didn't go off.

With my left hand, I reach inside my cut for my Glock and I point it at her, flicking off the safety and cocking the firing pin as I point it at her face.

"Well, well, well. What do we have here?"

The voice sends a sliver of ice through my veins. "If it isn't the ever-elusive Lily Beaumont," Rooster sneers my name.

I turn toward him, keeping my gun in my left hand pointed at Taz's head and I pull my second gun from inside my vest, my favorite gun, and point it at Rooster. I flip the safety and cock it.

"Drop it," a voice behind me says and I feel the barrel of another gun press to the back of my head. "Both of them," Opie growls behind me.

"Well, aren't you in a pickle?" Rooster gives me a wicked smirk.

I could kill Rooster and Taz before Opie would get his shot off, but what good would that do if I'm dead, right? Right.

I uncock the guns, holding them and my arms up while at the same time switching the safeties back on and I manage to tuck them back into the holsters under my cut before Opie can snag them from me.

"Get out of here, whore," Rooster snaps at Taz.

"Where's my son?" She screams.

"You didn't complete your mission. Loki is alive, and so is she." He cocks his head in my direction before his face lights up with his phone.

"She failed. Kill him," Rooster orders and Taz lets out a blood curdling scream as she falls to the ground on the other side of my bike.

Her gun is sitting at my foot and I kick it toward her. Her sobs continue, but somehow, I manage to do that without raising Rooster's attention. Opie may have a gun to my head, but I'd like to believe he'd be loyal to the Angels, even if they've threatened his son. "Where is he?" Rooster asks me.

"He, who?" I counter.

"Don't be a cunt, cunt. Loki, where is he?"

"How the fuck should I know?" I snap.

I notice Taz has gotten quiet. Her sobs no longer break through the night.

Loki

"SHE HAS KIWI. ALL BETS are off. Move, now, goddammit. Get him out of there before he gets killed," I bark into the phone over the roar of my engine as I'm racing toward Kiwi's house. I can't hear the reply but I hang up my phone. I may be a monster, but killing children is not high on my list of shit to do. Millions of children are raised without a mom or dad and Hunter will survive that. Taz, on the other hand, will not.

She crossed a line. Tried to kill me and is trying to kill my old lady, the sister of Tryke, the niece of Big Daddy and Sticks. No one will get away with that. Not now, not ever. They let Tryke's 'murder' slide at Tryke's behest. He wanted to do things the right way and since it was actually me who shot him, and besides, if they'd gone after the person responsible, I'd have gone down. Tryke wouldn't stand for that and neither would Big Daddy, and especially not Sticks.

I understand now why Sticks championed me so vehemently. By the time this all went down, Kiwi was pregnant with my daughter.

Anger colors my vision again and I kick it up a notch, taking the corner down our street far faster than I should have and I fishtail out on the other side. I manage to right the bike, but my heart rate triples. "Fuck," I growl.

I roll up in front of Kiwi's. The lights are off, the two cars are there, but no bike. "Fuck, fuck, fuck," I roar down the street. If she was really concerned about my whereabouts, about what was happening between Taz and I, she may have gone to my place.

As I draw closer to my house, fear rattles my nerves.

I'm less than five hundred yards away when I hear a shot ring out. Followed by two more. I open the throttle and go charging for my house.

Kiwi

"DUMB BITCH," ROOSTER GROWLS. I glare at him, both guns pointed at him. My heart is pumping a million miles a second. There's a bike roaring down the street. I'm certain it's Loki, but I don't bother to check. "Not a very good shot, are you?" he sneers.

I aim and fire, clipping him in his foot. He screams as the pain registers. "Say again?"

"You missed, cunt." I aim for the other foot.

"Want to lose both of them?" I growl at him. "Or just your life?"

My gun in my right hand is pointed at his head, my left at his right foot, the one I've not shot yet.

It's eerily quiet now.

"Drop it," I hear someone, Loki, growl at someone.

Taz shot Opie in the shoulder, knocking the gun free and giving me a window to fire back. I didn't know whether or not Rooster was armed, so I shot him first, clipping him on his shoulder with nothing more than a flesh wound.

I promised Loki that I'd let the Angels have their way with Rooster.

"Kiwi, you alright?" Loki asks.

"Perfect," I say back to him. "I behaved," I tell him and he lets out a nervous laugh.

"How so?"

I give Rooster an evil smirk. "I clipped his shoulder, just enough to slow him down. But then he got a smart mouth on him so I shot his foot. He thinks I missed."

He laughs then he snaps, "Drop it, Opie." "You don't want to do this, man," he says and I don't want to turn away from Rooster, so I don't know what's happening. "Taz, you alright?" he asks.

"No," she barks. "He told Gunnar to kill Hunter," she sobs.

"Hunter is safe," Loki says and I breathe out a sigh of relief. "I promised you we'd rescue him."

"But you...I didn't do what you...you said?" she sputters.

"If you know anything about the Angels at all, you know children come first. I couldn't have called them off, even if your life depended on it, he's safe," he says.

"Babe, can we save the small talk?" I ask.

"Just trying to get her to stop pointing her gun at you, baby."

My heart rate speeds impossibly faster. "Drop it, Taz. Don't make this worse than it already is. Hunter is safe. Rooster is here..."

I'm interrupted by Taz screaming, "Shut up, you dumb cunt! You don't know shit!"

I take a deep breath, steadying myself. It's killing me to not pop Rooster in his kneecap and take him down, but I'm afraid if I fire then she will too. Though I don't think she could hit the broad side of a barn if she did.

The quiet night is cut with the roar of motorcycles drawing closer. "You're out of time, Leslie," Loki says. "They show up here, you have a gun at her back, they're gonna take you out and not think twice about it."

"I need to know that Hunter is okay."

"Loki's already told you he's safe," Opie says through gritted teeth, his wound no doubt causing him some serious pain. Rooster starts to go white as he rolls to the ground. I roll my eyes.

"Bit dramatic, aren't we, Rooster?" My voice drips with sarcasm. "You're not dying. You have a flesh wound in your shoulder and I shot your foot. You're not even close to dying." I take another step toward him. Ignoring the fact that Taz has a gun pointed at my back and hogs are roaring closer. "For an evil son of a bitch, you're sure acting like a damn pussy. You're not even armed. What the hell kind of bullshit is that?" I snicker. "Oh, that's right, you have people do your dirty work for you." I'm about ten feet away from him now. "Get up, cocksucker," I growl.

The pussy acts like he's been shot through the heart as he slowly gets up.

"If you think those bikes roaring down the street are going to save your ass, you've got another thing comin'," I tell him. "You see, we all know about your little skimming game. About the millions you've stolen from the club." His eyes flare. "About the hits you put on Tripp, Tryke and Loki." He's finally up to his knees, I want him on his feet. "Stand-up, motherfucker," I order him. He glares at me. "What, can't stand taking orders from a cunt?"

"Kiwi," Loki warns.

"Get. Up," I emphasize.

He finally rises to his feet, though awkwardly. "Taz, you're out of time," I shout over my shoulder. "You gonna lower that gun?" I ask her.

There's no answer.

"The choice is yours, Taz. Live for your son or die because you're stupid," Loki snaps at her.

"Here," she screams. I can't see them and I brace for a shot, but none come.

"Got it," Loki says.

"Good." I take one step toward Rooster. I fire once, hitting his other foot. "That's for my mother," I say with conviction as he cries out and falls to his knees.

252

WICKED REVENGE

"Kiwi, don't," Loki shouts.

I fire again, this time clipping his left shoulder. "That's for my father." Rooster's hand comes up, leaving his other shoulder only slightly exposed. I narrow my eyes and fire another round. "That's for Tryke," I growl as he falls to the ground as Loki's arms wrap around me.

"Easy, he's down, alright?"

"I didn't kill him," I mutter.

"No, baby, you didn't kill him," he whispers in my ear.

"I got my revenge," I breathe out as the biggest weight lifts from my shoulders.

"You did," he returns in my ear as the roar of bikes gets deafeningly loud as they pull up in front of the house. Engines start turning off.

"Mommy!" I hear a scream and I turn, bringing Loki with me just in time to see Hunter put on the ground at Tryke's side.

"Hunter," Taz yells and she runs toward him.

"You got him," I breathe and then everything goes black.

CHAPTER TWENTY-FIVE
Loki

"WHAT'S WRONG WITH HER?" I ask anyone who will answer me.

Cowboy comes to stand in my light. "Is she breathing?" he asks and I nod. "She bleeding?" I shake my head. "She have a pulse?" I gently wrap my fingers around her neck, feeling her heart beat strong, maybe a little too fast, but it's there. I nod. "Then she's just experienced an adrenaline surge." He gives me a smile. "She'll be fine. Some people can't handle the adrenaline."

I nod, but look back at her peaceful face. It's like she's sleeping. I frown.

"What the fuck did she do?" someone growls, and I look up to see Big Daddy surging through the crowd of bikers.

"She got her revenge," I tell him at the same time Rooster groans on the ground.

"Well, fuck me sideways," Big Daddy says as he gets an eyeful of Rooster. He's fucked in four corners and has no hands to try to suppress the pain. It's almost comical to watch. "Get him out of here," Big Daddy orders and Sketch and a couple of his ATF buddies come over and assess the situation. Sketch laughs at the moron on the ground.

"Darius Rufus Beaumont, you're under arrest for extortion, bribery, kidnapping, false imprisonment, assault with a deadly weapon and the murders of Kevin and Lillian Beaumont and the attempted murder of Kellen Beaumont..."

There is a collective gasp at the words 'attempted murder of Kellen Beaumont' followed by some murmurs from the guys. I can't make out all of them, but they're all pretty confused. "Kellen's dead," someone finally says.

"No, I'm not," Pyro says from the back of the crowd of people. I can't see him from here but hear the collective gasp and chatter that follows through the mass of Angels standing around.

Movement in the corner of my eye catches my attention and Sketch and his buddies pick Rooster off the ground. "I don't know how you're gonna explain this one away," one of his guys says.

"I'll just tell them she missed," Sketch mumbles but they help Rooster to the SUV they showed up in. Sticks, Big Daddy and Cowboy laugh at Sketch. He knows damn well she didn't miss.

My attention is drawn back to the crowd of Angels in the street.

"Why?" I hear someone ask.

"For this very night. The night where we take down the man who was destroying this club, destroying the name we've spent the last five decades trying to build into a good, reputable name," Tryke says.

"What now?" someone hollers.

"Now, you name a new Pres," Sticks says. "Tomorrow, noon, clubhouse common room. Those wishing to make their bid, prepare. Those with nominations, you'll have your chance to voice them and three hours to decide. At which point, the Veterans will vote on your nominations and if need be, the members will have their chance." Sticks puffs out his chest a little. "Then tomorrow night, we party," he announces and there is a collective cheer among the men, some fist to chest pounding. Some people approach Tryke. I can't hear the things they're saying, but no one seems disappointed to see him. It makes me smile. Everything has fallen into place.

Too bad Kiwi isn't awake to see it.

The crowd disburses. Bikes fire up and roar off down the street until there's just our little circle left. I'm still sitting on the ground with Kiwi in my arms. Her guns are on the ground at my side. "We have a problem," Pixie finally says to me.

"We didn't want to let the others know, but we don't have Gunnar," Big Daddy shares.

"We found the boy alone in the warehouse," Tryke says.

"Where the hell is he?" I growl.

There's a collective shrug among the men standing before me. "What about Rooster's house? The money?" I ask.

That's when I notice Whistler, and a couple of the Tucson guys are missing from the circle. "We sent Whistler in to collect," Tryke says. "We have it."

"All of it?"

"Aside from the stacks we caught Gunnar stealing on the tape, yeah, it's all there," Big Daddy confirms.

"Now we just need to find Gunnar," I growl.

"We're working on it. Sketch has some of his guys on it too," Sticks says. "Get her inside, tuck her in. She's gonna be out for a while."

"I think I should take her to the hospital," I say softly.

"She'll be alright," Tryke says. "Mom used to faint when shit got too real, too." He smirks. "Just let her sleep it off, she'll be fine in the morning."

"God, I hope so," I grumble and awkwardly try standing when Tryke comes over and scoops Kiwi into his arms. "Thanks," I tell him.

He smiles wider at me and I stand up. I take her back and he opens the front door. I carry her down the hall and lay her on my bed while Tryke stands at the door. I carefully remove her vest, her corset isn't as easy, but I manage. I leave her topless and then pull off her boots and jeans. Leaving her in only her underwear. I kiss the top of her head. "I'm so proud of you," I murmur.

Reluctantly, I leave her to sleep it off and follow Tryke out to the living room. "You really love her?" he asks me.

"More than anything in the world since she was three."

"That's gross, man." He scowls at me.

"It wasn't like that, and you know it." I shoulder check him.

"Take good care of her and we won't have issues." His voice is soft, but definitely threatening in his Tryke way.

"I'm gonna marry that girl one day," I tell him.

He busts out laughing. "You said the same shit when she was born and

256

we were nine."

I laugh with him, "I knew it then."

He holds out his hand and I take his forearm and he takes mine before we bump chests. "You didn't have to come out to them," I tell him. "You could have crawled back to your hole and they wouldn't have been the wiser."

"Yeah, well, I feel better about it and I really fucking hate this haircut," he laughs.

"The scar?" I ask him.

He shrugs. "It was my own fault," he mumbles. "I could have it removed or reduced, but I kind of like it."

"The chicks dig it," I tease him.

He laughs and we leave the house, locking it up as tight as we can.

"I want someone on the house," I say when we rejoin the guys outside.

Big Daddy cocks his head toward the shadows where Axel is sitting on his bike. One of our highest ranked Veterans and the next in line for Sergeant-at-Arms, should I vacate the position. "We trust him?" Pixie says.

"Implicitly," Tryke adds. "He's the one responsible for my being alive. Not to mention half the shit Sketch has to take out Rooster."

I concur with his assessment just as someone's phone rings. Big Daddy pulls his phone out, answering it. "Whistler, what's doin'?" he asks.

He shakes his head. "Fuckin' Christ, alright."

"What's up?" I ask when he disconnects the call.

"We got nothing on Gunnar. No clue where he took off to."

"I might be able to help with that," Tryke cuts in. "We have to go back to the house though."

"Lead on," Pixie says and we all mount our bikes. I can't help my eyes roaming over Kiwi's bike as I go for mine.

"What happened to Opie?" I ask.

"Whistler has him now. Looking for Gunnar."

I cringe. Whistler got his nickname because he likes to whistle while he interrogates you. When the whistling stops, you're dead.

I climb on my bike, looking back at the house again. It's dark and quiet, no lights, no movement and I want nothing more than to be inside with her right now, but I have a job to do. I have to make sure she and my princess are safe, forever.

CHAPTER TWENTY-SIX

Loki

WE PULL UP TO TRYKE'S place and Pixie, Sticks, Big Daddy, Cowboy, Tryke and myself dismount and head inside. "What are we looking for exactly?" Pixie asks.

"I put a GPS tracker on Rooster and Gunnar's bikes. As long as they weren't discovered, we can pinpoint his location."

"And if he's not on his bike?" I ask.

Tryke grins at me. "Then I have his car and his cell phone."

"And if none of those come back?" Sticks asks.

"Then we're fucked," Tryke grumbles.

"Killjoy," Big Daddy says. "Pull 'em up. I'm losing patience with this."

"On it," Tryke says as he sits at his bank of computers in the living room. I never understood half this shit, but he's definitely got everything he needs to do what he's doing. Big Daddy spared no expense when it came to all this shit. Tryke had his own nest egg, but the club paid for it all. Some of the equipment came from Sketch and the ATF. We'll have to return it eventually.

He clicks some buttons and the big screen comes on. I can't tell what's happening, I'm too stupid for this shit, but as long as he knows, we're golden.

I'm watching the screen when three feeds come up, one in Rooster's office at his house, the safe sitting open, no doubt the way Whistler left it. The next is the clubhouse, which is rotating between cameras. Apparently, a bunch of the guys went back there because the place is crawling with people.

"What's gonna happen with Taz?" I ask.

"She's banned from the club," Cowboy says.

"That's it?" I ask. "he tried to kill me, nearly killed Kiwi, and you're only gonna ban her from the club?"

"Don't push it," Sticks snaps. "She did what she did because she didn't have a choice. For whores like her, banishment from the club is a life sentence. Short of killing her and leaving her kid without a mother, there ain't much we can do besides have her arrested. Attempted murder of you, plus assaulting your old lady would carry at least a twenty-year sentence. So again, we banned her from the club. Shifter's not far behind."

I nod. I guess it could be worse. I want her dead, but not at the expense of Hunter living his life without his mother. Bad enough his father's a bastard when it comes to him and Taz.

My eyes roam down to the third screen. "Is that..." I step closer to it, "Kiwi's house?" I ask him.

"Yup, installed it a few days ago," he tells me.

"When?"

"I'm pretty sure you were rocking her world," Pixie adds and I look at Tryke in time to see him shudder. I swallow my chuckle as I turn back to the screen. The cameras at Kiwi's switch between inside and outside the house. One of them lands on Piper's room. I can see she's sound asleep, oblivious to anything else going on.

A fourth camera pops up. "Jesus, ya fucking voyeur," I grumble as my house pops up. The feed flips between different cameras before landing on my bedroom and Kiwi sleeping. "Can you change that?" I groan as I see Kiwi sleeping, on her back, her tits out.

"Leave some clothes on her next time," Tryke says and the camera shifts, flipping through the feeds. On the outside camera I see Axel on his bike smoking. "Alright, here's his phone, though it's off. The last location was the warehouse." He clicks some keys. "His truck is showing parked at his house." Another camera pops up and I assume it's Gunnar's place.

"Fucking pig," Cowboy grumbles and I have to agree with him. It either looks like the man hasn't got a clue what a rag is, or he's never around there long enough to do anything about it.

"We can go back through the footage later," Tryke says. "If he was there, it might give us a time frame on how far away he is. But he didn't take his cage." Our term for cars – you're caged in, no wind in your face, no open road beneath your feet. There's some more clicking on

260

the keyboard. "And this is his bike..." he pauses, drawing out the word slowly. "That's impossible."

"He found the GPS?" Big Daddy asks.

"Had to, or he got rid of his bike, which I don't see happening."

"When was the last time anyone saw him on it?" I ask.

"The funeral," Pixie says. "We were all riding."

"He had to have found it, though I don't know how that's possible," Tryke says. "It's nearly fucking invisible and...shit." Something dawns on him. "He swapped his wheels. I clipped it on a spoke."

"Well, there goes that," I grumble.

"Wait," Tryke says. "His phone just came back on."

"Where?" Sticks asks.

"Triangulating now, give it a sec," Tryke says distractedly as he watches his monitor.

"How'd you even get the phone's GPS anyway?" Cowboy asks.

"Church," Tryke says.

"Ahh," Cowboy says as if that answers everything. It sort of does. Phones aren't allowed in church; therefore it would be easy to snag it because they're all in a box while we're in our club meeting.

"Okay, got it," Tryke says and the screen changes to a map, covering the cameras. "He's outside Pixie Sticks," he says.

"Prolly went to check and see if I was dead, which means he has no idea what Rooster was doing."

"We got eyes on Taz?" Pixie asks.

"No," Big Daddy snaps. "What happens to her now is her problem. If something happens to Hunter, it's her issue unless Shifter comes to us, and even that's a stretch." Big Daddy is pissed and I can't say I blame him. Taz fucked up royally tonight. Not only did it get Rooster shot by Kiwi, but gave Sketch more problems to deal with than he should have. I should be grateful he's not pissed at Lily because he has every right to be.

"We ridin'?" Pixie asks.

"Let's do it," I add.

"Can you bring this shit with you?" Sticks asks Tryke.

"Yeah," he says before closing one of his computers and tossing it in a bag.

"Then let's go," I say as I head for the door.

IN THE DARKNESS

I LICK MY LIPS AS I watch her chest rise and fall.

Her tits exposed, nipples hard.

My cock is throbbing, but I'm biding my time, waiting patiently for the right moment to strike.

I finally have her in my sights.

It's time to take down the cunt who showed up and ruined everything,

Kiwi

"MMM," I MOAN AS LOKI'S beard tickles my back. His body presses against mine. Still clothed, that's disappointing.

I lull in and out of consciousness as Loki continues kissing and licking up and down my back, but it's weird. The beard feels too long, the lips too rough and the mouth too wet. "Loki," I moan.

"Guess again, bitch."

Before I can react, my mouth and nose are covered by something and I'm breathing something in with a noxious smell. My head starts swimming, and my world spins into blackness once again.

262

CHAPTER TWENTY-SEVEN

Kiwi

MY HEAD SHOOTS TO MY right.

Pain registers.

My head shoots to the left.

My cheek is on fire.

I taste pennies in my mouth.

My head flies back to the right.

"Wake the fuck up, cunt."

I hear the smack, my head flies to the left, the pain ignites in my cheek. I groan in pain.

"Much better," the voice snarls.

I try to open my eyes, but they're so heavy. My mouth is dry and it tastes like I've stuffed my mouth with metal, but it's not blood, not exactly, I slide my tongue along the roof of my mouth, trying to wash away the taste.

"Chloroform, effective but disgusting," a voice says. It's softer than the original voice. I try and place it, but my brain isn't functioning like it should.

The last thing I remember was shooting Rooster, then Loki wrapped his arms around me and then nothing.

Images flicker in my mind, but I can't make sense of them.

I finally manage to open my eyes and the room is dark, except the spotlight I'm sitting in. It reminds me of some mafia movie I watched years ago.

Another smack causes my head to jerk back to the right, the pain more intense. "Fuck off," I growl and spit. My cheeks are on fire. Blood fills my mouth. My tongue slides along my teeth, still intact. Then my tongue slides along a scrape on the inside of my cheek and I taste more blood.

"Where's your boyfriend?" a gravelly, nasally voice asks me and I stiffen. It's Gunnar. It was Gunnar who took me, but from where?

How'd he get ahold of me?

"How the fuck should I know?" I say through swollen lips.

My head is whipped to the left and I grit my teeth.

"Try again, cunt," Gunnar snarls at me.

"How the fuck would I know?" I say again.

This time I brace for an impact that doesn't come. Gunnar steps into the light. His face is red with anger, his beard full of shit like he's been kissing gravel. "Where's Rooster?" he asks me this time.

I shrug as best I can. That's when I realize my hands are bound behind me, tightly. The pain of my bindings cuts into my wrists as I try and move. I test my legs, they're bound too.

All of a sudden, my nipple is being pinched, hard, and pulled outward. I cry out. I realize now that I'm topless, no shirt, bra. I look down my body and I can barely see the thin black panties I'd put on this morning. "Where's Rooster?" he says again, grabbing hold of my nipple again, pulling and twisting harder. It burns as pain shoots through me and I thrash under his touch.

"I killed him," I growl at him.

"Bullshit," he says before connecting with my cheek again.

My blood begins to boil.

I test my bindings again and pain shoots through my arms as I do. My shoulders are aching. I look into the darkness and someone else is standing there. I narrow my eyes to focus on who it is, but I can't see.

"He's someplace you can't get to him."

"Try me, cunt."

"What's your deal with him? You guys butt buddies?" I sneer.

That earns me another yank on my nipple, but this time it's the other one. I cry out in pain.

WICKED REVENGE

"You want answers?" I say. "Ask your fucking lackey, Opie, he was there. How the fuck you think he got shot?" I growl.

"Where's Rooster?" Gunnar growls again.

I turn, spitting blood and saliva in his face. "Go to hell, motherfucker."

The next thing I know, my head is being pushed back by my chin. Cold metal presses up hard against my jaw.

For the first time ever, my life flashes before my eyes. Loki, Kellen, Piper, Emily, Sticks, Pixie, Tucson, Boulder, school, you name it. The last picture I see before all hell breaks loose is Piper and Loki together.

I feel a sharp blow to my temple and blackness consumes me once again.

CHAPTER TWENTY-EIGHT
Loki

"THERE'S NOTHING HERE," I SAY as we comb through all of Pixie Sticks property. "No one," I say as I come out of the last room in the back. It was dark as night when we got here, no sign of life anywhere. No bikes, cars, nothing.

"Hang on," Tryke says as he whips out his phone. I don't know what he's doing, but he moves out of the hallway and into the parking lot. Then he comes back in again. "There a basement here?" he asks.

"Not that I know of," Cowboy adds. "There's a storage area below the store, but we checked that."

"Check it again. Look for any other doors down there. The phone is showing in this building," Tryke says confidently.

"Come on," I say to Cowboy and we go back into the store. We're not inside the store three steps when my phone starts ringing. I look at it. "Hold up," I tell Cowboy and I answer it.

"Yeah, Axel, what's doin'?"

"I need an ambulance." Tis voice is weak, shattered.

"What happened?" I growl.

"Shot…" Then I hear the phone crashing to the ground, it bounces off the pavement and I go tearing through the back of the store and down the hall.

"Axel's down," I scream as I launch through the back door. "Call the EMTs," I shout as I kick over my bike, and take off toward the house.

Axel's down.

This is not good.

I don't bother to wait and see if anyone comes after me, I don't give a shit. I blow every stop sign, stoplight and traffic law in Roswell and I make it back to my house in less than six minutes. The ambulance hasn't arrived when I nearly lay my bike down. I notice my truck is gone from the driveway. Forgetting Axel, I tear into the house and go straight to the bedroom.

"Fuck," I scream. The bed is empty, no sign of Kiwi. "Kiwi?" I holler. No response. "Fuck, fuck."

There are sirens blaring and motorcycles roaring down the street when I bolt back out the door and find Axel.

He's alive, breathing, but barely. "When?" I ask him.

"I don't know…" His voice barely above a whisper. "Twenty, thirty minutes after you left," he adds.

"Who?" I ask him.

"Gunnar," he mouths.

"Fuck," I growl. "Come on, Axe, say with me." I smack the side of his face, firmly, but not to cause him more pain. His eyes flutter open again.

"Tryin," he breathes. "I didn't see…already in house…" His breathing is short and ragged. Finally, the ambulance pulls up and following behind them are bikes.

The paramedics take over and begin working on Axel. "Save him," I growl before I return to my bike. Sticks is there. "She's gone. He took her."

"Who?" Sticks asks.

"Gunnar," I breathe. "I'm going back to Tryke," I tell him. "Find that fucking phone."

Sticks nods. I notice Big Daddy talking to the paramedics who are loading Axel into the back of the ambulance.

I can't seem to move. My mind fills with thoughts of Kiwi, Piper, Emily, us, them, her. *Where the fuck is she?* I ask myself, trying in vain to think of any place Gunnar may have taken her. "The phone's a decoy," I snarl.

"What?" Sticks says.

"The phone, it turned on, we went looking for it. Gunnar knew we were on to him. Hence the GPS on another bike. His phone turning on…" I pull my phone from my cut and pull up Tryke's number.

He answers and I snarl, "Get out of there, now. It's a trap!"

I hear his bike fire up. "Location D." he replies as he revs his engine and disconnects.

Tryke

I'M BARELY ON THE STREET when the loudest noise I've ever heard explodes behind me. A massive blast of heat hits my back and I stop, turning my bike hard as Pixie Sticks goes up in a giant ball of flames shooting toward the sky. "Motherfucker," I growl and take off before the cops show up. "Fuck, fuck, fuck," I growl.

I call Loki back. "Code Red!" I scream.

Loki

I ANSWER THE PHONE.

"Code Red!" comes across the line over the roar of Tryke's engine.

"Fuck!" I shout as the ambulance fires up its sirens and takes off down the street.

"What the fuck?" Sticks asks.

"Tryke called a code red," I say and every face glares at me.

"Why would he do that?"

That's when something catches our eyes in the sky in the direction of Pixie Sticks. There's a ball of flames flying into the air before dissipating. It takes a good fifteen seconds before we hear the resounding boom. "Shit," Big Daddy growls.

"Call it," Sticks orders.

I do exactly that, texting all members, Roswell, Tucson, Boulder, and the smaller charters – with three exceptions- Rooster, Gunnar and Opie. They were removed yesterday.

WICKED REVENGE

CODE RED! Building Down. Evacuate All Buildings. Location Delta.

I hear Pixie, Sticks, Big Daddy and Cowboy's phones go off. The call has gone out. "Let's move," I order.

CHAPTER TWENTY-NINE
Kiwi

THE BUILDING WE'RE IN RATTLES loudly and shakes all the way down to the foundation. If it wasn't for the massive explosion that followed, I'd have thought it was an earthquake.

"Aww, looks like your boyfriend went looking for you." Gunnar snickers, "too bad he's dead now."

I spit in his face again, "fuck you," I growl.

He slaps me again.

Adrenaline spiking through my veins again and the pain isn't nearly as bad as it should be, "tie her to the bed. She needs a real lesson." Gunnar orders the other man in the room with us. I haven't been able to figure out who he is, and frankly, I don't care, not anymore. Gunnar leaves the room through a door straight ahead of me. The space is mostly empty but there are a few filing cabinets and what looks like an old desk next to one of them, behind the man approaching me is a table line with instruments. From this angle, I can't make them all out, but it doesn't look pretty.

Now's my chance to escape. I take a deep breath as the man comes into the light. I haven't a clue who the man is, I've never seen him before. He's not even wearing a Wicked Angels patch. I narrow my eyes at him as he comes close to me.

He squats down before me as if he's going to try and undo my bindings and instead, he leans forward and runs a fat, wet tongue over my nipple. Disgust and fear creeps into every corner of my body. I watch the man's pupils dilate as lust consumes him. Fuck.

He opens his mouth again and I try to squirm away from him and the next thing I know, I'm crying out as pain ignites in my right breast as he bites down so hard he breaks the skin.

Hissing and breathing hard through my teeth, trying to find a way to process the pain he's inflicted on me. I need to find my head, I need to get out of here.

He looks up at me with the evilest smirk I've ever seen in my entire life, blood, my blood, dripping down his chin. Then his hands are at my thigh, my breathing halts as I wait to see what he's going to do next. I expect him to come north, to touch me down there, but instead, he traces his callused fingers down my leg. His touch makes my stomach roll.

Breathe, I tell myself over and over again. You can do this. I chant in my head. The pain in my breast a reminder of this vindictive asshole. A reminder that I need to get out of here. I need to get myself safe. I can do this.

His hand finally reaches my binding at my right ankle. I notice that he's put himself in a vulnerable position, but I debate on whether or not connecting with his crotch is a good idea. Anyone this sadistic would probably be more turned on by a kick to the junk. But I have to do something. I test my wrists and I realize they aren't bound to the chair. Good.

I need my other leg free. I can't go anywhere if I don't have that. He frees my leg and the blood rushes into my foot. It's painful as it does.

The man before me stands and side steps to the other leg and squats again. He leans forward, repeating the process of licking my nipple. I don't fight him. I let him do it. This time, he sucks it into his mouth and bites on it hard. I flinch but fight the urge to pull away from him. I don't want him biting me again like he's already done.

I don't make a noise. No approval, no disapproval, nothing. I shut down. He continues licking and sucking while his hands trace patterns on my legs. His fingers coming awfully close to my sex and I try in vein to pull my legs together. He pinches the inside of my thigh, hard and I scream. Reflexively my legs fall open and his fingers brush the outside of my panties and I cringe. Oh god, this cannot be happening to me. I cry, but say nothing.

Growing bored with what he's doing, his hands trace down my leg and I suck in a deep, relived breath. Bracing for what I'm about to do. He finally frees my nipple and my ankle. The blood rushes into my foot, the pain is almost unbearable this time, but I've got to do something if I'm going to get out of this. I lift my leg and connect the bottom of my foot with his crotch. He grunts. I push on him and he falls down. I lift my arms and stand up, pressing my foot hard and firmly into his crotch. He laughs.

I lift my foot and stomp down, hard once, twice, and finally a third time I connect and he doubles over in pain.

I move out of his reach and move toward his head. He's squirming on the ground trying to reach me but he can't, I stay out of reach and he's fighting with cupping his balls or reaching for me. When he goes back to cup his shit again, I lift my foot and connect with his nose.

Blood spurts out and I both hear and feel the crunch that happens when I do. I lift my foot and bring it down again, but I miss. I dance forward and connect with him again. This time I catch him in his eye socket and he falls still. I throw down one more blow on the side of his face for good measure. My heel connecting with his temple.

Now that I'm not in the spotlight anymore, I can finally see some of what's in the darkness and my eyes roam over to the table I saw, over by where this asshole was standing. I notice several tools on the table. I go to the table, hoping to find a knife or something. I look over the shit that's there and some of it doesn't make any sense. There's a twisted piece of metal that's at the end of a poker like you'd use in a fireplace. I shake my head and look down the line of shit and finally, at the end of everything is a knife. I turn around, grabbing it with my hand. It takes me a couple tries because I can't see where my hands are behind my back and on the table, but I manage to grab the hilt of the knife and I do my best maneuver my hands enough to cut my bindings. It doesn't work and I drop the knife.

I go back the chair. My eyes roaming over the idiot on the ground. He's still passed out but I catch a glimpse of something under his shirt. Thank fucking god he's got a gun.

When you watch movies, you see people get out of handcuffs by bringing them around their asses, then their legs coming through. I have to tell you that it's not that simple to do. Especially when you're cursed with a longer torso and out of time. I stand up, bending over, trying to hook my arms under my ass. It takes a couple tries and an enormous amount of pain in my wrists but I manage to do just that.

I sit down carefully, but I tweak my wrists in the process and I cry out. "Stop," I scream, "no," I add as I grunt and groan trying to move my hands down my thighs. My shoulders are burning like nothing I've ever felt before I can see blood dripping from my wrists.

I grit my teeth and push them forward before I'm able to move one of my legs enough to get it to fall back to the ground. Once that one is out, the other comes out quickly. I fall to my knees and knee crawl my way back to the knife. I pick it up and get it turned around and tucked under the cable ties wrapped around my wrists. Unable to get the leverage I start to panic. Gunnar is gonna come back in here any second. With the blade hooked under the tie, I lift my hands to the table, catching the hilt on it and pushing up. The knife pulls on my bindings and my wrists ignite in a warm rush of pain and blood, but the tie snaps. Freeing my hands.

The knife falls to the ground.

The door kicks open.

I have two choices, charge the asshole and hope for the best or dive for sicko's gun. My eyes go from Gunnar to sicko and back to Gunnar. He's staring at me dumbstruck. He can't believe I managed to take down his number two.

I use his distraction to dive toward the sick bastard. Gunnar springs into action just as my hands land on the waist of the assholes jeans.

Then Gunnar is jumping on me, pinning me to the ground. My ribs explode in pain and I feel the crack of at least two ribs as I scream in pain. My air cut off by his heavy weight on my back.

I bring my foot up, trying to kick him, but I miss. Fuck.

His hand goes into my hair and he grabs it, hard, pulling so hard I see stars as he wretches my head back. I feel his hand come to my chin. Fuck.

I hear the grinding of bone in my neck. I cry as pain ignites every nerve in my body.

I don't know how I do it exactly, but somehow, I manage to extract asshole's gun from his waist and Gunnar's hand comes away from my chin as he tries reaching for it. His hand still in my hair, pushes my head forward, giving me reprieve from the pain and allowing me to focus. He leans forward, further crushing my back, ribs and lungs beneath his weight. I squirm, throwing him off balance just enough to put him back on his knees. His hand in my hair pulling my head back up. "Fuck," I cry out as I finally manage to pull some air into my lungs.

I get the gun in my right hand, his left reaching for it.

I tilt my right hand back, the barrel of the gun pointing backward toward him and he scurries off of me to my left to get away from the gun. I roll to my right, bringing the gun around. A shot rings out. Pain slices into my leg. "Fuck," I growl and start firing the gun as I bring it around, I catch his shoulder, my focus returns and I fire three more shots. Each one into his chest as he jerks and slumps against the chair I started in.

CHAPTER THIRTY
Sketch

"I'M HERE NOW. THERE'S NOTHING left," I tell Big Daddy on the phone. "It's completely obliterated. The fire department is working to put out the fire. Are you sure there was no one in here?"

"No, I can't say for certain. We swept through every room and there wasn't anything, but we had Gunnar's phone tracked to that location and Tryke thought it might have been in a basement that no one seems to know about."

"Shit," I say. "Alright, I'll keep you po…" I stop when I hear a gunshot ring out behind me. "Shit," I growl into the phone. Then I hear another one, followed by three in rapid succession. "There's someone else here," I mumble.

"On our way," he snaps and the line goes dead.

"In there." I point to a building about a hundred and fifty yards away from Pixie Sticks. Three of my guys and I go running toward the building. There are lights casting weird shadows on the building from fire trucks, flashing lights, cop cars, and it makes the building look ominous in a way I wouldn't expect.

Then a door bursts open. A naked woman comes stumbling through the door. Some light swings around and catches her just right. She's holding her arms around her chest, her breasts exposed, blood dripping from one of them and my stomach rolls. No pants on, blood running down her leg, no shirt, only a pair of barely visible panties. The light hits her again and I see her bright green hair. "Kiwi!" I roar.

Her head comes up; her eyes are wild in the light. Fear rips through her and she starts backing away. "Lily, it's Sketch," I tell her and she stops. I charge toward her, catching her just as she starts to collapse onto the ground.

I motion for my guys to go in the building, their guns drawn, tactical gear on.

Lily starts crying. "Loki," she sobs.

"On his way," I tell her.

"Oh, thank god," she whispers before she falls weak in my arms.

"I need an ambulance, now," I shout as loud as I can.

Loki

"WHERE IS SHE?" I SCREAM as I climb off my bike. Sketch comes toward me. I see blood on his flak jacket. "Is that hers?" I growl.

"She's alive," he tells me and my whole world explodes in color of happiness and relief. "She's hurt pretty bad."

"What did they do to her?" Sticks interjects.

Sketch shake his heads and look at Sticks. I grab him by his vest and shake him. "What happened to her?"

He looks at me and braces before he says, "She's alive. She's been beaten up pretty bad. Her face is a mess, she has a couple cracked ribs and…" he pauses.

"And what?" I snap.

"She was naked," he breathes and my world goes red.

"I'm gonna fucking kill them," I growl.

Sketch's lips twitch with a grin. "She already did," he breathes. "Well, one of them. The other is in pretty bad shape."

For some reason, I bust out laughing harder than I have in years. "That's my woman," I roar. I should have known she could take care of herself, but Jesus, this has been the worst possible night of my entire life.

The next thing I know, my head is flying to my right. "Fuck," I growl at Tryke. "What the fuck?"

"You're losing it, man." He glares at me, waiting for me to settle down. "Get your shit together and get over to the hospital," he tells me.

"I need to get Piper." I find some clarity in my mind. It's not much, but

276

it's enough to start thinking straight.

"Go to the hospital," Tryke orders. "I will bring Piper up later. When she's ready to see her." He tacks on with a glare.

I sober completely and nod. "We'll be right behind you," Pixie adds. I nod again, making my way to my bike. As soon as my ass hits the seat, I take a deep breath. She's alive. I'm alive. Gunnar is dead, Rooster is in jail, Piper is safe. Lily is safe.

I never imagined I'd feel such relief when this was all said and done. It's like the biggest burden has finally lifted from my shoulders and I feel like I can actually breathe for the first time in a very long time.

I drive toward the hospital with a small smile on my face. The sun starts to rise and it's the most glorious thing I've seen in years. The smell of fresh air and sunshine is more beautiful than I'd ever considered and it's because she's safe. She's alive, she's forever going to be safe because she's my old lady. She's my everything, and she can handle herself.

My smile fades the moment I see her lying in the emergency room hospital bed. Her face is a mess with bruises on both sides of her face. There's blood pools under the surface of her skin making her look even scarier. Her hair is matted and a total mess.

. Her shoulders are bare, naked and exposed, but there's a sheet covering her from the chest down. That's when I notice a bandage peeking out the top of the sheet covering her. I move toward her and I pull the sheet up. My vision swims when I see the bandage at the side of her breast, her nipple is covered under the bandage.

"She's alright," someone says and I snap my head in their direction. There's a short, broad-shouldered woman with short brown hair and brown eyes. She's wearing scrubs and a white jacket with a pleasant smile on her face. She extends her hand to me. "I'm Doctor Marx. I treated Lily tonight."

"What happened to her?" I breathe.

"She has a fractured rib and two that are cracked." She bites her lower lip. "I'm trying to avoid ruining that beautiful tattoo," She gives me a small smile. "I have faith this will work." With her pen she points at Lily's wrist and I notice bandages around one, then look at the other. "She was bound so tight they cut into her skin. We'll assess her for nerve damage when we wake her up. She has the same on her ankles."

With each word Doctor Marx says, my blood boils with the need to kill the motherfucker who did this before I remember he's already dead.

Doctor Marx continues, "She was shot in the thigh."

"Fuck," I growl, anger raging so hot I want to punch something.

"It's more flesh than anything, again, when she wakes up, we'll run some tests, it went straight through," the doctor says and I try to suck in a full deep breath in as she continues, "Her face is bruised up, but there are no fractures. She's a tough girl," she adds.

I point to her chest. "And that?"

Doctor Marx gives me a sad smile. "She was bitten hard enough to break the skin and she has a deep laceration on the side of her breast."

Anger slices through me so hard and fast my hands bend the side rail on her bed. "Relax," Doctor Marx says. "We have a plastic surgeon on his way in. We will do everything we can to cover up the bite."

"What about the other guy they brought in with her?" I ask through gritted teeth.

"Do you know him?" she asks.

"No, but he did this to her," I tell her.

Doctor Marx gives me a satisfied smile. "Then you'll be happy to know he died about ten minutes ago."

Relief takes over and I sit in the chair next to the bed. I gently grab her hand and brush my thumb over the back of it, letting her know I'm there.

"She'll be alright, physically. It's just gonna take some time for her to heal."

"How long will she have to stay in the hospital?" I ask.

278

WICKED REVENGE

"We've given her some sleep meds, she's gonna be out for a while, and we're waiting on the plastic surgeon, so a couple days, maybe a week, depends on how quickly she recovers." Doctor Marx shrugs. "I imagine it will be sooner rather than later."

I nod my understanding and Doctor Marx does her exam. She lifts the sheet at the end of the bed and checks Lily's reflexes and I'm relieved when her foot twitches. The other one too. Then she moves to her hands and does the same thing. Lily's hand twitches. She takes the one I'm holding and while it takes a little longer for it to respond, Doctor Marx seems satisfied with the results and turns to leave.

"Are you her husband?" she asks.

"Boyfriend," I correct her.

She nods. "Is she on any medication?" she asks.

I shake my head. "Not that I know of," I tell her, and it's true, I have no clue.

"Birth control?" she asks.

"She said she wasn't on anything." My heart starts pumping a little faster in my chest. I can't tell if its panic or fear or something else entirely.

"Is there any chance she could be pregnant?" Doctor Marx asks me.

I just stare at her for a moment before I gently squeeze Lily's hand. "Um, maybe."

"We can run some tests to be sure," Doctor Marx says softly.

I just nod, not sure what to say to that and the doctor goes to leave, "wait," I say to her. She stops, looking back at me, "was she…uhm…was she…down there?" I manage.

Doctor Marx gives me a sympathetic smile. "We found no evidence to suggest that. She was still wearing her panties and we checked for any signs and there were none," she reassures me. "We'll ask her when she wakes up to be certain, but I think you're in the clear." She winks and leaves the room.

My heart, which had leapt into my throat a few moments ago, settles back in my chest and slowly returns to its normal rhythm.

About thirty minutes later a nurse comes in, checks Lily's vitals and does a couple of things, including drawing blood from her IV. "What's that for?" I ask her.

She looks at me, her eyes widen briefly, but she hides her reaction quickly. I know I'm attractive, but shit. "Doctor Marx requested some additional blood work," the nurse states.

"What for?" I ask.

She cocks her head at me. "Pregnancy," she states deadpan and my heart jumps back in my throat.

"How…how long will it take…to um…"

"Find out?" she finishes for me and I nod. "Maybe an hour." She shrugs and leaves me alone with Lily again.

I don't know whether it's the prospect of her being pregnant or the fact that she could be pregnant and she went through all this that has me freaking the fuck out more when Sticks comes into the room. "Jesus," he groans. "She looks like shit."

"Ya think?" I say.

"She gonna be alright?" he asks and I explain her injuries. He, like me, blew a gasket over her being bitten, but he let it go when I remind him the fucker's dead.

"Who was he?" I ask.

Sticks shrugs. "We're not sure. But Sketch is looking into it. We think he might be a blood relation to Gunnar."

I roll my eyes. "I never want to hear that name again," I grumble.

"The rest of the guys are here, most of the club too." He comes to stand next to me. "Why don't you leave me with her and go talk to them?"

"Why can't…" Sticks gives me a look that says to shut the fuck up and do what he says. I gently squeeze Lily's hand before I let it go and stand up. Sticks promptly replaces me in the chair and I head toward the waiting room. As I draw closer to the doors, I hear a lot of noise on the other side and I push through the door.

"Jesus H," I grumble when I see close to fifty burly, badass bikers in the waiting room of Roswell Regional.

There's a collective hush that comes over everyone as some of the guys notice me. Tryke comes forward first. I don't say anything to him, I don't have to, and he wraps his arms around me. "She's gonna be fine," he whispers.

"Yeah, man, she is," I breathe back. His arms tighten a little more before he releases me.

"She's alright," he tells everyone and I catch the nurses jumping when the guys all cheer.

"Piper?" I ask Tryke.

"I'm going there next."

"She's gonna wanna see her," I tell him. "But not yet. Whether Kiwi wants it or not, she's in bad shape."

"You got it," he tells me.

"I'm sorry guys," a petite little thing comes up next to us, "I'm gonna have to ask you guys to leave."

"Like hell we're leaving. One of ours is in there," Big Daddy barks.

"If you're going to stay, you need to sit down and be quiet. Your loved one is not the only patient in this hospital," The nurse fires back.

I snort. Big Daddy turns red, but Whistler cuts him off. "She's not one of us," he gently reminds Big Daddy. "And she's right. Some of us should get out of here."

"Whistler's right, they're not gonna let y'all back there," Cowboy adds. "And there ain't much we're doin' besides standin' round causing a ruckus. Drinks on me," he finishes and again the guys cheer, none of them giving a shit that it's eight in the morning.

A bunch of the guys pat me on the back as they file out of the emergency room doors. I'd love to see the parking lot right now, full of bikes scaring away anyone coming to the hospital.

After all the guys leave, Whistler, Pixie, Tryke, Big Daddy and Cowboy are all that's left. "She really gonna be alright?" Big Daddy asks.

"Physically? She'll be fine. She's got a broken rib, two cracked ribs, a through and through in the thigh, and more cosmetic damage than anything. She's pretty bruised up," I tell them.

"The other guy?" Cowboy asks.

I give them all an evil smirk. "Dead," I share and my smirk is matched by theirs. "Not sure of the details, just know it was about ten minutes before I got here."

"Good," Pixie says.

"I know you don't want to leave her," Tryke chimes in, "but we got the vote at noon."

I sigh. "Can we put it off for another day?" I ask.

"Nope, gotta be done today," Big Daddy says. "You want to make a bid for it, you have to be there."

I look at Tryke and say, "I think Tryke should."

Tryke shakes his head. "My time came and went, I ran instead of fighting, no one is going to want me as their Pres."

I snort, "I wouldn't be too sure about that."

He shakes his head.

"Noon, clubhouse," Big Daddy says and I nod. Family may come first, but the Wicked Angels were my family long before Lily was.

"Go to Piper, please," I implore Tryke.

He nods. "On my way." He squeezes my shoulder and heads for the doors.

"We got Tucson and Boulder rollin' in," Pixie says.

"Why?" I ask.

282

Pixie cocks his head. "New pres." He smirks and leaves me to Whistler, Cowboy, and Big Daddy.

"I'm gonna hang out for a while," Big Daddy says. "I'd like to see her."

I nod and give him the room number. He goes back to see her. "I'm gonna go to Iron Wings. Come by and I'll liquor you up, you look like you could use it," Cowboy says before taking off. Leaving me alone with Whistler.

"You get anything out of Opie?" I ask when we're alone.

"I got all kinds of shit, including where the rest of the money is hidden."

I narrow my eyes at him. "I thought we got it all."

Whistler snorts. "Apparently, we weren't the only ones Rooster was skimming."

"Jesus Christ." We walk toward the chairs and sit down.

"It will be up to whoever gets Pres, but Big Daddy wants to allocate the money we recovered to rebuilding Pixie Sticks and that compound. He's also going to make sure Lily and Piper get some of it, then whatever is left over can be used for whatever Roswell needs."

"I think we're good," I tell him.

"He's making some serious changes to all the compounds. Including cameras and security systems. He refuses to see another building blown to smithereens and it's time the Angels caught up with the times." Whistler is pretty insightful when it comes to shit, and I learn that more and more the longer we talk. Then he asks me, "You get Pres. What's the plan?"

I shrug. "I want Tryke as Veep, Axel…shit, have we heard anything about him?" I ask.

Whistler smiles. "He's upstairs, but he'll be fine. Why?"

"I want him as SIA."

"Good choice," Whistler agrees.

"Treasurer."

"You're gonna laugh at me," I tell him.

"Not likely."

"Kiwi."

"You're shitting me, right?" He's not laughing.

I'm the one who laughs. "I'm not sure I can ever trust anyone with that position again and if Tryke takes Veep," I shrug, "he can't do both."

"Says who?" Sticks joins us. I look for Big Daddy and deduce he's still with Kiwi.

"Um, Angels law," I tell him.

"Fuck that," he grumbles as he sits down across from us. "He can do both, at least until you find someone you can trust."

"Did you hear who he wants?" Whistler asks.

"No, who?" Sticks raises an eyebrow.

"Kiwi," Whistler says.

"No, shit?" Sticks asks me.

I nod. "Not sure I trust anyone else," I tell him. "She's smart, knows more about this club than any of us possibly imagined. She could handle it," I tell him.

He frowns. "I like the idea of progress, you know this, but I doubt it will fly with D," he says.

"I know, but it's worth a shot. Regardless, Cowboy would be a good bet, he's just got Iron Wings and…"

Big Daddy joins us and says, "Maybe it's time to turn over a new leaf at Wings."

"How so?" I ask.

"Sticks is right. I would never sign off on Kiwi as Treasurer. I'm all for forward progress but books and logistics are always handled by members. You've got a pool to choose from and if Cowboy is who you want, then roll Iron Wings to someone else. Loni's 'bout done," he says. "I'd imagine she'd put in a bid for something else once the presidency is assigned. She tried a couple years ago and Rooster refused."

WICKED REVENGE

"Who'd run it?" Whistler asks the question I was thinking about.

"Kiwi," I breathe.

Big Daddy smirks at me. "It's a win-win," he says and he's right. I can keep Kiwi close, but not too close.

We talk for a few more minutes before I return to her room and sit by her side. I take her small hand in mine and give it a gentle squeeze. Her fingers twitch in mine. I look up to find her eyes are still closed. I stand up, lean over her and kiss her forehead. "I love you, Lily," I breathe.

CHAPTER THIRTY-ONE
Tryke

WALKING OUT OF THE HOSPITAL is a bit surreal. I'm beyond relieved that Lily is gonna be okay. I don't know what I would do if I lost her.

I'm lost in my own pity party when I hear, "Py..Tryke..Pyro, fuck, man, what am I supposed to call you now?" I chuckle as I turn to see Tracker and Viker standing near their rides.

"Tryke," I tell them both as they approach me.

"It's good to have you back, brother," Viker says as he takes my arm and I take his.

"Thanks, I'm not sure everyone else feels that way, though."

Tracker smiles. "You'd be surprised."

"How'd you guys find out anyway?" I ask them. I blink, my contacts irritating me.

They both laugh. "These dumbasses are worse than a lady's aide society with their gossip and shit," Viker says.

I can't help but laugh. It's true, they are. "Hey, you gonna put your name in?" Tracker asks.

I shrug. "I'm not sure anyone would want me as Pres."

They both scowl at me. "Why the hell not?" Viker asks.

I give a humorless snort. "Because, when shit got real, I let the idiots win," I tell them both. That's something I've had to live with the last six years. Instead of fighting back, taking Rooster out immediately, I ran.

"Fuck that, It's rightfully yours. You should put your name in," Tracker urges. "Ain't no one going to challenge you."

"Loki might," I say. "He deserves it, he's busted his balls for this club for years."

"Maybe, but he's not a Beaumont," Tracker says stoically.

"Technically, he is," I remind them.

WICKED REVENGE

"How so?" Viker asks.

"He colored my sister."

"Skit's your sister? I thought she...when your parents..." Viker whispers like it's a conspiracy.

"I needed her out of the lifestyle, away from the club. I needed to keep her safe," I tell them.

"Understood, brother," Tracker says.

"No one blames you, and no one doubts you," Viker tells me.

"That's good to know," I share and we part ways to our individual bikes.

I toss a leg over my bike while I blink repeatedly. My contacts have never irritated me like this before and it's annoying as fuck.

Instead of going straight to Lily's house, I go to mine. After last night, I need a shower. I stand naked in front of my bathroom mirror, staring at myself. I don't even recognize the man looking back at me. His hair's too long, his eyes too brown. I reach up and stretch my bottom eyelid, my vision blurs as I press a finger against the contact and extract it. The bright green of my eye shines bright behind the brown coloring of the contact. I repeat the process on the other eye and I'm now staring at someone who better resembles myself, but still, it's not me.

Walking out of the bathroom, I go into my closet and pull down my shaving kit. Ever since I came back as Pyro, I haven't used a shaver, but I've always kept one on hand and I need it now. It's time to make Pyro go away and bring Tryke back to life. This is the best place to start.

I return to the bathroom and plug in the shaver and I flick the switch. It kicks on and the vibration in my hand is a reminder of what I'm about to do. I smile at myself and lift the hair on the side of my head, the one with Lily's tattoo and I press the shaver to my temple and swipe it through, leaving a nearly bald streak in its path. I come back, closer to my ear, and repeat the process.

287

I keep going until that side of my head is bald and free of hair, then I start on the other side. I haven't touched the back yet. It's been six years since I've cut my hair. Here's hoping I don't fuck it up.

Ten minutes later and I'm looking at my hair again in the mirror. The top is still too long, but I kind of like it. I can't see the back, but it feels alright. I have a nice thick stripe of hair running from my forehead to the base of my skull. The mohawk is much longer than I've ever had it, but I kind of like it like this.

"There you are," I say into the mirror. "I've missed you."

For the first time in my life, I regret the scar on the side of my face and I wish there was a way to make it disappear. But unless I'm going to have surgery, it will be a permanent part of my face for the rest of my life. I take a deep breath before I step into the shower.

About thirty minutes later, around ten, I'm headed toward Lily's house. My scruff has been shaved off, my hair fixed, sort of, and my contacts are gone.

When I pull up in front of Lily's, I see that someone brought her bike back here from Loki's and it makes me smile. She can keep riding it. I know Loki won't stop her and if Loki is willing to let her ride, there ain't a brother in Roswell who would make her stop.

In hindsight, it was probably ridiculously stupid of me to think she'd stay away from the life, but I'd hoped.

The front door opens and Piper stands there as I kill my bike. "You're not Loki," she says sadly.

"No darlin', I'm not. Is Emily here?"

"Duh," she says as I approach her.

I laugh. "Do I know you?" she asks me as I step up the front steps.

"No, but I know you," I tell her with a smile.

288

WICKED REVENGE

"Are you sure?"

"What makes you ask?" I counter.

"You look like mommy's brother." My heart picks up a beat in my chest. "But mommy said he died," she says sadly. "I never got to meet him."

I kneel before her. "What if I told you that I am your mommy's brother."

Her eyes widen and she lights up. "Are you really mommy's brother? Are you really Unkie Kellen?" she asks, hopeful.

"I am, Piper."

She gasps, "You know my name?"

I can't help but chuckle at her. "Yeah, I know your name because I'm your Uncle Kellen."

She pushes through the door and slams me with a massive hug. Her arms wrap around my neck, holding on for dear life. "So, you're not dead?" she asks softly.

"No, baby, I'm not dead," I tell her.

"Piper, what are you doing?" a voice says as a woman comes to the door. My eyes lock on hers, they're a beautiful shade of blue. Her stick straight black hair cascades down her back. My heart stops in my chest. "Who are you?" she asks, but her voice comes out as more of a whisper and I smile at her.

"I'm Tryke," I tell her.

She shakes her head. "That's not possible, he's dead."

"No, he's not," Piper champions for me, turning around to face Emily. "This is my unkie Kellen. I know it is."

"It's a long story," I say by way of explanation. "I came to talk to you."

"Is everything alright?" she asks, concern in her voice.

"Hey, Piper, can you do me a favor?" I ask.

"Anything."

I smile at her eagerness. "Can you give me and Emily a minute to talk?"

"I know, I know, adult stuff," she mutters as she squirms out of my arms and she ducks inside the house.

I look past Emily and see that Piper has moved into the dining room. "Lily is in the hospital," I tell her. She gasps and covers her mouth. "She's alright, just a little beat up, but she's gonna be there for a couple days."

"Okay…" she says, unsure of what else to say. "Can we go see her?"

I can't stop my features from scrunching up. "I wouldn't recommend it, at least not for a few days. She's pretty beat up. I don't want to scare Piper."

She nods in understanding. "I can handle Piper, but what should I tell her?"

I shrug. I haven't the first clue about what you tell kids in situations like this. "I don't…I have no clue," I admit..

Emily smiles at me, her eyes roaming over my cut and lower. My cock hardens in my jeans and I pray to god she can't see it. "Kiwi is usually pretty honest," she says as her eyes make their way back up to my face. I bite the inside of my cheek to stop from blushing like a moron.

After I regain control, just a heartbeat or two, I say to her, "Well, I will leave that up to you, but she's going to be fine. She needs her rest and some time to recover."

"What about Loki?" she asks.

"He's fine. He's at the hospital with her…" I realize that we're still standing outside and I'm not sure I like this. "Can I come in?" I ask.

"Absolutely," she says, opening the door for me to step inside. I walk up to her, putting myself right in front of her. She's much shorter than I am and her breathing catches in her throat. Her eyes, staring into mine, dilate, and I smirk.

"See something you like?" I ask her.

"Uh huh," she breathes before her face turns bright red and she breaks our eye contact. I smirk. Taking the door from her hand, I close it gently. Piper is singing in the dining room, some Adam Levine song, Animals, I think it is, with no music playing. I shake my head and press Emily against the wall. I'm not touching her, but she's trapped between me and the wall.

"And what would you like to do with it?" I ask her.

"Lick it from head to toe."

My mouth falls slack, my cock hardens further and I move in closer to her, dipping my head so that my lips are mere inches from hers. Her breathing catches in her throat and she tilts her head closer, trying to get me to kiss her. I leave her hanging for a moment, but then I slant my lips over hears.

Electricity flies through me. My cock jumps, my heart skips and my breathing falters the moment our lips touch.

She wraps her arms around my neck, pressing her body against me and I growl into our kiss before wrapping my arms around her and lifting her. She wraps her legs around me and I press her against the wall. Our lips never stop. I slide my tongue along her lower lip and she opens for me. I press my tongue into her mouth and she starts sucking it and flicking her tongue.

I groan again and press my hips into her sex. "Oh god," she wimpers as she tears her mouth from mine.

"Animals, like Animals," rings out from the kitchen and it's like dumping ice water over me. I let Emily back to the floor.

"Wow," she breathes.

"Wow is right," I agree.

I lift my hand, brushing the backs of my knuckles down her cheek. "I better go," I tell her.

"Okay…" she breathes.

I pull back, putting distance between us, and her vision clears, her mind returning to herself and she looks at me like I've just stolen her virtue. I smirk at her. With my eyes on her, I say, "Piper, baby, I'm leaving."

She comes running in and she looks from me to Emily and back to me again. "Already?" she says. "You just got here."

I smile and break eye contact with Emily to look down at Piper. "I know, baby, but I got business to take care of."

"Will you come back?"

I look at Emily again when I answer, "Oh yeah, I'll be back."

"Good," Piper exclaims and she hugs my leg.

"See you later," I say to both of them, but I'm looking at Emily with a look I hope says it's a promise. Her mouth falls slack and her chest rises quickly for a moment.

"See you later," she breathes.

I walk out of the house, my hand going to my cock, shifting it. It's hard as fucking steel and climbing on my bike isn't going to be fun like this, but I do it anyway. I look at the time on my phone, just before eleven. I have enough time to swing by the hospital before the meeting.

CHAPTER THIRTY-TWO

Loki

"HEY MAN, WHERE YOU AT?"

"I just pulled up to the hospital," Tryke says into the phone. "Wanted to check on her before I hit the clubhouse."

"She's still in the emergency room, but they're working on getting her a bed. Loni is with her now."

"Why aren't you with her?" His tone is accusatory.

"I need a shower, a change of clothes and to grab some stuff before I hit the clubhouse. Loni said she'd stay until I got done. The doc said they were gonna keep her out a while longer," I tell him. Loni was insistent on staying with her while I went to deal with club business. She knows how important today is. She's been around long enough to understand that. Besides, I'm pretty sure Cowboy made her do it.

"So, you're not here?"

"No, I just got back to my house."

"Emily's hot," he tells me.

"Dude, she watching my kid," I tell him with a scrunched-up face.

"And you're doing my sister, so what's your point?" he snickers.

"Touché," I laugh.

"Alright, I'm gonna run in here, I'll see you at the clubhouse," he says.

"Yeah, alright," I tell him and we hang up.

My eyes roam over to my bed and the cut lying across it. A smile spreads across my face as I think about how I'm going to do this today.

As much as I want to be Pres, it's not my place. Never was. It's always belonged to Tryke and he, more than anyone else, deserves it. Though if the club voted me in, I wouldn't be surprised and I'd have no problem making Tryke as Veep. I know he'd take it without a second thought.

I leave the cut and go for the shower. Remembering the last time Kiwi and I took a shower, sadness creeps over me because god knows how long it's going to be before we can do that again. Jesus, that's if she even wants to. I growl in anger as I get in the shower.

About an hour later, I'm pulling up to the club. Everyone is here. There's even a few extra bikes from Colorado and Arizona here. I grab the bag from my side saddle and tuck it under my arm.

When I walk in the door, I'm greeted with a lot of 'hey man', 'how you holdin' up' and 'how is she' as I step up to the bar. The prospect is quick with a shot for me and I slam it back.

"You see him yet?"

"Nah, you?"

"Yeah, he…I don't know, he doesn't look any different." Two of the Arizona members are talking. I look over at them and I recognize them immediately. They were once Roswell members, but after Tryke's death they rolled on to Arizona. Rooster put a lot of bad tastes in people's mouths so they did what they had to and bailed. "They give it to him, you coming back?" the one guy who remarked about looks says.

"Fuck yeah," the other one says and my reason for doing what I'm about to do is solidified. Roswell has been a small unit for the last six years. We used to be close to Tucson in size, but Rooster ruined all that. I'm eager to get us back on track.

The bell rings behind the bar and I see someone stand up on something toward the hallway. I look and it's Big Daddy. "As," he shouts, and the crowd quiets. "As many of you know, Gunnar is dead." The crowd erupts in cheers to the point of deafening. Big Daddy puts his fingers in his mouth and whistles loud enough to settle them down. "And that Rooster is officially in ATF custody." The roars and cheers are louder over that statement than they were for Gunnar. Big Daddy whistles again after he gives them a minute to celebrate, and they settle down. "That means, on this day, we must choose a new Roswell President."

There are several people shouting, "Loki and Tryke", a couple people shout, "Pyro: and there's some chuckles. "Enough," Big Daddy barks.

WICKED REVENGE

"You know how this goes. Since we no longer have a Veep, it passes to the Sergeant to make the first nomination." Big Daddy's eyes meet mine. "He can either nominate himself, or he can choose someone else. This person must be at least a Veteran member of this clubhouse and must have been a full member of this club for ten years. Once they announce their person, the Treasurer and Senior Veteran may confirm or deny and offer their own nominations. Now, you may not know this, but Axel, your Senior Vet, was shot last night. He's alive, breathing and wide fucking awake, but they won't let him out of his bed just yet. So, I've already spoken with him in regard to his nomination." Big Daddy's eyes move around the room. I can't quite see who he's looking at. "Once the nominations are in, the Veterans will go to church and cast their votes. Get me?"

The entire common room, including myself erupts in "we get you," before settling.

Big Daddy's eyes come back to me. "You're up Sergeant-at-Arms."

I nod and walk toward where he's standing on the box. He greets me by taking my arm and I take his before we fist each other's backs. "How's she?" he asks.

"Still sleeping," I tell him.

He nods and I step up on the box. I scan the crowd once, twice, before coming back to a man I haven't seen in six years. His contacts are gone. His green eyes look at me with familiarity. His hair cut short on the sides, long through the middle. I nod to him. "Many of you assholes expect me to nominate myself." I start to unravel the bag to a chorus of laughter. "But I'm not." There's a gasp among the masses. "Ten years ago we lost the best President Roswell's ever had, and ten years ago the club should have been passed to the rightful successor. However, ten years ago, we were younger, dumber and full of more cum than we are now." This gets me some more laughs. "And it wasn't the right time. So, my nominee did the right thing, unwilling and unprepared to take the throne, he stepped aside to learn, to understand and to have a solid grasp on who it is at the top. When he was ready to make that step, someone put a hit on him." My eyes find Tryke's again. "In an effort to protect himself, and his sister, he did what was best for his family."

"His sister?"

"She's dead."

A shiver runs through me. "No, she's not. Most of you have had the pleasure of meeting her as Skit or better yet, my old lady," I tack on.

"No shit?" someone says.

I smile. "She, in case you didn't know this, is the reason Rooster is in ATF custody and the reason Gunnar is dead," I tell them and that starts some murmurs and whispers, but I talk over them. "Regardless of that, Tryke, it's time for you to stand up," I pull the cut from my bag, "and take this cut back. Take back the real man you are, and step up to be our President."

Tryke stands up, his eyes are full of emotion, just like mine, as he makes his way through the crowd. Many of the men grab his shoulder and give him encouraging messages to welcome him back.

When he finally reaches the box, I step down. He grabs my arm and I grab his. "Thank you, brother," he whispers in my ear. I smile.

I take the cut and shake it out. "Take it off, man," I tell him.

He smiles and removes his Pyro cut and he hands it off to someone. I open the front of his Tryke cut and hold it for him. He smiles and slips his arms inside one at a time. Then he grabs the front and pulls it down, snapping it, and the entire common room erupts.

Big Daddy, Whistler, Sticks, Pixie and Cowboy greet him, welcoming him back to the club as Tryke before Big Daddy shouts, "Treasurer!"

Tryke rolls his eyes but steps up on the box and the crowd quiets without any prompting.

"I'd prepared a big long speech about the man I wanted to nominate today." His eyes come to mine. "He deserves it. He kept this club together in my absence. He kept me sane and he's taken on my sister as his old lady and that alone deserves some serious recognition," he teases and most of the guys laugh. "And he does deserve the job. You all look up to him, you all turn to him for guidance when you need it and most importantly, he's been there for each of you when I couldn't be. But if I nominate Loki, it feels like we're both swapping our nominations. So, at this time, as Treasurer of Roswell, I hold my nomination."

"Fair enough," Big Daddy says.

"Dick," I tease Tryke as he steps down.

"Cocksucker," he laughs.

"As I'm standing in for Senior Vet, I offer you no speech or anecdotes but Axel, Senior Veteran of Roswell Wicked Angels by proxy, hereby nominates Loki as president," he bellows.

I shake my head. "I knew that was comin'," I mutter.

"So with one nomination each, Tryke, do you wish to offer your nomination?" Big Daddy asks.

"No, I will leave it to the Veterans to decide."

"Fair enough," Big Daddy smirks. "Veterans, to church," he orders and there are fifteen of them, sixteen with Axel, but he nominated, therefore he cannot vote again. The fifteen members of our Veteran squad move through the common room. Cell phones are dropped in the box on the wall and they move into the conference room next to Rooster's old office.

"You could have sealed the deal, one way or another," I say to Tryke. "Why didn't you?"

He gives me a sad smile. "Because it's not my decision. Pyro's sure, he's been around long enough, but Tryke hasn't," he says with a hint of regret.

"You did what you had to do," I remind him.

"I feel like a fraud," he says honestly and I look at him.

"You cut your hair, you ditched the contacts, you're no fraud. If they vote you in, it's going to be because they can see what you are as Pyro and as Tryke," I tell him. "Jesus, this shit's too fucking heavy, I need a fucking drink," I mutter and Tryke laughs.

"I'm buying," he laughs.

"Ha!" I say and we walk to the bar.

The prospect sends us two whiskies sliding down the bar and we grab them. I hold mine up. "To whatever happens," I say and we clink glasses.

"You're my Veep," he breathes.

"You as well," I tell him. "No question."

"We stick together."

"Always."

We shoot our whiskey down and put the glasses on the bar.

We spend the next hour drinking and shooting the shit with the guys before Sticks finally comes out. "Loki, Tryke," he barks and Tryke and I look at each other.

"Here goes," Tryke says.

A smiles spreads across my face we walk toward Sticks and the hallway.

"They're indecisive, but they agree on one thing," Sticks says after we walk down the hallway, getting away from the common room.

"What's that?" Tryke asks.

"They want both of you," he tells us.

"That's a given," I reply. "Either way, he's my Pres or my Veep. So, regardless, they get us both."

Tryke nods. "It's only fair that way."

"Alright, we'll tell them." He turns to leave for the room we use for church or private club meetings. "Oh," Sticks turns toward us. "They're curious about who you were going to nominate."

Tryke doesn't say anything but his eyes roam over to me and Sticks nods. "I'll tell 'em," he says and he disappears into the room.

"I thought this would be easier," Tryke says. "I figured they'd go straight for you."

WICKED REVENGE

I shrug. "I didn't think that at all. Once it was out that you're alive, I knew it would cause them to pause and think a little more. If you hadn't come out, technically, the club would have passed to me because of Kiwi and they all know that. But, with your return, you're rightfully Pres by code." I grab his shoulder, squeezing it. "Honestly, I'd rather you have it," I tell him.

"Why?" he asks. "I haven't done anything for six years."

"But you have, the name on your cut doesn't change what you've done for this club these last six years. Not to mention, I've been Sergeant, nothing more than an enforcer. You've at least had your hands in the books. That's got to count for something," I add.

He only nods.

The door at the end of the hall opens and Sticks comes back out. He says something to the guard on duty, who happens to be Pixie. He nods and goes into the room and Sticks comes down the hall. "They're voting now." We nod. "I need a drink." Sticks smiles.

"That bad in there?" I ask.

"Nah, they have some valid points. Big Daddy convinced them that regardless, they're going to get both of you. It's just a matter of who they respect more." His eyes roam to Tryke. "The club is rightfully yours and if you want it, Big Daddy and I will overturn their vote."

"I don't want that. I want them to choose me, or Loki. Who they decide on is the man they respect. I can't be a Pres if I don't have their full attention and respect."

"That's why he deserves to be Pres," I say with a smile playing on my lips.

"Agreed," Sticks says and pushes between us on his way to the common room and that drink he wants.

Tryke and I stand there quietly while we wait for Sticks to return or for someone to come out and tell us something. My phone vibrates against my chest. I pull it from my pocket and my lungs seize when I see Loni's name across the screen.

"She alright?" I ask.

"She's fine, still sleeping. They moved her to her room. She's in four oh three."

"Thanks, Loni."

"Anytime. How's it going over there?" she asks.

"Still waiting."

She chuckles. "It's a miracle you guys get anything done over there."

"Yeah, yeah, keep me posted," I tell her.

"Will do."

We hang up. Tryke's eyes are on me for an update. "They moved her into her room, four oh three."

"She still out?"

"Yup, they said they'd keep her down for a while. Or until I get back there."

Tryke nods in understanding but doesn't say anything else.

It's another fifteen minutes before Sticks walks back past us. He claps both of us on the shoulder as he passes before disappearing into the room. A few minutes after that, Pixie comes out. He smiles at both of us before taking up his post. "I need another drink," Tryke says as he turns back toward the common room. I turn to lean against the wall. My mind wanders over to Kiwi and what she's going through. I hope she comes out the other side of this intact. Then my mind wanders to Piper and what she must be going through. I want to call Emily, but I don't have her number and that irks me in a way I don't expect.

I start pacing the hallway, making sure to stay clear of the door. That's what Pixie is here for- to keep people away who shouldn't overhear anything. Usually that's Axel's job but he's still in the hospital.

About ten more minutes pass, I've managed to calm down. Vowing to rectify the situation with not having Emily's number as soon as this is over. I want to see Piper and I need to get back to Kiwi.

Tryke comes into the hallway at the same time Big Daddy and Sticks exit the room. They both look satisfied as they walk toward us.

"We have a President," Big Daddy says, "and from my understanding, we have a Veep?" he raises an eyebrow.

I nod, "regardless of decision." I tell him. My heart beating faster in my chest. I want it, but I'm not sure I want it if it means taking it from Tryke, he deserves it.

"Good," Big Daddy says, but he says nothing further.

"Are you gonna be a dick or are you gonna tell us?" Tryke cajoles.

"I'm thinking about it." Big Daddy smirks. "You two sure you're gonna be alright with the outcome?"

"Absolutely," we both say together.

"Now, who?" I ask.

He looks at Tryke and says, "As it should be. Congrats."

I smile wide as Tryke takes Big Daddy's arm, "It's official. You're it Tryke."

"Thank God," I breathe a sigh of relief.

Everyone laughs. "Thanks," Tryke says.

"Ready to change that patch?" Sticks asks as he hands Tryke a President bar. Then he hands me a VP bar. "Now the two of you need to decide who you want for Treasurer and Sergeant, since you're vacating those spots."

Tryke looks to me for my pick. "Cowboy for Treasurer, since these two won't let me have my first or second choice," I laugh.

"Who's that?" Tryke asks.

"You, obviously. All the shit you did with finding this crap, I'm not sure anyone else could be that good," I tell him. "But they won't let you do both."

"Second choice," Tryke says.

I laugh, "You were my second choice. But your sister was my first."

He narrows his eyes at me. "Why her?"

"Because I don't trust anyone else. Though Cowboy has proven his loyalty time and time again and I think with you at the head, he'll be on his game." I nod.

"Cowboy it is," Tryke agrees. "And Sergeant?"

"Axel."

"I agree with that. We can move Viker up to Senior."

"Sounds good to me, man," I tell him.

"There's some other changes you two are going to have to deal with," Sticks says. He'd brought them up at the hospital. "Loni wants out."

"I can't blame her for that. That bar's a handful. But who do we hand it over?" Tryke says but looks at me.

I shrug. "That's your call, but you know she'd take it."

"Agreed. We'll give it to Kiwi," Tryke says.

"Then it's settled," Big Daddy says just as the door to church opens and the Vets file out. Each of them congratulate Tryke and myself as they pass into the common room. There are cheers coming from them as they do because they know it's over and the Roswell Wicked Angels have a new president. A rightful president.

Big Daddy and Sticks make the announcements after talking to Cowboy about his new position. He agreed, without a second thought, and the rest of the clubhouse was made aware of the changes at the top. No one objected and everyone congratulated us both when it was over.

It's nearly three-thirty by the time the group disburses with plans in place for a party tonight. Though neither Tryke nor I feel like partying, we'll do it because we have to.

Tryke takes off for the hospital to check on Kiwi and I go to the house.

As soon as I pull park in the driveway, Piper comes outside. "Loki," she squeals. I'm barely off my bike when she jumps at me. I catch her and lift her up.

"Hi baby girl." I smile at her.

"Where's momma?"

I catch Emily standing at the door. "What did Emily tell you?"

"That momma was busy."

I nod and take Piper in the house. "Everything okay?" Emily whispers.

"It's fine, she's fine."

Relief rushes into Emily's features and I see now what Tryke was going on about before. Emily really is a beautiful girl and I'm surprised I hadn't noticed it before. Then again, I was too focused on Kiwi to see anyone else.

I sit down on the couch with Piper in my lap. "Pipes, baby, mommy got into a bad fight last night." She starts to cry. "Oh, don't cry, she's gonna be just fine."

"You sure?" she says, her chin quivering.

I smile. "I'm sure. She's gonna be gone for a couple days."

"I wanna see her," she cries.

"I know, sweetheart, and you will, just not today, okay?"

"When?"

I look at Emily. "How about in the morning?"

She sniffs. "Okay, daddy."

My heart explodes in my chest as I look at her. She called me daddy. Not Loki, but daddy. I kiss her temple. "Love you, Pipes."

She wraps her arms around my neck and she settles her crying. I lean back against the couch, holding her until she's ready to get up. For being five, she's an amazing creature, but I have to remind myself that she is only five and sometimes I need to be careful with what I share with her.

She stirs and climbs down from my lap. "Can we go for our ride?"

I smile. "How about I take you in the morning, before we go see mommy together?"

"Okay," she smiles wide and runs off to her bedroom.

"She'll be alright," Emily says.

"She's a tough kid."

Emily smiles. "That she is."

"I need your number," I tell her.

"Sure," she says and I pull out my phone, punching it in as she gives it to me.

"I'm going to go up to the hospital." I shoot her a text that just says 'Loki'. "And I just texted you my digits. Call if you need anything. I'll check on her later. If I don't crash at the hospital, I'll come back here."

"Sounds good."

"You need anything before I go?"

She shakes her head. "No, we're good."

I nod and go into Piper's room to tell her bye. She's playing with some dolls on the floor. I stand there watching her blonde curls bounce as she moves her dolls around. It makes me realize just how innocent and young she is and for the first time since the transfer of power to Tryke, I feel relieved that he got the job and not me.

I've lost five years with her. I'm ready to make them up and so much more.

"I'll see you in the morning," I tell Piper.

She looks up at me. "Okay, daddy."

I smile wide at her and step into her room. I kneel and kiss the top of her head. "Later, Pipes."

"Bye, daddy." She says it again and my heart explodes.

CHAPTER THIRTY-THREE

Kiwi

MY EYES FLUTTER OPEN.

Then closed.

Open again.

Closed again.

Jesus, what's wrong with me?

I open them again and I see someone, someone I haven't seen in years. "Am I dead?" I breathe.

"Why would you think that?" the voice I hear is my brother's though it's raspy and gravelly in a way that makes me think of my dad.

"Because you're here," I say.

"I've always been here," he says.

"You look like you," I say and then I try to move. "Ow, oh my god, ow, ow."

"Don't do that. You'll hurt yourself."

"What the hell happened?" I ask, a little irritation in my voice.

"You don't remember?"

I close my eyes. My head is pounding, my face is on fire. My ribs feel like I've been railroaded, then the night before flashes through my mind. Rooster, revenge, bed, Loki. No, it wasn't Loki, it was Gunnar. I shudder. "Ow," I say again. Then my mind flashes to the room, the guy, I shiver again. "Dammit," I breathe through the pain. "I remember," I murmur.

"Good," Kellen says.

"What did you do to yourself?" I ask him.

"Which part?" he asks.

"You look like you, except that scar."

"I took out the contacts, cut my hair, and got my cut back," he says with pride. My eyes roam over his chest, and the air in my lungs freezes.

"President?" I ask.

Kellen smiles wide. "Voted on this afternoon. Rooster is in custody, Gunnar is dead, thanks to you," he tells me. I smile but my cheeks hurt.

"Loki?" I ask.

"Veep," he says and I give him a smaller smile that doesn't hurt.

"Piper?" I say, sadness creeping into my tone.

"At home, safe, with Emily." I notice a rush of breath escape him when he says Emily's name. I narrow my eyes at him.

"What about Emily?" I ask.

"Don't worry about it," he says with a tone he used to use when I was younger and he wanted me out of his business.

"Nice try, jerk."

"She's a fucking hot piece of ass, okay?" He blushes, like, he actually turns red.

"Uh huh, she is," I tell him. "She's twenty-three, you know?"

He shrugs. "Since when do I care."

I laugh. "Ow, oh god, don't do that," I grumble.

"You're the one who laughed, silly girl."

"I know. But Emily? Really?"

He shrugs again. "I've met her once," he grumbles, but I think there's more to it than that.

"Uh huh, sure." If I could and it wouldn't hurt, I'd shake my head.

"Don't be like that," he argues.

"Like what?" I ask.

"All little sister on me."

"Oh, believe me, you ain't seen nothing yet. But I will warn you, she's the best fucking babysitter on the planet, if you fuck her up so much she runs off, I will kill you myself." I narrow my eyes and my head roars.

"Yeah, yeah," he mumbles.

"Where's Loki?" I ask him.

"He was gonna stop by the house, see Piper. She's really a great kid, Lily."

"Stop making me smile, it hurts," I tease him. "She's an amazing kid," I tell him. He nods. "She okay?" I ask.

"Perfectly fine. Emily knows what's up, and I'm assuming Loki is giving an update."

"I want to see her," I say.

He takes a deep breath. "That's not the best idea, bean." He uses my old nickname and my heart skips in my chest.

"Why not?" I snap.

"Because your face looks like it's been used as a punching bag."

"Oh," I breathe.

"Give it a day or two, let the swelling subside, then one of us will bring her up," he tells me.

"Okay," I say quietly.

My eyelids start to get heavy and I start blinking.

"Go back to sleep," Kellen says. "Heal up. You've got work to do."

"I do?" I ask sleepily.

"Yup, but we'll talk about it later."

"S'oka…" I slip back into sleep.

I don't know how long it is before I open my eyes again. My hand is sore and yet really warm. I wiggle my fingers trying to figure out why, when there's a shift on the bed. "Kiwi," a voice whispers.

I turn toward it and my eyes take a moment to adjust. Loki is staring down at me. "Hi," I breathe.

He stands and leans over me, gently placing his hand on the pillow beside my head. "Hi," he breathes. I can see relief in his eyes as he looks down at me. "How are you feeling?" he asks.

"Tired. I hurt like a bitch," I groan.

He stands up straight, pulling his hand away from me and I pout. "What happened?" he asks.

"Gunnar happened. Him and some other piece of shit," I grumble.

"His brother," Loki tells me.

"That's one sick motherfucker," I snap.

"He's dead," he tells me.

There is a gentle calm, a peace and sweet relief that washes through me as his words register in my mind. "Did I…" I don't finish.

"Don't worry about that," he tells me.

I don't argue with him. I'm not in the mood for it. "So, what's wrong with me?" I ask him.

"You have two cracked ribs, one's broken." I figured as much. "You have some damage to your wrists and ankles, but I think they're going to be just fine."

"I remember he bit me," I whisper and Loki's face turns blood red with rage.

"Don't worry about it. The plastic surgeon said he can fix it." I nod slightly. "Did he do anything else to you?" his voice is strained.

I lift my right hand, the one that doesn't hurt as much and I see the bandage around my wrist, no doubt from the cable ties, and I press my palm to his cheek. "I won't give you details, because you don't need that in your head," I tell him softly. "But no. I took him out before he got the chance."

"Thank god." His voice is soft but relieved and he leans down, kissing my forehead.

"I'll be okay," I reassure him and he nods his head.

"You don't have a choice," he tells me.

"What do you mean by that?" I scowl at him. It hurts so I let it go.

He doesn't say anything as he brings his hand down to rest just above my pelvic bone.

"Oh, god." I breathe. "Seriously?"

He smiles so wide it lights up the entire room. Tears prick my eyes and then one escapes before I can stop it. He leans down and gently kisses it away. "They drew blood, and ran some tests. The doctor said it's really early, but the signs are there."

"Loki, I…"

"Shhh," he hushes me. "It's alright. I told you before, I didn't care."

"But I do. I won't do it again, alone," I tell him.

"You're never going to be alone again." He gently presses his lips to mine. I kiss him back as best as I can. He pulls back, his eyes are alight with wonder and desire and so many unnamed emotions that I can't possibly put into words.

"Okay," I breathe. I nod slightly. "Okay," I repeat.

He smiles wide before pressing his lips to my head. "I love you," he whispers.

I suck in a gasp and pain shoots everywhere. I groan, "Ow," and I breathe through it.

He gives me a smirk. "That's not the first time I've said it." His smirk turns to a grin and I raise an eyebrow in question. "Granted, you were passed out…" he chuckles.

"So not fair," I tease him.

"It's true," he tells me. "I've loved you since you came home from the hospital. I just didn't know it then. When I named you Kiwi at three, I was twelve and I knew that one day I was going to marry you." He takes a deep breath and continues, "That night, in the garage, I knew I would have my colors on your back, no matter what the cost." He kisses my forehead again. "When you walked back into my life, I knew it was meant to be." He reaches for my hand.

He lifts it gently and I look down as he slips something on my ring finger. His eyes flash to mine. "Now you have my ring, my patch and my brand," he says in a commanding tone.

"Caveman," I mutter.

He throws his head back with laughter.

"It's not funny," I tell him deadpan.

"What did I do wrong this time?" he asks through his laughter.

"You can't even propose to me right."

"I'm not giving you the chance to say no," he snickers and presses his lips to mine again but pulls back before he gets too carried away. "Now heal, I need my woman."

"Caveman," I breathe.

Sleep consumes me again shortly after that.

CHAPTER THIRTY-FOUR

Loki

FOUR WEEKS LATER

IT'S OFFICIAL, SHE'S PREGNANT.

The dumbass, shit-eating grin won't leave my face as I walk into the clubhouse. Tryke called me about twenty minutes ago, said it was important, so I dropped Lily and Piper at home. She's still recovering but on the mend. Her face has finally returned to normal with only some slight yellowing in the cheekbone area, but she's covering it with make-up, which is good, because every time I see it, I fill with rage. It makes me want to dig up the asshole that did it and kill him again, only I wouldn't give him the satisfaction of bullets.

I knock on Tryke's office door. "Come in," he says from the other side.

Big Daddy, Whistler, Sticks and Pixie stuck around for about a week after Tryke was officially sworn in. They wanted to make sure he was settling in okay, that, and I think they wanted to see how Kiwi came out of all the shit that happened to her. She's a strong woman. There's no doubt about that, but I keep waiting for the other shoe to drop. Sometimes I can't help wondering if it's an act for me.

Then she does something completely random and it makes me think otherwise.

"What's goin' down?" I ask Tryke as I step into his office.

He nods in the direction of the door. "Close it."

I look Tryke over. He cut back some of the length he'd left when he originally cut his hair, it's still long and chocolate brown, but I can see his lighter roots coming from his scalp.

After Kiwi got out of the hospital, Tryke spent a lot of time with her. At first I thought it had to do with Emily, but it was never about the black-haired beauty who works for Kiwi. It was about her.

I'd catch them up late at night talking. Mostly about life after we faked his death. She was letting him back in and it made me happy to see them repairing their relationship. She and I have had several heart to hearts and I finally learned where she got all her mad, crazy skills from. Sticks wasn't going to leave her defenseless. So, he taught her how to fight, how to shoot. He had no idea she'd become such an excellent shot.

"I'm not sure whether we have a problem or if we have answers we've been waiting for," he says cryptically.

"Meaning?" I ask.

"Rack."

"What about him?"

He moves the brown paper off his desk and sitting under it, laid out nice, is Rack's missing cut. "Where in the hell did that come from?" I snap.

He hands me a piece of paper and I look at it front and back before reading it.

We can't apologize enough for what happened that night. And we understand that this isn't going to make what happened right, but we feel it's important to return this to you.

You see, Rack was not our target that night. He was simply in the wrong place, at the wrong time.

We've honored his memory by hanging his cut in our house, waiting for the day it could be returned to you.

That day has come.

You see, our target that night was Rooster.

He fucked us over with some of our local contacts. Making business impossible and costing our house lots of money. It was time he paid the ultimate price. It was also time, as we understood things, to have a new Pres is Roswell. We figured we could handle both for you.

But we failed.

WICKED REVENGE

So, as a gesture of good faith, we return to you the cut of your fallen. He went down a hero and will forever remain that way in our eyes.

All we ask in return is that you send us Rooster and Gunnar's so that we may add them to our wall of disgrace.

Hex

Critical Chaos President

"Well fuck," I snap.

"That's what I said too," Tryke adds. "We haven't destroyed their cuts. I think the least we can do is send them on."

"I want their patches," I tell him.

"For what?"

"The Wall of Dishonor."

"You know I hate that thing," Tryke says.

"Maybe, but it's a reminder to all of us that trust is earned, never given. That honor and brotherhood stands above all else," I remind him.

"Truth," he says, his green eyes meeting mine. "SD it. Strip the bars and send them back to CC."

"What about business with them?"

Tryke shrugs. "We severed ties when I took over. I think it might be better that way. We're doing fine without them."

I nod in agreement. "At least we have our answer," I tell him.

"We do," he says somberly. "We'll burn it this weekend."

Neither one of us says anything for a minute. Tryke pulls himself back together.

"How's my sister?" he asks.

I smile wide, much like it was when I walked in the door. "Pregnant,"

I tell him.

He narrows his eyes at me. "You waste no time, do you?"

"Nope, not a second."

"How she feel about this?"

"She's apprehensive, and I don't blame her," I tell him honestly.

"Me either." He rounds the desk and comes to stand in front of me, toe to toe. "So help me God, Logan, you fuck this up and I will take you out. You get me?"

I smile. "I get you, brother. But she's got my ink, she's wearing my colors, and my ring. I assure you, I'm going nowhere."

Tryke throws his arms around me in the biggest hug the man has ever given me. "Take good care of her," he whispers.

"Always," I tell him.

He lets me go. "Uncle? Again?" He raises an eyebrow.

I shrug. "We both get a little redemption this time around," I tell him.

"How so?"

"We both get to watch this one grow up." I smile.

"Truth," he says before returning behind his desk.

We talk shop for an hour before I leave and head to Kiwi's. I have something for her that Tryke gave me. Though it was an argument, I agreed to give it to her for him.

Piper comes running out when I pull up. "Daddy," she squeals.

No matter how many times she says it, it makes my heart melt. "Hi, Pipes. Where's momma?" I ask.

"She's laying down. She's not feeling good."

I pick Piper up and bolt into the house, charging down the hall and into the bedroom. Kiwi is on the bed, curled on her left side, away from me. "Kiwi," I say and she rolls toward me. She smiles. "You alright?" I ask her.

"I'm fine, just tired. Why?"

"Piper said you weren't feeling good."

"Mommy threw up," Piper chimes in.

"I'm fine, baby, just like I told you before," Kiwi says and she puts her arms out and Piper squirms out of my hold before curling up next to her. "Mommy's gonna be doing that a lot for a while."

"Why, are you sick?"

Kiwi's eyes meet mine and I shrug. "No, baby, I'm not sick. I'm pregnant," she tells Piper.

"What's that?" Piper asks. Her innocence warms my heart.

"It means that in a few months, you're going to have a baby brother or a baby sister."

She squeals, "I want a baby sister!" Then she hugs Kiwi who flinches a little.

"Easy, baby, remember mommy's still sore," I remind Piper.

She pulls away from Kiwi. "I'm sorry, mommy, I'm just so excited."

"Me too, baby," Kiwi says to Piper but she's looking at me.

"Pipes, why don't you go find Emily?" I suggest.

"Okay. Can I tell Emily?" she asks.

"Sure, baby," Kiwi says and Piper gets off the bed.

"Emily," she hollers as she runs out of the room, and I close the door behind her.

"You sure you're okay?" I ask as I kick off my boots, and climb onto the bed.

"Perfect," she says as she rolls over toward me. She reaches up with her face and presses her lips to mine.

"Not fair," I growl. "My hand is getting boring."

She chuckles softly, then she hitches her leg over mine as she pulls herself on top of me. She grinds her hips against my cock and it grows harder and starts throbbing.

"Kiwi," I growl.

She leans down, pressing her lips to mine again and her hands go to my sides and she pulls them up to cup her breasts.

"Lily, please," I beg. "I can't take this anymore, so please…"

Her eyes find mine. "I'm off restrictions, cleared, free to fuck your brains out," she growls and claims my lips again. This time, I cup her breasts, careful of her right one.

Before she left the hospital, the plastic surgeon had his way with her scar and now there are two, still healing, pink semi-circles. Eventually she wants to get them tattooed over, but for now, they're healing nicely. I roll her nipples and she hisses.

I stop. "I'm don't want to hurt you," I tell her.

She smiles. "You're not. You just knocked me up. My tits are sore."

"Oh," I breathe. "Let's see what we can do about that." I reach for the hem of her shirt, pulling it up and she lifts her arms and I toss it to the floor. Hooking my thumbs in her bra, I pull it down, exposing both of her beautiful nipples. Before I do anything, I kiss her scar. She shudders above me and I suck her right nipple into my mouth, massaging it gently with my tongue. She moans above me. Having her soft, flesh in my mouth again is heaven and my cock pulses between us. She grinds her hips against mine and I groan. Releasing her nipple with a pop, I move to the other one and repeat the process. Giving her a soft tongue massage against the sensitive buds has her hips moving against mine.

After a few seconds, I release her left nipple with a pop and reach around her back, sliding my hands along her warm flesh. "I can't wait 'til you say, 'I do.'"

She laughs softly, "I'm pretty sure there's not much left. Between the patch, the ink, the engagement ring and the child inside me, I'm spoken for."

"That's not the same," I grumble as I unhook her bra. She shifts, sliding

316

her arms through and putting it on the floor with her shirt. I wrap my arms around her softly and roll her onto her back. "Not even close to the same thing, baby."

She smiles. Her hands go to the hem of my shirt, pulling it up. I sit up, letting her pull it off and toss it on the floor with everything else. She leans up and kisses her lily on my chest then her fingers trace the chain of my dad's dog tags.

"You're wearing too many clothes," I grunt.

"Caveman," she laughs.

"Your caveman," I remind her.

"All mine." She lifts her lips to mine and I moan into her mouth as I press my denim-clad cock into her shorts covered slit.

"You're wearing too many clothes," I grumble and pull back, reaching for the waist of her jean shorts, tracing my fingers over her pelvic bone as I do. "Is this safe?" I ask her.

"Perfectly," she says. "Now, clothes, off," she commands.

I glare at her with mock irritation and she laughs again. This time harder and she winces. "Are you sure you're up to this?"

"Shut up, caveman, and finish it." She says the two words that always turn the animal on inside me and I unbutton her shorts, sliding them and her panties off in a rush before lying between her legs. I slide a fat tongue through her sex.

My eyes roll up in my head as her sweet nectar hits my taste buds. My cock throbs with a desperate need to be buried inside her. Her hand slides into my hair, holding me there, and I suck her clit into my mouth as she cries out softly.

"God, I missed you," she breathes and her hips twitch with each of the little nibbles I'm giving her clit. I slip a finger inside her sex and it clamps down on my digit as I flick her clit with my tongue.

Desperate to make her come so I can stick my dick in her, I start alternating between sucking, flicking and nibbling until I feel her body go rigid. Her hand in my hair tightens, almost to the point of pain, and she cries out my name as she shatters beneath me.

I extract my finger and slow my pace on her clit as she grinds out her orgasm on my tongue. When she jerks and settles, I rear up, unbuttoning my fly and sliding my jeans and boxers down to free my cock. I move closer to her and she grabs my cock and strokes it a couple times. Pre-cum forms at the tip and she wipes it up with her thumb before using it to move her hand more freely. The sensation sends my legs trembling and I take my cock back from her, stroking it twice before lining up with her cunt and pushing inside. I take it easy, not wanting to hurt her.

She wraps her legs around me and pulls me into her hips. "I won't break," she breathes. "Please, I need to feel you."

With that, I push myself inside her all the way. Sliding home. Warmth, love, happiness, desire, and pure lust race through my veins as she moans below me.

I start to grind in and out of her, her body trembling beneath me, our eyes locked on one another. "I love you," she breathes.

"I love you," I groan as I press my lips against hers, my cock sliding slowly in and out of the only place I ever want to be, ever again.

She's my home, my family, my life. Everything I've ever wanted wrapped in one beautiful, tattooed, colored hair, sexiness amplified package.

She stole my heart the day she was born.

She cradled my heart close to her until she gave it back to me so I could love her, forever and unconditionally until the day I die.

"Finish it," she breathes. And finish it, I do.

EPILOGUE

BECAUSE I LIKE TO KEEP YOU HANGING ON...

TWO MONTHS LATER

Emily

"HE WAITS ANY LONGER AND I'm gonna be as big as the house," Lily grumbles as we're sitting in a bridal shop where she's trying on dresses.

"I think he might like that," I tell her back.

She looks at me. "Good point," she says before looking down at her body. She's not showing per say, but she's definitely pregnant, at least to anyone who knows her well.

I made the remark because any chance Loki gets, he's kissing on her belly, on her, on Piper, it doesn't matter. Watching his behavior has made me insanely jealous and it makes me think of Tryke.

God, that seems like it was a lifetime ago.

A lifetime ago that he forgot all about me.

He'd come to the house to tell me about Lily being in the hospital and before he'd left, I'm pretty sure I fell in love with him. At least the idea of what he had to offer, but since then, nothing.

It makes absolutely no sense to me and I'm trying my best to put it out of my mind, but it's hard. Especially when he's at the house constantly.

"Alright, Em, what about this one?" Lily asks me.

"Wow," I breathe, taking in the strapless, A-line wedding dress she's currently wearing. It shows off her back tattoo, the one of the tribal wings she has with its low-cut backline. "Have you looked at yourself yet?" I ask her.

She shakes her head. "I don't want to fall in love with something like this then have him wait another three months to finally walk me down the aisle," she grumbles.

"I think you should look in the mirror, Kiwi," I urge her. Her hair is no longer black and green like it was when we first moved to Roswell a few months ago. Now it's blue and it's fitting for her. She can pull off the crazy colors and I love how excited she gets when she wants to change it.

"You think?" she questions.

I nod vigorously.

Finally, she steps up onto the pedestal that's centered in the three-way mirror of the boutique we're in. "Open your eyes, woman," I tell her.

"I can't," she laughs.

"Yes, you can, because if he doesn't walk you down the aisle in the next month, you make him wait until this dress looks just like this on you," I tell her. It's truly the perfect dress and it screams for both the sweet Lily and biker's woman Kiwi.

She slowly opens her eyes and then her eyes widen as she takes in the entire dress.

There's a small train on the back, but the dress is literally, nothing. There's three tiny fake buttons that come down between her breasts, and a small satin band under them that is met in the back on either side of a long eloquent line of buttons that runs from the top to the end of the train. It fits her like a glove. "This is it," she says with so much excitement I can't help smiling at her. "It's perfect," she squeals.

"Then we're all set."

An hour later and we're leaving the shop. The dress is a perfect fit, for today at least, and we leave with it. She also got a beautiful choker necklace and veil to go with it, though she's hesitant on that part of it, she bought it anyway.

WICKED REVENGE

While she was paying for it, I snuck off to send a text.

We got one, fits perfect, buying off the rack.

Then as she was just about done, I send off another one.

Leaving in five.

I didn't get a response to either one of the texts, I didn't have to. I know what he's up to.

"Where to?" I ask her.

She yawns. "Home. I need a nap."

I smile at her, but I know a nap is not in her future.

We arrive at home and there is no sign of Loki. "Where'd he go?" she mumbles as we pull in the driveway.

I shrug. "No clue." Liar.

Piper is with Loni and Cowboy, for now. They have their own tasks to handle when it comes to the spritely six-year-old.

Her birthday was a couple weeks ago. She's loving school more with each passing day. I decided to put off college until at least the next fall semester. With all the changes happening around the house, I knew Lily would need me, and she reluctantly agreed to let me wait 'til next term. That made me happy.

We're walking into the house when Kiwi stops dead in her tracks. "What's this?"

I smile. "You must be Kiwi," someone says.

"Who are you and why are you in my house?"

I smile at Lara. "Let me take this," I tell Kiwi as I scoop her dress from her arms.

"I'm Lara. I'm going to be your stylist today."

I hide my laugh. "Stylist for what?" Kiwi asks.

Lara smiles. "Your wedding day."

Kiwi turns to me, her eyes wide with fear. "You knew?" she accuses me.

"I have no idea what you're talking about," I tell her as I trot off to her bedroom with her dress, necklace and veil. Once in her room I go to her closet, now half full of her stuff, the other half full of Loki's. He lives here, for the most part, full time. That is until the house is finished.

About a month after Kiwi got out of the hospital, Tryke, her brother, and the love of my life – he just doesn't know it yet- gave Kiwi a gift from her uncles. It was a fat check for a million dollars. Kiwi nearly passed out and Loki about had a heart attack.

The note said it's what she should have received when Kellen had been 'killed' but no one knew she was still alive. So, she's putting the money to good use and having the house she once shared with her family rebuilt. It's where Loki, Kiwi, Piper, the baby and I will be moving before the baby arrives.

On my way out of the closet, I catch my reflection in the bathroom window. I stare at the woman staring back at me. A woman thriving, living a life that makes her happy, about to go to school to do what she's always dreamed of doing. But the reflection in the window doesn't match the woman underneath it.

The woman underneath the mask is shattered, lonely, and living lies she's told so many times it's starting to blur realities.

Anonymity has been my game.

Running from my past has been my goal.

First it was Boulder, where I befriended a woman who would quickly become my best friend. A woman I would bond with only to later find out we were hiding our pasts from those around us. The woman who took me in, treated me as her own, and offered me a job as the nanny to her beautiful daughter. Who would later move me farther away from the past I was running from when she brought me to Roswell.

Now, with my past buried, my future laid out before me, can I give into my one true desire? Hand myself over to a man I know nothing about because he makes my insides go squishy and my brain misfire?

What will happen when all my secrets are revealed?

I shudder at the thought.

In the window I see Emily Jefferson, nanny, friend and fraud.

In my heart, in my soul, I am Amelia Black, scared, alone, and on the run from a man who will stop at nothing until my heart stops beating.

ACKNOWLEDGEMENTS

Rachel, Emily and Shelley - Thank you, from the bottom of my heart, for reading Wicked as I wrote it. I know I left you all hanging horribly, but as you can see, it was necessary and hopefully worth it. You feedback is invaluable. I cannot wait to share the next one with you.

Mandy - Your honesty, no matter the good or the bad, it what I count on to write these stories. This book is no exception. I have forever saved that one special text message from you telling me how riveting this story is. You fill my heart with warmth and make me feel like I really can do this day after day.

Ashley - your excitement and enthusiasm about this book made me even more excited to finish it. I'm honored that you were so engrossed you forgot you were supposed to be working on it too.

Dana - I think the fabulous cover speaks for itself, but thank you for putting up with my crazy and my excitement.

PJ - My beautiful goddess, thank you for making this book sparkle with your charm and for everything else you've done for me with this release.

Wicked Wenches - You Are My Rock Stars!

Z-Team - Hope you enjoy this new tale of the Wicked Angels.

Mom, Thanks for all your love, support and never ending encouragement. You keep me going.

Zoey

ABOUT THE AUTHOR

BEST SELLING Erotic, Paranormal and Contemporary Romance author Zoey Derrick comes from Glendale, Arizona. Zoey, was a mortgage underwriter by day and is now a romance and erotica novelist full-time. She writes stories as hot as the desert sun itself. It is this passion that drips off of her work, bringing excitement to anyone who enjoys a good and sensual love story.

Not only does she aim to take her readers on an erotic dance that lasts the night, it allows her to empty her mind of stories we all wish were true.

Her stories are hopeful yet true to life, skillfully avoiding melodrama and the unrealistic, bringing her gripping Erotica only closer to the heart of those that dare dipping into it.

The intimacy of her fantasies that she shares with her readers is thrilling and encouraging, climactic yet full of suspense. She is a loving mistress, up for anything, of which any reader is doomed to return to again and again.

www.ingramcontent.com/pod-product-compliance
Lightning Source LLC
Chambersburg PA
CBHW050548260626
47157CB00002B/476